THIS
WILL BE
FUN

THIS WILL BE FUN

a novel

E. B. Asher

AVON

An Imprint of HarperCollins*Publishers*

THIS WILL BE FUN. Copyright © 2024 by Bridget Morrissey, Emily Wibberley, and Austin Siegemund-Broka. All rights reserved. Printed in the United States of America. No part of this book may be used or reproduced in any manner whatsoever without written permission except in the case of brief quotations embodied in critical articles and reviews. For information, address HarperCollins Publishers, 195 Broadway, New York, NY 10007.

HarperCollins books may be purchased for educational, business, or sales promotional use. For information, please email the Special Markets Department at SPsales@harpercollins.com.

FIRST EDITION

Interior text design by Diahann Sturge-Campbell
Hand lettering on half-title and title pages by Kate Forrester

Library of Congress Cataloging-in-Publication
Data has been applied for.

ISBN 978-0-06-337136-1

24 25 26 27 28 LBC 5 4 3 2 1

To all the heroes in the group chats,
who save the world for one another

THIS
WILL BE
FUN

Before

Galwell the Great was almost sad they would be saving the realm tomorrow.

Not, of course, because he was reluctant to defeat the dark powers wishing to rule over Mythria. He stood on the bluffs overlooking Queendom, the realm's capital, where they would lay their siege in just one more day. The sight of Mythria, the land he loved, corrupted with evil wounded his heart. Gone were her green hills, where one could nearly feel the magic flourishing. Instead, foul power had seeped gray into the landscape. Over the mountainous Queendom, dreamlike in peacetime with her white stone parapets, dark shadows loomed.

While night was falling, the sky surrounding the queen's castle offered little in the way of sunset. Clouds of perilous magic churned, lightning crackling ominously within.

No, tomorrow he would become a hero. He would live up to the name bestowed on him as a young boy from whom everyone knew to expect greatness.

Galwell the Great.

The name never felt burdensome to him—perhaps because he was admittedly quite strong. Magically so. It was his gift, the hand magic of strength. Never did he chafe at the expectations of others, either. His noble birth, his prodigious might, and, above all, his goodness made him a person people rallied behind and believed in.

He didn't mind that. Galwell the Great did not fear that he would fall short tomorrow. He knew he and his three companions—his sister and his two closest friends—would prevail. Mythria would be saved. Evil would be destroyed. The four of them would be heroes.

. . . but then what?

Prevailing, Galwell felt, was rather the problem. What was a hero's purpose after the villains were vanquished? Who would Galwell the Great be then?

They were the sort of existential questions he'd never contended with before. What waited past the edge of greatness? Marriage to his betrothed, the princess, he supposed, although the idea gave him only the pleasure of honoring the promises his parents made in his youth. Thessia was a nice enough princess. They would have a fine life. He would be true to her because it was the right thing to do, and doing right was all he would have to hold on to when heroism was no longer needed.

True was his surname, after all. Not "the Great." Perhaps the honorific would fade into obsolescence. Perhaps he would remain just—Galwell True.

The idea frightened him in ways swordfighting, horsemanship, and infiltrating dark fortresses did not. Would it be enough?

It would have to be. Heroism demanded sacrifices.

Wind whipping his long auburn hair, he knelt in the dirt, offering up a silent prayer to the Ghosts, the heroes of Mythria's founding thousands of years ago. Life lasted long past his twenty-seven years. Ghosts, grant him the wisdom—

"Galwell, please come inside."

His sister's voice interrupted his reverence.

"Beatrice and Clare are bickering over the last of the stoneflour loaf," she went on. "It's simply too much veiled flirting to tolerate. You must stop them."

He turned and found Elowen True crossing her arms, her characteristic scowl on her face. He privately considered the contrast of her fiery red hair with her closed-off demeanor a little ironic. She did not open up easily, and, seven years her senior, Galwell considered their closeness one of the greatest blessings of his life.

He grinned. "Have patience with them," he counseled gently. "You're not much better to be near when that Vandra comes around."

While Elowen harrumphed, he knew she was not really annoyed. Putting a hand on her shoulder, he returned with her to the cave where their group was camped out.

Inside, Beatrice and Clare were indeed sitting far too close for people who purported to hate each other.

Clare Grandhart glanced up, looking half relieved for the distraction, half dismayed. "Galwell, at last!" he greeted the other man. "Please say you weren't just standing on a cliff looking majestic as you contemplated destiny or something else stuffy."

A bandit and mercenary they'd brought on for part of their quest, Clare had not yet left despite claiming to have no heroism in him. When asked why he hadn't merely taken his payment and departed when his job was finished, he had offered only weak excuses. *Farthings would hold no value if the realm was destroyed*, he'd pointed out—his gaze lingering on Beatrice the whole time.

Despite Clare's jesting, Galwell the Great-for-Now made no habit of dishonesty. "I'm always stuffy, Grandhart," he replied.

Beatrice plucked the final bite of stoneflour loaf from Clare's hands. He did not protest.

Galwell had known Beatrice since childhood. She possessed powerful magic, like Elowen, and the two had quickly become best friends. Naturally, this made Beatrice his friend as well. The daughter of peasants, she held gifts farthings could not purchase— wry wit, unflinching rebelliousness, and an insatiable lust for life.

"Not tonight you're not," she protested. "This could be our last night. We should have fun. Wine, anyone?"

She held up the bottle next to her—the end of their provisions. The quest had gone on longer than anyone anticipated.

While Galwell would not keep his companions from enjoying themselves, he could not let her words stand.

"It won't be our last night," he said.

Everyone looked to him.

"We will prevail. I have confidence in every single one of you." He fixed his gaze on each of them in turn. "Beatrice, my oldest friend—smarter, fiercer, and more resilient than any a soul I've known. Clare, my newest friend—while I've not known you long and though you try to hide it, you possess the rarest gems of loyalty and kindness. And Elowen, my other half, whose heart is so strong her love is a gift to all on whom she bestows it. There isn't a force in Mythria that could break the bonds that hold us together. It is why the Order will fail."

Everyone was silent for a moment, as they often were after Galwell's speeches.

Clare spoke up first. "Ghosts, you're good," he commented. "A hero already."

What more? Galwell's inner voice queried. "We all are," he said instead. "There will be songs written about each of us four."

With firelight flickering on the cave walls, the weight of their futures settled onto them. They would make history. Perhaps when they died one day, they would join the Ghosts of Mythria legend. It was Galwell's greatest wish.

Yet in his friends' eyes, he saw how the scale of their fate frightened them. They'd found greatness without having the word linked to their names their whole lives. It made them greater, in his view.

"Songs," Clare mused. "I do hope mine are dirty."

As usual, Clare cut heavy moments with humor. It was not a skill Galwell possessed, and he appreciated Grandhart for it.

"I hope mine are folksy. Something sung with only a lute and a single husky female voice," Elowen said. "That would suit me very much."

"Mine should be something you can dance to," Beatrice declared.

Three pairs of eyes turned to Galwell.

He rarely did not know what to say in front of a crowd. However, his companions' easy joking banter sometimes eluded him. It was not because he was older than them, he knew. In his heart, he recognized he was just different. Responsibility had robbed him of frivolity. Heroism demanded sacrifice. Heroism demanded he remained apart. Friendship required the opposite.

"What do you want your songs to be, Galwell?" his sister prompted.

"If you don't answer," Clare joined in, "I'll be forced to commission the first song about you to be titled 'Galwell the Glum.'"

"Oh, or 'Galwell the Galling,'" Beatrice contributed.

Clare eyed her, impressed. "Good one."

"Thank you," Beatrice replied.

Galwell smiled, glad to see them getting along. It encouraged him. "Very well," he ventured. "My music should be . . . simple. Something a child could sing. Happy and hopeful."

Elowen nodded, approving of his selection.

"However, I welcome 'Galwell the Glum' and 'Galwell the Galling' into the Mythria canon," he went on, emboldened. "As long as 'Galwell the Gaseous' is never sung."

The remark left everyone stunned. His friends exchanged glances, until Elowen spoke up. "Did you . . . just make a fart jest?"

Clare burst out laughing. "He did! Mythria's greatest hero partaking of flatulence-based humor the night before he saves the realm!"

Beatrice wept from laughter.

Into the night the four shared one another's company like it was one more ordinary eve on their extraordinary quest. The wine was indeed passed around. Several stanzas of "Galwell the Gaseous" were indeed composed. They did have fun.

When the fire finally started to die, Galwell felt he knew what waited past tomorrow. Yes, he was a hero, but he was also a friend. He knew what he could hold on to, in victory and forevermore—the people in front of him.

Ten Years Later

1

𝕭eatrice

B eatrice was drunk in the bath.

She deserved to unwind, she told herself. The bath she'd run in her . . . *cozy* new cottage was the only comfort she'd found in her dismal week. Divorcing the lord of her village was not easy. Soaking in the scented water provided her a much-needed distraction from the many headaches life was causing her.

She'd managed something sort of like unwinding—she was lucky one of her only friends in the village marketplace was the home-goods potioner, who offered her generous discounts on her finest concoctions. Roselia petals! Honeyjade oil! Content, she immersed herself in lavender foam.

Until she realized her favorite robe, enchanted to stay warm, *somehow* wasn't in the chest of her things her ex-husband's footman had delivered last night. Of course it wasn't. The bastard would "borrow" her enchanted robe every chance he got, though he would never own to it.

Well, he may have gotten the manor, but he wasn't getting the robe.

The conviction pulled Beatrice, wine-tipsy, out of the bath. Was her new quest petty? Possibly. Was her fury frivolous? She, who once fought great evil, who fended off hordes of enemies, marching in pursuit of her favorite bathtime garment? Perhaps!

It mattered not. These days, Beatrice clung stubbornly on to every flash of feeling she could find. When life left one little to care about, one could care very deeply about very little.

She'd nearly reached the door, hastily dressed, when she remembered she had no money. Her ex-husband was the nobleman, not her. Without his finances, she had no carriage, no servants. Nothing.

The surprise stung in the same dull way she was getting used to. Nothing in the life she found herself living resembled the one she had expected growing up.

When she was twenty years old, Beatrice, with her three closest friends, had saved the realm of Mythria from dark magic summoned by the Fraternal Order. She'd followed the famous Galwell the Great into the fray.

They were heroes! everyone said.

Beatrice could only ever remember how they'd failed. How *she'd* failed.

Fate was punishing her, she suspected. She felt like everything wrong with her life now—her divorce, her current finances—was unpredictable penance for what she'd done wrong *then*, the way one never could know where rain would pool underneath leaking rooftops.

The thought made her want to pour more wine into the glass perched on the tub's stone rim. Why not? *Wine not*, she half-joked to herself. She could crochet the saying onto one of her new pillows.

No, damn it, she scolded herself. If she couldn't fix her life, *she could have her robe*.

Not wanting to lose her nerve, she swung open her cottage's front door. With the sun just starting to set over the green hills, she *walked*, carriage-less, across the village, heading for where she once called home.

Ignoring the whispers from the spinning women who paused in their garment making outside the marketplace, she continued with her head held high. The brewers behind the brewshop counter hesitated over the foamy concoctions they were producing with hand magic for customers on dates or on their way to nighttime work. Uriel, the old weaponeer, just stared, his eyes like dull crystals watching her while his forge cooled under his distracted ministrations.

Not much of note happened in Elgin, the hamlet where her ex-husband's family had lived for generations. It was sort of the point, for Beatrice. Mythria was no small realm. The castles of the land's nobles stood impressively on its valleys and mountains, small villages surrounding them like the hamlet where Beatrice grew up. Monstrous and marvelous creatures existed in its shadows and outskirts. Magic flourished in every corner. Her quest with Galwell, Elowen, and Clare had carried her far from her humble hometown, from the elegant streets of Queendom to the horrific Grimauld Mines.

Never to Elgin, though. The country village's wide roads held no shadows where memories could hide.

In the earliest days of her courtship with Robert, she'd found its ordinariness beautiful. Then, with time, comforting. Then, just familiar.

Now, it was nothing but the reminder of the gossip her evening robe quest would cause.

Without stumbling despite her drunken state—*great job, Beatrice*—she managed to reach her destination on the edge of town. The manor.

Her manor, once.

The home was half built into the hillside, with the upper floors rising into the sky. In the center grew a grand oak, with the house's walls constructed and enhanced with hand magic to accommodate the plant's massive limbs.

In front of the door, Beatrice hesitated, her disheveled state giving her the slightest pause. She was not proud of how she looked. In flattering light, her shoulder-length hair shone like bronze. Now, she imagined it looked more like dead weeds. She was sure a drunken pink had swallowed the freckles in her pale, round cheeks.

Was there soap in her hair? There definitely was.

Furthermore, from the unevenness of her stride, she suspected she was wearing two different boots.

Let everyone who called her a hero see her now.

But what could Robert do if she looked like shit in front of him? Divorce her a second time? She swung the door open, mind made up.

Instantly, she stilled.

From inside the house drifted minstrel music, punctuated by raucous laughter. She even recognized the song. It was the popular verse of the day, written about the deeds of Clare Grandhart. Creeping across the empty gallery up to one of the interior windows, she peered past the courtyard, into the grand hall, where—

Robert was having a fucking banquet.

Near the long table piled high with the feast, people were dancing in elaborate costumes. There were masks. Her ex-husband was putting on the party of the season . . . to celebrate their divorce.

While she was drinking wine in the bath.

Good for him! Good for Beatrice! Everyone should celebrate divorce.

While the separation of her life from Robert's was exhausting, it honestly did not sadden her. She'd married him because he was meek, which she mistook for kindness—and, yes, she'd married him somewhat for his title. She'd dreamed of marrying into nobility from her humble birth, especially since her closest childhood friend, Elowen True, grew up wealthy. After their quest, marrying rich felt like the one thing Beatrice could take from saving the realm.

Robert had played his part well in their courtship. He'd portrayed himself to be everything the last man she'd let into her heart wasn't. Polite, patient, even noble.

Nothing like Clare.

Within the walls of their home, however, she'd swiftly learned nobility and politesse only extended to court and reputation. Under the impartial presence of the old oak, Robert was . . . petty, jealous, and, worse, boring.

She wished she'd been the one to leave him. In the end, he'd denied her even this satisfaction.

Like he was denying her her robe.

In order to retrieve the garment, she needed to go upstairs. Unfortunately, the main stairs were right in the middle of the festivities. She would *not* let Robert's guests see her—the savior of Mythria—with soap in her hair and mismatched boots. Imagine if they thought her heartbroken. Over *him*.

No. Servants' stairs it was.

She would just have to reach them without being seen. Starting for the hallway, she noticed footmen on the other end of the passage.

She refused to let her confidence falter. *Yes*, she was drunk. What of it? Clare had been drunk when they'd snuck into Castle Corpus. She only needed to get upstairs outside the watchfulness of the de Noughton manor's footmen. She was Beatrice of the Four—she'd stolen the Orb of Grimauld from the Orb Weavers.

Next in her heroic legacy would be this robe!

She sprung for the servants' stairs. Even wine drunk, in mismatched boots, Beatrice no-longer-de-Noughton was nimble. She mounted the winding stairs swiftly, swung right, followed familiar corridors under limbs of the oak—until, just like she'd planned, she found herself in her old room.

She was startled by the unpleasant feeling in her gut the moment she stepped inside. How did she not notice it in years of living here? Fortunately, the room provided her the perfect distraction.

Her pink robe, draped over Robert's bed.

She snatched up the soft garment. Pulling on the sleeves, she welcomed their sudden warmth. It was perfect. Reveling in the enchanted comfort, she strolled out of the room—

Only to find footmen spilling from the servants' stairs. Well, she had not gone unseen, then.

Following the footmen were—worse—guards. She was too drunk for guards. While she could not fight them, however, she could flee. Rerouting, she wove through the house's hallways. Finding the main stairwell wasn't difficult. Her robe snug on her shoulders, Beatrice descended the stairs.

From her wine fog, she suddenly remembered why she had avoided the main stairs in the first place. They were crowded with guests celebrating the end of Beatrice's marriage, sipping wine from the manor's fanciest glasses. Her head ducked, Beatrice evaded the guards while keeping herself inconspicuous. Until—

Halfway down the steps, she collided with someone. Someone large. Someone male. Someone whose jostled drink flung flecks of wine into her soapy hair. Well, she couldn't look *worse*.

"Shit, sorry—" she started.

"Beatrice."

The sound of her name—in *that* voice—stunned her motionless like not even the realm's darkest magic could.

She looked up. For the first time in ten years, her gaze met with the eyes of her closest-guarded fantasies, his irises crystal blue like the waters of the Galibrand Strait, though the storminess in them held more in common with the cruelest winds of Mount Mythria. The years had not drawn on him. He was intolerably handsome.

"There you are," Clare Grandhart said.

There you are? Like he was looking for her? Here, at Robert's banquet? Or here, in front of him, despite the years and the distance they carefully maintained, entrenched in rage neither of them would ever forsake? *There you are, at last.* She didn't know.

Oh, she was struggling. Only resilient instincts, combined with the power of inebriation, kept her coherent in the face of the man who'd occupied her dreams and shattered her heart. "Did you expect to find me at the party being held in honor of my eviction?" she said witheringly.

With her own words, she faltered, realizing. When her eyes went wide with indignation, Clare smiled, politely grim or perhaps grimly polite.

"Did you journey here to *celebrate* my divorce?" she shouted.

In fact, the notion of handsome eligible men coming to this party eager to cheer her singlehood rather pleased her. What did not was the idea of *this* man. If there was one person in Mythria who had no right to revel in Beatrice's new relationship status, it was Clare Grandhart.

He watched her carefully. When she shouted, she could have sworn she caught something flicker in his expression.

Unfortunately, her exclamation had the one result Beatrice did not wish. The musicians halted with resinous squeaks of their strings. Everyone stared. Here was Beatrice of the Four, in her favorite enchanted robe, standing drunk, uninvited, in the middle of her ex-husband's banquet.

Whatever emotion crossed Clare's expression was gone in fleeting moments. While the guests gawked, he only shrugged. "I was invited to a nobleman's party," he offered with unconvincing nonchalance. "If I happened to notice the name and the neighborhood on the invitation . . . well . . ." Once more, his warmthless smile. "Your ex-husband's idea of roasted grawk likely wouldn't have justified the journey. Commemorating *your* unhappiness, however . . ."

She gaped. Not in surprise, exactly. Nothing Clare was saying contradicted the way she understood them to have left their ruined relationship. She'd just never expected to feel his unforgiving disregard in person. Why end their decade of spiteful silence *now*? She could hardly believe the golden-haired, glaring ghost of her past was here.

"You and Robert should form a club," she returned. "Beatrice's Greatest Mistakes. You could wear sashes." The words tasted deliciously bitter on her tongue. It was unconscionably tempting to keep going, to open up old wounds on the staircase of her freshest injury. To see just how much she could *hurt*.

Clare leaned forward, like he, too, was pulled to the pain pulsing between them. To yell, to curse, to clench, to dig his fingers in deep, to—

He glanced to the side. Conjurists were conjuring their image, preserving the way their heads leaned together forever. It would reach Mythria's gossip pamphlets forthwith, she knew. The scribes would love this. The Four's contentious couple, reunited and . . . fighting.

Curious or not, masochistically or otherwise, Beatrice did *not* want to deal with conjurists. She stepped back, forgetting she was on the stairs.

Clare caught her.

The closeness hit her white-hot, hurtling her past and present into one impossible collision. How could his hand, on her for only one steadying instant, feel *exactly* the way she remembered when everything else was devastatingly different?

Then he released her. The moment was over, its hint of chivalry—of fucking compassion—erased. In its place, however, Beatrice was darkly delighted to notice him uncomfortable. It felt like points scored in a game she didn't understand.

While she waited, Clare squared his shoulders. His demeanor, she noted, was changing. Inexplicably, he was putting on something like formality. It fit him like poorly smithed armor.

"You—look well," he said, standing straighter for their spectators.

Beatrice knew Sir Clare cared for his celebrity more than he cared for anything or anyone. The three of them had been offered knighthoods in recognition of their quest. Beatrice wanted no involvement with the guilt-ridden spectacle. Elowen had by then practically vanished from the realm. Only Clare showed up—strutting and smiling for every scribesheet.

Beatrice, however, cared nothing for the scribesheets. She didn't then, and she didn't now. She wouldn't play nice just so he could look gallant. "*Do I*, Clare?" She gestured to her pink robe, to the calamity of her hair. "Do I look well?"

"I didn't say you were dressed well . . . but you—" He coughed. "You're lovely as ever."

The compliment soured her stomach more than too much wine. How dare he try to be *nice* to her in front of an audience. What an absolute scoundrel.

"Same old Clare Grandhart. Enjoy the party," she said loudly, intending to leave him behind for the second time in her life.

She stepped *successfully* down the stairs while everyone watched.

Beatrice heard murmurs of *"Claretrice,"* which made her want to shrivel up. She'd on occasion heard the "couple name" Mythria's popular scribes had coined for her and Clare's unfortunate liaison during their quest, like they were shadow play stars or something. It grated on her, one more way her heartbreak had become nothing but the source of others' entertainment.

The herald in the great hall's entrance was likewise struggling with the surprise of her presence. "Esteemed guests," he started unsurely, speaking to the crowd. "Lady Beatrice of the Four, hero of the realm!"

With her confidence starting to ebb, Beatrice reminded herself she'd faced worse. She stopped and managed to curtsy. "Just 'hero of the realm' is fine," she said loudly. "No longer a lady."

When she surveyed the room, she caught the eye of Robert, standing motionless near the roast. She recognized the look of quiet fury vibrating on his face.

In her ex-husband, she'd eventually noticed the hunger she knew to lurk in other meek men. To be looked up to. To have women listen to him. When he couldn't make himself look grand, he settled for making others look small.

"No longer much of a hero, either, by the looks of you," Robert remarked loudly.

Uncomfortable laughter rippled over the room. Despite the arrow her ex-husband had successfully shot into one of her sorest spots, she didn't let her features fall. "Well, sharing your bed for eight years certainly required heroics," she replied.

When new laughter rang out, she watched Robert seethe. His features screwing up, he waved one finger forward, summoning guards.

Beatrice flung up her hands in surrender. "Don't bother," she said. "I'm leaving."

"Beatrice—" she heard Clare say.

"*I'm leaving*," she repeated harshly.

With whispers following her—damn "*Claretrice*," gossip she knew every guest would eagerly share for probably months to come—she pushed her way through the crowd, head low.

The entry hallway was in sight, the cooling forgiveness of the night within reach—when, *damn it*, she felt a grip on her elbow. It could only be Clare's. Frustrated, she whirled.

Leaving her caught off guard by the depth in his eyes. They looked . . . earnest. Sincere. Rogues weren't supposed to look sincere. Men who hated you weren't supposed to look sincere.

"Can we begin again?" he started, his voice rough, like he was inexperienced in the subject matter.

She laughed. "It's ten years too late for that."

His jaw tensed. "I mean tonight. Let's have peace. People change. *I've* changed."

"You're standing in the middle of my husband's divorce banquet," she seethed, "saying *you've changed*? Why would you want peace with me anyway?"

The combative smolder in Clare's eyes—this, she recognized. "Because we'll have to see each other at the queen's wedding soon. We should be civil," he said.

Surprise left the half-drunk Beatrice without words.

Clare went on, sounding flustered and half frustrated with himself. "It's—I—we shouldn't mar the festivities with our discord," he explained. *Mar? Discord?* She wondered why he was speaking like the fancy characters in shadow plays. "We must mend our . . . fighting, and go to the wedding properly. It's what . . ." He faltered. "It's the right thing to do," he finished.

Beatrice narrowed her eyes. She could not understand why Clare Grandhart was offering this play of propriety.

However—drunk or not—she finally knew what to say.

"I decline your suggestion of peace," she informed him, "on the grounds that I'm not going to the queen's wedding."

In the weeks since she had received the formal invitation to the wedding of Mythria's Queen Thessia, she had not once stopped feeling horrible for discarding the heavy paper, deciding instantly she would not attend.

She wished Queen Thessia nothing but joy on her wedding day. While they hadn't spoken in years—one more effect of Beatrice's guilt, one more reason for it—she did consider the young queen one of her few real friends. Beatrice found the thirty-two-year-old ruler of Mythria uncommonly caring even despite everything she'd lost.

Nevertheless, Beatrice couldn't stand to see her former friends, her former flame. Couldn't stand to relive everything they went through. Worse, the wedding would coincide with the Festival of the Four, the upcoming celebration of ten years since the deeds of Beatrice, Galwell, Elowen, and Clare. Beatrice did not need magic to foresee scribes on every corner chasing them for interviews, fans screaming their names . . .

Just more commemoration of the worst thing that had ever happened to her. No, she would not be joining the festivities. She couldn't.

Confusion contorted Clare's eyes. "You have to go," he said.

"I don't, actually," she informed him sharply. "Good night and have a good life!"

She strode for the door.

He gripped her arm once more, gently firm. Urgent. She shook off the heart-racing memories the contact left her with.

"You don't want to forgive each other, fine," Clare said, his voice low, his effete diction gone, the rogue she remembered leaping out in his whipcrack sentence. "But don't rob Thessia of her happiness. Not after all she's been through."

The hurt of his reference stunned her. She lifted her eyes to his once more, feeling betrayed. It shouldn't have surprised her, in hindsight. Betraying her was something of Clare Grandhart's specialty. In the look they shared, of secret wounds, the hallway full of gossiping guests watching them disappeared.

"The Beatrice I knew would've come," he pronounced.

She wrenched her arm from his grip.

"You were half right. I guess *some* people change," she said.

Then she proceeded out of the house she once called home.

The manor's front door closed behind her before she let hot tears sting her eyes. She hated how Clare had pushed on regrets he *knew* would hurt, which they did. She hated how true her ex-husband's words rang. What was she left with? Just fame for something she did a decade ago, already drying up.

Fame, and guilt.

In the deepest part of her heart, Beatrice felt the prickle of scars from wounds of memory she refused to let close. Ones Clare had touched with familiarly effortless fingers.

Many in Mythria possessed magic of one of several types. Hand magic was useful in controlling the material world, whether in the form of culinary gifts, powers to shape metal, rock, or other materials, or gifts of manipulating the body. Heart magic pertained to understanding or controlling matters of emotion or inclination. Head magic related to gifts of memory or perception.

While some magical gifts were minor or specific enough that they weren't much different from simple skill—intuition in the kitchen or resonance on the harp, for instance—others could yield considerable, rare power.

Beatrice possessed uncommon head magic. With her gift, she

could revisit memories of her own, or others, like she was living or reliving them herself. Which she'd become obsessed with doing, immersing herself in just one memory, over and over. Robert de Noughton had grown impatient with her exhaustion, her irritability, her preoccupation.

She didn't care.

For while everyone knew Beatrice had helped Galwell the Great defend the realm, no one knew he'd died because of her.

The guilt never let Beatrice go. Galwell was special. He wasn't just her girlhood crush, her best friend's brother, or her lover's best friend.

He was . . . hope incarnate. In the eyes of many, he was the man on whose example Mythria could become kinder, stronger, nobler. He was their hero.

He was dead now. Because of Beatrice.

Every night in bed in the room she just revisited, she would return to the battlefield where she would relive the moment when he died before her. It was part masochism, part vain hope she might understand what she could've done differently. She'd found a hundred little things that could have prevented his death, and yet, still, she could not stop submerging herself in the memory, searching for respite.

Tonight, of course, would be the same.

Don't rob Thessia of her happiness. Not after all she's been through.

Beatrice clenched the tears from her eyes. Reminding herself she was no hero made her feel honest. Remembering whom she'd failed, however, just hurt.

It wasn't just Elowen, who'd lost her brother, then eventually forsaken the entire fabric of her life. It wasn't just Mythrians, whose idol was gone. Thessia had been betrothed to Galwell the Great. Oh, how she had loved him. Beatrice remembered the fawning

look in the young royal's eyes, full of feelings Beatrice fondly recognized from her own youth.

She remembered the princess's scream when they returned from
the final fight with the Order, the gutted sound of someone who'd
known bad news was coming. It was pretty much the only thing
Beatrice remembered from their day of victory.

She sighed out loud, hoping it would ease some of the pressure
in her chest. No, she was not the hero the people of Mythria deserved. Still . . . Clare's words rang in her head, consuming her
completely in the way only he could. If she was not the hero the
realm deserved, she did not have to be a coward, either.

Not when her cowardice would wound Thessia.

In the end, she came to the worst conclusion. She hated it when
this happened. Infuriating or not—ridiculous or not, showing up
here to her ex's divorce party—posturing or not, Clare Grandhart
was *right*.

This wedding was her chance to be part of letting light into
Thessia's life instead of darkness. If she were to hide from the celebration, she would close the door on sharing Thessia's joy, maybe
for the last time.

She couldn't. She needed to go to this wedding. Guilt would
weigh on her forever, but she could give her kindest efforts to one
of her only friends in the world.

This time, she honestly didn't know if she'd lived through
worse. She just knew she'd live through this.

2

Elowen

Elowen True lived high above the ground, her dwelling built atop the most precarious branch of the tallest tree in the isolated woods she called home. Reaching Elowen required—among other things—traversing a cursed forest, climbing three formidable ladders, and pledging loyalty to a prickly brushwalker named Morritt. It was a nearly impossible task, getting to Elowen's front door. Which meant Elowen never had human visitors.

Just the way she preferred it.

She did, however, have shadow plays. They were stories performed by the best actors in Mythria, conjurated for viewing five times a week via head magic. Elowen had begun watching them as a child. At thirty, they were the sole thing from her youth she'd held on to. Her favorite was called *Desires of the Night*. It followed a family who spent all of their time fighting with one another and romancing their various love interests.

Desires was Elowen's window into the world she'd left behind. She could immerse herself in the viewing experience without fear of accidentally absorbing any of the emotions. Elowen had been born with a heart magic gift of sensing people's feelings through close proximity and soaking up their emotions through touch. Elowen hated her powers in general. Emotions were so fickle, for one. People could feel one way and act another, and it seemed to be more of a burden than a benefit to know how often their hearts betrayed their heads. With her shadow plays, however, Elowen never had to physically carry the characters' disappointments or their failures. She could be completely alone while still witnessing the full range of emotions life had to offer.

And she could interact with other fans using a magical message tapestry without ever having to let them know who she really was. She was just an anonymous, impassioned *Desires of the Night* fan to them, not Elowen of the Four, lauded hero of the realm.

As the latest episode of *Desires of the Night* started to come to an end, the conjuration swelled, dramatic music building for a huge reveal—Elowen's favorite character, the long-dead Domynia, had been resurrected!

Elowen shot out of her armchair. "Ghosts alive!" she cheered as tears streamed onto her daygown. "She's back!"

When the shadow play had first killed off Domynia years ago, Elowen had purchased all of Domynia's original costumes in order to cope with the loss. It had cost Elowen a small fortune—all of the farthings she had ever saved in her life, to be exact.

Elowen's message tapestry pinged constantly, her fellow shadow play fans reacting to the reveal. Right as Elowen set out to respond, someone knocked on her front door. Her *nearly impossible to reach* front door.

"Elowen?" a booming voice called out.

When Elowen first moved into the treetops, she'd fashioned several weapons of protection and hidden them around her strange, cluttered home. Beneath her armchair was a sword made from a stick. Elowen wrapped her hand around it, tamping down any anxieties she had about interacting with someone face-to-face, much less attacking them. It had been ages since Elowen had a combat lesson. She used to be a decent fighter.

She used to be so many things.

Elowen found that the longer she had to think, the worse her fears became. The intruder needed to be confronted quickly, so Elowen, gripping her wooden sword, took three long strides to her front door and threw it open.

She did not know whom she expected to find on the other side, but it was certainly not a man with muscles the size of boulders and eyes the color of precious dumortierite. He was the kind of person others would call strapping, covered in dirt with bleeding nicks and scrapes all over his face. The damage managed to perfectly showcase the many struggles he'd faced to reach Elowen's door. He wore the royal crest on fabric that pulled taut across his bulging pectoral muscles. A guard of Queen Thessia. Seeing him, Elowen could sense his feeling of triumph. It was no small feat to reach her door, and he surely assumed the hardest part was over. If she could read minds instead of feel hearts, she'd know what brought him to her home in the first place. The Festival of the Four, most likely. But no, all Elowen could do was sense how thoroughly pleased he was with himself, and that did her no good at all.

"Ugh," Elowen said, all her fear morphing into rather potent frustration. "Please go home."

"I'm afraid I can't," he thundered. His voice had bass notes so rich it actually vibrated the creaky floorboards. "I almost lost my life reaching you."

"That sounds like a personal problem." Elowen moved to close her door.

The guard pressed an impossibly strong hand against it, keeping the entryway open. He peered his gemstone eyes at her, squinting them into something like a smolder. Elowen knew the expression well. The men on her shadow plays were always smoldering like this at their love interests. She sensed the man wanted to woo her.

"*You're* my personal problem," he said.

Ah, yes. He even had the disposition of the shadow play performers. That stormy, defiant energy. This man was practically designed to make certain people swoon. Not Elowen. No man had ever made her so much as look twice.

Women, on the other hand . . .

"I am no one's problem but my own," Elowen assured him.

The guard laughed like she meant it to be funny, when in fact she meant it as truth. "Surely you know how difficult it is to reach your dwelling," he said. "Many have tried and failed. I am the first to complete this valiant quest." He pressed his large hand over his heart, expecting Elowen to be as impressed with him as he was with himself.

She was not. She was annoyed.

"I come with an invitation for you," he continued. "You have been cordially invited to the wedding of our royal highness, the honorable Queen Thessia of Mythria."

Elowen swallowed back her surprise as hot tears pricked at the corners of her eyes. Once upon a time, Queen Thessia—then a princess—had planned to marry Elowen's older brother, Galwell. Thessia and Galwell were the peak of romantic tragedy. Every shadow play attempted to recreate their sad story. Thessia was a kidnapped princess in danger. Galwell was the noble hero who rescued her, then died while attempting to save the realm afterward. On paper, it was perfectly heartbreaking.

In reality, Galwell had been too virtuous to admit he didn't love Thessia the same way she loved him. Not that it mattered anymore. He'd been gone ten years, and there was no one in all of Mythria who would be interested to learn that the most famous tragic love story of all time had actually been a lie. Only Elowen carried the burden of knowing that particular secret.

Even without the personal drama attached, Elowen could not believe Thessia would dare invite her to a *wedding*. Weddings were about love and community and the promise of the future. Three things Elowen had very intentionally removed from her life.

"I decline," Elowen told the guard matter-of-factly.

Frowning, the guard looked down at the shiny, sturdy paper in his hand announcing Queen Thessia's upcoming nuptials. "Queen Thessia said securing your attendance was required."

Elowen closed her eyes, giving herself a moment to think. She wanted to see her brother, and the only place he still lived was inside her mind. Galwell the Great, once known for having the most impressive, flowing copper hair anyone in Mythria had ever seen. Elowen's hair was equally as long and thick, yet Galwell was the one who received all the praise for it. That was the case for most everything when it had come to the two of them.

If the roles had been reversed—Galwell living while Elowen perished—and Elowen's former romantic interest had invited Galwell to a wedding, he would have gone. He probably would have hosted the after-party. But it was Elowen who lived and Galwell who died. Elowen was not forgiving, even when she should have been. After all, if Thessia hadn't gotten kidnapped, Galwell wouldn't have felt compelled to go on a valiant quest in the first place. He wouldn't have believed he needed to save the realm.

He would still be alive.

"My *no* has turned into *never*," Elowen said as she slammed her front door shut.

"If you don't attend, the queen will cut off your hero's salary, effective immediately!" the guard yelled from the other side.

"I bid you good day!" Elowen shouted in return, fighting off the rise of panic that swelled inside her. "Best of luck with the brushwalker! He will want to collect your fingernails on your way out, if he hasn't taken them already!"

Elowen pressed her back into her door as her mind raced. In recognition of how they'd saved the realm, the queen had offered Elowen, Beatrice, and Clare a monthly payment as a gesture of thanks for all they'd done to protect Mythria. Beatrice had rejected it outright. Clare accepted heartily. Elowen took it with no small amount of shame. She didn't like being beholden to the queen, but the money allowed her to live the life of solitude she desired. It was rather expensive to have all her essentials delivered to her treetop home via carrier birds.

Without that stipend, she had no other viable options. Her parents were well-off, but they refused to support her isolation. She'd have to live with them again to gain access to their money, which would be fine if they weren't so *social*. They threw parties and held gatherings and made up a thousand reasons to invite friends over for random events. Elowen had barely tolerated it as a child. As a full-grown adult? She'd rather wither to dust.

Just then her small magical tapestry let out a different ping— the sound of someone messaging her privately. *You're the biggest* Desires *fan on here*, the note read. *Do you know anyone who makes good replicas of Domynia's original costumes? I'm desperate to get my hands on them now that she's back. I'll pay anything.*

Elowen's eyes went wide. If she sold her Domynia costumes, she would have more than enough money to sustain herself for at least a year, if not longer. Best of all, she would be free of her ties to Queen Thessia.

What incredible fortune. Her shadow plays never let her down.

Elowen's hands shook as she used magic ink to scribe a response. *I can do you one better. I can give you the real costumes.*

Deal, the other person wrote immediately. *Do you happen to be near Featherbint? That's where I am.*

Elowen gasped. *Featherbint is very close to me. I could give you the costumes today if you wanted. We can discuss the price there.*

That would be a complete delight. Let's meet at the bookshop in an hour! I'll be the woman seated in the back. I'll have a purple hemalia flower on my cloak.

Granting herself no time to consider her actions, Elowen gathered up the costumes and put them inside a large satchel. She threw on her darkest cloak, pulled up the hood to cover her red hair and fair skin, then shielded her eyes with dark sunshifting spectacles.

In her humble but correct opinion, everyone else had exaggerated the struggle of reaching her treetop dwelling. It was not *that* difficult to enter or to exit. With the proper shoes, a satchel full of trimmed fingernails for Morritt, a steady soundtrack of hummed tunes to chase off the threat of head magic nightmares, and the spine-tingling adrenaline rush of losing your sole source of income at the exact same time that your favorite character returned to your favorite shadow play, it was a downright breeze.

"People are so dramatic," Elowen muttered as she passed the strapping guard. He was screaming, dangling from a thorn-riddled vine at the edge of the cursed forest. He would be released soon. The vines never held anyone for long. They weren't evil, just mischievous, which made them misunderstood by most. Elowen herself had hardly broken a sweat, and she only had two lingering nightmares attach themselves to her. No matter. They would keep her other nightmares company.

Featherbint was a tiny village of specialized shops such as a used horseball shoe store and a rare crystal boutique. At high noon, the sun shone directly onto the faded paint that covered every build-ing, emphasizing the years of neglect. The village hadn't seen an update since Elowen last ventured through years ago.

Glancing through the bookshop's unwashed window, Elowen saw a woman sitting alone in the back. Her hair—which blocked her face—was a shade of freshly polished black tourmaline that matched her elegant apparel. The exposed parts of her warm brown skin had been coated in a shimmery lotion that made her seem to sparkle. There was a purple hemalia flower woven into the hood of her cloak.

Elowen's heart started to beat in double time. It had been a long while since she'd gotten anywhere near an attractive woman. At-tractive women were, regrettably, her biggest weakness.

Elowen left on her sunshifting spectacles as she reached for the bookshop's front door. It was rude to wear them indoors, but she couldn't risk someone seeing the birthmark beneath her right eye. Many said it was heart-shaped; in reality, it was just a tiny blob. It would be recognizable as Elowen's all the same. And her eyes, blue as her brother's had been. They'd show her hand faster than her hair ever would. She'd become Elowen of the Four again. People would shout. They *loved* to shout at her. Things like "Use your magic and touch me!" or "Can you *feel* how much I love you?"

It would be disastrous.

A tiny bell chimed when the door opened. The fellow fan's eyes shot up at the sound. Elowen looked away, overwhelmed by the intensity of the gaze and the sense that this woman felt . . . excited? Was that right? It seemed like a level of eagerness that went beyond what Elowen would expect from even the biggest of *Desires* fans. Elowen was very glad to have the spectacles on her face. They dis-guised the heat that crawled to her cheeks. If this attractive woman found Elowen attractive, too? The situation would move beyond disastrous into something far more terminal—it would become *charming*.

Elowen hated being charmed.

She walked forward with her spectacled eyes fixed on the ceiling, examining the rotting wooden beams that held the bookshop together.

"What? No greeting for an old friend? I really hoped you'd smile at me. I rather like your smile, and you so rarely offer it."

Either the nightmare that had attached itself to Elowen had begun altering her reality, or her lack of sleep was creating the same effect. The glass of the storefront had obscured Elowen's ability to see what was now very clear—it was not a fellow *Desires of the Night* fan sitting alone in the bookshop. It was another woman entirely. A woman with the world's most dazzling face, complete with tiny dimples that pinpricked into the umber of her smooth, perfect cheeks.

"*Vandra*," Elowen whispered in disbelief, yanking the spectacles off her face. The name fell out before she remembered she'd planned to never say it again. It had been her own self-inflicted punishment. She was no longer allowed to delight in the way those syllables tasted. *Vandra*. Such a perfect name. Delicious and bright. Like biting a cold bramberry on a hot day.

"The one and only," Vandra responded proudly. She stood up to reveal herself in full, putting her hands on her hips as if to say, *Here I am, take it all in.*

A beat of stunned silence passed between the two women. There was no one else in the bookshop, Elowen realized with distant concern. Where was the bookseller? Where were the other patrons? Had Vandra done something to them?

"My dearest, it's not polite to stare with your mouth open,"

Vandra said. "If you keep on like that, it might hurt my feelings. I so hate to have my feelings hurt."

Despite the clear instructions, Elowen continued staring anyway, unable to quiet her shock. The bowed lips. The dark hair and eyes. The bosom. A heaving one, at that. It was all there. Vandra Ravenfall, the dangerous and delightful assassin, stood in front of Elowen for the first time in years.

Their shared past roared to life. Stolen kisses between campsites. Nights fumbling in the dark together, touching one another with feverish urgency, knowing at any moment someone would come looking for Elowen and they'd need to split up. They never had to speak about what they were to each other, because there was never anything to communicate. They were adversaries who enjoyed each other in their downtime. When the quest ended, Elowen hadn't even said goodbye to Vandra. Why would you bid farewell to someone who wasn't an official part of your life in the first place?

Dazed, Elowen turned on her heel. "I must be on my way at once," she announced.

"I'm afraid you won't be going anywhere without me," Vandra called out after her. "Certainly not when you look as lovely as you do."

The compliment tripped Elowen up. Vandra's relentless flirtation had always unmoored Elowen, a feeling she distinctly disliked. It was worse when Vandra touched her, as she did now, putting a hand on Elowen's shoulder.

Fuck. Elowen hadn't been touched in so long. It felt tingly and strange and overwhelming. It rooted her in the moment. This was not the work of nightmares or curses. This was *real*.

Worse, it felt good. Too good. Elowen had spent a decade convincing herself she enjoyed constant solitude. She believed that she required no other human interaction to have a fulfilling life, and day by day in the trees, she proved herself right. One single touch—full of history and passion—exposed the fragility of her beliefs. She hadn't really been living. She'd been surviving. Now that she remembered the difference, she had no idea how to recover fast enough to convince Vandra to leave her alone.

"You see, Queen Thessia knew you would be the hardest to get. She tasked me with the distinct honor of bringing you to her wedding in case her other plan failed. Naturally, it did," Vandra explained. "I was told I may have to give up my fingernails to get you, and I'm thrilled to be able to keep them. I quite like the shade of pink I had them charmed. Don't they look lovely?"

Just then, Vandra pressed her mouth to Elowen's ear, and the insistent pressure of the contact made Elowen feel all of Vandra's desire, hot and urgent. "It's been quite a long time, hasn't it? It's wonderful to see you," Vandra cooed.

Elowen's knees nearly gave out. She had to disconnect from their shared touch, or she'd do something unforgivable, like run her finger across Vandra's cheek. Or slip her tongue into Vandra's mouth. Instead she wiggled out from under Vandra's hand, freeing herself from Vandra's desire. She focused all her attention on the cursed forest in the distance. She needed to run. She hadn't done it in years, but she had to try. Adrenaline and delirium were surely a great recipe for success. She could make it happen.

"Don't tell me you're thinking of running," Vandra said. "I've just had my boots waxed. I'd hate to get a nightmare stuck on them when I don't need to."

Elowen turned around. "I can't go with you," she reasoned, as if that would be enough to stop Vandra from chasing her. To explain more would be to expose Elowen's own loneliness. Elowen could admit it to herself, but she could never say it aloud.

Vandra frowned. A rare sight, and done more for effect than an expression of truth. "Aren't you pleased that I work for the queen now?"

"I'm insulted," Elowen said honestly. "I can't believe my supposedly sovereign ruler would ever hire the likes of someone such as you."

Elowen hoped to cut deep, and cut deep she had. A glimpse of real emotion burst forth on Vandra's carefully trained face. The quickest shadow of hurt, gone as fast as it came. Truthfully, Elowen hadn't even meant what she'd said.

Ten years ago, Vandra had been hired by a rather annoying man named Bartholomew, one of Galwell's childhood nemeses who wanted to thwart Galwell's quest. It was a unique job for Vandra. She hadn't been tasked to kill Galwell, only to inconvenience him so that Bart could rescue Thessia first and be declared Mythria's hero instead. Vandra found the Four at every turn, adding an extra layer of difficulty to their already difficult tasks. Sometimes Vandra succeeded, throwing the Four off the trail for a day or two. Other times, she failed. Vandra conceded the losses with grace all the same, knowing full well she planned to meet up with Elowen afterward so Elowen could make some concessions of her own. Bartholomew, for his part, never came anywhere close to rescuing Thessia, and last Elowen heard, he hadn't paid Vandra for her services, either. She was certainly a nuisance to the Four, but she was never a bad person.

Dangerous, on the other hand? She'd always been that.

"Talent is talent, my darling," Vandra told her, settling right back into her natural cheerful state. "She asked me to do whatever is necessary to get you to the wedding, so long as it didn't involve violence. Which was irrelevant, of course, because I don't do violence anymore. Much has changed since last we saw one another."

She leaned in, cupping her manicured hand beside her mouth as if telling a secret. "That should intrigue you, by the way. I am not the woman you once knew."

Her breath, so close, pricked up the hairs on Elowen's neck.

Vandra was indeed different from how Elowen remembered her to be. Ten years could do that to anyone, but this went beyond what Elowen would have expected, had she known she'd see Vandra again. She'd always been a bubbly, self-assured person with a flair for spontaneity. The self-assuredness still existed, but the rest of her energy had settled.

She seemed . . . steady. Her emotions didn't bounce around as quickly as they once had, and her attention remained fixed on Elowen without wavering. It did intrigue Elowen. More than she wished it would.

"Queen Thessia wanted me to use my mind to gather you," Vandra continued. "So I developed a scheme far wiser than anyone else could ever dare dream up. All it required was advanced knowledge of the subject. The subject being you." She took a weighty pause. "No one else in Queendom knows you like I do."

"You don't know me at all," Elowen hissed out instantly, fighting to ignore every romantic feeling Vandra threw her way. Just because Vandra no longer worked as an assassin did not mean she'd given up on using her distinct charm to manipulate others. After all, killing bad people was only one small part of her previous occupation. Most of her work involved luring the bad people out, earning their trust only to betray them in the end. Now Vandra was using that gift to get Elowen to attend the wedding, and that hurt.

"Thessia would've sent me to get you in the first place," Vandra explained, ignoring Elowen's comment. "But too many men volunteered for the job. The one who reached your dwelling? His name is Carl. When he sent an urgent conjuration saying you rejected the invitation, I knew it was my time to shine. You see, I've been following you on the *Desires of the Night* tapestries for years. I knew if I could just lure you out of your little treetop, I could get you to the wedding . . ."

"You've been watching my activity on the message tapestries for years? That's a violation of my privacy," Elowen snapped, desperate to sound tough when all she really felt was vulnerable. She had worked so hard to stay hidden. She didn't use her real name on the tapestries. In fact, she'd concocted an alter ego with an entirely different life. Vandra finding her anyway really *was* a feat. Elowen would have been impressed, if she wasn't so exposed. And she would have been flattered, if she wasn't so terrified of letting Vandra get closer to her. Why had Vandra bothered to keep an eye on Elowen at all? They'd both cut each other off with no contact.

"Of course I've been reading your messages," Vandra said. "You're right to think I don't know you anymore. But you can't deny that we once knew each other quite *intimately*. And I'm being honest when I say I might just want to know you again."

It was Elowen's turn to ignore the comment. There was no need for Vandra to lay it on this thick. "Is your plan to kidnap me against my will?"

"It would be lovely if you'd consent to it," Vandra replied. "It would make things so much easier for us both, as this is ultimately in the name of a joyful affair. I love weddings myself. And you and I both know you don't have any other options. You need the monthly salary."

Elowen looked down at her sack of Domynia costumes, now useless. "Let's get on with it, then," she said, outmaneuvered. "Go ahead and take me."

Vandra let out a gasp of delight. "You're really letting me kidnap you?"

"I am," Elowen replied. She was not the hero Mythria believed her to be, and frankly, she never had been. That had always been Galwell. Elowen was just a tagalong sibling who followed her brother everywhere, even straight into a realm-saving quest. When she was younger, she'd been less aware of her own limitations. She was willing to try things even when she wasn't sure she'd be successful at them. That was no longer the case. Elowen possessed no ability to outsmart a woman as cunning as Vandra. Not without sufficient preparation. She had walked herself right into a trap, and in that moment, she had neither the time nor the energy to come up with a way out of it.

Beaming, Vandra threw Elowen over her shoulder, a move that resulted in Elowen staring directly at Vandra's perfectly full rear end. What a view.

What a situation.

3

Clare

For the third time this month, Clare Grandhart recognized neither the bed in which he woke nor the woman who slept next to him. When his eyes fell on brassy curls splayed on white sheets, his heart leapt.

Beatrice?

No. He remembered now, the feeling not unlike falling from his horse. Last night had not gone at all the way he had hoped. Two days ago, when he'd heard Beatrice *de Noughton* was divorced, Clare had used the revelation to push past the grudges they held against each other—hers callous and unjustified, his entirely reasonable, of course—and do what he knew the queen's wedding invitation demanded. He jumped on the first wagon to Elgin.

When Beatrice met him bitterly on the stairs, he let his worst impulses grab hold of him. They were easier than . . . whatever other feelings she might provoke in him. Feelings she certainly would never share, never even entertain. Very well—he could unentertain them the same way. If Beatrice wished, they could exchange remarks like they were crossing swords.

Had he expected she would run into his arms after so many years apart?

Ghosts, no.

Had he thought the years of silence between them might have resulted in Beatrice missing him even a little?

Possibly.

He shouldn't let her rejection sting. Clare was no stranger to Beatrice's disdain. He had everything he could possibly want—fame, wealth, companionship both sexual and friendly, a lovable eagle named Wiglaf. So what if *one* woman in all of Mythria despised him!

She was his decade-old—no, he would not say heartache. Beatrice was his decade-old *headache*. How dare *she* hate *him*, when Clare's callousness or promiscuity was nothing compared to the way she'd wounded him? It wasn't the end of the realm, especially to someone who had literally faced down the end of the realm.

And yet . . . to Clare, it might as well have been.

He hadn't expected the knifelike urge in him the moment he saw her. How much he wanted her, even when he couldn't forgive her. How desperately a part of him hungered for *her* forgiveness, her pride, her care. He wanted her to be the living proof that he was worth loving.

He needed to put her out of his mind. Focus on everything he *did* have. Like the lovely lady currently in his—or *someone's*—bed. With hungover effort, he connected the naked shoulders half exposed from the coverlet with the woman who'd refilled his drink after Beatrice had walked into the night. He'd been hurting. She'd promised to distract him.

They'd had fun. Or, *she'd* had fun. Clare Grandhart always made sure his partners had fun.

Him, on the other hand . . .

He exhaled, hating the discontent quietly pervading his chest, spoiling the golden morning.

It wasn't this lady's fault, of course. It was him. It was *Beatrice*. It was how he had everything *except* what he wanted. Who he wanted. It was how, in ways he could not fully understand, he'd started to feel he was only playing the character of Clare Grandhart, protector of Mythria and one of the Four.

He was forgetting his lines more and more these days. Which wasn't good, not when he clung on to one consolation every day of his unexpected life.

Clare Grandhart was a hero.

He held on to the idea when everything he *wasn't* caught up with him. If he wasn't the man he hoped he would be—horseball player, healer, father? Never mind. He was a hero. If he wasn't sure he was happy?

If Beatrice didn't want him? Fine. He was a hero.

If he wasn't good enough? If he wasn't loved?

It didn't matter. He was a hero.

He *needed* to be a hero, especially with the anniversary coming up. He needed to make up for Galwell's absence. Galwell was who Mythria deserved. He was the brave one, the gallant one, the kind one. The one people followed.

The one people loved.

Clare knew he was a badly drawn copy, but he was trying. It was why—as Clare had nearly confessed in inelegant, fumbling phrases—he had made his way to the de Noughton manor. Inventing noble reasons for forgiving Beatrice in order to pretend he didn't want to, deep in his wounded heart. Galwell would have forgiven her, Clare reasoned. He would have put his friends first, his queen first.

And then Clare encountered Beatrice herself, and his desire deepened. The unbidden, insatiable need to prove himself to her, even while he could not forget every reason he had to hate her. He didn't know why the esteem of the woman he'd devoted the decade to resenting meant everything to him, no more than he knew how the realm's magicians had mastered sending conjurations from coast to Mythrian coast.

He just knew, if he could prove himself to *Beatrice*, the woman who'd once known him best, he might finally feel like the hero the rest of the realm deemed him.

He wrestled the familiar feeling down. He'd dealt with worse. Dragons, nightwalkers. What was a little existential uncertainty? What he needed was something at which Clare Grandhart excelled—distraction. Perhaps he could spend the day with—

With . . .

Fuck. He was forgetting more than his lines now. He looked down, focusing on the woman's pretty freckled shoulders, her curly hair. Horrible realization opened up in him. He could not remember her name. He was mortified. *Morgana?* No . . .

While at heart he knew himself best suited to the role of dashing rogue, Clare valued the women he slept with. He never considered them just people to fuck. He learned their names, where they were from, what they enjoyed reading or what sports they followed. Forgetting this woman's name was damning proof he wasn't himself.

Isabella? No. *Velaria?* No.

He was frustrated with himself. How goddamn often would he make the same mistake? Leaping into other women's arms when the one he wanted left him heartsick?

"Good morrow," his companion said sweetly.

"Mm," he returned.

With his mortification mounting, wisdom he recalled from debauched drinking evenings with friends from his banditing days entered his head.

If you can't remember her name in the morning, take her to the brew-shop. She'll give them her name to call out for her order.

"Morning brew?" he suggested.

The woman paused *just* long enough to imply she might be interested in morning something-else. When Clare pretended to be sleepily oblivious, guilt gnawing his insides, she smiled.

"I'd love to," she purred.

Only a little relieved, Clare dressed himself, lacing his tunic while the woman wrapped herself in the elegant dress hung from the wooden hook on one wall of the room. "I assumed you would sneak out with the morning light," she commented.

Following her to her door, he scoffed. "Most of the rumors about me are wild exaggerations. I've even been known to make brunch on occasion," he said.

In moments like this, he found it unnervingly easy to put on the charm. A half-grin, a rolled-up sleeve, a hand run through his hair. Mixing truth with what felt like lies. He'd perfected the moves over the years, using them to hide from the mistakes he made a decade ago.

Of course, his looks didn't hurt. Or didn't help, depending on how one viewed things. Clare Grandhart was well over six irons in height, sculpted of lean muscle checkered with scars over which women liked to run their fingers. His sweep of golden hair was deceptively cheerful to his enemies, charming to his romantic pursuits. His crooked smile was legendary.

It worked now. Her cheeks flushing with delight, his companion laughed while she led him out her home's front door.

The greenery surrounding Elgin's small homes hurt his eyes in the morning light. The village was not large, and he had walked its main roads on his way to the de Noughton party. He couldn't keep himself from imagining Beatrice here, wearing her usual smirk, in Elgin's shops or on the same roads.

He would never know peace, would he?

The village didn't suit her, in his opinion. The Beatrice he had known was social, vibrant, even unruly—someone who preferred her wine from seedy taverns, not stuffy estates.

She should have lived somewhere like—for instance—Clare's home in the flourishing city of Farmount. Clare had moved there after saving the realm, knowing he could make his living handsomely by lending his name to vendors who wanted his endorsement. Weaponeers, drinking halls, fancy cigars. Perhaps this made him shallow—well, no news to him. Beatrice had told him years ago he would never be noble, not like Galwell, the first man she ever loved.

She was right.

Elgin did, however, have what he was looking for this morning. Recognizing the street they were on, Clare directed them toward the brewshop. The heads of passersby swiveled in his direction. Whispers started. Glances of lust or envy from men and women.

Unsurprised, Clare nodded respectfully in return. Even existential dread aside—not to mention his hangover—he couldn't muster more enthusiasm for the renown.

"Pardon me, sir," came a small voice next to him.

Clare paused. He was used to recognition, especially from children like the one standing in his square-shouldered shadow, holding—

"I, um," the boy started. "My father said you could, um, sign my collectible Clare Grandhart card."

Clare smiled. Now *this* part of fame, he genuinely liked. Making people happy. Inspiring the young.

What was more, the request in itself delighted him. Clare had, in his youth, collected Hero Cards with the painted likenesses of great Mythrians. There were points on them, skill levels, so on. You could play games, engaging your cards in pretend combat with other collectors. It was one of the greatest honors of Clare's life when he was notified that the card craftspeople were putting Clare Grandhart cards into circulation. "Your card," he repeated. "Yes, I would be honored."

With a flourish, he produced from his tunic the thick-nibbed quill he was never without. In handsome letters over his likeness, he enthusiastically inked the name everyone in Mythria knew.

Sir Clare Grandhart

"Now," Clare went on, his smile conspiratorial, "if you'll pardon me, good sir, I'm with someone this morning."

The crowd, of course, followed his cue to glance at the violet-eyed woman. Like he expected, she preened, enjoying the second-hand fame. *Good*, he said to himself. It was the least he owed her in return for his dreadful issue with her name. Clasping her hand in his, he returned her smile. He was determined to prove to her he was decent.

The noble pleasure of this resolution offered him only moments' relief, until his companion asked with poorly feigned innocence, "So, what are you doing next week?"

He stiffened. He understood instantly the intent of the question, one he'd heard from the lips of plenty of lovely women. Clare Grandhart didn't do second dates. He wasn't suited for second dates—not with Beatrice, not with the woman he'd woken up with this morning. He could only pull off the performance of noble hero for so long before those close to him saw through to what he really was. *Not good enough*. One fun, drunken night was all he was worth.

"I travel to Queendom for the festival, of course," he replied, grateful for the honest excuse.

His date's eyes lit up. "I've always wanted to see the festival in the capital."

"You should attend," he replied hastily. "I'll unfortunately have no time to myself, but I would be very happy to see you in the crowd." Once more, not a lie. Just a ploy. Keep the door ajar and people will glimpse enough to never want to come all the way in.

Or so he hoped.

Fortunately, they had reached their destination. Forcing the winningest smile he could muster, Clare held open the door for her. He followed her in, the spicy smell improving his mood instantly.

Harpy & Hind was Clare's favorite brewshop. Everyone's favorite brewshop, really. In the years since their founders first set up shop in Queendom, the women had expanded their enterprise, opening up nearly identical locations of their shops in villages everywhere in Mythria.

While every brewshop could craft the usual varieties of dark brew, foamy milkbrews, or sugared brews, Harpy & Hind was known for the creative whimsy of their concoctions. Pumpkin brews, nut-spice brews, holiday flavors. Right now, however, the promise of their delicious potency was not what drove him. In moments, he would know his mystery woman's name.

Her hand in his, he strode decisively for the open counter—only to abruptly pivot, yanking his date's arm forcefully toward the other brewmaster. "Apologies," he said. "This line is, uh, better."

She eyed him, but if she saw the cause of Clare's change of mind, she stayed silent.

Clare positioned his date so he could turn toward the wall to speak to her, keeping his back toward the rest of the room—and the all-too-familiar brunette waiting for her drink.

Beatrice. Here.

Of fucking course she was here, he chastened himself. Yes, Clare could perhaps have foreseen she might come to the *one* Harpy & Hind in Elgin, *the most popular brewshop in the realm*, on this summer morn like every other villager here.

Perhaps she didn't see him, he hoped ridiculously.

Calling on the stealth that saw him through the Grimauld Mines, he turned just enough to catch Beatrice in the corner of his vision.

Only to find her looking directly at him. Their eyes locked. The corners of her lips flickered in victory. Her eyebrows rose imperiously.

It was almost comical, Clare could admit. Last night, he had caught her in mismatched boots and a pink robe, which, for the record, was unfairly hot given how fuzzy it was. Now the scales were even once more. She was catching him fresh off a one-night stand.

Not that Clare wasn't entitled to one-night stands. He certainly owed Beatrice nothing. Still, he hated how the impression of him she was getting here would only fit the opinion she had of him— rake, scoundrel, disgrace.

He stepped up to the counter, determined to ignore his ex. "One large nut-milk caramel foam brew, please," he requested. He unleashed his usual smile. "For Clare Grandhart."

Clare knew other men disdained the sweet, intricate brews they considered *ladylike*. Not him.

"Of course, sir," the hand magician said.

Clare nodded, waiting.

No one spoke for a moment.

Realizing, Clare faltered, glancing to his companion. The whole point of this Ghosts-forsaken errand.

"Oh, nothing for me," she said.

What?

No. Sir Clare Grandhart didn't give up this easily. He'd saved the realm once, with resourcefulness and persistence. He needed only call on them now.

"Please," he insisted, leaning charmingly on the counter, coating his voice in sugar. "It's on me. It would be my pleasure. You must"—he glanced at the menu, improvising—"you must have the pumpkin-gingerroot cream. It's the only thing I've ever tasted half as sweet as kissing you."

The line was risky. He hoped his date wouldn't roll her eyes. Distantly, he heard a familiar snort of derision from the other side of the shop.

Instead—*yes*. "Fine. One small pumpkin-gingerroot cream, please," she said.

He paused, waiting for her to give her name.

She did not.

The brewmaster smiled pleasantly.

"I must step outside quickly," he commented, thinking fast, then placing farthings from his pocket on the counter. "I need to check on my eagle. Could you collect our drinks?"

She blinked, no doubt surprised by his sudden urge to see a bird. Celebrities were often eccentric, though. She turned to the brewmaster. "Of course. Put it under Sir Clare's name and I'll collect them both."

Clare hesitated.

"Go. See your eagle. I'll be right out," she said happily.

This was the dark night of the soul. All was lost. His quest would fail.

"He wants you to give your name for the drinks, Viola."

Viola! He was saved! By the most lovely voice, one belonging to a majestic Ghostly visitation, no doubt, to—

Beatrice?

She walked up beside them, her own drink in her hands. "He's forgotten your name, and he's brought you here in hopes he could learn it without you ever realizing," Beatrice said, her tone thick with gloating.

Not waiting for a reply, she strode off. A conquering hero who has laid waste to all her foes.

Clare turned to Viola. "So sorry. Would you excuse me for just one moment, Viola?" Wincing, he followed Beatrice.

On the street, Clare gave up subtlety entirely. "Beatrice," he called out.

Of course, she ignored him. She strode into the middle of the road.

Groaning, Clare ran to her side. "Stop," he demanded when he caught up to her.

He was, he'd discovered on his way out of the brewshop, furious once more. *Fuck heroism.* He had much, much more to say to her than posturing pleasantries.

"Is there nothing you won't ruin?" he found himself exclaiming.

Lo and behold, Beatrice *did* stop. He recognized the moment the same spark struck in her. *Fuck civility. Fuck silence.*

She held herself rigid. Her hair was loose and wild, the way it always was after her baths. *She was beautiful.* The angles of her face stood out strikingly in the morning light. Were her lips always a shade shy of purple? He'd forgotten in the ten years since he'd last tasted them.

"I offer my deepest regrets, Sir *Clare*. Your discord gives me not inconsiderable grief," she replied, her voice deathly low.

Was she . . . mocking the way he spoke last night? In hindsight, he knew he'd overemphasized the courtliness of his phrasing.

"I would never have intervened had I known your liaison with my former neighbor Viola was serious," his ex continued. "I wish you lifetimes of happiness. She's lovely."

Headache was not the word, either. She was his *everythingache*. "It's—not like that," Clare retorted.

"Like what?" She crooked the arm not holding her drink onto her hip. Waiting for him to say it.

He looked to the skies, wishing his eagle really was nearby. Wiglaf followed Clare at a distance, preferring to hunt on his own, then swooping onto Clare's shoulder in hopes of some salted meat from the market. It was very cute, and frankly, he set Clare at ease in stressful situations.

"It was only one night," he said, letting his breath out in defeat.

Beatrice grinned. "Just like old times, right?"

"No." His voice was tight. There was too much history in their words. Too much they weren't saying, too much he so desperately wanted to say. Years of resentment covering over pain from which neither of them had healed, like wounds dressed with heavy stone instead of silk.

"Clare, it's fine," Beatrice said, finally dropping some of her spite. "Really. Go. Take Viola to the wedding. She'd make a great date. I'll even share a drink with her and give her some words of wisdom on being with Clare Grandhart."

"We were never together— Wait." He stopped himself, realizing what she'd said. "You're coming to the wedding?"

Beatrice looked to the side, clearly frustrated to have betrayed herself. "Don't make this a thing. I'm coming to the wedding. We'll hardly see each other."

The sun seemed to shine brighter. Was that Wiglaf in the clouds above? From fury, Clare glimpsed the shimmering filament of . . . hope. *Beatrice is coming to the wedding.*

No. Beatrice and hope *couldn't* overlap in his mind.

Not when he knew her heart held nothing except poison for him. The event would only remind him of the hatred that endured in their relationship. Beatrice and him, side by side, witnessing declarations of undying love, expected to share wine and dance together, while she loathed him and he determinedly returned the resentment . . .

The wedding would be torture.

"I'm not going for you," Beatrice warned him, "and we'll never have peace between us."

Clare was good at withstanding torture, though. He could do this. For Galwell. Yes, it was only for Galwell that he would force himself to take Beatrice's arm while the harps played. Only for Galwell would he compliment her dress. For Galwell, he would hold her close, brush his nose along her neck, lose himself in her dark eyes.

"I'll see you at the wedding, Beatrice," he promised her. "Save me a dance."

He turned back to Harpy & Hind, feeling strangely light.

"I certainly will not!" she called behind him.

He raised his hand in farewell. He would see Beatrice again. He would see Beatrice again.

When he walked into the brewshop, Viola was waiting for him, her expression pained. She handed him his drink.

"Clare . . ." she began ominously.

"Viola, I'm so sorry for . . . all of that. Truly, you didn't deserve it." He put heart into his words, no longer seeking to charm, just to be sincere.

She smiled weakly. "I had a really fun night last night. But I think I'm going to skip the festival."

He nodded. "I understand. I'm sorry. Again. I was drunk, but I shouldn't have forgotten your name. It's no excuse."

She blinked, the apprehension in her eyes replaced with confusion. "You didn't forget my name," she said simply. "I never gave it to you. Honestly, it's very sweet how much effort you put in to learn it this morning. Under other circumstances I would love to see you again."

Clare felt his mouth open unbecomingly. His quest was . . . in vain? He had to hold in a laugh. Let Galwell see him now. Sir Clare, the hero no one actually needed.

As Viola started to walk away, a thought seized him. He didn't want to make things work with Viola. He was grateful she was moving on from him.

Yet, if it wasn't forgetfulness of her name, why *didn't* Viola want to see him again? Was it something he did? Was his morning breath bad? His skills in the bedroom diminishing? *Ghosts, please let it not be that one*. He had to know. Knowing Beatrice would be at the wedding made it, for some inexplicable reason, pressing to learn. He hurried after her, catching up to her at the door.

"Can I ask why? Why don't you want to come to the festival?" he asked. "I respect your choice completely. I just . . . want to know."

She smiled and laid a friendly hand on his shoulder. "I thought everything that happened between you and Beatrice was in the past, but seeing you two together . . . I can't be the woman to get in between *Claretrice*." She patted him like he was an eagle with a wounded wing, then walked off.

Claretrice?

Clare watched her go, confounded. He considered the gossip pamphlets' couple name no different from the legends of Old Mythria that historical scribes would recount. Captivating? Perhaps. Lost to the past? Certainly.

He sipped his nut-milk caramel foam brew. What Claretrice? There was no *Claretrice*, never—

His wondrous brew distracted him. It was *delicious*.

The simple pleasure calmed his nerves and eased his hangover. What couldn't the Hind do? In the reprieve, he found his focus sharpening like steel under the weaponeer's whetstone. He remembered what was important.

He'd woken this morning wanting the chance to prove his character to Beatrice. Whether he *enjoyed* the celebration of love with her mattered not. What the wedding offered was *exactly* the opportunity he wanted. Indeed, the Ghosts could not have presented him a more ideal one.

Finishing his drink, Clare left the shop. When he stepped outside, Wiglaf descended from the skies, making the delightful *ka-kow* sound that Clare, when completely alone, had been known to repeat to his dear pet.

While he fed Wiglaf from the bag of jerky he always kept on him, Clare hummed, realizing he found Elgin beautiful. Was there really a chance three of the Four could reconvene, even for just one night? Thessia had assured him Elowen would come. Now, with Beatrice's notice, Clare had reason to hope. What if he, Clare Grandhart, with nobility and grace, could reunite them peaceably?

The very idea made him feel . . . like he could face down any evil in the realm. Ever since the Four separated, he'd struggled to compensate for their absence, to fill the emptiness that losing friends closer than family left in him.

If he could rejoin them, maybe this week he would not find the role of hero so difficult after all.

4

Beatrice

The wagon smelled of old roasted gryphon shank. While the wooden seat thumped under her on the uneven road, Beatrice could easily imagine some previous rider stuffing his face with the sinewy meat, leaving the scent of grease pervading the wagon.

Beatrice had never once traveled on Wagons-For-You. She'd only heard of the new convenience in dialogue on shadow plays or from the slurring mouths of younger people outside of Elgin's tavern. It was the preferred method of casual transportation for those in foreign cities, or on late nights when drink rendered hometown streets unrecognizable. Everyone in possession of their own wagon could sign up to contribute to the service's expanding network of drivers for hire.

Their promotions promised rides in luxurious convenience. In fact, neither point was consistent with Beatrice's present experience.

Convenience? She'd recited the simple summoning spell on the Wagons-For-You posters everywhere in town, clutching her five farthings' fare together like the instructions described. She'd then proceeded to wait *nearly thirty minutes* before her farthings emitted the green firefly-like lights indicating her wagon was nearby.

Luxurious?

Only if one really liked the scent of gryphon shank.

Still, Beatrice reminded herself, the ride was preferable to nothing, which was what her family was left with when she was young. When they couldn't scrape together fees for established carriage services, there were no other options. The steep fares sometimes meant the difference between seeing loved ones one last time or not.

Her situation changed when she met Elowen. Though born to commoners, Beatrice caught the eye of her village's noble family with her unique head magic—including the children, Elowen and Galwell. They embraced Beatrice, especially Elowen. From then on, when Beatrice wished or needed to leave the small stone walls of the village, Elowen would have the finest stallion outside Beatrice's door the next morning.

In the years since the Four saved the realm, Beatrice could have bought her own horse if she hadn't declined Queen Thessia's offer of payments to the heroes of Mythria. Whenever Thessia gently insisted, Beatrice pretended she'd had enough of taking money from friends in her life. The real reason, though, was that she didn't want payment when she'd caused so much pain.

She'd similarly rejected the offers she received from vendors who wanted her fame in exchange for farthings. She didn't want those opportunities to carry her into contact with Clare, who'd pounced on them like she knew he would.

Instead, she married noble. She hosted dinner parties. She used Robert's carriage for consultations with dressmakers or home decorators—not much more. In order to forget what she'd gone through, she remembered what she'd dreamed of when she was the poor village girl whose gifts her parents didn't understand.

Until she just . . . couldn't.

Did she regret walking the slippered, candlelit path right into her contemptuous divorce? In some ways, yes.

In the end, though, it was worth it to avoid Clare.

Nevertheless, Beatrice could not now call on the de Noughton carriage. She'd returned home from Harpy & Hind yesterday in uncommonly poor spirits, spent the day restless, then put herself to sleep in her usual manner. She knew the practical particulars of the journey, namely how she would reach the royal castle, would not be easy. Destitute from her divorce, her only choice was the cheapest means possible.

Leaving her here, in her very first Wagons-For-You, in the company of the old woman snoring next to her. The young couple on the bench across from her—still in their wedding finery, presumably embarking on their honeymoon—were canoodling shamelessly.

On the bench next to them, Beatrice spied with displeasure the latest issue of *Mythria Magazine*. The cover was a printed conjuration of Clare and Beatrice on the stairs of Robert's manor. **Claretrice—as in Love as Ever!** proclaimed the headline.

Beatrice resolved to discuss Mythria's declining journalistic integrity with the queen.

While the bride looked preoccupied with her husband's wandering hands, Beatrice nonetheless wished to ensure she escaped recognition. Letting her hair curtain the front of her face, she sought to blend into the carriage wall. She diverted her gaze from the shiny cover, not needing to see the intense way Clare was looking at her nor the embarrassing flush in her cheeks.

Fortunately, Beatrice's head magic did not only work to impress local nobility. In circumstances like these, her magic could offer the perfect escape.

She closed her eyes. Fighting to ignore the uneven journey of the wagon, she slowed her heart rate, concentrating on more comfortable times. Fonder memories.

The magic began to work. She knew when she no longer smelled greasy roast gryphon, the stomach-churning scent changing into the sweet summer ripeness of roselia flowers. The thumping terrain under her went next, becoming soft grass. The head magic of prophecy was uncommon but not unheard of in Mythria. Beatrice's gift to peer through the mists *backward* was far rarer.

The insides of her eyelids melted like morning dew into the vision of the loveliest place she'd ever been. The roselia fields near her village, where her parents would pick from the swaying white field only the purest-petaled flowers for their stall.

Beatrice did not expect this refuge to make her want to cry.

In hindsight, she wasn't surprised. She should have known the first time in years she used her gift for peace would only remind her of what she now used it for instead.

She exhaled unevenly, pulling herself together. For this wagon ride, what she needed was escape.

Thump. Under her, the wagon hit bumpy ground, threatening to break her magic.

She pushed herself to relax. Her head magic worked best when she was calm, centered. It was why her bedchamber provided such ironically perfect conditions for relived repetitions of the worst day of her life.

She summoned from her memories the moment when she was most relaxed—with her magic, she could call on not only specific scenes, but certain *feelings*, for which her powers would produce forth the corresponding memory. Without knowing which moment she had in mind, she wished for peaceful, contented calm.

Relaxation emerged in the form of firelight, the feeling of crisp sheets under her. It was like she was physically transported in time, but in a dream, where she could only watch what she was doing from outside-inside of herself. Still, every detail was perfectly rendered. Every smell, every flicker of light.

In the memory, she was pressed close to a warm body. His smell weakened her instantly, instinctively. Deep, welcoming. Like dark woods under the night sky.

He was kissing the skin of her shoulder, where sweat lingered, his mixed with hers. Relaxation was no longer the word for what she felt. Supple warmth softened her limbs. The insides of her thighs welcomed the impression of fingers, urging her to unravel. Lips followed, in the same places. Gently rough.

The memory's resonance returned to her now. While she'd been touched in those places since, she was certain she had never been touched in those *ways*.

Invitation on her lips, she lifted her head to face him, coming eye to eye with—

Clare Grandhart.

She jerked out of the memory magic forcefully, her head knocking into the wooden plank of the wagon behind her.

The hard thud caught the notice of the honeymooning couple, who paused their handsy proceedings, for which she was distantly grateful. Wincing preemptively, Beatrice could feel the very moment recognition flickered into the bride's eyes.

"Ghosts alive," the woman gasped. "I knew it was you."

Beatrice shifted in her seat. *Ugh*. Even in the magic sex dream she was having in the middle of her Wagon-For-You, Clare was still managing to screw with her. Fate was being unkind to her.

"No, no," she replied hurriedly. "We've never met. I'm just passing through." Perhaps if she protested enough—

"No," the bride insisted. She held up the magazine. "You're Lady Beatrice of the Four," the woman insisted, pointing to Beatrice's conjurated image in her hand. "We're traveling with a *hero*!"

Of course her voice shrilled with the final sentence. The predictable effect resulted. The groom's eyes went round. The old woman next to Beatrice startled up out of her slumber. She now wished she were trapped in the stone prison under the Southern Sea instead of here.

Frustrated, Beatrice reached out, snatching the magazine from the bride's hands. She rolled the glossy parchment up and stuffed the magazine into the pocket of her skirt. Confiscated, the pages could do her no more harm!

The starstruck woman offered no resistance. "Can I have your autograph?" she inquired eagerly.

"No, I don't do autographs," Beatrice replied.

When the disappointment of the dismissal flickered in the woman's eyes, remorse hit Beatrice's heart. She intended no disrespect—with her upbringing, she understood very well how it felt to be looked down on by those you looked up to. Clare *loved* doing autographs, she knew. Even so, she could only ever find them unsavory.

Why should she commemorate how she cost Galwell his life by signing something for a stranger?

"*Wait.*" Renewed exhilaration lit the honeymooner's features. "Can you use your magic on us? I have a question about something in the past."

Now Beatrice wished she could render herself invisible. Or even spontaneously combust.

Unfortunately, however, her magic of reverse prophecy was known throughout the realm—and throughout this wagon, apparently.

Exasperated, Beatrice foresaw hours of conversation just like this on the long journey to Queendom. She *needed* to procure separate transport, somehow. If only she had—

Wait.

"I'll gladly use my head magic for your purposes," Beatrice replied. "For a fee."

The girl faltered. "Aren't you . . . rich?" she asked.

"I'm in a wagon with you," Beatrice pointed out. "Are *you* rich?"

Beatrice didn't need Elowen's gifts to see excitement spark in the bride nor the way her groom shifted uncomfortably when she shoved her hand into her satchel. "It doesn't feel very heroic to charge commoners," he ventured.

"You're right, it isn't," Beatrice said. "It'll be twenty-five farthings." Not enough for conveyance to match the de Noughton carriage, but enough, she guessed, to pay some local farmer with spare time to drive her the rest of the way.

While the woman collected the coins, her husband continued to look nervous. "We saved that for our honeymoon, love," he reminded her.

The observation earned him only his bride's narrowed stare. "Hiding something, Kolton?"

"Yrice," the man—Kolton—started, reaching gently for his wife's hands. "The past is the past. We're embarking on our future. The rest of our lives. I can't wait to spend every day with you. It's like I'm finally awake and everything that came before you was merely a . . . waking dream."

He leaned forward, staring into her eyes. When Yrice did the same, Beatrice saw her chances for compensation melting like the mush in the couple's gazes—

Until Yrice's expression hardened. "It was no dream," she said. "And I want to see it."

Beatrice hid the smile she could not help. "I'll need your hands," she said. "Whose past will we be entering?"

"His," Yrice replied. Her gaze rounded on Kolton, sword-sharp. "Give her your hand," she ordered.

Kolton complied.

Holding one of each of their hands in hers, Beatrice repeated the psychological preparation she did with her own memories, closing her eyes, evening her heartbeat. She would enter his memory through her connection to him, bringing Yrice with her by the same means. "Is there a day or a feeling I'm looking for?"

"Helena's banquet," Yrice intoned.

Cracking one eye open, Beatrice caught Kolton gulping nervously. She clenched his hand in her grip, expecting his resistance. Not only did she need Yrice's farthings—she was no great supporter of inconstant lovers.

With her magic, she delved into his memory, which produced forth the desired destination. Unlike with her own memories, which she could replicate more fully, when she entered someone else's, the limits were more distinct. With the girl by her side, hands enjoined, they walked into the crowded, candlelit scene, separated from the events by gossamer distorting veils. Music was playing, lanterns strung up in the small square where couples were dancing. The edges of perception were hazy, outside of what surrounded past-Kolton himself.

He was dancing with Yrice, whose head rested on his shoulder. It looked rather romantic, until Kolton whispered in her ear, earning bashful giggles. Then it looked *very* romantic.

While Beatrice watched, though, the memory-Kolton separated from Yrice to walk from the dancing square to the drink barrels. Beatrice led Yrice by the hand, following him.

Beatrice knew what they would find. She knew what she would have found if she'd entered Robert's room when he was "painting" village women he'd hired to "model," too. She'd never much cared. She'd felt worse betrayals.

Yes, indeed, behind the barrels, they found Kolton. What he was doing with some flaxen-haired woman who was not Yrice—Helena, presumably—was decidedly *not* dancing.

Beatrice was relieved. She would get paid!

Without warning, the wagon lurched violently. The movement startled Beatrice out of the conjured memory. While Yrice in the wagon looked furious, the emotions of the memoryholder or the conjurist never interrupted the magic in this way. The cart really was rocking.

"I knew it!" Yrice cried, wrenching off her wedding ring. "With Helena! My best friend!"

"I can explain—" Kolton mustered.

He didn't get the chance.

With sounds like hammer strikes, arrowheads slammed into the wood of the wagon, their tips piercing through the planks. Instinctually, Beatrice grabbed for Kolton's collar, flinging him to the side just fast enough to evade the next volley.

"We're under attack," she said, fearing it was unclear.

When gasps went up from the other passengers, she stood, glancing over the wagon's walls. The coachman was slumped over, his corpse arrow-riddled. She saw, surrounding the speeding horses, what her sinking heart had expected.

Outlaws.

The outlaws' arrows flew past her—while she knew she was vulnerable, she needed to stop the horses. Springing forward, she seized the reins. When she pulled sharply, the creatures slowed but would not stop nor turn no matter how hard Beatrice pulled. When one outlaw rode up near them, sword held high, the steeds surged forth in uncontrollable surprise, the reins yanked from Beatrice's hands.

With the iron-masked men surrounding them, she rummaged under the seat, grasping—*yes*. The crossbow she'd hoped the coachman kept on him for circumstances like this. Slinging the weapon up, she shot, her bolt finding her intended mark in the face mask of the nearest outlaw.

She was surprised by how readily muscle memory sprung to life in her. Drink-inclined divorcée or not, she possessed more combat experience than the gryphon's share of the realm's foot soldiers. Years of dinner parties, it turned out, could not vanquish the Beatrice who'd fended off the Order.

Still—glimpsing farther down the road, she saw other outlaws gathering. They intended to trap the travelers.

The horses did not slow. They charged forth toward the waiting brigands. Beatrice needed to get everyone out of the wagon.

Cradling her crossbow, she leapt back into the rear seating where she'd ridden. "Everyone, heads low!" she instructed urgently. Reaching for the old woman first, Beatrice looked for the softest patch of ground onto which she could toss her when—

When one horse, unlike the others, sped into the fray. Beatrice couldn't help pausing, watching the rider cut down outlaws, his sword wheeling, cords of muscle stretching in his forearms. He fought dirty, yet made his maneuvers look like poetry, the combat equivalent of sultry rhymes slipped under your door—kicking up dust with his horse's hooves, then using the diversion to grab the man nearest him, only to fling the outlaw with one powerful throw right onto the sword of the distracted outlaw next to him.

While Beatrice watched, he emerged from the dust cloud, the sun striking his stunning features. Beatrice faltered, realizing—it couldn't be.

"Clare Grandhart!" Yrice shouted exuberantly.

Oh, Ghosts no.

"I think I may faint," the young wife went on.

"It's not *that* impressive," Kolton grumbled.

Beatrice was furious. Three run-ins in as many days? None as terrible as right now with him looking . . . the way he looked. Like he was made for exactly this moment, his shining hair windswept in perfect waves, his lean musculature poised for combat.

Beatrice was surely cursed.

She prepared to jump from the wagon to the ground, figuring she could evade his notice if she slunk off stealthily, her heart pounding in her chest.

She was livid.

"Mythrians, fear not. I have rescued you," Clare called out, his voice vaulting over the field like he practiced rescuing people. He pulled his horse up in front of the wagon. Of course, *then* the steeds stopped. What was Beatrice, chopped gryphon liver? "Is anyone injured?"

With his words, Yrice fainted—right into Beatrice, who caught her swoon. The movement unsurprisingly drew the eye of Clare. While Beatrice stood, helpless under Yrice's sagging frame, the famous hero squinted in the sun, focusing on her.

"Why, hello again," Clare pronounced, directly to her. Oh, how she remembered his unhidden pride. The way swordplay brought him to life. "We must stop meeting like this," he remarked.

No, no, no.

Gently, she laid Yrice on the seat, where Kolton leapt on the opportunity to tend to her. Spinning on her heel, Beatrice leapt from the wagon and strode into the road.

While Clare urgently promised the other passengers he would return to them posthaste, Beatrice took off, storming down the incline—right for where she'd seen the outlaws gathering, intending to lay siege to their wagon.

"Is anyone left alive?" she cried out. "I'd very much like to be kidnapped now!"

5

Elowen

lowen planned to flee. She really, really did. The first decent chance she got, she was going to hike up her cloak and sprint through the Mythrian countryside, escaping this situation for good. The problem was, while galloping on horseback together, Elowen had to hold on to Vandra. And when she held on to Vandra, she *felt* Vandra. And Vandra Ravenfall radiated bliss.

It had been hours since Elowen consented to being taken. Thanks to her very close proximity to Vandra, Elowen had since absorbed every last bit of Vandra's good mood. To Elowen, Vandra's feelings were already more potent than other people's. Perhaps because she'd once touched every last bit of Vandra with not just her hands, but her mouth. She used to delight in all the ways she could unravel her. It was the best part of what was mostly a punishing endeavor, questing across Mythria to rescue Thessia and then save the entire realm.

Touching Vandra again felt like being pulled up to the surface after a life underwater. Elowen found herself doing ridiculous things such as marveling at the beauty of the sunset—a stunning pink, reminiscent of rhodolite—and adoring the caress of the wind on her face.

They were riding atop the same horse Vandra had ten years ago, a striking fellow named Killer, who was black as obsidian, from his coat, to his mane, to his eyes. In the past, the sight of him lit up

Elowen's heart. His presence indicated Vandra was nearby, which meant aside from the real trouble that lay ahead, some fun trouble awaited Elowen. That was what Vandra used to be—fun trouble. Near the end of the quest, Elowen and Vandra's late-night adventures had become an open secret among the Four. It was a source of light teasing from Beatrice and Clare. They would make a game out of keeping Elowen from leaving for the night, desperate to get her to admit where she was going. Galwell was more earnest in his approach.

"Who is she to you really?" he'd once asked.

"It's nothing to worry about," Elowen had responded.

"I never said I was worried." Galwell leaned closer. "I just want to see you happy."

Elowen hated those memories. She'd spent years whittling the shape of them until they were far too sharp to revisit, because to think on them too much would remind her of everything she'd given up when she fled to the trees. But there she sat, clutching Vandra's waist, smelling the jasrose oil on her neck, thinking fondly of their shared past. Fondly! What a cruel joke! Elowen True was fond of nothing but despair!

"What a lovely sunset," Elowen found herself saying, right when she meant to hiss out some insult about . . . something. She couldn't remember what.

Vandra, already warm with joy, grew warmer yet. She tugged gently on the reins until her horse came to a stop. "That's why I took the scenic route. Best view in all of the land."

It was the first time they'd been still since departing. The countryside came with its own kind of quiet, so very different from the noisy treetops where Elowen resided. Elowen had grown accustomed to the shake of wind through leaves or the never-ending bustle of animals scurrying from branch to branch. Down in the valley, between rolling verdant hills, the shimmery pink sky fading with every passing breath, it was so quiet Elowen could do nothing but marvel at her own contentment.

"You have no idea how lovely it is to be near you," Vandra said.

Yes I do, Elowen thought, feeling all of Vandra's fulfillment.

"Yes you do," Vandra remembered, right on cue. Her laugh pressed against the silence. "How could I ever forget the ways in which you can feel me?"

Elowen jerked back. Free from touching Vandra, a wave of resentment instantly flooded in, restoring the coldness of her heart after hours exposed to Vandra's unbearable brightness.

Elowen leapt down from the horse, and grabbed her satchel once she was on the ground. The quiet no longer felt like peace. It was cruel in its patience, granting far too much room for Elowen's loud, angry thoughts to stomp around. *How could you do this? Why didn't you let go sooner? What good can come from returning to this realm again?*

Elowen set out to find a cave. Yes. That's where she was headed. Someplace dark and chilly where she could tuck herself inside for days, surviving on nothing but patches of grass for food and a healthy dose of misery for company.

"You know I won't let you get away," Vandra called out.

Elowen would have to do something to rid herself of Vandra. Kill her? That sounded dreadful. Elowen didn't want anyone to die. And blood was so messy. She just wanted to be left alone. When she was alone, she was centered. She could remember how much the realm had hurt her, and why it was she shouldn't return to it.

She did not dignify Vandra with a response. Vandra would find a way to be charming in return, and it would chip away at Elowen's already damaged armor.

When Elowen was younger, she kept people at a distance as a test of sorts. Were they truly loyal, or did they just want something from her because of her wealthy parents or her impressive brother?

Now Elowen kept people at a distance because growing near to them came with far too much pain. The better you knew someone, the harder it was to lose them. Elowen had already lost the other half of herself in Galwell. The better half, really. She'd lost her only real friend in Beatrice, who'd never even considered Elowen a friend at all. She'd lost her purchase in the world. And now she'd even lost her sole source of income. It was amazing how she'd helped save the entire realm and she'd come out of it as nothing but a loser.

Elowen could not stand to lose anything else.

She walked until the sunset turned to dusk, with Vandra and the horse a few paces back. From her satchel of Domynia costumes, a series of pings started up—another private delivery on her message tapestry. Elowen rummaged through her bag until she found it.

Please talk to me, the message said. *Though I do quite like my view back here.*

You told me you wanted to purchase my costumes, Elowen responded, fighting to keep her body from tensing. She did not want to give Vandra the satisfaction of seeing the effect she had. *You lied. We have nothing else to discuss.*

"I will buy them from you," Vandra called out. "For whatever you want me to pay."

I want none of your money, Elowen wrote. Speaking aloud to Vandra always managed to get her into trouble. Perhaps writing would be safe. *And I'd never sell these precious pieces to a pretend fan. You don't deserve them.*

"I truly love *Desires of the Night*," Vandra said.

Elowen whipped around, no longer able to hide her fury. How

dare Vandra mock her interests, pretending to enjoy the very shadow play Elowen had loved since she was a young child? She expected to find Vandra with a mean-spirited smirk on her face. Instead, Vandra looked genuine, though Elowen could never know for sure, which only brought more frustration.

"See?" Vandra said. "I mean it. Just like I mean it when I say I don't want to hurt you."

It was utter agony, knowing people's emotions but never knowing their *intentions*. What was it Vandra really wanted? She'd already succeeded in dragging Elowen toward Queendom so she could attend Thessia's wedding. Yes, Elowen was currently fleeing, but they both knew it was a fruitless exercise and Vandra would get her back on track. So why was Vandra still flirting with Elowen along the way? Their entire past relationship had been built around stolen moments on opposite sides of the same quest. Under these new circumstances, Elowen could not even imagine how they could mimic such a situation. Or why Vandra would wish to in the first place.

Elowen whirled back around, newly furious. "Too late!"

She heard Vandra pick up her pace. "How have I hurt you? Please tell me. I am quite invested in learning more. Much like my investment in *Desires of the Night*."

Elowen hated this. She did not want to lay herself bare. There was nothing she could say other than she did not want to be seen, or known. She wanted to be safe. And Vandra was not safe. Not at all.

"I can't get into this," Elowen said.

Vandra fell back, letting the distance grow between them again. "Ah, yes. There's the Elowen I once knew," she said. "It's funny how I'd almost forgotten. My memory can be so forgiving when my heart feels such excitement."

Elowen ached at those words. She knew she was being difficult. Now she had confirmation from Vandra. But she couldn't apologize, because that would build a bridge between them, and Elowen could not bear to bring herself closer to Vandra, especially when she'd so swiftly proved that she'd only ever cause Vandra pain.

"This is precisely why I'm single again," Vandra lamented.

With one sentence, Vandra had managed to pique Elowen's curiosity in the exact way she could not ignore. She had a whole host of questions. *Who have you been with since you knew me? What happened? How do I compare?* They were the wrong thoughts, and Elowen scolded herself for having them. They were never anything serious. She had no claim over Vandra. Still, she had to comment, saying, "I'm sure your breakup was more their fault than yours," because it seemed to be the kindest, truest, and safest statement she could make on the subject.

"For someone so committed to ignoring me, you do paint me in the most generous of lights," Vandra responded.

Ghosts. Elowen had done the opposite of what she intended. Further proof she shouldn't be roaming the realm with Vandra this way.

"She was the one who broke up with me, I'll have you know," Vandra continued.

"Why?" Elowen asked. She attempted to make the question sound harsh, judgmental even, so Vandra wouldn't think Elowen was being flattering again.

Vandra came up to her ear again. "It's sweet you think I'll tell you all my secrets," she whispered.

With that, silence fell over the two women again. Good. The less talking, the better. Hopefully it would nurture the small amount of bitterness Vandra had let creep into her cheerful facade.

Maybe with every step, she'd resent Elowen more and more, until, finally, she abandoned her altogether.

The pings started up once again. Elowen nearly tossed her tapestry to the hills. "Stop messaging me!"

"I'm not!" Vandra protested.

Confused, Elowen looked to her tapestry. It was a reminder—her heart-healing appointment was about to start.

"*Fuck me*," Elowen muttered.

"Really?" Vandra asked. "On what condition?"

Elowen shot her a glare. At that moment, nothing was worse than Elowen being inflicted with horniness. "Please grant me some privacy," she pleaded. "I'm begging you."

Vandra smirked. "I do love it when you beg." Her grin widened, even more dazzling than Elowen remembered. She was so good at bringing things back to playful. She never let a bad moment linger. It was a large part of what made her so dangerous. You never knew her true aim until it was far too late. "See?" she said coyly. "You know me just as well as I know you."

Vandra did not know everything, but she did know Elowen's weaknesses. *Intimately.* And she was, regrettably, playing on every single one. Elowen hadn't meant to let her guard down around Vandra, but somehow, she had. She could never do it again.

A few paces ahead, right where the curve in the road began to straighten, sat a quaint-looking inn. It was the first sign of civilization they'd seen in a long while.

"How perfect," Vandra commented. "We need lodging for the night. We're nowhere near Queendom yet. We can stay here. You and me in our own bed. Doesn't that sound delightful?"

"We will be getting *two* rooms," Elowen snarled.

"Even better," Vandra said. "I love to have enough space to

freely move about. Though we've certainly made good use of tight spots when necessary." She winked.

A conjuration alert appeared in front of Elowen. It was a powerful head magic that had made it possible to communicate with anyone in the realm. In the last ten years, the wisest magicians in Mythria had found a way for the residents to tap into that magic source wherever they wanted instead of needing a specific conjuration device. All anyone had to do was snap their fingers and accept the conjuration to start a connection with someone or something else, and they could pinch and poke the air to change the scale of whatever they'd conjured.

Elowen snapped her fingers to accept the incoming personal conjuration.

At once a soft-voiced woman flickered into place, seated in a chair that did not exist on the wide-open road. "Elowen," the woman said, alarmed. "Where are you?"

It was Lettice, Elowen's heart healer. Every seven days, Lettice and Elowen met via live conjuration appointment to discuss Elowen's feelings.

"Hello!" Vandra responded cheerily. "Elowen and I are traveling through the countryside! I kidnapped her! With her consent, of course!"

Lettice could not hide her widened eyes, nor could she compose herself quickly enough to stop her jaw from dropping. Elowen fought off the urge to laugh. No dark thought or despairing memory ever seemed to shock Lettice. Of course Vandra relaying her successful kidnapping would be what finally did it. It *was* kind of funny.

Ever since their first meeting, Lettice had been suggesting Elowen make an attempt to return to society, and Elowen had been gently but firmly dodging the request. She claimed she had all she needed in the trees. She grew her own fruits and vegetables out on the porch, and every few days a carrier bird delivered whatever other essentials Elowen required. She had shadow plays to entertain her and the queen's salary to support her. Now all of that was gone, and here Elowen was, stomping through the hills with the very woman whose name she refused to speak in her appointments, but whose presence she referenced often, calling her a nuisance, or a thorn in Elowen's side.

"Sorry to intrude," Vandra continued. "I suspect this is a private matter. I need to check us into our rooms anyway." Vandra walked right up to the conjuration. She dropped her voice to a stage whisper. "Do me a favor and be sure this one doesn't attempt to run off." She pointed to Elowen. "She loves to do that. And she used to say *I* was the theatrical one. She has a wedding she must attend, so leaving now will do her no good, and she knows it." Vandra blew a kiss. "All my love!" She strutted toward the hitching post beside the inn, her black horse following closely behind.

"Elowen, is everything all right? Do I need to call the royal guard to help you?" Lettice asked once Vandra had gone inside.

This time Elowen *did* laugh. "I'm quite certain the guard won't help, seeing as Vandra is now a member. She's taking me to the queen's wedding."

Lettice fought off another gasp. "I wasn't sure if you'd heard the news. I'd hoped we could talk about it."

Elowen waved her hand. "There is nothing to say."

This was Elowen's favorite response to Lettice's many inquiries. And yet Elowen was the one who'd set up the heart-healing appointments for herself. She wasn't exactly sure why she'd done it, only that she'd grown tired of being the only person subjected to her own thoughts and feelings. Unfortunately, that did nothing to convince her to share most of those thoughts and feelings with Lettice. She'd talked through some—as much as she could manage—but she resisted saying it all. Because when Elowen spoke certain things out loud, it always seemed sillier than it did in her head. Too small to be as big of a deal as it was. And Elowen hated to feel that small.

"Will Beatrice be attending?" Lettice asked. Elowen could not sense emotions through conjurations. Not magically, at least. Still, she could feel Lettice straining to conceal her genuine curiosity. As her heart healer, Lettice wanted Elowen to mend her friendship with Beatrice because it was the healthy thing to do. As a Mythrian, Lettice was clearly *dying* to know why the famous Beatrice and Elowen no longer spoke.

"What great fortune!" Vandra shouted from inside the inn, loud enough to distract both Elowen and Lettice.

Good. Elowen wasn't planning on answering Lettice anyway.

Vandra peeked her head outside. "We got the last two rooms!"

Lettice tapped her finger on her cheek. "Is this the woman you've told me about? The one whose name you won't share?"

"No," Elowen said.

"Maybe this is good," Lettice said softly, ignoring Elowen's answer. "Maybe you can have some fun for once."

"I hate fun," Elowen responded. "And I won't be having any." She snapped her fingers twice, effectively ending the conjuration.

Vandra came back outside with two keys in hand. "Did you have a good appointment? I use a heart healer as well. They are quite transformative. By the way, which room would you like? One is the corner, with windows on either side, and I know you prefer a scenic view."

"Stop pretending you care about me!" Elowen shouted, unable to withstand another moment of Vandra's thoughtful attention. "I am here. I am going to the wedding. You have done your job. Can you just leave me alone along the way?"

"Why do you assume that's all I want?" Vandra asked. She did not bother to conceal her hurt. "I know you've been away from society for a while, but surely you have not forgotten that people who care about one another do things like ask each other questions."

Elowen knew Vandra desired her. That had been clear from the first moment they met, ten long years ago, when Elowen caught Vandra leaving decaying meat around their camping tent in an attempt to get carcass hawks to swarm them on the way to the Grimauld Mines. Elowen had gone into that interaction expecting a confrontation, only to end up with her tongue down Vandra's throat and her hands grabbing her waist, eager for more. But Vandra *caring* for her? That couldn't possibly be true. In ten years, neither one of them had ever attempted to reach out. How could Vandra possibly care for her?

While Elowen stood there stunned, unable to respond, Vandra took the opportunity to dig in deeper. "We have a chance to do what we couldn't ten years ago. We are no longer adversaries. I am not here to thwart you. Do you really wish not to know me better?"

"I don't want to know you at all," Elowen lied, and for once, she considered herself lucky to be the only one with the ability to know how much her head and her heart disagreed.

6

Clare

In fifteen years of valiant deeds, Clare hadn't often *not* known what to do. He'd pulled himself out of poverty in the Vast Plains by sharpening his skills in thievery. He'd faced monsters that caused others to soil themselves, isolating the creatures' weak spots with finesse. Where others failed, he rarely had.

Even more rarely had he found himself rendered speechless.

Now, watching Beatrice walk into the waiting clutches of bandits instead of facing him, was one of those times.

Striding straight into the fray, she looked stunning. *Fuck*, he loved it when she strode into the fray. It was like every quality of hers he couldn't help noticing in their recent meetings was gloriously on display. The years had only made her more beautiful, giving her face more freckles, rounding her hips—hips swaying with every step down the grassy incline into certain danger.

Sure, she was a little dirty, a little disheveled from recent events. In Clare's honest opinion, it only made her hotter.

He'd made messes of their past few conversations, he knew. His emotions had overcome him like superior swordsmen. He should only have felt wounded rage, and yet she left him with infuriating urges to prove himself. When presented with the chance, dread feuded with hope in him until each was exhausted.

In fairness, he consoled himself, how could he have done otherwise? This was *Beatrice*. The woman for whom his wayward passion had been left to steep for ten years with her uncompromising spite, and they had melded mysteriously—like the dark potionmaking in which the witches of Megophar were rumored to indulge—into feelings Clare Grandhart was embarrassed to give names.

But he knew what they were, slithering in his veins like smiling snakes, ready to stop his heart.

He'd spent the past decade rehearsing what he would say if fate ever reunited them, fighting imaginary fights with imaginary Beatrices during his morning exercises or under Wiglaf's nonjudgmental gaze.

Considering you only speak to me when the world is ending, what is it this time? The Nightbiter Plague?

How can you hate me for throwing away a few months when you were ready to destroy much more?

You can't trust me? Beatrice, how could I ever trust you?

I've missed you. I think about you so much it's like your head magic has become mine.

Of course I loved you, damn it.

Then the wedding invitation had dashed his imaginings. Their reunion reshaped into diligent duty, the vain, insecure effort of one Clare Grandhart to uphold his own myth. He'd clung on to the rogue hope of proving himself in Beatrice's eyes. Instead he'd only managed to fumble everything.

Well, he wouldn't fumble this rescue!

She was no longer far from the thickets where the cutpurses waited to ensnare the wagon's passengers. It was what his resourcefulness needed to reengage. Right. Danger.

He leapt from his horse, rushing to her side.

He'd done much rushing to her side in the past couple of days, he recognized. He grudgingly doubted he could ever free himself of the instinct. Despite himself, he supposed she remained his favorite destination to rush to.

When he caught up with her, her stride did not change. "This isn't happening," she informed him flatly.

"Walking away won't make it stop," he replied.

She glared, right into his face, her fury unflinching. He found it not unlike staring into a sunrise—glorious.

"I was *not* just rescued," she insisted. "By *you*."

He could not help smiling. *Yes*, he counseled himself. *Yes, this is good*. Noblemen's parties weren't his home field. Daring rescues were. "It really was quite a dangerous situation," he observed.

She stopped sharply. He watched her ready some slashing remark—the only manner of reply she had left for him—then seemed to restrain herself from such squabbling. For the record, he would have welcomed the slashing. He preferred squabbling over silence if confronted with the choice. "What are you doing here?" she demanded.

"What was I doing on Queen's Road? The same thing you were, I imagine," he replied. "Going to Queendom."

His plain logic only infuriated her once more. She strode straight off again—into the foliage ahead. Clare intuited what was coming but was too far away to reach her. Sure enough, from the rustling shrubbery, out sprang the waiting outlaws.

Clare went motionless. Beatrice did, too, evidently deciding she did not *really* wish to be kidnapped.

"I see," she whispered out of the corner of her lips, her *fucking mesmerizingly kissable lips*. "You are as bad at rescue attempts as you are at honesty."

Her words startled him out of sexualizing her frustration. "Honesty?" he repeated indignantly.

Past the pounding in his heart, he distantly noticed the outlaws' leader pause, removing his iron mask to reveal grizzled features. Clare did not know whether the men hesitated in recognition of their famous captives or out of politeness, permitting their prey to cease fighting. Or perhaps the outlaws just smelled good gossip.

Whatever their reason, nothing would change Clare's stubborn need to justify himself. "I never lied to you, not once," he insisted.

"The first words you ever said to me were lies!"

"Beatrice, the first words I said to you were a *pick-up line*!" He wrestled with his flash of ire. Heroes out to demonstrate their valor did not, he imagined, snap at even infuriating, infuriatingly lovely women. He glimpsed the outlaws' leader sheathe his sword now, his men following suit. Clare hadn't intended to forestall the bandits with relationship drama. He merely did not resent the result.

"Exactly!" Beatrice replied hotly. "Line, lie. What's the difference?"

The foremost outlaw raised his sword like he was raising his hand in class.

"What line did you use that worked on the likes of her?" he inquired.

Clare said nothing, despite very, very much wanting to. Bragging, he intuited, would do him no favors.

"He said," Beatrice answered flatly, "'Are you a time-walker, because I see you in my future.'"

The bandits nodded, suitably impressed.

Clare bowed his head in modest gratitude. "Not strictly speaking a lie, since here we are," he said. But when he glanced to Beatrice, he found her unamused. Sobering, he cleared his throat. "It's not my fault you walked away from our . . . encounter thinking something I never said."

"*Encounter?*" Beatrice exploded. "Oh, like I'm some woodland sprite—"

"You do sometimes sound like one—"

"WE SLEPT TOGETHER!" she shouted over him.

Clare swallowed. He saw the outlaw's scarred eyebrow rise. "Perhaps now is not the time—"

"Oh, no." She rounded on him fully, stabbing one finger into his chest. "You do *not* get to bury this conversation just because these enterprising outlaws have decided to capture us. How convenient for you!" She stepped closer. "I'm sure you'd rather run. It's what you do."

Finally, his pride escaped him. "Fine!" he returned. "You want to get into it? Let's get into it, Beatrice!"

He couldn't help saying her name. It was like sucking on sour candy.

He welcomed the chance to finally "get into it." On the Four's quest, they'd only ever danced in circles around the subject of their first liaison. Neither of them had wanted to discuss it, not when they knew the quest might cut their lives short, nor when their relationship on the road started to grow fonder despite their inauspicious start. What they had started to build was too fragile.

Now, however, they were survivors. Survivors who hurt each other.

Clare felt grimly ready for the fight. Eager to expose old wounds to the light of day. "We slept together and I made you no promises," he continued. "Yes, I snuck out in the morning but I had work to get to, which you know very well."

"It sounds like there may have been fault on both sides," the outlaw ventured.

Clare flung his hand in the man's direction. "Yes! Exactly!"

"Then answer me *this* honestly." Beatrice's voice dropped into its deadliest register yet. "If said *work* hadn't been the job Galwell hired you for, which neither of us knew would bring us into close contact for months, would you have *ever* tried to contact me again after our night together?"

Every one of the outlaws halted. Clare noticed a few eyes behind the iron masks exchanging glances of genuine interest.

In the hush descending over them, Clare sighed. He hated it when this happened. Frustrating or not—hating him with what he maintained was profound injustice or not—she was *right*.

He had met Beatrice at a tavern. He was only in town for one night before he took on a dangerous but exciting job for Galwell the Great, who needed someone who could lead him and his two companions to the Grimauld Mines to retrieve the Orb.

Clare was one of the few Mythrians who had ever escaped Grimauld with his life since its ill-fated excavation had uncovered the ghastly Orb Weavers, once dwelling undisturbed in the darkness under the mountain. Northern Raiders had captured him while he was pursuing a job and hauled him into the mines to be devoured. He had escaped, barely.

His fellow bandits—his friends, the only ones he'd ever known then—had not.

Galwell the Great, a nobleman's son whom whispers of legendary magic followed, heard rumors of one of Grimauld's only survivors. He hired Clare, who couldn't have cared less what magical object Galwell sought in the mines. Reckless and restless with grief, Clare spent the night before joining Galwell's expedition with the gorgeous woman he'd noticed in the local tavern—Beatrice.

He had left with the morning light, his custom with women in his youth. Only when he reported to Galwell did he discover one of the young nobleman's companions whom he was about to lead into Grimauld was none other than his attempted one-night stand.

With inquisitive outlaws surrounding him, Clare both wanted

to explain himself and feared the same. He'd received nothing from Beatrice except spiteful silence for the past decade. He did not know if his heart could withstand her rejection of the real reason he fled from their wondrous first night.

Cowardice decided for him. He would make no such confession. "We can't *know* what we might have done in the past . . ." he muttered instead.

The outlaw leader winced.

His men readied their swords as if to say, *You're dead either way, friend*—until Beatrice held up a halting hand.

"*No,*" she said. She rounded on Clare. "Answer. The. Question."

Clare Grandhart was, once more, speechless.

The iron masks surrounded them, swords stayed for the moment. He would likely die with the woman who captivated his dreams hating him, never knowing the full truth.

He would *not*, however, die with lies on his lips.

"No," he finally mustered, feeling much like he had when those raiders hauled him into the mines, presumably never to return. "No, I had no plans to contact you."

Beatrice did not sneer. She did not rage.

Instead, the strangest calm seemed to fall over her. "Thank you," she said.

"But we didn't really know each other then, Beatrice," he added, desperate for her to see the truth. He didn't like the look in her eyes. Didn't want to imagine what lies she was whispering to herself using his honesty.

"Oh, I knew you perfectly after that morning," she said, her voice unnaturally smooth. "You've proven me right over and over. At the funeral. Yesterday."

He winced, hating the comparison.

"What I did . . . after the funeral," he ground out, grimacing at even the reference of his infraction, "was not the same. My actions were wrong. But they were nothing next to what you did."

He felt it now. The dangerous calm of closing in on the real fight, the unforgivable fight. Their relationship had progressed despite the unfortunate misunderstanding of their first meeting. On the road with Galwell and Elowen, it had flourished, even, into passion and perhaps something more.

It had never recovered from what happened at Galwell's funeral. If the past decade was any indication, it probably never would.

"Tell me my feelings were unfounded," he went on. His words were a challenge, one he desperately wanted her to rise to. To fight with him, and work out how they'd hurt each other so they could begin to heal.

He did not, however, have the chance. Because they were surrounded by outlaws. While his feud with Beatrice had escalated, Clare had failed to notice he and she were no longer holding their captors' interest. Well, Ghosts forgive them for getting into deeper context instead of sticking to scribesheet gossip! Honestly, did criminals have no respect for emotional honesty?

Nevertheless, Clare could not find it in him to resent the men holding him captive—for he had once stood in their place himself. Growing up with nothing on the Vast Plains, he had survived on petty banditing, constantly confronting and raiding from other like men.

When the masked men lunged forth, thinking them distracted, he had only one embarrassingly unhelpful thought. *I'd rob myself if I were them.* He was no longer them, though. He was—

"STOP."

The voice Clare was startled to hear ring out was Beatrice's. He looked over, finding her menacing their foes fearlessly, hand outstretched, holding—

His quill?

Glancing down, he realized the implement must've been jostled loose from his pockets when he caught up to her. Beatrice stabbed the feather forth threateningly, so startling that the nearest outlaw slipped on the road, feet flying out from under him, depositing him in the dirt.

She glowered. "You mean to murder us and sell our possessions for money," she presumed to the group's leader.

He narrowed his eyes. "*Murder* isn't a word we like, ma'am," he replied.

"Me neither," Beatrice returned. "Do you know who you've just threatened? This is Clare Grandhart of the Four. Hero of the realm. Face of Spark's Sport Potions. *Mythria Magazine*'s five-time winner of Sexiest Man Alive."

"Six-time, actually," Clare supplied. Past the guilty pleasure of Beatrice knowing of his accolades, he noticed hesitation commingling with curiosity in the eyes he found peering through the iron masks. The outlaws had not recognized him, he knew then. Men like these didn't spend much time in cities, so he understood why they could not identify the heroes on sight. But even those living in the grasslands had heard the songs of the Four.

"Only three living souls know what deadly magic Clare possesses," Beatrice continued. "Would you like to make it six? For, oh—how long would you say?"

She looked to him.

He could hardly comprehend what was happening. Of course, he knew what she was doing. They'd performed this old ploy on enemies in the past with unmitigated success. Hearing her invoke it now—well, it was the second time lately his heart combined hope and Beatrice in the same cauldron.

The ruse required he hide the emotion. He shrugged one shoulder. "Three seconds," he replied laconically.

"Excruciating death in three seconds?" Beatrice repeated. "Impressive, Grandhart." He knew her words were for show. Still, they . . . made him feel things.

Fortunately for them, they made the outlaws feel *other* things.

The eyes behind the iron masks grew nervous, postures stiffening with ill-concealed fear. Clare glared. He knew how this went—knew how he would have reacted in his own cutpurse days.

"Or," Beatrice entreated, her voice now sounding more sweet pumpkin-gingerroot cream than venom, "Clare could use this quill to sign your swords. Then you could sell his signature for far more farthings than the junk on this wagon."

Startled out of his shadow play–worthy show of ferocity, he glanced over. Beatrice smiled invitingly, enticing their erstwhile performers.

Her freckled cheeks. Her chestnut eyes. Her smile.

His heart nearly exploded.

The outlaws exchanged glances. "How do we know you're really Grandhart?" the outlaws' leader posed. His men hummed in recognition of the perspicacity of their commander's question.

Clare had no response to the query. In his daily life, it never came up.

Beatrice, however, faltered. Her smile changed into a reluctant grimace. Clare could only watch quizzically as she pulled from her skirts—a rolled-up magazine? With unhidden embarrassment, she unfurled the shiny parchment. Good Ghosts, he recognized the cover she displayed for the outlaws. He'd noticed it in news-handlers' shops yesterday.

Claretrice—as in Love as Ever!

The men looked from magazine Clare to real Clare. Without the faintest hesitation anymore, one stepped forward, reaching eagerly for the quill.

Clare grabbed the magazine, which Beatrice rendered freely, like she wanted nothing more to do with the damn thing. Where had she gotten this? he wondered with no meager interest.

Then the first enthusiastic bandit ventured up to Clare, quill in hand. While Beatrice strode past him in satisfaction, headed for the wagon, Clare called on muscle memory he found, if he was honest, readier than that used for swordfighting. When each iron mask presented their scabbard or satchel, he did his usual, swooping the name *Sir Clare Grandhart* onto each piece with spirited but recognizable penmanship.

Only in the idle task did he feel the quiet emergence of complicated feelings.

In truth, Clare's magic wasn't deadly. It wasn't even useful. In fact, it was embarrassing, so embarrassing he never told Galwell or Elowen or Beatrice what it was—despite nightly prying. Somehow, their joke of naming outrageous gifts he could have had changed into rumors, murmurs starting to spread of Clare's unspeakable gifts. They'd realized it was only in their interest to feed the whispers.

Beatrice revitalizing their old ruse reminded him of how keenly he'd hidden his laughable powers from them. Yet . . . it reminded him there were parts of their quest where they'd had *fun* together. They'd . . . become friends. They'd found undeniable passion with each other. They had even kissed, deeply, with desperate need, the night before they went into battle. It was the greatest kiss of his life.

He'd felt hope then, too. Until everything had gone to shit. Still, they had a history. One he hadn't stopped thinking of in ten years.

One she evidently remembered, just like he did.

She'd revived their ploy like it was second nature, he couldn't help pondering. The idea occupied him through his signatures, lingering with him while he returned to the wagon. One of the wheels was broken, and Beatrice was mounting an elderly woman onto one of the wagon's horses.

Only when she'd sent the creature off following the other horse—on which rode a young couple seemingly in the middle of a shouting match—did he realize something.

"There's no horse left for you," he remarked.

He felt Beatrice reining in some sarcastic reply. *With powers of observation like those, Sir Grandhart, you should join the Secret Guard.*

He was disappointed. Everyone knew sarcasm was flirting's little cousin.

"They're going to be screaming at each other all the way to Devostos," she said stonily, nodding in reference to the departing couple. "I'd rather walk."

"Ride with me," he proposed. *Heroic chivalry would not let her go unaccompanied*, part of him remarked. *You really want to ride with her*, reminded another.

"Absolutely not," she said.

Clare paused. *What*, he pushed himself to wonder, *would Galwell do?*

He grabbed his horse's reins. Instead of mounting up, he fell into step with the woman whose very memory enchanted him.

"What are you doing?" she asked.

"Walking with you," he replied cavalierly. "We have to talk and we're going to the same place. On foot, it should be—oh, five days?"

No sliver of sunshine passed the storm clouds in her expression. "Just ride your horse, Clare."

"A gentleman would never ride while a lady is on foot. Isn't that your taste these days?" he pried. "Gentlemen?"

The same laugh, mirthless. "You're no gentleman," she assured him.

He hid his smile. She couldn't quite manage to make the reply sound insulting. "A lot can change in a decade," he replied.

"Not that much."

"Let's see," he went on convivially. Was he . . . enjoying himself? Was he flirting? Were swordplay and signatures not the only muscle memories waiting in him? "I adopted a pet eagle," he started. "His name is Wiglaf. He likes rabbit and salted grawk. I also bought a boat. My favorite color is now green. It used to be blue, as you know. My shoe size went up a half. Isn't that strange? Nevertheless, you know what they say of shoe sizes. Oh, and I have this ringing in my ears when it rains—"

Beatrice humphed loudly in frustration. However, she did not stop walking. Inspiration coming to Clare, he unrolled the magazine he'd pocketed earlier.

He whistled—one of the many popular songs written in his own honor—while he flipped to the pages he wanted. **Claretrice—as in Love as Ever!**

"'Eyewitnesses from the event confirmed what every Mythrian has long suspected of our favorite famous questing couple,'" Clare read out loud. "'With soul-deep glances and longing heat in their every moment in each other's company, every observer, casual or committed, could confirm, without doubt, the yearning love Claretrice share has endured—'"

"Ghosts eat me!" Beatrice's outburst rang out over the road. She snatched the magazine from his hands and promptly hurled the parchment into the forest.

Clare could not help grinning.

"We'll ride the damn horse," she declared.

Pleased with himself, he mounted up with swift ease, sitting near the back of the saddle. When Beatrice stepped near, her eyes like dark lightning, he offered his hand to help her up.

She ignored him, straddling the horse herself with the unpretentious confidence he'd known her for.

Once she was up, he found her ass nestled right between his legs.

Perhaps this was a very foolish idea, he noted to himself, dazed. Oh, what the decade had done for her. Every curve was like magic. They sneered while they invited, reminding him how far out of reach she was even when she was literally pressed up against him.

Which she was. In fifteen years of valiant deeds, Clare Grandhart had escaped wild gryphons with gashes running the length of his shoulder. He'd ridden days down mountainsides while hunger racked his insides.

Yet this was the most punishing ride he'd ever suffered on horseback.

Their bodies bumped together with every uneven bit of road. Her hair danced in his face, her warmth unbelievably close. They mocked him with memories of how he used to drift off with her smell just feet away—he didn't sleep well once in the months they traveled together, tortured by fantasies. Every one of them returned to him now.

He wondered if he knew now how his old friends felt, ripped into pieces in the darkness under the mountains.

Despite the visceral desire building in him with every sway of her hips, he reminded himself to be a gentleman. Their history was double-sided. She'd rejected him because he was a thief and a lout.

He was a hero.

The instinctive voice in his head reminded him why he was really here. For her. Perhaps he could prove he wasn't the reckless rogue she remembered.

He wanted to try. Which left him—saying nothing, ignoring the ferocious firmness in the front of his pants. *No more flirting, either, damn you*, he chastised himself. He hadn't forgiven Beatrice. Nor would he, he imagined. He had nothing to do now except suffer.

Heroically, of course.

His eyes scoured the landscape for relief until—*finally*. Given Clare would've probably stopped in the Forest of Vrast for some release from the journey's uncommon rigors, the roadside inn emerging past a curve in the road was frankly idyllic. "We should stop here for the night," he said.

The strain in his remark did not go unnoticed. "Uncomfortable back there?" his companion inquired.

"Of course not," Clare replied unconvincingly. "I'm perfectly comfortable. I could do this all night."

When he caught the smirk she flung over her shoulder right in his face, he was forced to concede he could not do this all night. In fact, he could probably only manage for—three seconds.

"Liar," she said. Nevertheless, she steered the horse deftly over to the inn's hitching post, where Clare found his eyes clinging to the obsidian-colored horse stamping its coal-black hooves in the mud.

"Hold on," he noted, distracted in earnest. "Do you recognize that horse?"

"Yes, he was my maiden of honor," she replied dryly. "No, I don't *recognize* it. It's a horse."

Clare was now intrigued enough that he only distantly registered the emergence of flirtation's little cousin. "We've seen it before," he insisted. "I know it."

"Is that your magic? Horse recognition?" Beatrice inquired. "Did we pass it on the road ten years ago and now you'll never forget its face?"

Only the reference to their old joke pulled him from his contemplation. "I don't remember you being this hilarious," he said, because he didn't dare speak more.

Beatrice hopped off their horse. "What can I say? Ten years free of you have made me joyous and quick to joke," she replied over her shoulder, striding in the inn's front doors.

Clare found himself smiling. Very well, it wasn't *all* heroic suffering.

He followed her inside, giving the black horse one last glance.

7

Elowen

Elowen wished she'd been born a teleportationist. This was now the third precarious situation she'd needed to escape in one single day, and she had only her clumsy feet to help as she ran from the sight of Clare and Beatrice arriving at the inn.

All Elowen had wanted was to enjoy a nice, silent meal after her rigorous heart-healing session and intense conversation with Vandra. She stole one single glance out the pub's window, Ghosts only knew why, and there were two of the last people in all of the realm that she wanted to see.

Elowen tossed her satchel of Domynia costumes onto the bed and locked herself in her room, breathless. Fucking Beatrice. What was she doing traipsing around with Clare after all this time? Had they become lovers again? Did they plan to overshadow Thessia's wedding by publicly unveiling their own relationship?

Elowen had been reading too many gossip pamphlets. There was only so much to do in the trees. At some point, Elowen had developed a fondness for keeping up with other people's relationships, and Claretrice still remained at the forefront of Mythria's gossip cycle. From what Elowen had read, Beatrice was newly divorced, and Clare never kept a woman for longer than a week or two. Elowen didn't know why she indulged in the Claretrice speculations when she knew firsthand how inaccurate the pamphlets could be. After all, they believed Galwell had been desperately in love with Thessia. The gossip pamphlets were practically shadow plays with how much drama and intrigue they injected into the stories they published. Perhaps Elowen took pleasure in knowing her questmates hadn't found any real contentment in the years since their victory, even if it wasn't all true. Reading about them *certainly* had nothing to do with wanting to keep up with their lives.

"Everything well?" Vandra called out as she knocked on Elowen's door. She let her voice show no trace of the earlier hurt she'd exposed. In a strange way, it made things worse, knowing how well Vandra could disguise her own pain.

Though Vandra had no officially known magic, Elowen found Vandra's ability to always seek out the light even more powerful, because it came not from a gift she'd been born with, but a choice she'd made and stuck to for the entirety of her life.

When Elowen did not answer, Vandra jiggled the handle. "I hope you know this lock stands no chance against me, though I'm willing to humor its existence a little longer if you tell me why you've used it. Does it have to do with what we discussed earlier?"

Elowen looked around the room for something heavy. There was only a bed and a dresser in the small space. Elowen pushed the dresser with all her might, devastated to find that the sturdy wooden thing had no interest in moving.

"I'd like to have my dinner sooner rather than later," Vandra continued. "I may be older and wiser now, but an empty stomach still distracts me."

"I eat my meals alone," Elowen told her, lost in thought. The scribes would go wild if they knew Claretrice arrived together at a countryside inn. Maybe Elowen could become a scribe informant? Then she wouldn't need to go to Thessia's wedding to reinstate her hero's salary.

No. She could never do that. Her own empty stomach was clouding her judgment.

When Vandra laughed, the sound jarred Elowen back to her current reality. She found herself regretting the door between them. She couldn't see the way Vandra threw her head back and squeezed her eyes shut, losing herself to every pleasure in life with fullhearted commitment.

Ghosts. She couldn't think like that. It would only make things worse.

"What's so funny?" she hissed.

"Either you let me into your room, and we enjoy a meal together on the bed, seeing as there is no other furniture in there, or you and I go to the tavern and dine," Vandra replied. "Perhaps you don't want to know me, but you *do* have to be around me. I can't have you sneaking out of the window and roaming through the countryside alone. It will be a tedious and unnecessary time killer for us both, and I don't want to miss any of the pre-wedding festivities."

Elowen pinched the space between her brows. She did need a drink. And she would never share a meal in bed with Vandra, despite what her body sometimes told her to do. "What if someone out there recognizes me?"

Vandra laughed again, as if Elowen had told a joke. "If you ever took your eyes off the ground for more than a moment, there might be a chance someone here would know it's you, but you must have everyone's footwear memorized by heart. No one can see that lovely birthmark beneath your eye to confirm your identity. Of course your hair is well-known. Though you're not the only person in this realm to have luscious red curls. Yours *do* bounce more than the average Mythrian's. Hard to say if that's an opinion shared by those who haven't had the privilege of running their hand through your hair."

Elowen shuddered, and not in distaste.

After a long pause, Vandra continued. "The cloak you're wearing is the same one they use for all your portraits. And the way you *stomp* about. It's unforgettable. Such a forceful tread for one of the most notable heroes in the realm, famous for sneaking about to defeat the darkness. Not to mention all those throaty sighs you let out, forever displeased. Utterly distinct. Could only belong to you."

It bothered Elowen that Vandra had noticed all of that. Elowen hadn't been making eye contact so that people would pay her no mind. She couldn't bear the thought of playing the role of hero for the masses on a regular weekend. With the Festival of the Four so near? It would be a legitimate nightmare, worse than anything the cursed forest offered up. Since she hadn't been gifted the ability to turn invisible, she did her best to go unnoticed instead. All it had done was grant Vandra the permission to study her closer.

When Elowen looked to her satchel, inspiration struck. She put on one of the costumes.

Domynia's pants were tight, made of faux-grawk skin, and they hugged Elowen's curves like her body was a long-lost friend of the fabric. The top was even more salacious. First, it was lilac, a shade Elowen never wore. Second, it squeezed around her rib cage so much that her bosom spilled over the top, even with a gauzy white blouse beneath it. The people of Mythria knew Elowen was stormy and wore thick cloaks and stomped about. Domynia's cloak was lilac, too, matching her bodice. If Elowen was so predictable, would she really wear *this* out to a crowded tavern?

She opened the door and strutted past Vandra, who wasted no

time letting out a low whistle. She found the first open table and sat down, making a point to scan the crowd. From what she could see, Beatrice and Clare were not in this part of the inn. A small victory.

"People are certainly looking at you, but not because they believe you are—" Vandra hesitated, seeming to realize that saying Elowen's name aloud would be a bad idea. "Well, you."

Good. The plan was working. Elowen's heart was beating so hard she could feel it in her throat. Probably because of the heaving bosom.

"I'll order for us." Vandra got up to head toward the bar.

"No," Elowen snapped, reaching for Vandra's hand. She wanted to prove she was not predictable. Or at least show that she was self-sufficient. The jerky motion made the lilac cloak fall from her head, exposing her red curls. Out of habit, she grunted in frustration, then stomped.

"Could it really be? Elowen of the Four?" someone whispered in reverence.

"I believe so," another person confirmed.

"It is!" a third said, louder. "I can see the birthmark under her eye!"

The chatter rose. Patrons came closer to their table. Elowen's heart magic went wild, sensing the emotions around her. Desire. Excitement. Genuine awe.

They'd recognized her, all right.

Vandra laughed her usual laugh. Head thrown back and all. "Do you hear this, Riv?" she asked, looking right at Elowen, whose name had never once been Riv. "They think you're Elowen True! Must not be fans of *Desires of the Night*, because you're clearly dressed as Domynia. Or they've never seen a redhead with large breasts before. Their loss, frankly." She winked.

The patrons, who were so certain only seconds ago, emanated

confusion. How was it possible that Vandra had fooled them into believing the truth was a lie? Another facet of her impressive gift.

"If you're going to stare at her, the least you can do is buy her meal. Mine, too, seeing as we're together." Vandra put her arm around Elowen, then dared to plant a kiss on her cheek.

Elowen's skin burned at the point of contact, where she'd absorbed not just desire, but . . . was it affection? It had happened too quickly for Elowen to be sure. She longed for more touch, and she hated herself for it.

The other patrons kept staring.

"Go on now!" Vandra said, shooing them away. "We're starving, and we'd like something sweet and spicy to eat! With two ales to wash it down."

The first person who'd guessed Elowen's identity nodded and headed to the bar. The second followed, pledging to get the drinks. The third just shook their head and went back to their seat. At that, Vandra released her hold on Elowen and returned to her side of their table.

The distance did little to calm the heat that burned under Elowen's skin. She shook her head to clear her thoughts, which had *obviously* been clouded by Vandra's energy, because suddenly all Elowen wanted to do was talk to Vandra. And touch her. And hear about every single detail of her life.

"Who is Riv?" she whispered, coming back to consciousness.

The patron returned with food for them both, prepared by hand magicians skilled in cooking entire meals in a matter of seconds. Vandra took an eager bite of her sugar-crusted hotcakes topped with spicy dollpeppers. "River. One of the best assassins still in the game. Looks nothing like you." She winked again.

The deception had worked well. Impressively so. The second patron brought them their drinks, and the rest of the guests in the tavern went back to their usual activities, paying no mind to Elowen and Vandra.

"Is River your ex?" Elowen asked carefully.

"Oh no," Vandra replied. "It was never like that with Riv and me. When I joined the Deathrose Guild a few years ago, we met through one of their member mixers. It was a paint'n'sip night, actually. Quite delightful. She and I ran a lot of cons together in our heyday. She'd understand."

When Elowen last knew her, Vandra freelanced her jobs, taking on whatever people offered her, so long as the pay was good and the mark was worthy of her talents. When Elowen asked her why she had basically agreed to be a menace to Galwell, Vandra had said, "Because he's the furthest thing from irredeemable—nothing like my usual marks. I thought it would be an interesting challenge, and I knew he would be able to handle it with grace."

"I didn't know you'd joined the Deathrose Guild," Elowen said. The guild was quite prestigious, known for pursuing the worst people in Mythria.

"Of course you didn't," Vandra said, chewing her meal with a smile. "You were in hiding."

"I wasn't hiding," Elowen protested. "I was taking a well-deserved break from society."

"And I was moving up in the realm. Or down, I suppose. Depends on your perspective." Vandra shrugged. "Doesn't much matter anymore, because I quit the guild altogether."

It was strange to consider how much had changed for Vandra when Elowen's own life had been effectively paused since saving the realm. If Elowen had to sum up the last ten years, it would take about three minutes. She suspected it would take the rest of her lifetime to learn all of Vandra's history.

"All the same, thanks for helping get those people away from me," Elowen said.

Vandra waved her off with a fork. "Don't mention it. They were getting in the way of my meal."

Elowen could sense regret emanating off Vandra. Invoking River's name had hurt her somehow, yet she'd done it without pause. Elowen's gloomy heart grew gloomier. Why was Vandra so damn endearing?

"I should tell you that Beatrice is here," Elowen said, wanting to even the score. Ghosts forbid she find herself indebted to Vandra. Her voice dared to shake a little. How embarrassing. "I didn't want to see her, so I ran off."

Vandra looked about. "I heard she finally split from Robert de Noughton. What a dreadfully average man. Did you ever meet him?"

"I haven't spoken to Beatrice since Galwell's funeral. I'd hoped to keep it that way, though it seems I won't be so lucky."

"It's very hard to drift apart from friends." Vandra's smile lacked its usual luster.

"Beatrice was never my friend," Elowen said, harshly. When Vandra did not engage with the statement, continuing to look at Elowen with an understanding kind of sadness, Elowen could not keep hold on the sharpness of her own anger. "I wondered if time would make it easier. Doesn't seem as though it has."

"We love to trick ourselves into believing time softens all our blows."

"It's only ever made things worse for me," Elowen said.

Vandra grinned. "Don't you dare give time all the credit. You're unusually good at making things worse all on your own."

Elowen couldn't help but laugh in return. When Vandra joined in, the two women locked eyes. There was a spark between them so intense that Elowen wondered for a moment if a hand magician had lobbed a fireball at their table.

No. It was just the intoxicating glow of a genuine connection being made, of truth flowing from both sides of the table.

"Why did you leave the Deathrose Guild?" Elowen asked.

Vandra's eyes lit up, surprised by the question. Elowen knew she was revealing herself to have been dishonest earlier, but she couldn't help it. She *did* want to know more about Vandra. In fact, she'd spent ten long years fighting the urge to wonder about Vandra, and now that she was here, eating her sweet-and-spicy meal, the least Elowen could do was find out some small details about her life. It was certainly better than discussing her non-friendship with Beatrice.

"My parents don't know what my job is," Vandra said. It was not the route Elowen expected, and her curiosity only deepened. "All my life, they've believed I work in fashion."

"You are always well-dressed," Elowen noted, because it was true. Vandra's clothing never failed to look impeccable. She was currently dressed all in black, typically a rather uninteresting ensemble. On her, the different textures of the fabrics and the precise fit of the pieces looked utterly distinct among the crowd.

"I am," Vandra confirmed. "Right now my parents believe I am a live-in fashionist for the queen, not a guard. It's easy to keep the secret from them, because they are all the way out in Devostos, and they don't really pay attention to anything beyond their robust bingo community."

"Why do you lie?" Elowen asked. This conversation had already taken so many surprising turns, she had to keep seeing it through.

"Before I was born, my mother's sister was murdered by a man who had also killed many other women," Vandra said.

Even while saying something so painful, Elowen sensed that same steadiness from Vandra that she'd felt when she first saw her again. Vandra lacked any hesitation, even through this difficult topic. She was just . . . open.

"I'm sorry," Elowen whispered.

"Thank you," Vandra replied, receiving Elowen's regrets with sincere appreciation. "They'd figured out this man's patterns and particularities, but no one caught him. And my whole family made their peace with that somehow. Not me. Once I was old enough to get around the realm alone, I fixated on finding him. And I *did*."

Elowen gasped. She hadn't intended to become so engrossed, but Vandra drew it out of her.

"I accomplished what entire knight forces had not done," Vandra continued. "That was how I learned I have a unique talent, and word spread of my work among underground networks. When my parents heard the man who'd murdered my aunt was dead, I thought they would be thrilled, or at least relieved. I'd finally brought them justice. But they were sad. They grieved my aunt all over again. And I knew I could never tell them it had been me. I didn't want them to see me differently for it."

Elowen understood very well how hard it was to have other people change their perception of you because of the loss you'd experienced. She, too, had changed from her grief, and she had no control over how the entire realm received her for it. She would always be Galwell's little sister to them. The tragedy followed her like a persistent shadow, visible in every light. If she'd had the choice, she would have asked not to be seen differently for it, either.

"I set out to find only the worst of people, hoping to prove to myself that my talent was worthwhile. And sometimes I got tasked with little side quests along the way, like how you and I met." Vandra paused, letting the moment sink in. "By that point, the Death-rose Guild had been asking me to join for years, and I'd been turning them away, not wanting to make my job that legitimate. Then Galwell died, and I realized that I no longer wanted to work alone."

It struck Elowen then how Vandra was one of the only other people outside of the Three who knew Galwell at all. Vandra had seen his heroics up close, but she'd also seen his failings. She'd caused some of them, in fact. While it bothered Elowen how often strangers used her brother's death as a reason to alter their own lives, she found it rather touching that his absence had affected Vandra in such a way.

"That quest had brought me a sense of community, even if it came from antagonizing the four of you at every turn," Vandra continued. "I thought the guild could provide me that in an even deeper way. As the years ticked by, I realized that so much of my life had been built around deceit, and no one knew the real me. When I left the guild, it only proved my point. They'd all cared about what I accomplished as an assassin, using it as fuel to be even better themselves, but no one cared that I was gone. Except for River. So now I'm finally trying to get what I've never really let myself have—a life I'm proud to tell my parents about."

"I see," Elowen said, taking it all in. She had known small fragments of Vandra's life. That she was an only child. That she always tried to make monthly dinners with her parents, even while questing. Now she saw the bigger picture. How Vandra's sunshine facade disguised so much more than even Elowen the heart magician had seen. "I would be proud of you, if I were your family," she admitted.

Vandra blushed. "Thank Ghosts you're not," she said, flustered by Elowen's sincerity.

Elowen bit down on her lip, preventing herself from saying anything more. She'd thought by choosing to eat the meal in public, she would avoid any *intimate* moment that could be brought on by eating together in bed. Yet somehow Elowen found this to be an even more vulnerable affair. Worse, Elowen found herself not just moved by all she'd learned, but deeply invested in Vandra's hope for a better life.

8

Beatrice

W e're booked."

The innkeeper did not hesitate. In fact, the dour woman had hardly laid eyes on Beatrice, instead glancing past her to the line of people waiting to check in elongating into the creaky, firelit lobby of the roadside inn.

"Please," Beatrice pressed. "You must have something. Even rooms with"—she grimaced—"only one bed? We'll make do—"

"No," the innkeeper replied. "No beds. No rooms with no beds. I'm sorry, but—" The woman gestured to the crowd of guests. "Festival weekend is our busiest of the year. The entire realm's traveling to Queendom to celebrate the Four. Now with the queen's wedding . . ." Stress furrowed gorges in the innkeeper's brow.

Beatrice had grown up accepting the hand she'd been dealt was always smaller than those around her, and it was a mark of pride that she had never asked for more. Sure, she would marry a boring nobleman to briefly raise her status, but she would never *beg*.

Even worse than begging was using her celebrity for advantage. Absolutely abhorrent to her.

Nevertheless . . .

Without a room in this inn, Beatrice knew she would consign herself to the worst of fates. She would need to *camp out with Clare*. She couldn't stand the very idea of the cool night surrounding them, the carpeting of grass underneath them, the music of wild things filling the night. The sound of him drifting to sleep. The seclusion. The closeness.

Out of the question.

Which meant Beatrice knew what she needed to do.

She leaned forward onto the rickety table, lifting her gaze from beneath the hood of her cloak, despising herself. "Yes, well, I'm journeying for the festival myself," she said. "You see, I'm Beatrice of the Four."

The innkeeper snorted.

"Heard that one before," the woman replied, sounding grimly glad for the humor she found in Beatrice's entirely honest proclamation. Beatrice now deeply wished she'd not flung the copy of *Mythria Magazine* into the woods. The innkeeper did not even look up from the bedsheet she was magicking stains out of.

Incredible advertisement for your inn, Beatrice could not help thinking. *They could change the sign out front. The Inn of the Spotty Sheets.* Of course, she knew she would prefer sleeping in that suspiciously stained bedding over sleeping beneath Clare's cloak with his arm as her pillow and his chest as . . .

She shook her head with vengeance.

"Maybe it'll work on someone in the dining room and they'll offer you their room," the innkeeper went on, jutting her chin in the direction of the loud room off the lobby, where guests clamored and the worn wooden floorboards were damp with drink. "If not, I recommend getting a table in the tavern. We won't kick you out come midnight if you want to sleep on a bench, but I'll warn you—the rats hate cuddling."

While she waved on the person behind Beatrice in line, Beatrice could only gape in horrified silence.

Wood for her pillow, the scent of stale mead filling her nose while she struggled to sleep . . .

Or the calm of night, the lullaby of the forest quiet, with only the company of the man she used to love . . .

Rats it was, then!

Reluctantly leaving the line, Beatrice found her way into the tavern. She was no stranger to the raucousness of rooms like this one. Beatrice's childhood was pockmarked with unsupervised stretches in strange locales while her parents sold their wares. Her later youth included sneaking from her family's home to carouse with visitors at her village's seedier waypoints. She loved the voyagers' stories, their daring . . . how wide their worlds were.

On her quest with the Four, nights of journeying had led them on occasion into roadside refuges, though with Galwell's financial resources—not to mention his natural charm—the nights never ended with sleepless hours on unyielding wood.

Everything is worse now, isn't it? she could not help reminding herself.

She needed no further reminding when she found Clare seated at one end of the room, steaming bowls of delectable stew in front of him.

He pushed one toward her when she sat across from him, their knees inescapably close in the cramped booth.

"It's—" He paused, like he was wrestling with himself. "Your favorite," he muscled on. "Honeyspiced pigeon."

In no mood for his politeness or for contemplating its reason, Beatrice slid the bowl carelessly to the side. "My tastes have changed," she informed him. While the statement was not untrue, its relevance to the present situation was. She *loved* honeyspiced pigeon stew.

Clare shrugged and dug in. While Beatrice reached for the wooden jug of wine, Clare watched, new wariness clinging in his eyes.

"Don't tell me Clare Grandhart gave up drinking," she chided him, enjoying once more the indulgence of mocking him. "Do the alleyways of Mythria finally know peace from your late-night inebriation and urinations?"

Her delight dampened like the floorboards of the crowded, mead-smelling room when Clare did not scowl, or retort, or roll his eyes. He did nothing in the manner of how rough men were supposed to respond when you insulted them. "I wish I could drink the way I used to," he conceded while spooning his warm, lightly sweetened, zesty—all right, she very much wanted some stew. Damn his generosity. "I'm not a young man anymore, though," he went on.

"No, I suppose you're not," she replied with good cheer.

When he exhaled in frustration, she hid her victorious smirk in her goblet. He'd clearly determined to be "gentlemanly" toward her, she'd noticed. Well, she would not make it easy for him. Wherever his unusual modesty was coming from, she was determined to dispel his every false pleasantry. It would be her game for the evening! Like Ogre's Chess, if Beatrice found Ogre's Chess fun.

Why should I do otherwise? she heard herself wonder with viciousness she'd never brought to Ogre's Chess. Clare, she remembered, was not just her unlikely journeying companion, not just the mismatched outlaw who'd recognized her.

He'd hurt her. Sneaking out after their first night together was nothing compared to what he'd done after Galwell's funeral. How deeply he had wounded her in her darkest days.

Oh, she knew he blamed her. It didn't matter. Ghosts, it didn't even matter if he was *right*. When pain was the only prize one had, one clung on to it stubbornly. Clare had wounded her in the very depths of her confusion, her loneliness, her misery.

It was enough. She didn't need to question or second-guess. She would never forgive him—she, who had endless practice in never forgiving.

Clare composed himself with his next mouthful of stew while she glared.

"I'm sorry you're going through a rough time," he said.

No. Ghosts no. Pleasantry, she could spurn. With resentment, she could spar. Pity, however? Out. Of. The. Question.

"A rough time indeed," she replied hotly. "Stuck in a tavern with *you* and no rooms for the night."

Clare held on to the upper hand. Casually he waved off the problem of their lodging. "I meant with respect to your divorce," he replied evenly, leaving her fuming. Nightwalker shrieks were preferable to *him* speaking with equanimity. "You're clearly taking it hard," he commented.

"I am not!"

He glanced up. She could not decide whether she liked the flicker of humor in his eyes. It did not feel exactly like claiming Ogre's Chess pieces.

"You're halfway to drunk on an empty stomach," he observed. "Not two hours ago you were in a wagon-share smelling of gryphon shank. You recently crashed your ex-husband's banquet in a bathing robe and mismatched boots."

She fumed. She'd hoped he hadn't noticed the boots.

"For your information, Clare," she replied, "I've never been happier."

Her companion made no reply, instead only raising one eyebrow in challenge. He was goading her, the way she'd watched him deceptively draw opponents into fights he would win. She knew she should ignore him—but she refused to let Clare Grandhart think she regretted a single one of her choices over the past ten years. Points of pride were exceedingly few in Beatrice no-longer-de-Noughton's personal ledger. She needed to hoard them where she could.

"Divorce was necessary," she heard herself retort, "and happy. He'd long since stopped pleasing me in the bedroom, and I feel I've experienced everything there is to experience in nobility. I was"—she'd started enjoying the honesty now, not to mention the haughtiness—"bored."

Now Clare smiled. His crooked smile, one she shouldn't imagine kissing, lips spiced with honey—

"Robert didn't satisfy you sexually, then," he remarked.

"He was better than some."

Clare's smile didn't change. The doubtfulness in his eyes flickered like fire on winter nights. "Not better than all, of course."

She held his gaze. "Asking about anyone in particular?"

With calloused fingers, he cracked his knuckles. "I've no doubt *one* night stands above the others in your memory."

I've no doubt. He was putting on gentility even now, playing with diction. It pissed her off, making her want to strike him off-kilter. Forget Ogre's Chess. They were jousting on dragons. She pretended to consider, like she needed to sift through dozens of unforgettable nights of lovemaking.

Of course, she didn't. There *was* one night she could never forget, pleasures lingering in her memory in vivid detail even without her head magic gifts. Her not-really-one-night stand with Clare. In the days following, on the Four's quest, they had only ever worked up to kissing, once, before their final confrontation with the forces of darkness. In the meantime, had she wished for other nights like their first?

Well . . . she would never say. Like she would never confess he'd given her the greatest night of her life.

"Hard to say," she demurred. "I didn't know *what* I wanted

in the bedroom until more recently. My youthful indiscretions were . . . ungainly."

Crack. Clare did violence to his next knuckle.

It delighted her. She was consuming him in fire now. Was he imagining the endless possibilities of what she wanted in the bedroom? Was he remembering how she sounded when she wanted them? Was he wrestling with the idea—a lie, of course—that others had given them to her, instead of him?

"I could have told you what you wanted, Beatrice," he replied. "I knew very well what you liked."

She flushed, shocked. Insinuation was not the same as invoking their history outright.

Quickly, she felt foolish. How often had she watched Clare outspar opponents with unconventional strikes? She could recall several one-eyed gnarlivores who'd learned the lesson she just did. She reached for the stew, looking to end the inane exchange here.

It was the wrong move. Clare smirked.

"I reckon not all of your tastes have changed," he said, nodding at the stew.

His words themselves flustered her like not even his crowing comment could. *I reckon.* No noble ever used the rough slang. While his pretend politesse enraged her, she hated how the reemergence of his roguish accent affected her in . . . other ways.

She offered him only silence, congratulating herself on her wisdom. Ignoring him watching her in victory, she cast her eyes elsewhere—

Only for them to land on a voluptuous woman with raven hair.

Clare could read the moment disturbance entered his dinner companion's demeanor. He sat up straighter.

"Vandra Ravenfall is here," she said, speaking quietly and clearly, her focus never leaving the assassin.

He did not raise the alarm, reacting with perfect calm. "Where?"
He set his goblet down, carefully not following her gaze.

"At the bar, on my right," she replied.

"Armed?"

"Can't see from here, but—"

As it happened, they finished the final words in unison.

"Assume she is."

The unintentional harmony grated on Beatrice's ears. She
frowned—until Vandra headed their way, carrying a pitcher of
drink. "She's going to walk right past us," Beatrice observed, urgency replacing her irritation.

Relying on an old practice of theirs, she reached out, placing
her hand on Clare's knee under the narrow table. She did not know
what unnerved her more, the readiness of the instinct or the heat
rushing into her with the contact. With just the lightest of pressure, she could feel how muscular his leg was.

His eyes locked on hers. He nodded.

When Vandra was a step away from them, she lifted her hand
from his leg with reluctance she did not enjoy recognizing. Clare
sprung quickly from his seat, trusting Beatrice's timing completely. Before he could have seen Vandra for himself, he had his
dinner knife raised to the woman's throat in one smooth motion.

"Speak your purpose, assassin," he commanded.

Vandra Ravenfall did not look intimidated. Nor did she look
surprised to find herself under Clare's knife. She *did* look well,
frustratingly. How had her skin lost none of its radiance, her figure
none of its definition?

"Clare Grandhart," she stated pleasantly. "You know, I really
must thank you. Your ale is my favorite. I order it by the case."

Clare didn't release her, although Beatrice could tell the compliment pleased him. *Of course* Clare had slapped his likeness on

an overpriced line of ale. It was called something ridiculous like Hero's Reward. Just one of his many sponsorships over the decade.

"I've been a fan of your work as well," Clare replied coolly, not that anyone in the tavern was paying them a moment's notice. Scuffles and brawls were practically on the menu in places like these. "The disappearance of Archibald the Limb-Cleaver had you written all over it," Clare went on.

Vandra grinned, delighted. "That was a fun one. Many fond memories. I figure it may be relevant to mention at this particular moment, though, that I've given up killing for contract."

Clare exchanged a look with Beatrice. They'd learned better than to trust Vandra Ravenfall on their quest to save the realm after the first time she'd lied to upset their plans.

"You expect us to believe you're no longer an assassin, and yet you just happen to be at the same inn as two of your former marks?" Beatrice asked.

Vandra nodded eagerly, paying no mind to the knife's edge jutting into her skin. "It's a perfectly logical coincidence! See, I'm here on behalf of the queen, escorting a guest of hers to Queendom. I imagine the palace is your destination as well. As this is the main road to Queendom."

"Who are you escorting?" Clare didn't take his eyes off the assassin to look around the room.

"Funny you should ask." Vandra's voice lowered just slightly, delighting in the drama. She had been an assassin for fifteen years, after all—the instincts didn't die as easily as her targets. "An old friend of yours."

Beatrice's breath stilled in her lungs. She felt trapped, with danger closing in. Terror flooded her system, sharper than when she'd once awoken in the night bound in enemy hands and with her allies beaten and unconscious.

No. Not Elowen.

She couldn't face her former friend. Not after their fight, the funeral, Galwell. Everything. When she'd agreed to come to this wedding, she never thought Elowen would descend from her home in the trees for it. She'd been counting on Elowen's reclusive bitterness to shield Beatrice from her own shame.

Before Beatrice could run or hide or do some other cowardly action befitting the circumstances, Elowen True herself stepped forward from the room's plentiful shadows, seeking her traveling companion and finding her under Clare's dinner knife.

Shock rounded her features for a heartbeat before her eyes slid to Beatrice. She looked away immediately. No curiosity for her former friend. No interest in her welfare. Beatrice was something hideous. Something she wished she could unsee. A nightmare you prayed to wake from.

Beatrice, however, couldn't look away. For one, her former friend wore rather un-Elowen-like clothing. If Beatrice did not know better, she would say she *recognized* the dramatic, figure-sculpted garment. Was Elowen . . . dressing up as a character from the shadow play they watched as children? Surely not.

Outfit notwithstanding, Elowen looked . . . hardened. Her skin was paler than Beatrice had ever seen it—paler than that time in winter when they both got the poxworm flu and had to stay inside for weeks with only each other to entertain themselves and care for. Her hair was long, standing out in fiery contrast to her pallor. There were circles under her eyes, but her cheeks were tinged with the pink only Vandra could inspire. She was beautiful, of course. But distant. Untouchable. Like one of the Ghosts alive the mystics wrote about.

When Clare saw Elowen, he released Vandra. It was sloppily done. Ten years ago, Galwell would have reprimanded him for leaving them open to attack. Clare used to be rash about things like this, though—his love for the people he held dear. He rushed forward to pull a startled Elowen into his arms.

"It's good to see you, kid," he said thickly.

Elowen blinked. Beatrice winced. The nickname hung heavy between the remaining three of the Four. People who would have once died for one another, who now didn't know how much of each other even remained.

This *was* a nightmare.

"I'm not a kid, Grandhart," Elowen said, warmth at last coloring her voice. She'd said it to him a hundred times on the road. As Galwell's younger sister and the youngest of the group, Clare had enjoyed teasing her. "I wasn't a kid ten years ago and I'm hardly closer to one now," she continued, laughing slightly.

Clare smiled at the sound, rendering himself unfairly handsome. For more than one reason, Beatrice finally had to look away.

"Look, we're all reunited," he said grandly.

Beatrice's stomach twisted, knowing what was coming.

"Not all of us," Elowen replied.

It was as if she'd summoned the ghost of Galwell into their midst. Beatrice had watched him die thousands of times. She felt the impact of the killing blow all over again with Elowen's words, how pain had ripped through her when Galwell fell.

Their reunion wasn't happy. How could it be when the Four could only ever be the Three? Being together was only a reminder of whom they'd lost.

Even Clare seemed to struggle under the weight. He cleared his throat, his weird posturing returning once more to his demeanor. "We don't have any lodging for the night," he informed Elowen and Vandra formally. "We'll be heading on to make camp on the road. Perhaps we could all share a drink together before we go?"

"No. I'm tired," Elowen replied quickly.

"*Elowen*," Vandra gasped, an assassin offended by her charge's rudeness. She turned to Clare, apologetic. "We took the last two rooms. Oh, but you should take one!" She brightened as she seized on the idea. "I owe it to you after, you know, the trouble I caused you. Quite often, if I remember. Indeed, nearly incessantly."

The real Clare peered out once more in his realization of the offer's good fortune. "Yes, I'd say it'll settle the score," he replied. "Right, B?"

What game was he playing, invoking their old nicknames? She could only glare. Of course, Elowen did the same.

Oblivious, or, likelier, uninterested in their resistance, Vandra promptly handed over a heavy, rusted key.

"You two have this one," she proposed, indicating Beatrice and Clare, "while Elowen and I can—"

"Absolutely not," Elowen replied curtly, the rosiness in her cheeks deepening.

Vandra grinned gracefully, like the color in the other woman's cheeks was reward enough. "Fine. Very well. You and Beatrice—"

"*No.*"

The word joined Beatrice's voice with her former friend's. The overlap was, regrettably, perfect. The unfortunate instance of their unity struck Beatrice like hearing the first notes of a melody forgotten from childhood.

Yet Beatrice's dismay was nothing compared to what she felt when, in the next moment, her eyes locked with Elowen's. It was no glancing gaze. What she saw in the glare of her childhood confidant, once her dearest companion in the world, was—

Utter loathing.

Her heart cracked in places she did not know vulnerability could be found. She chewed down on the waver in her lip.

Clare, of course, noticed.

He deftly passed her the key. "Why don't I catch up with the kid," he said, "while you watch the assassin?" He was no longer playing the nobleman. He was doing something far worse—he was showing her real kindness. *Sir Sensitive, knight of Mythria over here*, she wanted to mock him. Except she couldn't, not entirely, not when gratitude overwhelmed her.

She could only nod, silent.

The plan mollified Elowen. "Follow me, Grandhart," she summoned him gruffly. Unhesitating, intuiting the slightest pause would destabilize the fragile peace, he followed.

Without another word, they were gone, drawn into the dark of the inn. Beatrice watched, evaluating the two people who broke her heart. She did not know which one had done it worse.

"Well, roomie?" Vandra prompted her. "Shall we?"

Upstairs at the inn was not unlike downstairs. Noise of every manner rang from the rooms, whether the doors were closed or open. Prayers to the Ghosts in devotion and exclamations of ecstasy in the midst of nocturnal carousing. Music, from craftspeople practicing their lyrics and parents singing to cheer their children. Well, it was not as if Beatrice planned on sleeping.

Vandra led them to the very end of the hall. The room she unlocked for them was narrow—"cozy," one might say. All considered, an assassin was the roommate Beatrice preferred to the alternatives. Nevertheless, she was not naive. When last she saw Vandra Ravenfall, she'd been disclosing the Four's plans to the irritating Bartholomew.

"I want to see how you got Elowen to come with you," Beatrice demanded.

Vandra hesitated. "Using your magic, I would guess?"

"I hardly trust you," Beatrice returned. "If Elowen is here against her will . . ."

While the note of warning inspired nothing in Vandra, her roommate's concern for Elowen did. Vandra cocked her head in curiosity, then presented her hand.

"Gladly," she said.

Her palm in Vandra's, Beatrice reached out, her head magic unraveling the world. The raucous inn vanished under the gossamer veil of the past. Finally, she saw—Elowen's home, high in the forest over Featherbint. Everything was desperately present. She felt *pulled*, like the memory of her friend drew her into the vision the way no solitary recollection or visitation for strangers could.

She watched the past days play out. How Elowen was coaxed down from her home. How she encountered Vandra. The former assassin's story was clean—and yet disturbed her like no deceit ever would.

For the magic revealed how Elowen had lived.

In her darkest moments, Beatrice would imagine the circumstances in which their quest—*her* failure—had left her former friend. Elowen's sorrow. Her solitude.

She no longer needed to imagine them. Vandra's recollection of her espionage on Elowen revealed every painful detail. The heartbreaking quiet of Elowen's secluded home. Elowen, who used to have "sleep outside" parties with her where they would confide every detail of their lives while wrapped in coverlets inside Elowen's family's stables sharing sugary delicacies—who now went nearly every day without speaking one word out loud. The nervousness in the way she moved. The fear hiding in her eyes, driven there when fate robbed her of what she held dearest in her heart.

No. Not fate.

Elowen had lived isolated in her grief, for *years*. Because of Beatrice.

9

Clare

Chivalry, Clare Grandhart found, was a real pain.

He did not experience the sentiment figuratively. Very real pain presently pervaded his shoulders, neck, and spine from the joyous position of sleeping on the wooden floor of the inn where they decamped for the night.

It was embarrassing, honestly. The swordsman and scoundrel, aching like the old men who posted up in his neighborhood pubs. In his youth, he could sleep for hours on the stone floors of the dungeon cells in which he not infrequently found himself. His duskjay-feather pillows and sleeping-spelled drapes in his Farmount home had wrought this misery on him.

Nonetheless, chivalry was chivalry, and it was in keeping with the gentlemanliness Clare would practice on their journey. When he and Elowen had reached their room, it dictated ceding her the narrow bed wedged into their quarters.

The escape from the company of Beatrice, however, had been welcome. *Very* welcome. He'd faced nightwalkers and gnarlivores and precipices of eroding rocks—yet he did not know if he would have survived the night sleeping next to her. Huddled for warmth under the dark starlit sky, wrapped in the sweet shroud of her smell, her soft—

He definitely would not have survived.

Instead, the evening he passed with Elowen had been pleasant enough. She had not protested when he consigned himself to the floorboards. She *had* protested, in her way, when he peppered and prodded her with questions. How did she find the cursed forest? Was she excited for the wedding? How was her journey? Elowen had replied sullenly, ending conversation after conversation with monosyllabic replies or sometimes just grunts.

It had been just like old times!

Clare was unashamed of how deeply it overjoyed him to find himself once more spending a unilaterally chatty evening with the flame-haired girl he'd once considered as close as a sister. It was, he'd confided in himself while he rolled and repositioned on the worn oak of his sleeping situation, a reunion for which he had not let himself yearn. The famous life he'd found in Farmount had helped him forget how fiercely he missed Elowen. How much he missed *them*.

When his former companions had absconded into the forest and into nobility, respectively, he had, in part, embraced the public role of "hero" in response to their retreat from it.

Or, Elowen's retreat. In the days following Galwell's funeral, when the pain of what Beatrice had done was still fresh, he could not have cared less about what discomforted Beatrice.

Elowen, however—he knew grief had forced her into isolation. Mythria needed a hope they could hold on to, and Clare had stepped onto the stage so she did not have to. His flaunted life had not earned him only purpose in his days, coin in his coffers, and a gaudy knighthood. In occupying the role of hero in part *for* Elowen, he felt a connection with his old friend, even when, deep down, he knew none existed.

Now, it had earned him a creaky pain in his left hip.

He rose with the morning sun, wincing. The hubbub in the inn hallway, the cacophony of parenting, entertainment, prayer, and sex—in, he hoped, separate rooms—had subsided, leaving only the upbeat shuffle of morning journeyers on their way.

While Elowen slept, and ignoring the stabbing hip pain, Clare quietly went downstairs. The tavern, now the morning meal hall, was rich with the smells of sweetspiced sausage, corncakes, and four varieties of eggs. Clare helped himself, liking the look of the dawnlark eggs, and headed to one of the open seats.

And waited.

She arrived looking refreshed, her wooden plate heaped with pink-salted eggs. She sat, her eyes lit with eagerness for the day.

"The innkeeper gave me your message," Vandra said.

Clare said nothing in reply. He was inopportunely in the midst of a mouthful of eggs.

Vandra smiled. "Early breakfast with Clare Grandhart," she went on. "I imagine people would pay a fortune for the pleasure."

"They do," he remarked, swallowing. "I sometimes auction off my meals to raise money for charitable causes."

Vandra looked indulgently interested, like his explanation was the setup she was entertaining in expectation of the punchline. She flagged down the drinkmaid and, once she'd ordered a dark brew with cream, returned him her focus. "What charities does a former outlaw support?"

"I have an eagle sanctuary, if you have farthings you'd like to devote to our wonderful creatures."

Her smile widened. "I suppose I can't make fun," she conceded. "Like you, I've given up my life of crime for the straight and narrow!"

Clare reminded himself to remind her to fund his precious eagles. Despite her insinuations regarding his past, his charitable endeavors were entirely in earnest. "How do you like it?" he asked instead, with no meager curiosity. While the intent of his morning meeting with Vandra was not chitchat, her cheerful ease interested him. He'd wrestled with his life's direction recently—how had Vandra found comfort in hers?

Well, she *doesn't have the pressure of upholding the desired image for sponsorships for ale or horseball apparel,* he comforted himself pettily.

Of course, she only shrugged. "You know me, Grandhart. I always make my own fun," she replied dazzlingly. "It matters not whether I'm assassinating an evil cultist or escorting a grumpy hermit across the land. I'm going to find the laughs!"

Now it was Clare who laughed. It was the finest eloquence he'd ever heard in a description of Elowen.

Vandra had not mischaracterized herself, either. The former assassin's demeanor—shining like the sun outside their window—was unique in her line of work. Clare knew this from personal experience, having encountered the Deathrose Guild on memorable occasions in his rougher days. Named for the Mount Mythrian flower with ebony petals like opening lips and thorns capable of stopping the heart, Vandra's cohort of former colleagues was . . . interesting.

"So." Vandra shifted in her seat like she was waiting for noblewomen's gossip of whose wife was sneaking around with the neighborhood weaponeer. "I expect you didn't invite me to breakfast so we could bond over our criminal pasts."

Clare finished off his dawnlark eggs. "Well, I'd hoped we might bond a little, but no." He placed down his fork, continuing delicately. "How—was Beatrice?"

His guest's eyes widened, her smile sharpening with accusation. "You're still carrying your massive torch for her? I remember staking you out and watching you watch *her* the entire night with utter longing." She shook her head. "Massive. Utterly fucking massive."

He could not help flushing. "No," he replied hotly. *Chivalrous men don't lose their cool*, his conscience reminded him. Nevertheless— Vandra calling him out on the complicated emotions hiding under his and Beatrice's betrayals of each other made him feel the way he did when pub rabblerousers contended the Farmount Falcons played inferior horseball to the Northwood Knights. He *had* to dispute her. "We're in the past," he insisted with warning. "Like you and Elowen."

"We're not in the past at all!" Vandra exclaimed.

The declaration distracted Clare from his indignation. "Wait, really? You've pined for her all these years?"

"Of course I have. Isn't she wonderful? She's the grumpiest human being I've ever met. I'd say the grumpiest *being* in Mythria, except I once had a cat who bit me whenever I ventured to pet her," Vandra replied.

"Does Elowen know?" Clare inquired.

"She knows of my ill-tempered cat, yes."

Clare pinned her with his gaze. "Not what I meant."

Vandra grinned. Her impishness softening, she looked down. "It's . . . complicated," she confessed. "We weren't there for each other many years. It hurt how easily she left everything— left *me*—behind. I knew she owed me nothing, of course." Vandra sighed, the rattling sigh of someone impatient with their own sorrow. "I wanted to leave her behind, too. It hurt nonetheless. Then . . . when I parted from the guild, I did a great deal of reflecting. Elowen was on my mind often," Vandra replied. "I couldn't forget her."

Clare stared into his dark brew. He knew something of the impossibility of forgetting, no matter how much misery entwined itself within the memories.

"Couldn't forgive her either, though, I suppose," he finally said.

"Oh no, quite the contrary," Vandra rejoined. "I forgave her easily."

He glanced up, uncomprehending.

Vandra went on. "After all, I could have reached out to her as well, and I did not. I refused to resent Elowen when I knew she could resent me in return." She regarded Clare. "In my old line of work, I learned one thing," she said. "People are not all bad or all good. We are both. And to be happy, sometimes you must forgive."

You must forgive.

Clare wriggled under her pointed gaze. *Yes, very well*, he wanted to say. *I know you mean me.*

He offered the only honest reply he could. "Some things cannot be forgiven." He knew not whether he meant what he or Beatrice had done. *Does it matter?*

Vandra said nothing, yet her expression made no secret of how his reply left her unsatisfied. The drinkmaid returned with the steaming mug of dark brew and a small cup of cream.

Clare watched in fascination while Vandra swilled the hot, spicy drink—then promptly pounded the creamer on its own like it was a shot of liquor.

While he contemplated the combination he'd just observed, which was not, to put it mildly, customary, Vandra made no comment on her unusual morning ritual.

"Well, while we are certainly in *no* way discussing Beatrice currently," she replied, "I will now answer your question. Beatrice was . . . wary," she explained. "She delved into my memories to confirm my story. I don't think she liked what she saw. How . . .

Elowen lives. She went to bed immediately, except I'm pretty sure she didn't sleep. She went very still for hours, unresponsive. Like she was . . . in her magic."

"Doing what?" he managed. *For hours? Sleepless?* Regardless of whether he could forgive Beatrice, he was discovering his instincts toward her hadn't changed. Worry pulled him like storm winds on perilous mountain paths. Unless he entrenched himself, remembering she cared nothing for him, they would push him over the edge.

Vandra shrugged. "I'm an excellent spy, but even I can't see inside someone's head. Memories, I'd imagine."

Memories.

Clare had been in his memories last night, too, but not like Beatrice. He knew his were only fumbling, forced-up recollections, nothing like the renderings Beatrice could revisit, yet they devastated him—which reminded him of the horrible power Beatrice possessed. How vividly she could see every failure, feel every loss.

His ordinary memories were enough—combined with the uncomfortable floorboards—to forestall hours of his own sleep. He'd found himself remembering the last time they were together, united on their journey. The quest. He remembered how Galwell's death drove them apart. If Galwell could, impossibly, have known what his death would do to them . . . Clare knew the fallen hero, their dear friend, would have been heartbroken.

He would be disappointed.

The conviction had given Clare new resolve. He'd woken in his upstairs room with a hurting hip *and* a new plan for the coming days.

It was why he'd invited Vandra here. He leaned forward, hiding none of his hesitation, none of his self-doubt. If Vandra felt he was only acting cavalierly, she would feel less of an imperative to go along with his plan. She needed to know he was serious.

"I was . . . hoping the four of us could travel to the palace together," he proposed.

Vandra's eyes narrowed, for once. She sipped her drink. "I'm not eager to forsake my one-on-one time with my prickly paramour," she said.

He'd expected that point. "After Galwell's funeral," he elaborated gently, "Elowen and Beatrice had a huge fight. I feel they should . . . talk. Heal old wounds. It would help them. You said you have forgiven her. Yearned for her, even. Mending her past might help her . . ." He measured his words. He did not want to promise what he could not deliver. ". . . return to herself," he finished.

Concern vanquished the cheer in Vandra's expression. She set down her mug. "Of course. Of course it's not just her brother's death that drove Elowen into the trees," she replied, pacing out each deduction in words. "Beatrice was her best friend. It must have hurt her horribly to lose not only her brother, but her oldest friend."

Clare nodded. While he knew Elowen was the route to Vandra's cooperation, he could not help considering how the rift had hurt Beatrice as well.

Oh, he didn't *sympathize* with her. How could he, when she knew exactly how she'd shattered his heart?

He couldn't, he told himself. He couldn't wonder whether she would never have settled for her miserable marriage if she'd held on to her dearest friend. He couldn't contemplate whether she would be less lost, or less inclined to losing herself in drink, if she'd had Elowen to hold on to. He couldn't concern himself with whether she would be happier.

Not when she hated him the way she obviously did. He could entertain none of those caring questions about her. Even if he occasionally wanted to.

"Why do you want to push them together?" Vandra queried. "It'll surely be a headache for *us*."

Clare straightened. He did not know exactly how to respond. Or, he did. He just did not know exactly how to respond in his own voice, his own person. Putting honesty into words he usually only employed for performance.

"It's the right thing to do," he mustered.

He felt the inquisition of Vandra's gaze on him, the full depth of her familiar scrutiny. She could see through him. How he postured greatness just to hold himself together. Hold everyone together.

She decided not to pry. The next moment, like the clouds parting in front of the sun, her cheerful resolve returned. "Very well! I like your plan, good sir. If Elowen and Beatrice can mend their own relationship, Elowen may more freely open her heart again. It is here resolved—we shall journey together on the road to Queendom."

She stood, drink finished. Clare joined her.

"A road voyage," she elaborated. "Road trek. Road trip. *Road trip!*" she repeated in delight. "That's the one, isn't it? Doesn't it just sound fun?"

It did not, to Clare, in honesty. He would, however, hold the course. It was his plan, which inspired commitment if not confidence. Galwell had been the Four's planner. Clare could only hope and welcome the presence of intercessors to his and Beatrice's hatred. "Then," he ventured, "we'll just need to find a way to convince them to travel together."

"Oh, we can't do that," Vandra replied instantly. "Fortunately"—Clare could only follow her out of the tavern, into the morning light dazzling over the greenery outside the inn—"I know what'll work instead. Which are your horses?"

Clare pointed, wary. "Why?"

Promptly, Vandra went to the hitching post, where she untied Clare's horse. Next, she loosed the obsidian-black mare. Exactly the one Clare had discerned! He made a mental note to tell Beatrice *I told you so.* In a very gentlemanly and noble way, of course.

Then, with one slap of the horses' hindquarters, Vandra sent the horses running.

"Lead him home, Killer!" she called out sweetly. "Have fun, you two!"

Clare watched the dispatch with puzzled horror. "Vandra . . ."

"Trust me."

He needed to now, he knew. He followed her, returning into the inn, where, with the growing group of guests waking up and hungry for dawnlark eggs, they found Beatrice and Elowen. The women were, naturally, standing as far from each other as possible while remaining in each other's sights. They looked up in guarded expectation when Vandra strode into the room.

Vandra did not disappoint. "Misfortune, ladies! Our horses have run off in the night!"

Faces fell.

"We know not how," Vandra continued. "However, we are in surprising luck, for the inn has chartered a coach for everyone going to Queendom. We can ride. Together!"

10

Elowen

Contrary to popular belief, Elowen did not take pleasure in being sour. Quite the opposite. Living a life attuned to everyone's emotions meant feeling everything, all the time. And there was quite a lot to feel in the cramped wagon sandwiched next to a beaming Vandra, with a rigid Clare and an unpredictable Beatrice sitting across from them. Whenever Elowen glanced up, Clare offered her a winning smile, yet she sensed nothing but worry coming from him. He was admirable in his attempts to disguise it, pointing out every so-called exciting feature the road had to offer.

"Do my eyes deceive me, or is that a flock of golden-tipped hamsterjays right there?" He leaned over to get a better look, pressing a hand on Elowen's shoulder to steady himself. She felt every bit of his eager nervousness. It was as potent as drinking three foambrews in a row. "I haven't seen any of those since I was a young boy. I thought they'd gone extinct."

Elowen turned to the small window behind her. "Those are rodents," she said.

Clare laughed good-naturedly. "Seems it might be time for ole Grandhart to make an appointment with a visionkeeper."

"*I'm Clare Grandhart, the newest face of Vision Glass,*" Beatrice muttered, performing a rather uncanny impression of him. "*With these spectacles, you, too, can see the world as a hero does.*"

Clare deflected Beatrice's mockery by pretending to hold a pair of imaginary glasses to his face. "I have been told on more than one occasion how striking I look in a pair of metal-rimmed lenses."

Right then, an unfortunate bump in the road knocked Clare's head into the roof of the wagon. He let out an agonized yelp, and Beatrice laughed heartily in return.

"It isn't funny," Elowen found herself saying. She did not mean to acknowledge the fraught relationship between Beatrice and Clare—or to acknowledge Beatrice at all—but she could not condone Beatrice celebrating Clare's pain.

The comment silenced Beatrice with surprising effectiveness. She leaned back into her seat and closed her eyes as if fighting off a headache. *Good. Let her stay quiet for the rest of this journey.*

"Golden-tipped hamsterjays aren't extinct," Vandra announced to the wagon, pulling her bag onto her lap to rummage around in it. "They migrated after the Fraternal Order froze Pollenberry Lake. You can find them along the Mythrian River." She held out her palm to showcase brightly colored candies, made to look like crystals. "Would anyone like a Sizzle Crystal?"

At least when Vandra attempted to soften tension, she came prepared with sweets. Elowen popped a handful in her mouth, appreciating how the crackling sensation required all of her attention. For a moment, she did not have to be the famed Elowen True of the Four, trapped inside a wagon with every living person who'd ever really mattered in her life. She was just someone enjoying a novelty candy.

"No Domynia costume today?" Beatrice asked, interrupting the peace as only she could. "I thought it flattered you."

Elowen squeezed her lips between her teeth. Sizzle Crystals fireworked against the roof of her mouth.

Beatrice paid no mind to Elowen's lack of engagement. "You know, they never should have brought Domynia back," she said.

"Why would Alcharis burst into tears at the sight of her? Her last act was betraying them, and they've spent the last however many years getting over that, and the moment they find out she's alive, they're *happy*?"

Elowen could bite her lip no longer. "They missed her!" she cried out, though the Sizzle Crystals made it sound more like *They mish'd sher*. She spit the candies into her hand so she could argue properly. "They were overcome with joy at the return of their long-lost love. It wasn't the time to hold her accountable for past actions."

"I don't care if it was supposed to be a heat-of-the-moment reaction, she doesn't deserve their forgiveness," Beatrice argued back. "Not when they've spent all this time suffering because of her. They should have been furious."

When they were young, Beatrice would come over so they could watch *Desires of the Night* together. She was always a more observant audience member than Elowen, spending hours considering the thoughts behind everyone's actions, whereas Elowen focused on emotions alone. It used to make Elowen feel like a less-intelligent fan. Beatrice could see things that Elowen never once even considered.

It was Galwell who had helped Elowen get over her insecurity, chalking it up to their different magics. Elowen was ruled by the heart, Beatrice by the head. Now that Elowen had lived through some of the worst agonies life had to offer, she'd learned it had nothing to do with magic at all. Beatrice believed happiness had to be earned, and it upset her when someone received it without just cause.

"I don't know why you're arguing this with *me* of all people," Elowen said. "As if my mind could ever be changed on the matter. Domynia is my favorite character, and she always will be."

Beatrice muttered something low enough that Elowen could not make it out.

"What?" Elowen snapped. She was all the way in, ready to see this fight through.

"I said, *Typical*," Beatrice told her, louder.

"What's *typical*? That you don't think anything good should happen to people who have made mistakes?" Elowen hissed.

"No. That you believe your opinion is the only correct one."

"You know what they say about opinions?" Clare interrupted. "They're like bums. Everybody has one."

"*Shut up, Clare*," Beatrice and Elowen said in perfect unison.

Vandra clapped her hands together. "Look at that. You two agree on something for once." She held the Sizzle Crystals out once more. "Last call for candy."

"I only meant to lighten the mood," Clare said. "I don't see the sense in being miserable at every turn. I recall a night around the fire when we pledged to have our nails charmed after the quest was over. Remember that?"

Of course Elowen remembered. And surely so did Beatrice. But it wasn't the point. Elowen didn't know what good came from pretending you were happy when you weren't. All it ever seemed to do was make people believe you had a higher tolerance for nonsense than you did. Poor Clare may as well have been a rug the way he laid himself out to be walked over, all for the sake of keeping a peace that could never be maintained.

"It seems our problems only start when someone speaks," Beatrice told Clare.

"Says the person who spoke first," Elowen couldn't help but remind her.

With a gusty sigh, Clare reached out his hand and accepted Vandra's candy offer, throwing the crystals into his mouth to escape a response. Elowen's own candy had melted into her hand now, a sticky swirl of colors on the inside of her palm.

"I was trying to make polite conversation," Beatrice said.

"What's polite about telling me my favorite character deserves a life of misery?" Elowen asked.

Vandra shifted in her seat. The quick brush of contact—Vandra's bare ankle tapping against Elowen's—showed Elowen how uncomfortable Vandra was with this. For some reason Elowen thought Vandra was impervious to the conflict in the wagon. Discovering that she wasn't put a pause on Elowen's fast-acting fury.

"You're right," Elowen admitted to Beatrice, much to the shock of everyone in the wagon. Even the man handling the horses up front fumbled the reins. "The problems start when we talk," she continued. "So let's take a pledge of silence, then. That will be better for all of us."

"Fine by me," Beatrice said.

"Very good." Elowen removed one of the sticky crystals from her hand to use as a paint. "In fact, I'll draw a line down the wagon. This will be my half, and that half will be yours." Elowen used the colorful candy to mark their division. "This line will act as an invisible curtain, preventing us from needing to entertain whatever is happening on the other side."

Beatrice folded her arms. "Wonderful. I don't even see you over there."

"Nor do I see you," Elowen said back.

"Perfect." Beatrice wanted the last word, and that irritated Elowen to no end.

She opened her mouth to get in one last jab—something clever that showed she used her mind just as well as she used her heart—

when she remembered the greater power existed in silence. That was how she had survived the last ten years, and it was how she'd survive the next few days.

In fact, if she had her way, she would never speak to Beatrice again.

11

Clare

He was certain nothing in history had ever lasted so long.

In the legends of the Winter War, where men fought with fearsome wights in endless darkness, none had endured the way he did. In the Nine-Kingdom Quell, when the ruling lands withdrew from each other instead of risking conflict, none knew the emptiness of isolation like he. No, Clare was convinced the wagon ride in which he found himself now outlasted every recorded instance of the endurance of Mythrian peril.

While he knew only hours were passing, they were hours of the stiffest, coldest silence. Of glares tossed like daggers and sighs wielded like armor. Elowen sat opposite Beatrice, neither of them speaking.

Contending with the outcome of forcing them into one wagon, on one journey, Clare was forced to confront one immovable, unfortunate fact.

He'd made a *grave* mistake.

The wagon eventually slowed. Moments later, the driver came around the rear. "Gotta hold up for dinner," he declared, sounding hasty to escape what was ongoing in his carriage. "There ought to be fun to be had in this village, though. Very *idyllic*, tourists say. Wonderful hot springs and decadent whitefish pies."

Clare wondered if the village had posters like he'd seen in Farmount for simple summoning spells one could use for delivery-persons to carry the local delicacies right to whatever lodging one found. He loved a good fish pie, if he was honest.

"No," Beatrice declared flatly. "No, we're not *vacationing* for the night. We're summoning Wagons-for-You."

"Can't," the driver replied. "Not out here. Sweetwater messes with the spell." He sounded proud, like he enjoyed pointing out the competing service's limitations.

The remark, however, did not endear him to Beatrice. "Can we pay you to recruit a second driver and *not* waylay us this eve?" she inquired irritably. "I want this journey over with."

In Elowen's glare, Clare recognized the expression of one who did not wish to concede she'd had the same idea. "Do you have the coin for it?" she replied. "I heard you were destitute. Again."

"Why don't you send an eagle to your parents and have them drop off the farthings?" Beatrice shot back at Elowen. "Oh, wait, you no longer speak to them, right?"

Clare was holding dearly on to the notion of delivered whitefish pies now. Perhaps he could commission spicesalted fried potatoes alongside.

"Ladies, please!" Vandra cut in, her cheer drawn with strain like the highest strings on a lute. Clare's spirits suffered further. If even the convivial Vandra was annoyed, the situation was dire. It called for . . . *oh, withering Ghosts*. It called for leadership. Something a chivalrous, heroic nobleman would display, whereas a knavish lout would only observe, dreaming of pie.

"No," he interrupted, mustering his voice into what he hoped passed for respectful command. "No, each of you. Cease. We're spending the night here. We will employ no secondary driver."

His ex's vicious gaze shot his way like venomed arrows from the nocks of the Forest of Vrast's unforgiving defenders. It was, however, Elowen who responded.

"Who died and made you the leader?" she demanded. "Oh wait."

Her gaze rounded on Beatrice.

Silence fell over the wagon. Beatrice did not rise to a retort. Instead, she wilted into herself. Where until now Elowen's remarks had struck her like sparks onto kindling, this one snuffed out the flame of her spirit.

Clare felt her pain as if it were his own. Figuratively, of course. He wondered if Elowen magically felt the wound for real.

He could not contemplate the possibility. He looked instead to the driver, who was uncomfortably watching his passengers fight. "Please," Clare implored. "Enjoy your night. Thank you for the smooth steering today."

The man did not need to receive further permission. He looked profoundly pleased to escape the crossfire.

With glares and eyerolls reserved for Clare, who really believed himself an innocent bystander in the current circumstances, Beatrice, then Elowen, then Vandra left the carriage and headed into town. In the peace of their absence, Clare stepped from the wagon onto the soft, sand-like dirt of the clearing, taking a quick measure of his surroundings. With woeful pangs in his heart, he wished he were here under pleasanter circumstances, for he loved the Western Coast.

The region was Mythria's dulcet preference of vacationers, a place of villages of sculpted sandstone where one could enjoy fair weather and delicacies from the fresh-caught creatures of the Sweetwater Sea. When he'd guest-performed on one popular shadow play produced nearby, he'd voyaged down with the rest of the cast. Amid the fried pestleshell sandwiches and laughs shared with the finest comedians in Mythria, it ranked highly among Clare's fondest memories.

While the coastal wind ruffled his hair, Clare racked his mind for how he could fix their infighting. *What would Galwell do?* he inquired of himself. Of course, no answer returned. Galwell would not have found himself in this fine, fine position because his calming presence always brought out the best in people.

Maybe his companions just needed to eat something, Clare hoped weakly.

He followed them toward the village, comforted that they were at least headed in the right direction and not running back to their homes on foot. "Hot springs could ease our weariness, could they not? We know Beatrice loves a bath," he called out behind them.

None of the women replied.

In the quiet, Clare came up next to them. He found them gazing skyward and followed their stares.

The TENTH FESTIVAL OF THE FOUR!
Come CELEBRATE OUR HEROES!

He had not even noticed the banner strung from the village's cream-colored rooftops. Or rather, he had, and had paid the paraphernalia no mind, used to festival adornment and, candidly, celebration of himself. Only now did he realize Elowen, who had isolated herself shortly after the Four's costly victory, had probably never once glimpsed such festivities. Beatrice, he understood, hid herself in her palatial estate to avoid the celebratory commotion.

"But . . . the festival isn't for days," Elowen said, half to herself.

Her stunned struggle hit Clare with quick sympathy. He returned to her side, speaking slowly. "Over the years, the festival has expanded," he explained gently. "People have started decorating earlier and earlier. Children are out of school for the whole week, there are parties every night in local squares, families travel to their home villages . . ."

"I'd hoped it would die down," Beatrice replied unevenly. "Instead, it's . . . worse."

Elowen's features wavered like marble melting, her face racked with fear. "I can't do this," she uttered. She shook her head nervously. "Not yet."

"My dear." Vandra placed a comforting hand on Elowen's shoulder.

Clare took them in. They'd both hidden from the commemoration of their quest for ten years for very real reasons, and now . . . they intended to face their fears for Thessia. He was overwhelmed with the feeling that these two women really were the heroes the banner over them proclaimed.

It demanded he offer them what heroism he—vain, celebrated Clare Grandhart—could offer. He had to find a way to spare them.

Unfortunately, right on the heels of his resolve, a shopkeeper shaking dust from rugs outside one of the nearby shops happened to look up. Her eyes locked with Clare's. Her gaze, of course, continued to the rest of the party.

He knew what would happen next.

"Great Ghosts!" she exclaimed. "*The Four themselves! Here in our village!*"

Her cries caught the interest of other village folk—the man vending what looked indeed like whitefish pies from his street stand, the couple emerging from a storefront where, the sign proclaimed, one could rent windwalkers for use on the Sweetwater's welcoming waters.

Clare realized the situation they were in. There was no stopping mobs like this when one has been recognized. He couldn't get them out of their predicament.

This was, however, the manner of heroism in which Clare Grandhart excelled. His skill with the sword was nothing, he'd learned in recent years, next to his ability for catching the spotlight his compatriots did not want.

He stepped forward, strutting with rakish glory. He could be the Clare Grandhart everyone wanted, even if they assumed it was because he loved the attention.

He did enjoy the attention, he could admit. Yet on many days, he would rather not be lauded as a hero when the real hero, the hero everyone wanted, was dead.

Nevertheless, Mythria needed a hero—even if only the delightful performance of one—and more importantly, Elowen and Beatrice did not owe Mythria a single scrap more of themselves than they were willing to give.

With the villagers' eyes on him, he waved. He squared his shoulders. He hit them with the crooked smile.

Ghosts, he was good.

"My friends," he cried out. "We four"—he winked, letting the crowd know he intended the cheeky reference to their numerical moniker—"find ourselves passing through for the evening. Surely one of you fine folk could route us in the direction of dinner and drinks? I do love your seafood."

The woman he shot his demons-may-care wink looked earnestly short of breath. Fearing she would literally faint, which Beatrice would never let him live down, he raked his gaze over the crowd. His constituency was growing, people peering out from doorways and over the village's sculpted rooftops. "Show them to the Visshark's Fin!" one voice ventured from within the crowd.

While Clare fixed the villagers with his most eager, expectant glance—which was not feigned, for Visshark-oil-fried crisps were delicious—the idea grasped the crowd. The elderly man near the pie stand magicked streaming light into the sky, illuminating their path to the pub.

Clare swept his arms out. "Drinks on me!" he proclaimed.

Everyone cheered.

Jubilant now, the crowd followed him down the lighted path into the village—bringing his companions with them. While Vandra protected Elowen from inquisitors, he caught sight of Beatrice's discomfort with the village folk surrounding her. He grasped onto the first question he heard called out—"What were the Grimauld Mines like?"

He vaulted his voice loudly, drawing the focus of even those flocking to Beatrice. "Oh, nightmares worse than the mind could possibly produce," he promised ominously. "Orb Weavers in every corner. The chittering sound of spiderlike limbs echoing over rough stone. The stench of rotting corpses . . ."

Captivating the crowd, he kept their focus on him with the perhaps slightly embellished account of their experiences in the mines. He was a good storyteller, he congratulated himself. Maybe he would pen his memoirs when he returned home. Or even invent stories for fans of his, promising such fictions that would surely excite the imagination.

When they reached the Visshark's Fin, Clare could not help warming to the place. He loved a salty, sea-spat tavern. News had evidently spread of the heroes' arrival, for the drinkmaid greeted him with goblets of ale and seductive eyes. He was, he knew, in for a long night of "heroism."

Fortunately, he was Clare Grandhart.

Downing his drink, he called on every muscle in him from years of celebrity. For the next several hours, he exerted them with practiced zeal. He stood on tables, regaling the crowd with exaggerated stories of his exploits. He led them in songs venerating his courage. He paid for round upon round of drinks.

He caught sight of Elowen slipping from the room, Vandra following her.

He didn't know how to feel when he noticed Beatrice remained.

She watched him with undisguised focus the entire while. He felt foolish when he drew encouragement from her gaze, when he fortified himself with the idea she might feel some gratitude for Sir Clare Grandhart's revelry. Certainly she wouldn't. Gratitude? For him?

Nonetheless—on the off chance she appreciated his holding the interest of the village folk, or the display of how his charm captivated the room—he continued his efforts.

Until his voice went hoarse.

How could this happen? He chastened himself when his first whispered syllables struck in the midst of his seventh song of the night. Was Grandhart's capacity for revelry going the way of his creaky hip? Calamitous.

Despite how his very presence delighted the Visshark's Fin, the inevitable consequence of Clare's hoarseness followed. The villagers grew distracted. With Clare out of commission, their focus found the other famous person in the room—Beatrice. He could only helplessly watch her in return.

He overheard Galwell's name in the questions they posed to her. Saw the guilt staining her impossibly lovely features. He observed her struggle with polite stiffness, fending off overenthusiastic inquiries. It was, as it happened, exactly what he *would* wish on his worst enemy.

And yet.

Perhaps he was feeling charitable. Perhaps he was making decisions drunkenly. He did not pause to question his own motives—he often didn't—and strode to the shadow-songbox, for he'd realized he did not need his own voice to help Beatrice. With one farthing contributed into the shining cauldron, hand-sized conjurated musicians would play whatever song one's heart wished.

He heard the opening notes of his chosen melody, and the years vanished.

The song he'd summoned was one they'd sung, the Four. The mid-tempo clavichord ballad was suited for swaying steps, its grand chorus inviting every listener to belt out the lyrics. On a campfire-lit night, Beatrice had conceded she could never resist dancing to the enchanting melody. Playing the song now was a dirty trick—one Clare delighted in employing when he crossed the room and offered her his hand.

She eyed his rough palm. The crowd congregated, pressing in on them.

He held her gaze, expectant.

When she placed her hand in his, he whisked her unhesitatingly into the middle of the room, where he swayed her gently in the firelight.

"Rescuing me again, Grandhart?" she murmured. She did not, he noted, muster much resentment in her voice.

"You were in dire danger of having to sign parchments, weapons . . ." he remarked. "Perhaps even body parts."

Withdrawing in grudging surprise, she regarded him. "How many body parts have you signed, exactly?"

"It's not the number you should ask about," he replied. "Rather, the type of body part."

When she laughed—really laughed—he could not help how

the sound cut through just a little of the resentment in his chest. Like a knife carved of opalicyte, dangerous and shimmering and invaluable.

It reminded him how easy things once were between them. Or—no, not quite. Things were *easy* the night they met. Then he stole away into the morning light.

The next months on the road were *not* easy, but they were . . . good. Every day in her company, the pair of them were contentious, even combative, yet passionate. They cared for each other. While their unstable new connection wasn't physical—not since the first night, not except that one kiss on the eve of battle—the pull they felt was undeniable. He had started to see, as if magic lights guided his path like the ones outside, how his relationship with her could lead past conflict into something he'd rarely dared dream of. *A future.*

Until everything fell apart.

He did not know if they could ever find their way past what happened. *Ghosts*, though, he could not help wanting to.

"When did you learn to dance like this?" she inquired in earnest curiosity, distracting him.

"I've learned many things, Beatrice," he heard himself saying. He wasn't nobly posturing, yet the honesty felt foreign on his lips. "I'm . . . better than I used to be."

Whatever reaction he hoped for, it was not what he received. Her smile flattened, her composure stiffening. He hardly heard her question over the now mockingly familiar music.

"Why do you think you need to be anything different?"

He had no answer. How could he, when he did not understand the question? Why *wouldn't* he want to be different? He wasn't good enough, not for her, not for his friends.

He wasn't Galwell.

She stepped from his embrace. Whether she intuited the subject of his introspection or not, he did not know. "Thank you for the rescue," she said, like a door he hadn't noticed until now had slammed in his face.

Spinning on her heel, she stranded him in the fawning halo of the crowd, naked in the light of their joy—halfway between who he was and who he wished he could be, and utterly lost.

12

Beatrice

She didn't deserve parades. Beatrice chastised herself the same way whenever the Festival of the Four was happening in Elgin, when she'd made excuses and stayed inside, ensconcing herself in her head magic. No, she did not deserve parades, or festivities, or interviews with scribes. She deserved none of it.

Yet here she stood, on a fucking *float* constructed of sea flowers of every Western Coast sort, processing down the village street.

The sun glared off the cream-colored sandstone walls of the seaside hamlet where they had found themselves, making her eyes water. From the sides of the wide road, villagers cheered. In front of and following them were other floats, some decorated or vivified with magic—elaborate wooden dragons lofting in paper-winged flights, horses enchanted to look like unicorns. She could not help nostalgia, watching the crowd's youngest children stare up in wonderment. Everyone except the very young knew unicorns weren't real.

The villagers' pleading had assembled on one float the remaining heroes of the Four, weary from yesterday's journey and yesternight's celebrating. The one fortunate side of their fame was the free-of-charge lodging they'd received in the comfiest inn in the village.

The town, they'd learned, was called Keralia, and its sunlit charm covered over young scars. When the Fraternal Order's hold had clenched hardest on Mythria, the Four had passed by Keralia on their way to Queendom. Many villagers remembered the fear in the streets every night of the Order's stay. Beatrice understood why the village celebrated the Festival of the Four with corresponding zeal. If she ever found something capable of chasing off her nightmares, she would cling on to it for dear life.

Their float's journey had started right outside the door of their inn. They now processed toward the heart of the village. Vandra, Beatrice noticed, followed them inconspicuously on foot, weaving through enthusiastic crowds with the float's progress. Beatrice envied Vandra, who, as she wasn't considered one of the Four, was not invited to join the procession.

If Beatrice glimpsed something somber and wistful in Vandra's eyes as she watched Elowen above . . . Well, in Beatrice's experience, wishing to trade places with others only ever earned wasted hours. It was Beatrice on the float, not Vandra Ravenfall. That was that.

Elowen, for her part, glowered at the crowd watching the parade, while Clare—of course—smirked and strutted and had them swooning. Refusing to do either, Beatrice found herself faking smiles, waving at people who considered her the salvation of the realm, to whom they owed their lives.

It was miserable. *I deserve none of it*, she reminded herself with every inch their float crawled down the village walk. *I deserve loneliness and guilt and shame*. It didn't matter how many lives were owed to her. She owed Mythria one she could never restore.

She owed her friends. She owed Elowen.

One couldn't rectify wrongs like hers with mathematics, she knew. No measure of victory could make up for one inescapable condemnation. Galwell was gone, and she deserved no one's gratitude.

She didn't deserve to dance the way she had last night, either. It was almost what angered her the worst—almost. She wasn't pleased she'd found a glimmer of joy in *Clare's* embrace. Clare Grandhart aside, she knew she deserved happiness in *no one's* arms.

She'd let her guard down. Let herself have . . . fun. *Never again,* she vowed. Especially not with him.

When the float slowed in the village square, she felt a flicker of hope—until she glanced up. In the fountained center of the seaside town was . . . them.

Of course the village where they'd paused in their journey had a fucking statue of the Four in the square.

Galwell stood in front, sword raised, his face heroic. Clare was crouched, ready to strike, his mouth carved forever into his usual smirk. Elowen stood near Galwell, her glare intimidating. And at the rear Beatrice found . . . herself. Her expression serene, like she knew she would prevail. Her statue looked like everything she wasn't. Confident. Strong. Happy.

She ripped her eyes from herself, hurting.

Vandra, Beatrice glimpsed in the corner of her vision, regarded the statue with the same inscrutable yearning she'd worn during the parade. Then cheers rose from the crowd, pulling Beatrice's gaze past the statue, where stood what she intuited was the estate of the village's lord or lady.

The woman who stepped out onto the sandstone portico certainly fit the part. Neither her sumptuous garb, casually fashionable in the way of Western Coast villages, nor her seashell jewelry held Beatrice's focus, however.

Not when she caught sight of the shining black orb in the woman's ringed hands.

"It is my distinct pleasure to introduce myself, the Lady of Keralia," she spoke warmly to the surviving members of the Four.

More cheers went up from the crowd. "What an honor it is for our village to host our own heroes, in the midst of our celebration of the anniversary of their victory, saving our realm from the Fraternal Order's darkness!"

More cheering. Keralians were a cheering-inclined people, Beatrice noticed. She wished she wanted to join them.

"Every year, we remember," the lady went on. "For in remembrance, we keep the past present."

This, Beatrice found, was exactly why she hated the Festival of the Four. Not just remembering what had happened. Rather, Beatrice loathed the idea it was even possible to forget. It infuriated her. The quest would not need commemoration for her—not when it would never, ever escape her memory, even for one moment. Imagining it would for others . . . Poisonous jealousy coursed in her.

She fumed while the lady went on. "We remember. We remember how easily men of status can change into creatures of evil. We remember how the Fraternal Order, once known for nothing other than gaudy revels and investing farthings in each other's castles, went from proud noblemen to conspirators out to overthrow our queen and destroy Queendom."

The Keralians shook their heads in condemnation.

"We remember who inspired the Order's darkness," the Lady of Keralia continued. "We know now how to recognize the face of evil. Todrick van Thorn."

Hearing his very name, Beatrice felt herself flinch.

Todrick van Thorn. The face of evil. Indeed, he was. Wide-smiling, raven-haired, devastatingly persuasive. The young nobleman's unique gifts suited him grandly in the Order's company. His head magic could rewrite reality in his vicinity, changing memories or enhancing, eliminating, or editing what was.

"He corrupted the Order. Changed complacent men into wicked

ones. He wielded loyalty like a weapon, camaraderie like poison. He reminded us"—the lady paused, indulging now in her dramatic rendering of history—"of how evil does not flourish in isolation. It spreads like the Nightbiter Plague. Like it spread from Todrick van Thorn to his friend, Myke Lycroft, his counterpart in villainy."

They were darkly perfect for each other, Beatrice remembered. Each needed the other. Each held the key to the other's devious design. Lycroft, a hand-magical weaponeer, could forge implements for the magnification and replication of others' magic, yet had no other magic himself. Todrick's magic could rule a revel, but not a realm—not without Myke to heighten his powers. They were the ultimate duo of destruction. Determined to dominate Mythria together.

"Lycroft crafted the instrument of the Order's plan—the Sword of Souls," the lady recounted raptly. "When charged with the pain of those who perished under the sword's stroke, the weapon could extend magic like van Thorn's without end. The Order kidnapped Princess Thessia before her coronation. With Thessia deposed, they would use van Thorn's magic to recast the realm into one under Todrick's unending rule. They would reach out with his powers not only to neighboring noblemen, but to *every person* in Mythria."

With her words, the village folk booed like they were receiving the decade-old news for the first time.

"Queendom would not even need conquest," the lady continued. "It would simply . . . vanish from memory."

Beatrice watched the villagers react, remembering with every sentence why she scorned the festivals. Was this fucking *theater* to them? Did these memories not shadow their every waking moment? *This isn't some grand old legend with a happy ending*, she wanted to scream out.

"Until the Four saved us!" the Lady of Keralia cheered. Right on cue, the crowd whooped with joy. "They rode into battle and slew Todrick van Thorn! The sword was lost forever! Lycroft sent into hiding!" The lady's celebratory exclamations sounded now like newshandlers' cries promising wondrous reportage.

Beatrice clenched her fingernails into her palm, desperate to interject what else the Four did. They'd lost their dearest friend. They'd destroyed each other. They didn't need to remember because they would never forget.

"Our village was freed," the lady continued, softer. "Fear fled our streets. We could cherish our neighbors, look forward to our sunrises. We returned," she said, "to life."

The hush her words cast over the crowd gave Beatrice pause. Villagers bowed their heads in quiet remembrance.

Watching their expressions, she wished she could feel their gratitude. She really did. She wanted to feel like the Four's victory was not only cheap fairy-tale pageantry for the people of Keralia. Perhaps it inspired them. Perhaps it instilled in them the idea to remember the wonder of every day hence. In ten years of hiding from the Festival of the Four, Beatrice had forgotten heroism could hold such meaning.

Instead, she could only remind herself of what the village's story left out. What the people didn't know. The truth of why, when the village of Keralia returned to life, Beatrice's own life shattered.

"We will never forget this day," the lady continued. "Like we will never forget the day the sun rose ten years ago and the queen remained on the throne."

She faced the group of them now. Beatrice's hands went slick with sweat.

"If we could request of you one more favor . . ." The Lady of

Keralia's voice was honeyed, like the mead Beatrice consumed too much of yestereve. Both were in danger of rendering her ill.

The lady held out the dark orb.

"Beatrice of the Four," she exhorted, "would you use our Conjurall to show us the day you slayed Todrick van Thorn?"

No cheers now. Only the hush of hope. Every eager eye found her.

Of course she recognized the Conjurall, one of many enchanted creations designed for those with head magic to project, for the viewership of others, the conjurations or insights of their magical gifts. The noblewoman wished her to project her gift of reverse prophecy for everyone to view the defeat of the nefarious van Thorn.

The lady lowered her voice, showmanship replaced with gentle inquiry. "Please," she implored. "Many in our village have found inspiration in your perseverance and your victory. It would be the honor of our lives."

Beatrice genuinely contemplated refusing. No matter the village lady's exhortations. Of course, Beatrice could project every detail for the village folk of Keralia, right down to the moment they defeated Todrick—the moment Galwell was killed. It would hardly disturb her now. She'd watched it thousands of times.

She could not, however, show it to Elowen.

Gracefully, Clare stepped up next to her. "Why don't I lead us in song instead?" he offered, exactly like he had last night. Repetition robbed none of the luster from his enthusiasm. It was kind. Noble, even.

It infuriated her.

Yes, her life had gotten messy. Yes, she loathed herself when she was not drinking her storm-clouded soul into emptiness. What she was *not*, however, was some damsel for the heroic scoundrel's rescuing. She was sick of his kindnesses. She pushed past Clare to jump down from the float, reaching for the Ominoccular.

"I'll show you one of our greatest victories instead," she promised. "The day we rescued the princess."

What a surprise—the people of Keralia cheered.

Placing her hands on the shining inky stone, Beatrice summoned the scene, letting her magic spill into the sphere. The vision unfurled out from the orb, the veils of the past parting in the Western Coast sky. Above them, nighttime reigned, the darkness deep in the forest where—

She saw herself. Running.

Beatrice the hero looked powerful. Like the statue in the square come to glorious life. Her footsteps flew over the uneven ground, threading past trees in her dash.

Elowen was with her. Clare too.

He rushed past her, wind whipping his hair. Grinning with wild light, he looked as handsome then as he did now.

In Elowen, however, the changes caught Beatrice up short.

Running ahead of her, Elowen was *laughing*. She looked giddy. Like she was exactly where she was supposed to be.

"Pick up your pace, Beatrice!" Clare called out in playful competition. "Last one to rescue the princess is a rotten duskjay egg!"

She could not even keep herself from grinning with him. "Surely you're not serious," she replied. "Is this how you escaped the Grimauld Mines? With immature schoolyard insults?"

"Now that you mention it . . ." Clare paused in pretend contemplation, his impressive stride never slowing. "Why, yes, I do reckon my shouting 'Your leg-pits stink of gryphon droppings!' did indeed help me escape."

Elowen giggled. No matter how heavily one felt the weight of responsibility, gryphon dropping jokes never got old.

"Never underestimate the power of a good quip," Clare counseled. "Or a catchphrase. I'd love to have a catchphrase one day."

"How about," Elowen chimed in, "*Clare Grandhart—loved by many, especially myself!*"

Hearing her own laughter, the Beatrice in the village square remembered why she only watched sad memories. Sometimes the joyous ones hurt worse.

"I like it," past-Clare replied gamely. "I like it!"

They descended into the wooded gorge for which they'd set out, watching for clinging nightmares in the foul pits where frightening dreams could live, continuing to flourish even once dreamers had stopped dreaming them.

The path steepened, level enough to run, yet perilous. Which meant Clare chose that moment to spin nimbly, jogging backward, facing the girls.

"Show-off," past-Beatrice declared.

He grinned. "Now who's immature?"

"What can I say? You bring out the best in me."

In the village square, Beatrice was not prepared for the fondness flickering over Clare's expression with her joke.

Nor was she prepared for the crossbow bolts whizzing by their past selves, striking their pursuers—pursuers that Beatrice had forgotten were the reason for their dash through the forest in the first place. The Conjurall revealed the three of them nearing the stronghold where Princess Thessia was being held, its obsidian spires reaching into the night.

In front, his stature majestic, crossbow in hand, stood Galwell.

He rattled off crossbow shots to scatter their pursuers, clearing his friends' path to the dark fortress, where he had boldly ventured first, volunteering his hand-magical strength in case the Order had placed monsters to guard the citadel. Beatrice could not help noting how perfectly Galwell it was. Ever selfless, ever skillful. Ever in the right place.

Evading the Order's minions with his help, the three of them crowded to Galwell's side. The hero's hawklike eyes scouted the forest line, where the ominous rustle of enemies went quiet.

"Should we wait until we know they're gone?" Beatrice inquired, out of breath, chest heaving from their sprint.

Galwell held his weapon poised. "No. Thessia needs us," he replied. "Legends never wait."

Clare's shoulders slumped. "Fuck, see?" he said to his friends. "That's so good. Thank you, noble sir." He clapped his hand heartily on Galwell's shoulder.

Innocently curious, the other man paused. "What's so good?"

"The usual, brother," Elowen said. "Clare is jealous of how effortlessly fashionable and impressive you are."

When Galwell smiled, it pierced Beatrice's heart.

"No cause for jealousy, Grandhart," he said. "There is greatness in you."

His words were sincere, like always. Their effect on the younger Clare was immediate. His careless facade faded, and inspiration lit in his eyes. He looked . . . to her. Like he wondered if she'd noted Galwell's complimentary words.

She'd forgotten the moment. Forgotten the way her past self had smiled slightly, her only acknowledgment that she could glimpse the same greatness in him.

Then, like she sought distraction from her own fondness, she'd stolen over to where one of their crossbow-struck enemies was expiring. Palm to the man's forehead, she summoned his memory with her magic "They're . . . they're in the third door in the corridor to the right," she called over, informing the group.

"I feel hostility past the door," Elowen commented, catching her own racing breath. "We should be ready for combat, or a trap."

"*Let them try!*" Clare cried out grandly.

Beatrice cocked her head. "It's a little trite," she said. "Not bad, though."

"I can workshop it!" Clare replied. "I'll have you know I considered 'I'm always ready.' It doesn't quite hit hard enough, I fear. It sounds like I'm a wandering salesman for emergency gear."

Elowen's face wobbled from withheld laughter. It did rather sound the way he described.

"Perhaps," Galwell interjected with patient good humor, "we could quip *after* saving the princess?"

"See, this is why you're the leader," Clare conceded. "Where would we be without you?"

In the village square, Beatrice felt her face go white. When she'd summoned the memory, she didn't remember it invoked the question they had spent the past decade unwillingly investigating. Elowen stiffened next to her. Clare looked to the ground.

While her magic played on, she could hardly stand to watch the completion of the memory. The Four stormed the fortress. They fought off attacks from every angle, finally reaching the third door in the corridor to the right, which Galwell kicked down. Finding Thessia chained, he freed the princess. *Hooray, them.*

The Keralians cheered.

Exhausted, Beatrice removed her hands from the Conjurall, the vision concluded. She smiled weakly for the festival crowd, mustering the warmest reception she could for their gratitude.

Until she caught sight of Elowen. Elowen, whom she'd intentionally spared the gutting vision the Lady of Keralia had requested.

Her glare was livid.

Without words or decorum, Elowen strode off their float. On instinct, Beatrice pursued her, no longer caring what the crowd saw. Noticing Clare stepping easily once more into the spotlight, she doubted the village would object to her absence.

Down one of the side streets, she caught up to Elowen. "What is wrong with you?" Beatrice demanded. She found she was enraged. "Would you rather I showed the moment your brother breathed his last?"

Elowen halted and rounded on Beatrice. "I'd rather you had shown something *real*," she practically snarled. "Not the farce you gave them. You made it seem like we were *friends*."

The cruelty of her words left Beatrice nearly unable to breathe. "We *were* friends," she managed.

Elowen scoffed. "Were we?" She stated the question flatly. "Why don't you go up there and show them the moment you shared with me how you *really* felt. The day our *friendship*, as you say, died."

Beatrice felt her fury coil within her. She knew she could withdraw, welcoming Elowen's ire. She could consider the other woman's hatred yet more deserved punishment. Or she could unleash what she'd kept hidden. What more could she possibly lose?

She didn't care enough for restraint, she decided.

"Did you never wonder why Galwell climbed the ramparts?" she inquired calmly.

Elowen faltered, not following the change in the conversation.

"I thought you didn't want to relive his death today," she finally challenged Beatrice.

"I relive it every day," Beatrice replied.

Elowen eyed her. They stared like duelists with swords raised until Elowen relented. "Galwell climbed the ramparts in our final fight with the Order to stop you from trying to sacrifice yourself. You'd found out how to disempower the sword and didn't tell anyone. I know all of this," Elowen said. "It was the very last conversation we had, when my brother was fresh in his grave."

Beatrice nodded. Elowen was correct. Unbeknownst to the rest of the Four, Beatrice had learned that the blood of a sacrifice, freely given, would quell the Sword of Souls. Of course, she'd planned to give her own life. What did Mythria need with one more daughter of peasants? What the realm needed was a vanquishing sacrifice.

"But did you ever wonder," Beatrice replied, "how he knew I would give myself over? How you . . . didn't know?"

Beatrice watched the question cloud Elowen's ire. While Elowen could not read minds or exactly determine when someone was being deceptive, her lifelong closeness to Beatrice had permitted Elowen's magic nearly such insight when it came to her friend.

"I knew you would be the hardest to lie to," Beatrice went on. "Your magic would pick up my deceit. I knew you would question me about what I was hiding. When you did . . ."

She hesitated. When she'd driven the conversation in this direction, she had not known how hard reliving their friendship-ending fight would be. It had looked small from a distance, yet was daunting close up.

She forced herself to continue. "I made *a* confession," she explained. "About how for years I had felt like your charity case.

How it had weighed on me. How after that day, I would be done with you."

Ghosts, was she nearly choking on the words, even now? Remembering how she'd hurt herself hurting Elowen, convinced she needed to for the realm?

Elowen's eyes widened. She was starting to understand. She shook her head, looking like she wished to run from Beatrice's story. Into the hills, or the forest, or wherever offered refuge. "My magic would have known if you were lying," she challenged. "*I* would have known."

"I wasn't, though," Beatrice managed. Confession, she found, was no load lifted. It was a chasm she needed to carve into herself. "Not entirely. What I told you had enough truth to fool even your gifts. I *did* feel indebted to you in ways I sometimes didn't know how to deal with. And . . ."

Now was the hardest part. Yet she would not shy from hardship, she knew—from sacrifice. The same miserable, inevitable urge compelled her now.

"After that day, I *would* be done with you," she said softly.

Stunned realization crossed the stone facade of Elowen's features. "Because you intended to die," she finished.

Beatrice nodded. "I knew it would hurt you to hear I wanted nothing more to do with you. It would be enough to keep you from seeking out the *real* truth I was concealing." Her voice wavered like struck steel. "I knew you loved me. You would stop me and let the world perish. I . . . had to trick you."

The Western Coast warmth dried her watering eyes. Elowen only watched, cauldrons of emotion churning under her unflinching gaze. "And Galwell . . ." she elaborated, reconstituting the past her former friend had carefully kept hidden, "Galwell saw through it, because he didn't have my magic, so he wasn't fooled the way I was."

Beatrice exhaled one racked breath. Wasn't honesty supposed to ease the heart? Instead, she only remembered the consequences of what she'd done more sharply. When she'd confronted van Thorn, ready to die under his enchanted sword, Galwell had interceded, literally. Reaching her with not one instant to spare, Galwell the Great had caught the swing of the sword she'd meant for herself.

Ever in the right place.

The strike would have slain her cleanly. It did not kill Galwell the Great cleanly. Larger and stronger, he had died slowly from the mortal wound—slowly enough that he could with his own sword impale the stunned van Thorn, killing the head of the Order. When Myke Lycroft, not far from the confrontation, had come upon them, he wept for his fallen friend—and his tears on the magical blade he had forged drained the Sword of Souls of its dark potency.

Sacrifice, she'd quietly realized, was not the only way the sword could lose its power. She'd made a horrible mistake. If Galwell had slain van Thorn in honest combat, the same would have happened—without Galwell's own death.

Galwell the Great had died for nothing, except for her.

"You should hate me, Elowen," she whispered. "Ghosts know it is your right. But I will not have you thinking our entire friendship was a lie any longer. It wasn't."

Under the Keralian sun, Elowen watched her. The other woman's face held the strangest combination of feelings. Loathing pity. Resentful regret. Embarrassment even now, remembering Beatrice's rejection.

It made Beatrice want to flee—so she did.

She strode off, ending the conversation, hating the memories she knew would never leave her side.

13

Elowen

Elowen's anger lived somewhere cold and damp inside her—a cave with endless pathways and no light coming through. She'd long ago accepted that the feeling would be there forever, so she'd learned to avoid the bottomless places where it had rotted her all the way through. Until Beatrice had now forced Elowen down one of the worst paths of all—the way their friendship had ended— and Elowen had no choice but to surrender to the depths of her fury.

"You were happy to die having me believe we had no real bond?" Elowen asked, gritting her teeth on the last word. At least anger motivated her. If she'd succumbed to the sadness instead, she'd have crumpled into a ball in the middle of the road. Instead she walked with clearheaded intention. Actually, she sprinted, because Beatrice was half an iron taller than Elowen, and she used that to her full advantage, her long legs covering ground in twice the time.

Elowen fought to keep up without heaving for breath. She refused to show the effort it required to match Beatrice's pace. She hadn't moved this fast in years. It didn't help that the memory Beatrice had projected on the Conjurall highlighted how quick Elowen had once been.

"It meant saving you . . . and the entire realm, of course. So yes,

I was," Beatrice informed her, as if that was an obvious choice for anyone to make.

Perhaps it was. But Elowen could not understand how Beatrice had gone on living—knowing the entire time that Elowen thought their whole friendship was a lie—and never correcting it until now.

"If I had known how you felt about what my family provided you, we could have worked something out to put you at ease," Elowen said. "These days, I have nothing myself. I understand it now, how uncomfortable it is to rely on someone else to help you through. Why didn't you tell me sooner?" She fought off the traces of pain in her voice.

Beatrice did not respond, which helped keep Elowen's hurt at bay. She could focus on her anger more when Beatrice did rude things such as ignore her.

"That's rich," Elowen said baitingly. "Saying nothing to me at all. Very mature."

"I have no answer that could ever satisfy you," Beatrice said. "I've done many things I'm not proud of." Finally she turned to look at Elowen, slowing her pace for once, only to pale in fear.

Elowen glanced back, hoping to identify the source of Beatrice's horror. A handful of men in dark cloaks were running toward them, half their bows pointed at her head, half pointed at Beatrice's. They were about to be attacked, and they had been so immersed in their fight they'd almost missed out on noticing.

Instinctually, the two women moved toward each other. There was no good place to seek immediate cover. They had to rely on each other for protection instead, crouching low and zigzagging together, hoping to reach one of the buildings in the distance.

Elowen stole a look at the attackers just in time to see a crossbow pointed at Beatrice's back. She threw herself atop Beatrice, crashing both of them to the ground as the arrow whizzed over-head.

Elowen's initial shock ebbed long enough for her to realize what was happening. She was *helping* Beatrice. Disgusted with herself, she pulled away, weaving her own topsy-turvy path to prevent the attackers from hitting her.

"What are you doing?" Beatrice yelled. The panic in her voice almost pulled Elowen back. But Elowen was a cold person. She had to be. If she acted out of habit, working with Beatrice like in the olden days, she would be giving in to the dreary tenderness in her heart, forgiving Beatrice for all the pain she'd inflicted. Sentimentality was worse than anger and sadness combined. It was a curse with no respite.

"Saving myself," Elowen informed her. "I suggest you do the same."

"Oh, darling, I'll be the one doing the saving today." Vandra sauntered to the middle of the road and shot off a round of arrows the same way certain hand magicians dealt cards—fast and unbroken, with an effortless precision that came off like an act of boredom.

Both Beatrice and Elowen froze in wonderment. Vandra hit each man in the same spot on their lower leg, moving on to the next before a single other person could return the favor. One by one, the attackers fell, unable to continue pursuing Beatrice and Elowen.

"That should do it," Vandra said. She grinned as she returned her bow and arrows to the quiver slung across her shoulder. She looked . . . well, she looked fucking *cool*. She really was a badass in the most heartbreaking of ways.

She pressed her finger gently into Elowen's shoulder. Her concern bloomed through Elowen's body, a garden of worry lit by the heat of desire. "I turn away from you for one moment."

Elowen's legs shook, and she wished it was still from anger. "Sorry," she muttered.

"I know one way you can make it up to me." Vandra cupped Elowen's chin in her hands.

Elowen found herself drawing nearer, and not from absorbing Vandra's emotions. The want that sparked low in her belly was a feeling she knew to be her own. Vandra's lips—pleading, present, right *there*—would be a refuge. And to touch her. Oh, it would be just the delight Elowen needed. It would be a relief.

That was precisely what sobered Elowen up.

She would not, could not, kiss Vandra Ravenfall. She'd already gone and gotten herself invested in Vandra's emotional well-being. If she gave in to the physical? Who knew what that would mean.

And besides, Beatrice was watching. How embarrassing.

Stumbling back, Elowen faked the kind of quick-pulsed anger she was known for. "How do I know you aren't working for them?" she accused, pointing at the attackers Vandra had systematically taken down. They were scrambling to stand up and run off. After a few steps, some of them collapsed anew, while others managed to keep going, hobbling down the hilliest part of the road until they were out of sight. "You didn't wound them fatally! Perhaps this was a ruse to gain my trust, only to betray me in the end!"

Elowen was no performer. She tried anyway. She was already haunted by Vandra's touch on her skin. If she got the privilege of experiencing Vandra again in full, it would be her undoing. Because Vandra Ravenfall was cunning, and beautiful, and relentlessly social. She could never be limited to someone as prickly and sullen as Elowen True. So even though Elowen knew all Vandra wanted was to create a new life for herself, to give up deception and become someone honest, Elowen still accused her of lying, because she knew that would sting the most.

Vandra's face knotted up. Mountains of hurt sprouted up between her eyebrows as she turned swiftly on her heel.

"Really? You're just going to leave?" Elowen called out, unable to get her own words and feelings to sync up.

"I'm not one of the Four," Vandra said. "I won't be missed."

Elowen fought the urge to respond. She didn't want Vandra close, but she couldn't bring herself to admit how much she'd hate for her to go.

"Actually," Vandra said, turning and walking back to Elowen, "I don't need powers to see through your feelings. When I go, you can tell me that you're not going to miss me, but that doesn't make it true."

Elowen blushed.

"You can pretend to think I'm dishonest," Vandra continued. "That won't stop me from chasing after those men and learning who they are and why they've attempted to harm you. And if I return with that information, and you confirm that it's real, and I still show up after all the ways you've tried to stop me from doing so, maybe then you will know."

"Know what?" Elowen asked, breathless.

Vandra walked off again, leaving Elowen standing there tortured, arrows scattered around her feet.

Even when Elowen tried to push Vandra away, Vandra still found a way through. Elowen needed to build her walls higher, so that eventually even the relentless Vandra Ravenfall would tire of trying to peer over.

14

Beatrice

Queendom was on the horizon.

Wonderful.

They'd ridden on from Keralia in uncompromising silence. Without Vandra, no one filled the wagon with informative remarks on migratory hamsterjays. Worse, without Vandra, Elowen's sneering had changed into stony sullenness, which Beatrice found she preferred even less. *You should hate me*, she'd said. Well, she had her wish, same as if she'd caught a woodland sprite.

She was foolish, Beatrice reckoned. If she couldn't change the way things were, she'd hoped she could find some measure of solace. Instead, unraveling the whole story to Elowen only hurt differently.

Wishing to fend off such ruminations, Beatrice preoccupied herself with vigilance. For the duration of the ride, she kept one hand on the crossbow the Keralians had gifted the heroes while staring out the rear of the wagon. The men who fired on them in the village were likely just outlaws, she reasoned with herself, considering celebrities easy prey.

Yet why did they fire to kill? she couldn't help wondering.

No explanations crossed her mind, and no pursuers crossed the wagon's path on the journey inland. The road wound upward, until finally—Queendom emerged. Beatrice laid her crossbow down, wishing every sort of menace could be faced with weapons.

The palace rose up from the mountains encircling Mythria's flourishing capital. The city was one of dreams, one for which every Mythrian held pride in their hearts. It combined the finest qualities of everywhere in the realm—the dulcet clime of the coasts, with gentle winds rolling down from the snowy slopes of the mountains, the sophistication of Farmount's lively reach, the very design of the architecture like something the sculptors of Featherbint would *ooh* and *ahh* over.

Of course, for Beatrice, it was no city of dreams. It was one of nightmares.

The Four's final confrontation with Todrick van Thorn had unfolded here, not far from the elegant white-stone castle, which made this place the location of many dark dreams from which she could not wake—until she did, sweating, panicked, and hoping her nocturnal fit had not woken Robert de Noughton.

As they neared the gates, the city's high walls reaching magnificently into the clear sky looked as imposing as the day the Four had faced down the Fraternal Order. The day she'd planned to sacrifice herself. While she knew they would not find an army of Order aspirants inside Queendom today, what waited for them instead was, in her estimation, arguably worse.

For nowhere celebrated the Festival of the Four like the royal capital.

The festivities in Keralia felt like practice, like the pony her neighbor lent her when she was first learning to ride. His name was Walter, in honor of the neighbor's grandson, who'd received a knighthood. Young Beatrice had joked the pony aspired to *neigh*thood. He was nineteen years old. He moved very slowly.

The past few days were the Walter the Pony of festivals. What waited for them now was a stallion, untamed, ready to drag them into oblivion.

With hesitant steps, they walked up to the walls, where incoming journeyers could ring the welcome bells. While Beatrice felt unprepared, she knew Elowen was faring worse. She did not know how Elowen typically spent the anniversary of her brother's death, but undoubtedly it did not involve the singing and dancing in the streets they were about to witness.

No matter what was stirring uneasily in Beatrice's own soul, she wished she could comfort Elowen. Inexplicable or not, despite Elowen's diligent unfriendliness, it was how Beatrice felt. However, when last they'd spoken, she was *grateful* when they were attacked, for it had ended the conversation. She doubted Elowen would welcome her consolation now.

"How many people do you expect have . . . already gathered?" Elowen's voice wavered.

Clare's reply was gentle. "Sometimes it's better not to know your odds, right?"

Ghosts, Beatrice thought to herself. It felt no different from walking onto the battlefield. Only now, there was no Galwell to inspire them.

Her fault.

"We might as well get it over with," she said, reaching for the welcome bells' rope.

She did not have the chance to ring them. Clare's hand shot out, clasping hers before she could.

"Or," he proposed, "we could sneak in."

Not even the curiosity flickering in her could distract her from the confusing heat of his hand clasping hers. *Perhaps* this *is his magical gift*, she contemplated. *Making my hand warm where his skin meets mine*. For the feeling certainly was not the doing of her own heart. Certainly not.

Rubbing the reminder of his touch out of her palm, she focused on his words. "Sneak in where?"

"Remember? The secret passageways?" he reminded her. "Under the city. How we got in when the Order's guard held the gates. Look, I know we cannot avoid the crowds forever. Still—it's something. We've had our share of . . . challenges on our journey, and maybe a night of solitude in our own chambers in the palace would fortify us for, you know, facing the entire realm."

Elowen looked like someone had fed her warm soup on a cold night. "You'll hear no objection from me."

While Beatrice wanted to say the same, nagging questions kept her from doing so. She studied Clare. What was he up to? Was he coming to their rescue yet again? "Why don't you enter in the front," she suggested, grasping onto her stratagem for uncovering his motives. "Elowen and I can use the secret passageways while you"—she gestured welcomingly—"revel in your fame."

Clare's gaze flattened. Except, was droll denial the only note she could read in his eyes? "Firstly, I have legitimate cause to worry that you and Elowen may in fact murder each other if left under the city on your own. Secondly . . ."

Now she saw it with certainty. The lonesome shadow hiding in his shimmer.

"I don't actually enjoy when I'm lauded for surviving the day my best friend died," he said.

She hid how the revelation stunned her. "You could have fooled me," she commented. He'd indulged in every opportunity to profit from their fame, had he not? Never once did she suspect he felt the same guilt of survival himself. How could she, when he squandered his survival on hawking Spark's Sport Potions?

"Yes, well," Clare replied with his voice's familiar edge, "you more than anyone know how convincing a liar I can be when I wish."

He had her clenching her jaw now. She should have known attempting real conversation with Clare Grandhart was like offering vegetables to wolverlings—useless.

"Ugh. Secret tunnels, please," Elowen interrupted them. "I can witness your tortured pining for each other no longer."

Embarrassment flushed into Beatrice's face. "There's no—"

"We're not—" Clare started in overlapping indignation.

"—*pining!*"

Elowen smirked. On another occasion, the expression would have looked like sunshine past parting clouds to Beatrice. Instead, she felt only oncoming dread.

"I know it's been a while, but you do remember how my heart magic works, do you not?" Elowen inquired. "I've felt the longing rolling off each of you since we got into the wagon. It's gross," she informed them. "It feels like . . . slime on my skin."

Clare reared up. "My longing is not *slimy*," he declared.

"It decidedly is," Elowen replied, having evidently recovered her spirits. "It sticks to you. Like slime. Gooey, glistening slime."

"Enough with the slime!" Beatrice demanded. Elowen was playing with them, she decided. Vexing them out of resentment or for distraction or . . . Whatever her intention, Beatrice was certain no *longing* lingered in Clare Grandhart.

She stole a glance at him for confirmation.

No, no longing. *Whew.* He looked angry, which comforted her. He strode off. She followed him until the corner hooked, finding them along Queendom's western wall. Clare hunched over, studying the stones.

He made no further movement. Instead, he grimaced.

He'd forgotten which stones opened the magic entry, she realized.

"Move aside," she ordered gruffly. Clare glanced up, uncomprehending. Nevertheless, he deferred to the command in her voice. He moved, only just enough to permit her to reach for the spelled stones. Was Elowen in her head, or did she feel his eyes on her while she moved two careful fingers over the correct stone? He stood right next to her.

"*Mm-hmm*. Feel that slime, Beatrice?" Elowen needled her.

Beatrice's face went red.

No protestation rose from Clare, however. Instead, she noticed he watched—her.

"Did you just now use your head magic to revisit how we opened the passageway?" he asked while the western wall's magic revealed the hidden entrance, the stones rearranging themselves in accommodation of the underground opening.

"No," she replied. "I didn't need to." Despite his prying, she was grateful for the inquisition, for it had replaced Elowen's embarrassing comments.

He cocked his head. "How could you possibly remember the exact stone spelled with the passage entrance?"

"Does it matter?" she said, evading the question. She'd relived the memory of the entrance stone nearly every night, for the Four had used the passageway on the day of their confrontation with the Order. She'd studied every detail of the day, including their clandestine entry. She knew every footstep up to the moment Galwell breathed his last.

Ignoring Clare's gaze on her, clinging like—no, she would not even concede the comparison in her mind—she started downward, into the stone passage leading underneath Queendom.

She felt uncomfortably like she *was* walking within her magic.

But every small change stood stark. The new wear on the flagstones, the dead dysfunction of one of the lining lanterns enchanted to glow with purple flame.

Clare and Elowen.

Her companions were not the stalwart compatriots in her magic memory, comforting each other with comedy and encouragement. They followed her silently, each of them undoubtedly remembering their last visit into the tunnels and the ghost that walked with them now.

The corridor wound and rose, eventually ending in another stone wall. Once more, Beatrice easily selected with two fingers the proper stone for the revelation of the passage's magical egress. Once more, she felt Clare's wordless curiosity.

What waited for them outside the passage vanquished his unspoken questions, however. The royal stables had not changed much in the past decade. New paint, new horses. Yet the structure was much the same. Much the way she remembered from the celebration of their victory here years ago.

They were inside Queendom.

She prepared herself, hackles rising instinctually. Even if they'd escaped the main streets, she was ready for a certain measure of fanfare from palace keepers and stablehands—applause, congratulations, songs of greeting from those participating in drunken stableside festivities. Stepping into the light, she stomached her reluctance.

Yet no song greeted them. No cheers. *Nobody.*

Gazing out from the stable into Queendom's nearby streets, she found the same. Every street was empty. Every home was shuttered. There was no celebration here, and the reason was obvious.

On every turret, mourning flags flapped in the breeze.

15

Clare

Ominous quiet followed them into the halls of the palace. It disturbed Clare in ways not many experiences ever had.

He led the group, having the greatest familiarity with the royal floorplan. He'd visited Queendom's castle on numerous occasions in the years since the Four's victory. While young Queen Thessia was not profligate with her parties, they were wondrous events—her coronation, her engagement, even one gala she'd graciously held for the Clare Grandhart Eagle Sanctuary. Wiglaf, he remembered with fondness, had relished the roasted rumprat spread laid out specially for the gala's feathered guests.

The hallway's grim emptiness now could not have compared less favorably to the queen's parties. With his every footstep, not caring how his soles soiled the cream-white carpet with dirt from the passageway, his hope descended into worry.

It reminded him of when he'd found Beatrice not far from here, the Fraternal Order's chief killed, and Galwell propped in her lap, his eyes vacant.

The welcome they received certainly did nothing for his encouragement. Footmen's and guards' eyes registered recognition when the three of them walked past in the castle's halls. No one, however, responded with excitement. Clare had meant what he said about the uncomfortable way celebration struck him, yet he very, very much would've preferred the clamor.

It meant, he knew, something horrible had happened. He could not fend off wondering whether *they* were cursed. Perhaps whenever the three of them were together, they summoned tragedy.

He dashed the thought away, which was darker than he often permitted himself. He needed to remain hopeful, he reminded himself. Their fire in the night, their champion of heroism.

If entering the palace was not easy, entering the throne room was harder.

Upon the former heroes' entrance, Thessia rose, her tearstained face pale. She looked regal even in despair. Not merely grieving—rather, the emblem of grief itself.

Clare considered her the perfect queen. She was lovely, he could recognize, without having ever felt pangs of desire for her. Her chestnut hair curled naturally, her green eyes shone like crystalline peridot—were she not the realm's ruler, he was certain she would have found fame singing or in shadow plays. In every conversation, her eager mind was evident. Her kindness was renowned, the sort of compassion won only through loss.

Her misery pained him. He was very fond of her, having gotten to know her during various events. They'd found themselves comforting each other for the sorrow they shared. If he needed to console her now for the second great grief of her life . . .

He did not know if he could.

He could not even muster the courage to ask what had happened, afraid to hear the confirmation yet again—for their queen, for Mythria.

Nor could the queen herself expound on her anguish. Instead, when she opened her mouth, only heartrending sobs ushered forth.

Recognizing her incapacity, one of the room's guards finally shared the racking state of affairs.

"The groom," he said gravely, "has been kidnapped."

Clare paused. The dread in his stomach vanished. Lightness pervaded his coiled muscles, relief expanding in him. Hugh had been kidnapped?

It was *wonderful* news.

Clare liked the queen's fiancé almost as much as he cherished the queen herself. Sir Hugh Mavaris had spent his early life as a simple foot soldier. When the Fraternal Order was vanquished, he eventually found fame in minor Carnivals of Combat the queen held for the city's entertainment. His renown led him to join the queen's corps of guards, where his keen observations on matters of security earned him a larger role in her council of advisors— where his nobility had earned him her heart.

He was not Galwell, nor did he jealously position himself as such. He was a man whose solid character did not dull his warmth or vigor—plainspoken without ignorance, honorable without naivete.

And most importantly in the present case, he was apparently not dead.

"I'm sorry," Clare finally ventured delicately, his heart racing with hope. "Hugh was *only* kidnapped? We feared he was killed! You've already hung the mourning flags!"

"*Only kidnapped?*" Thessia wailed. She fixed her gaze on Clare with indignation. "He's undoubtedly dead by now!"

Quickly, Clare understood the queen's frantic reaction. How the trauma of Galwell's death clung on to her. How fearsome patterns were pushing her off the edge of reason. In vain, he worked to wrestle his words into the help she needed.

Instead, it was Beatrice who interjected. "This isn't like Galwell," she insisted. Clare had never heard the patient comfort in her voice. "Galwell was killed in this city, for all to see. If whoever has your betrothed wanted him dead, they would have just killed him."

Now Elowen spoke up. "Surely someone could simply rescue your groom?"

Clare noticed the moment it happened. Something sharp snapped into place in the queen's expression. She was the intelligent monarch now, not the heartsick fiancée.

"Indeed," she replied. "Yes, I suppose *a hero* could rescue my Hugh. Or several. Three, maybe."

The room went silent, except for one member of the queen's guard, who coughed.

"If only there were any nearby . . ." Thessia went on.

Clare nearly laughed. He did not think the queen intended to manipulate them. It was just comically perfect how well, even in the midst of her panic, she'd managed to maneuver her new guests in exactly the direction she needed.

Almost instantly, however, discomfort set in. The queen needed heroes. Who she had was . . . them.

Galwell wouldn't hesitate, Clare reminded himself sternly. Ghosts, Galwell *hadn't* hesitated. When the Fraternal Order kidnapped Thessia herself, Galwell rode from Queendom in pursuit the next day.

However—every step and fractious night of their journey this week had forcibly reminded him he *wasn't* Galwell. The mere *road trip* quest he was leading was going disastrously. Did he really want a man's life—indeed, the life of a man loved by one of his dearest friends—in his clumsy hands?

It did not matter, he finally decided. Refusing would mean he was nothing except the heroic fraud he feared he was every day.

"We'll save him," he stated, not wasting one more moment on the potential of losing his courage. "Of course we will."

"Who do you mean, *we*?" Beatrice interjected.

"*We* most certainly will not," Elowen declared, their voices overlapping.

Clare plucked up his courage. His first challenge, it appeared, would be quelling his prospective questmates. "You know," he ventured, "the pair of you bicker often, yet you actually agree on most matters."

"No we don't."

"We do not!"

Clare felt himself grow headachey. Not only from road weariness, either. The conundrum of his companions would not resolve easily. Grudgingly, he faced the queen. "One moment," he requested. "If it please your majesty," he remembered to add. He would not have his questing efforts commence with royal impoliteness!

The queen only waved him on impatiently. *Have at it!* her gesture said. She retreated to the throne, where she sat, staring out the high windows like she was searching for something she expected not to find.

The sight of her, nerve-stricken, focused Clare. He needed to do this right. He lowered his voice to Elowen and Beatrice. "Please," he implored. "Would you forswear your queen? The life of her love depends on us."

"Clare." Elowen met him with the same seriousness. She was not, he could tell, replying out of petty indignation. It was real. "We're not qualified to rescue anyone," she said. "He would be better off if the queen's guard went to save him."

He understood her frustrating logic—and yet, he grasped desperately onto the chance he felt fumbling out of his fingers.

"How can you say we're not qualified? We faced down the greatest evil this realm has ever known," he insisted, half-pleading.

He *needed* this quest, he found himself realizing. Not only his friendship for Thessia compelled him. He'd come to this wedding in hopes of proving his worth—to Beatrice, to himself. He'd hoped he could manage the feat with politeness of diction and gentility of temperament, winning enough grudging respect from his former friends to put his insecurities to rest.

Instead, what he felt emerging now, like the ship's prow of his destiny appearing from the fog of discontent, was his hope compounding a hundredfold. *What if I could lead my very own quest?*

Finally, he had stumbled onto the chance to prove he was not fake. He was not worthless without Galwell. He was not just the imitation of the man he wished he was.

It was not a chance he was keen on giving up.

"Yes, we faced the Order once," Beatrice replied firmly. He could read the mournful determination in her voice. "*Ten years ago.* We're . . . not what we used to be."

Offering him no opportunity to object, she faced the queen of Mythria wearily, whose guarded gaze rounded to rest upon Beatrice.

"Ghosts grant the return of the future king, Your Highness," Beatrice went on. "May we please be shown to our chambers? Our journey has been . . . long."

Thessia's face fell. However, Clare knew she was not the manner of monarch who would order her former friends into peril. Wordlessly, she gestured for her footmen, who escorted the women from the room.

When they were gone, Clare approached the throne, where Thessia gazed emptily out. He remembered the days following Galwell's death. Clare Grandhart, famous and cocksure warrior, knew what he saw in her eyes. The feeling of how every passing moment was a struggle to keep from shattering.

"Thess," he murmured gently, "we'll do this. We'll save Hugh. The word of a rogue might not mean much, but you have mine."

Thessia eyed him. Exhaustion, fear, and determination wrestled in her countenance. "How do you plan to convince them?" the young queen finally inquired, nodding toward the door where Elowen and Beatrice had departed.

He did not know. Galwell would, obviously. Clare was learning to cope with not having everything the other man had possessed. Plans, intuition, fortitude.

What he did have was hope.

"Don't you worry," he promised her. "You need only concern yourself with preparations for your wedding. You will be married this week—I swear it."

16

Beatrice

Finally, blissfully, Beatrice was in the bath.

She closed her eyes, welcoming the warm embrace of the place where she found the greatest joy. Her sanctuary, where the wounds of the world faded under soapsuds in perfect water.

She needed the comfort, what with the unpleasantness she'd left in the throne room. Clare playing the hero, flattering himself with more grandeur, would have upset her enough. Instead, she had been forced to contend with watching the light flee Thessia's eyes when Beatrice refused to help her queen.

Still, she'd made the right choice. Who was she to try to save anyone?

The question's answer left her here, drowning her sorrows in the bath. She slid down the gentle curve of the porcelain, low into the bubbles.

No novice where baths were concerned, Beatrice was impressed with the queen's considerable pantry of products for guests to use in the tub—though not surprised. If Beatrice were queen, bath-time delights would be her first regal indulgence.

Her choices would not look that different from the queen's, judging from the feast of soaps, scents, and decorations waiting for her. It was like someone else had gone shopping *for* Beatrice, swooping up the entire stock from her favorite stand in Elgin. From metal spigots piped over the water, one could drop in scented Vesper oils—she'd gone with the creamcake scent, lending the water the sweet smell of frosted confections.

She had reached next for the enchanted candles lining the porcelain tub. They required no matches, only waving one's hand near them for them to ignite. Then, like she'd hoped, their magic started to work. Instead of ordinary scented fumes, shimmering smoke emitted from them—forming an image of the idyllic Mythrian sunset on the unremarkable walls of the bathing room.

Yet neither enchanted candles nor Vesper oils were the crown jewel of Beatrice's royal bathtime experience.

In the wide bowl next to the tub, she found Bath Bulbs.

Beatrice loved Bath Bulbs. For her twenty-eighth birthday, she'd requested literally nothing except Bath Bulbs. She'd received instead from Robert de Noughton a portrait of himself. No matter now, not when the royal bathing chamber provided her every variety she could possibly imagine of the chalky orbs. Each promised untold sensory delights from the combination of hand magic mixed with creative concoctions of ingredients.

She relished deliberating over the choice until finally—yes, none could surpass the glittery, lavender-hued option. Her decision was rewarded when she dropped the orb in. Not only did the water color the loveliest calming purple, the Bath Bulb sent up sparkles with each foaming heap of suds. They fizzed pleasantly when they struck her face.

It was perfection.

In the wonderfully scalding temperature, easing the tenderness in her muscles from the wagon ride and the trek up the mountain to Queendom, Beatrice opened the first page of the novel she'd carried in from the palace library.

Romancing the Warlock King, read the heavy volume's cover. She commended Queen Thessia's taste in literature.

Far from the contemplation of quests, far from nightmares, far from Clare's complicated gaze, she planned to reward herself for the rigors of their "road trip." She would read in the warm water until the heroine had been thoroughly ravished by this promising Warlock King.

Within the pages and the cake-scented water, her woes finally started fading. The generous writer wasted few chapters before getting to the good stuff. Beatrice was growing comfortable, her muscles unwinding, her stresses gone—

The door flew open.

In strode Clare Grandhart, swirling the sunset fog into wisps of nothing in his wake.

She shrieked in shock, quickly piling suds over herself to obscure her chest. Clare, damn him, watched her, something raw entering his eyes when the foam closed its concealment over her breasts.

"Get out!" she cried, unable to help feeling like some heroines had all the luck. They got smoldering Warlock Kings. She got *him*.

"Sorry. Can't," Clare replied. "Actually, I'm not sorry at all. Another lie. Apologies," he went on, his manner the very opposite of contrition.

Near to her tub was a stool where one could sit while lacing up one's shoes. Clare pulled the footstool over, seating himself comfortably right next to her.

She was aghast. Rogue he was. Unintelligent he was not. He understood exactly the position in which he'd placed her, she knew. She could not leave his company without standing up, fully naked.

It was likely why he was here.

"I thought you said you were a gentleman," she hissed. "In case you were unaware, this is highly ungentlemanly behavior."

His smile was lazy and one she hadn't seen in years. Pure devastating delight, sliding over his face like Vesper oils into water. The warmth spreading through her whole body had nothing to do with the bath.

"Your stubbornness and ill temper have worn my chivalry down. I'll redouble my efforts tomorrow," he promised. He leaned forward. "When you're fully dressed."

His voice was no sweet-scented oil. It was rough, yet it lit up her skin like no sudsy confection ever could. Oh, the way his voice worked on her. Even when her outlook on matrimony was its most hopeful, Robert de Noughton's polite inquiries into whether she would like to lay with him had done nothing for her desire.

Not like how Clare's uncouth charm was currently raising her temperature even hotter. Thank the Ghosts her cheeks were already flushed from the bath.

"You're here"—no matter the horror she tried to muster, her delivery only managed to sound hungry—"using my vulnerability to hold me hostage while you . . . what, convince me to go on your silly quest? Or did you merely wish for me to read to you?"

She held up her novel.

"*Romancing the Warlock King* is quite engaging, you know," she informed him. "I was just getting to the action."

The instant the words left her lips, she felt like she had when she'd spilled red wine on her favorite white slippers—may they rest in peace. Had she just flirted with him?

Yes, she decided. She was feeling reckless, and manipulative. Why should he, with his unannounced entries, have the upper hand? How much longing and lust could she compel *him* to reveal?

"I'll admit, it's an intriguing option," Clare replied. His eyes said he was imagining the way the pages' sultry words would sound in her mouth, and, oh, now so was she, and— "Perhaps I'll join you in there."

She held her head high, heart hammering. "What's it to me? Be my guest."

Now his jaw tightened. He paused, regarding her. War unfolded in his eyes, campaigns she watched from the protected ramparts of her heart. One man caught in furious combat with his own restraint.

"Careful, Beatrice," he warned finally. His gaze held hers. "We could pretend we're nothing to each other all the way to you beneath me in your sheets."

She had no choice then except to dunk her head entirely underwater.

Vainly she hoped he would have gone when she emerged, leaving nothing except sunset smoke hanging in the empty room.

He had not, of course. He remained—though, she noticed, he'd exchanged his raw guile for rumination. He'd just run his hands through his hair, tousling his sun-colored locks. Impatience hummed in her. He had, she reminded herself, very much overstayed his welcome. "I'm not going on your quest," she informed him, hoping the denial would usher him from the room.

"Did I bring up the quest?" He was playing innocent. It did not become him, she felt.

"Did you come here to reconcile with me?" she charged on vindictively. "Now? After what we did to each other? If that's your purpose, you'd have better luck with the quest."

She welcomed the excuse to invoke their shared hurt, inviting the memories into the room with them. What were more unwanted, undeniable guests? The pain met her like too-hot bathwater, distracting her from worse hurts.

Yet Clare did not rise to her sharp words.

Unnerving her, his expression turned serious.

"How did you know which stones opened the secret passageway today?" he asked.

His voice was not rough now. It was constricted, clenched with uncommon cold. The Four's quest had sent them to the Far Northern Mountains, where they were warned of snowsnakes who choked their prey in embraces of ice. Clare sounded like he had one wrapped around his throat.

"I remembered," she said, not following the change of subject.

Clare glanced down grimly.

"How often do you *remember* them?" His question was quiet, unlike she'd ever heard him. "How often do you return to . . . that day within your magic?"

Now she looked past him to the door. She could not meet Clare's eyes, prying impossibly gently. Instead, she focused on the too-hot water, the purifying zeal of the pain. It made her honesty come easily.

"Every night," she said.

In the corner of her gaze, she watched the revelation hit him, his frame weakening with the gut-punch confession. She did not care. She felt nothing. Feeling nothing was the only way not to feel *everything*.

"You can't keep living in your past, love," he replied. "Even with your powers."

Love. It was pub-speak for affection. Like "reckon," it was the sound of Clare speaking in his sincerest voice. His honest self.

It enraged her. The gentleness, the words of endearment, the *care*. How could he pretend he cared? He understood nothing of her guilt. Nothing of how, in holding on to her worst memory, she had found the only way she knew not to vanish into the darkness.

"You accuse *me* of living in the past?" she spat in retaliation. "You're the one living as a hero for deeds done a decade ago. I *tried* to move on," she reminded him. "I married. I made a life for myself. And for what? It all crashed down."

She descended deeper into the water.

"The past is all I have," she said. "It's all *we* have."

Clare shifted in his seat.

"If we go on this quest, it won't be," he replied.

He didn't understand. He didn't understand *her*. "We're over, Clare. We never even really began," she said.

He shook his head. "I don't mean *us*—though we could have that conversation, if you want."

Grasping onto the distraction, she welcomed its weight. "What is there to say? You slept with someone the day of the funeral—and you had every right to. We weren't together. You made it clear to me the morning you first snuck out of my bed."

Repeating what he'd done, how he'd wounded her, nearly left her gasping. Unlike memories of Galwell, the day of the funeral was one she never revisited. The novelty left the sting sharp, like a sword fresh from the weaponeer's forge.

It had wrecked her when she found out he'd sought comfort in someone else's arms the night of the funeral. How he'd discarded her when she needed him dearest.

Next to her now, he darkened. The emotion on him, replacing his shimmering charm, would never cease to startle her. Glowering, he looked like some sinister wraith wearing Clare Grandhart's face. "I know my wrongs," he replied. "I think about them every day of my life. What about yours?"

He paused. His voice was scathing, full of pain and loathing.

"You tried to sacrifice yourself," he said.

She scoffed in reckless resistance. "Like you would have cared if I'd succeeded," she challenged him, throwing her deepest fear into the room like a weapon aimed to kill.

Clare stood, furious. Before she could react, he was leaning over the tub, hands clasping the porcelain lip, knuckles white. Her heart pounding, she held his gaze. Daring him.

His eyes fixed on hers, he plunged his hand into the water.

When his fingers skimmed her thigh, she gasped. His touch continued up until he found—her hand. His grip clutched her urgently.

"Use your magic on me," he insisted, not caring that he'd submerged his shirtsleeve. "Watch the worst moment of my life."

"I—" She looked down. "I've seen Galwell's death often enough."

"A terrible day," Clare intoned. "Not the one you'll find, though."

Heated water or not, chills chased over her skin. She could not mistake what he meant. Nevertheless, she scoffed again, determined to reject every demonstration of care he attempted. "Do you mean the day you slept with another woman?" she replied. "Or the day the scribesheets printed the gossip and I found out?"

He did not flinch from her invocation of what he'd done. Perhaps he really had reckoned with his wrongs.

"She was . . . irrelevant," Clare said of the fling. No doubt noticing her reproach, he went on. "Yes, yes. Call me a rake for not caring for her. Ghosts know I've earned the description. But I didn't sleep with her to hurt you."

"Then why did you?" She hated the desperation in her own voice. Proof of how the question had been burning in her for ten years.

He met her eyes, and there was nothing sharp in his gaze. Only kindness and regret. "When you kissed me before the battle,

I thought . . ." He swallowed. "I thought it meant something. I thought it was a promise that after we prevailed, you and I would finally be together."

Beatrice felt suddenly cold in the warm water. She had never let herself relive that kiss, though even without her magic she could have recalled every detail. She'd held him back from the others, picked a silly fight over nothing just as an excuse to have him to herself, then she'd tugged his lips to hers in the midst of the argument.

He'd kissed her back, his hands cradling her face like she was something precious. The kiss was . . . everything she'd ever imagined, and she'd done some imagining. It overwhelmed her, confusing her senses. He'd smelled like the night sky. He'd tasted like music.

When she'd pulled away, he stared, his expression awestruck as she joined the others. It had given her the strength she needed to walk into battle. She would sacrifice herself knowing she'd had one last kiss with Clare Grandhart.

"I was wrong. It wasn't a kiss promising more. It was a kiss goodbye," he went on, softer. "The worst moment of my life was the funeral, when I found out what you had tried to do."

It had been Elowen, with the carelessness of the wounded, wrathful from their fight, who revealed it to him.

"I realized then that we had nothing," Clare continued. "I had been a fool, wanting something from you that you had never even considered. You weren't imagining our future. You were doing the opposite, imagining the future you never expected to have. I realized . . . I had to get over you." He looked down. "I got drunk. And for just minutes I used someone else to convince myself that I could."

Her fury flickered. He had wounded her enough she could

hardly contemplate listening to him. Yet . . . he wasn't entirely wrong. She had made no promises to him, for she had expected to die. She had rejected the idea of a future with him in the deepest way she could. With Elowen's revelation at the funeral, he knew it.

Fiercely, she remembered how she'd felt when she found out. Even if they owed each other no promises, dashed promises weren't the only way to hurt someone, were they? Instead of holding on to her—helping her feel like he was glad she was still here—he'd run in the opposite direction. How could he not have understood the depth of her regret? "You should have stayed," she said.

"*I* should have stayed?" he repeated, his voice incredulous. "You almost left me forever. Why do you care that I slept with someone else? If you'd succeeded, you would have consigned me to women who aren't you for the rest of my life."

How dare he, she fumed. While she'd struggled in mazes of memory, his vaunting had brought him fame and comfort. How dare he pretend she'd *consigned* him to anything?

"Well, I didn't succeed," she snapped. "And every gossip pamphlet I've seen over the years has shown me just how many other women you've *suffered*."

"You were married!" he roared.

They stared at each other, chests heaving with anger. She had nothing more she could say. Neither of them did. They'd said everything. It couldn't help. The past was the past.

He released her hand, understanding she would not use her magic. Withdrawing, he returned to the footstool. He looked empty, she found. Resolute in exhaustion, water soaking the rest of his shirt.

"This quest isn't about us," he said finally. "That's not why you should do it. You relive Galwell's death every day like there is a way to save him. There isn't."

She started to interject, reminding him no person in Mythria knew as keenly as her how Galwell was past protecting—

"But there is a way to save Hugh," Clare went on.

The point quieted her. She could only gaze down, where, in the opaque lavender of the water, she found her own pained eyes staring up.

"I know what you've gone through," he explained. "I've . . . wandered the same dark labyrinth myself."

She shifted, not entirely understanding him. With her movement, her reflection rippled, her features in the lavender water disappearing into wobbling shapes of color. He did not seem to mean Galwell, from the unexpected confessional note in his voice. She wondered what he did mean. However, she did not wish to seem curious, so she did not reply.

Whether understanding her unspoken incomprehension or just lost now in his own recollection, Clare continued.

"I lost every friend I had in the Grimauld Mines," he said. "Horrible, unimaginable deaths. Galwell hired me to be your guide because I was the only one to survive." He sighed. "You know how it feels to have the honor of being the one to live when others did not."

She'd known he'd lost friends in the mines, but she'd never considered how Clare had dealt with his own survivor's guilt. It was odd, she reckoned, how she could meet someone, even start caring for him, without entirely understanding the closed scars he bore from past wounds she couldn't see.

She had the sudden urge to cry. Knowing Clare understood what she'd endured . . . Was it the worst condemnation, or the greatest reprieve? She did not know.

"Galwell offered me enough farthings to make me rich," he said. "And I . . . didn't much care. Farthings could not purchase what I wanted—revenge."

She had to look up now.

"I didn't take Galwell's job for the money, or because I was bored." His gaze held hers. "I took it because I needed to rend the Orb Weavers limb from limb. I didn't care if I survived. In fact," he confessed, "I expected I wouldn't."

Her heart pounded. "But you did," she whispered.

"I did," Clare replied. "After I met you."

Curses could sound like poetry, she reminded herself. Damnation like invitation. She forced herself to laugh. "Please," she pressed him. "Don't expect me to fall for that. You had no intention of ever seeing me again. You said so yourself," she reminded him, recalling their confrontation with the outlaws of the forest.

Clare remained imperturbable. "I admit," he said evenly, "it was my habit to not stick around with the women who welcomed me to their beds. I couldn't. I was . . . too lost. I was lost when I met you, too, Beatrice. I thought I would die the next day. But I didn't. And . . . I kept living."

Beatrice could not reply. Not when his words revealed that what she'd done to him was exactly what he'd done to her. Kisses exchanged on the eve of destruction. He'd slept with her, expecting the Orb Weavers to eviscerate him. She'd pressed her lips to his, planning to sacrifice herself for the realm.

What right did he have to resent her, then? her mind stubbornly queried. Except he had plenty, she knew. Other than their self-sacrifices, their situations had been utterly different. Clare had no one except one-night stands when he'd sought his revenge on the Weavers. She had . . . friends. Family. Friends like family.

She had him.

I kept living, her relentless mind repeated his words. Her heart had made living feel like a punishment. How had he made the sentiment ring like a victory herald?

"With Galwell, with Elowen—with you—I came back to myself," Clare went on. "I couldn't save the friends I had already lost. But I could do everything I could to help save the ones I was starting to love."

His words scared her. She was used to her grief, her guilt. They were her constant companions, along with the memories she could never forget.

What Clare was offering her was something far more danger-ous. *Hope*. Hope that she might finally heal. Finally move on.

"What if I fail again?" Her voice was small.

"Then you'll return home and continue living the way you are now," he replied. "It's not the question you should be asking and you know it."

She hated how logical, how insightful, his words were. *Clare Grandhart? Insightful?* She wished they could joke on the subject. Instead, she could only confront the import of what he was saying. She did not know if she could handle the responsibility for a man's life again, yet she knew she needed to change. What if . . . *what if she succeeded?*

Could she finally close her eyes without racking herself with memories of Galwell?

Even considering the notion required every mote of strength in her. It required straining muscles she'd let collapse in exhaustion.

She hardly recognized the flicker of fight she felt in them. Something, some reckless impulse, made her push, forcing herself. Imagining what she might do instead of just regretting what she'd done.

It was terrifying. Yet she could not forsake the possibility, she knew. If Clare's improbable, damnable quest held even the faintest chance of delivering her peace, she would go. While she could never even the scales of life, restoring what she'd destroyed, if she had the chance to make the weight more manageable, she needed to chase it.

Decisively, she stood up, exposing her skin to the cool air and to Clare's gaze. Every inch of her.

She needed to have the upper hand on him in order to tolerate her next words. "You're right," she admitted, reaching for the robe nearby.

At the full view of Beatrice, Clare sat stunned. His mouth dropped open.

"About which"—his eyes roamed over her nakedness—"which parts?"

"Everything," she replied.

She wrapped herself in the robe. He lifted his gaze to hers.

"I'll do it. I'll save Hugh. Or try," she said. "And this quest is *not* about us."

17

𝕰𝖑𝖔𝖜𝖊𝖓

I cannot do another quest," Elowen said, pacing her bedchambers.

"*Huh?*" Lettice, her heart healer, had answered the surprise conjuration seemingly from her own chambers. She had rollers in her hair and a treatment mask on her face, and she was outfitted in one of those long floral sleepgowns Elowen's own mother always wore. It was barely nightfall, which may have made it odd to others. Not Elowen. She had spent much of her time in the trees preparing for sleep, so she understood the importance of committing to a long bedtime process.

"Clare has taken it upon himself to volunteer us for a rescue mission," Elowen continued. "He wants us to find Thessia's fiancé."

Lettice grabbed a pair of spectacles and fumbled them onto her face, smudging some of her pink facial oils onto the lenses. "Sir Hugh is *missing?*"

Normally, it would annoy Elowen to explain. Queendom had already gone into mourning. Surely news of Hugh's kidnapping had reached the rest of Mythria. If conjurists weren't already putting renderings of Hugh beside loving portraits of Galwell as scribes drafted up stories about Thessia's tragic love life, they would be within the next hour. But nothing about her life was normal at the moment. She couldn't remember how to be irritated by Lettice's ignorance.

Elowen explained the situation, watching as Lettice went from confusion to shock to fascination. Elowen appreciated how forthright her heart healer was with her own emotions. It was a large reason why Elowen continued her appointments. Though she could not magically feel Lettice's emotions through a conjuration, on a human level, she never sensed that Lettice said one thing with her words while feeling something else. Which was why she appreciated when Lettice validated her feelings, nodding as she told Elowen, "This is a momentous occasion. I'm glad you conjurated me."

"Sorry for the lack of notice," Elowen replied. She'd been so wrapped up in her thoughts, she hadn't considered whether her actions were appropriate or not.

"I told you long ago that you were welcome to contact me at any time. I am thrilled you finally took me up on that offer. And for quite a good reason. Is your . . . friend with you?"

The last time Elowen and Lettice spoke, Vandra had been there. Elowen didn't know where Vandra was now. She was confident Vandra could take care of herself. She had not lost any talent in the ten years since Elowen had seen her in action. If anything, she'd gotten better at wielding a weapon. She really was the best assassin no longer in the game. Still, Elowen worried. That was the problem with being around other people again. Not only did you learn their habits—such as Vandra's inability to eat a meal that didn't have something spicy and sweet, or her penchant for petting wild brushwalkers to see if she could get in some affection without being bitten—you developed concerns for them. It was exactly what Elowen did not want to happen on this trip. She did not want her heart to expand any further.

"She's busy," Elowen said. "It's been a terrible week. I have suffered countless indignities since leaving home." For the first time ever, she laid out everything, from the pain of learning why Beatrice had once told her that they weren't friends to the confusion of the situation with Vandra. "Nothing has gone right. There's no way I am equipped for a quest. I am meant to be alone in the trees where nothing can harm me." When Lettice did not immediately respond, Elowen's familiar defenses went up. "What?" she barked out. "Does my week not sound miserable to you?"

"It does sound difficult," Lettice confirmed. "I was just thinking about how brave you've been."

Elowen scoffed. "I'm not brave. I'm miserable. You're confusing me for someone else. Galwell, I suspect."

"Elowen," Lettice whispered with undeserved kindness. "I know you grew up in your brother's shadow. But you are a hero in your own right. I have no doubt you could do another quest. That's not to say you should. I just wanted to point out that you've accomplished so much in such a short amount of time. You told me long ago you didn't think you could live alone forever in the trees, but you couldn't bring yourself to leave them. Now you have. And it hasn't been perfect, but it *is* brave, continuing on as you have."

"What if I don't want to be brave?" Elowen asked.

"Well, then, is there anything that would make you not miserable? Maybe you won't go on a quest. Might you have a little fun, though? Is there any place on land you've truly missed?"

An image flickered to life in Elowen's mind—the Needle. It was a pub built decades ago by a queer couple who wanted a cozy hangout close to Queendom. The walls were covered with knitwork and other kitschy crafts, and the wooden seats had scribbles all over them, declarations of love written in the heat of the moment. It was the kind of place that felt like a secret, even though by night's end, it was often packed to the brim. There was just an energy of community and safety there, lovingly cultivated, that made the Needle special. In her younger years, Elowen had enjoyed spending weekends at the long crestoak bar, nursing a drink and people watching, sensing what others felt about their night, sometimes lucky enough to find a woman who wanted the same thing Elowen did. It was always a welcoming, soothing setting, a rare place where Elowen's heart magic felt like a gift instead of a curse.

"There is one place nearby," she muttered. "A pub."

Lettice's expression brightened. "Perfect! What if you went there and ordered yourself a drink?"

"Just one?" Elowen asked, skeptical.

"That's it," Lettice confirmed. "And if it's not enjoyable, then you can take pride in knowing you attempted to do something for the fun of it, not because you felt obligated to."

After some further back and forth, Elowen agreed, if only so she did not have to continue pacing her bedchambers. She was developing a stitch in her side.

* * *

When she walked through the Needle's painted door—still the same lavender shade from ten years ago—Elowen blinked thrice, confirming this was not another conjuration of the past. Everything was exactly the same, down to Elowen's usual spot in the back-right corner, unoccupied as if they'd saved it for her arrival. She took her seat and ordered a sprymint fizzy like old times. Her heart ached as much as it raced, the war between anxiety and familiarity waging on inside her. It was only one drink.

She could do one drink.

Since returning to the public, Elowen had come to expect other people staring at her. Not that she'd ever be used to the overwhelming pressure of the attention, but it was at least predictable.

They were typically awestruck and a little confused—could it really be the elusive Elowen True? She felt that attention on her now, though in this pub, it was not confusion. It was . . . something else. Elowen couldn't decipher it, and it filled her with adrenaline.

"Hey," a woman called out. When Elowen looked up, the woman waved at her. Elowen glanced around, bewildered. The woman grinned like Elowen was just who she hoped to see.

Elowen flushed with nerves, heat spreading through her cheeks and down her neck.

"Could I buy you a drink?" the woman asked. A fan of the Four, most likely.

Elowen held up her sprymint fizzy. "Already got one."

The woman nodded in understanding, though disappointment flashed across her face.

Elowen continued nursing her fizzy. She'd only gotten in two more sips when another woman tapped her on the shoulder. "Anyone sitting here?" she asked, pointing to the open seat next to Elowen.

"Not that I know of," Elowen said back. Her hands shook, yet she felt strangely powerful. Perhaps it was like what Galwell had experienced with his uncanny strength. Elowen had so much raw energy coursing through her, she believed she, too, could lift up heavy wagons or move giant boulders. "Though there are plenty of open spots all around the pub." She gestured to all the places that hadn't yet been filled.

The woman frowned. "I was hoping for this one." She put her hands on the stool next to Elowen and leaned forward.

"Would you like me to find you when I'm done, so you can take the seat?" Elowen asked. Perhaps this woman also liked the backs of rooms, where everything was quieter, more private.

The woman stood up straight, adjusting her top to cover the

cleavage that had spilled out when she'd leaned. "That's all right. I'll find somewhere else."

When the second woman walked away, the pubtender came to Elowen's end of the bar, laughing. Elowen looked down, checking to make sure she hadn't gotten mouthpaste on her cloak or forgotten to button her top.

"You're Elowen True, right?" the pubtender asked, still chuckling. She was older than Elowen, perhaps in her early forties, and she had a rich, velvety voice.

Sheepish, Elowen nodded. At least this woman had come out and asked it.

"I have to say, the portraits do not do you justice." The pubtender appraised every visible part of Elowen's skin, lingering on her lips before flicking her attention back to Elowen's eyes.

And suddenly, Elowen understood what she'd been missing. She could now identify the feeling that had permeated the space when she entered. The women around her were horny. *For Elowen.*

To cover her gasp, Elowen downed the rest of her sprymint fizzy in one gulp. In her teenage years, she had done better than most of her peers when it came to dating, though she hated to discuss her flings with others, so no one ever knew it. It became its own game, figuring out what other girls her age were queer and discreetly pursuing them. Finding an interested party had always been a subtle thing. Lingering glances. Well-placed compliments. A touch that lasted a few moments longer than it should. It had all been so long ago that Elowen had not immediately recognized it as happening to her in the present, perhaps because she'd assumed after she shut herself off from society that she'd become the prickly grump that everyone in Mythria pitied. The sullen little sister of the greatest hero the realm had ever known.

Her one drink finished, Elowen put down some of the last coins she had to her name.

"Please." The pubtender pushed the coins back to Elowen. "Drinks for you are on the house here. Permanently." She winked, and Elowen, fighting flattery, thought again of Vandra.

Fucking Vandra. If she wasn't the way she was, so interesting and unique and beautiful, perhaps Elowen would engage with any of the apparently numerous interested parties in the pub. Alas, there was only one woman who ever seemed to be on Elowen's mind.

All the same, Elowen left the Needle with a renewed sense of . . . Ghosts, was it confidence? She was so unaccustomed to the feeling that she did not know if she was even correct in labeling it, but she did have a certain lightness to her step. And the corners of her mouth may have been pulled upward into what others could call a smile. Lettice was right. Elowen *was* brave. And apparently she was also hot.

To certain people, of course. Queer people. The exact crowd to which she wanted to be desirable. And she was only hot under the right lighting of course, which was so infrequently achieved. Why people insisted on hanging their brightest magicked candles from the ceiling instead of opting for softer, lower lights, Elowen did not understand. The Needle knew the importance of a mood-setting wall sconce, and that had to have been a key contributor to Elowen's attractiveness in the space.

Being hot did not matter to Elowen in any meaningful way, but it still seemed notable. Hot people always had a misplaced sense of confidence. Smiling, Elowen jaunted through the mourning Queendom like she'd just been announced as the winner of a hand magician's mystery money ticket.

She wondered if this was how Vandra felt all the time. Though Vandra had earned her confidence. She had not only good looks and a beaming personality, she could kill you in a heartbeat.

Elowen returned to her chambers, planning to throw herself onto the bed and have a good long think about being desired by others. But mostly about Vandra.

The very Vandra who currently lay across Elowen's sheets, grinning.

"Miss me?" Vandra asked. She was propped on her side in her usual attire, tight-fitting leggings and a magenta corset atop a flowing black blouse, with shiny laced boots that came up over her knees. When she tossed her hair, long raven curls cascaded toward the bed, wild and loose.

Elowen did not gasp or scream. She stared. Because she *had* missed the sight of Vandra's face. To see her then felt a bit like a reward. For bravery. And hotness, perhaps.

"Yes," Elowen admitted.

"Really?" Vandra asked, sitting up.

It was so hard to get a real rise out of her. To be the one who made her gasp? It was more than a delight. Elowen nodded.

Whatever Vandra had planned to say, Elowen's admission derailed it. Vandra grasped for something—words, it seemed. She stumbled around until she said, "The Fraternal Order was behind the attack."

Elowen's mood darkened. They'd defeated the Fraternal Order ten years ago. Their leader was long dead. How could the Order be back?

"They've been rebuilding in the years since Todrick's death." Vandra paused, shifting on the bed. "I promised you I'd get the information . . ."

"I never doubted you would," Elowen hurried out, once again

admitting to her past dishonesty. Clearing her throat, she attempted formality. "Why did they want to hurt us?"

"I couldn't get more out of the men that attacked you," Vandra answered. "They hadn't been told much about whatever sinister plans are at play here. They were bottom-of-the-barrel henchmen. Complete losers."

Both women laughed.

"Sorry," Elowen whispered, gathering herself.

"For what?" Vandra asked.

"I shouldn't be laughing. Not after learning this. And how we left things . . ."

Vandra wiped the smile from her face. "I rushed here to tell you what I'd discovered, worried something may have happened in my absence, only to find you walking yourself home from the Needle, grinning." She spoke with none of her usual cheer. Instead her voice was low, serious. "I thought perhaps someone else had gotten you to smile that way."

Elowen almost gasped as she picked up on Vandra's emotions. Vandra was *jealous*.

"Other women did hit on me at the pub," Elowen said, watching as Vandra's muscles tensed with each word. "They wanted me."

Vandra rose from the bed to meet Elowen in the doorway. "What did you do about that?" she asked, pressing her hand against the frame and leaning forward.

Elowen put her mouth to Vandra's ear. "I turned them down," she whispered.

"Why?" Vandra asked, her jealousy warring with curiosity and desire.

Elowen pulled back. Vandra's eyes, full of honeyed sweetness, held something even more powerful than desire. She looked at Elowen with hope.

"Because none of them were you," Elowen breathed.

And with that, Vandra kissed Elowen. Everything dark floated away, clouds parting for a miraculous light, the kind that glowed up to the tips of Elowen's fingers. She knew no self-consciousness or anger. The urgency of their shared touch brought out the most ravenous side of her. She was lips on lips and hands roaming skin. Touching her, Elowen learned how much Vandra's lust was coated in tenderness. Care.

"My darling." Vandra grasped the back of Elowen's neck with one hand and her ass with the other, never afraid to apply the right kind of pressure.

In that moment, it was comical to Elowen that those other women thought they stood a chance. No one could ever compare to Vandra Ravenfall.

The kisses deepened, slow and lingering, until they were no longer kissing at all. They were pressed into the wall and resting nose to nose, just breathing.

"Hi," Elowen whispered.

"Hello there," Vandra replied. "Been a while."

"Has it? You feel exactly as I remember." It no longer scared Elowen to experience it. Perhaps that was the calmness Vandra emanated, absorbed by Elowen's magic.

"Are you saying you thought of me while we were apart?" Vandra teased. "All that time, all alone, I crossed your mind?"

"Some days, I thought of little else," Elowen admitted. Magical powers could not account for the trust Elowen felt. She was safe in Vandra's arms, and that safety gave her courage. "I'm going to do the quest," she decided.

"*Quest?*" Vandra echoed. "Does this have to do with Hugh being missing? I got some conjurations on the matter. I should have known they'd involve you." Her emotions shifted, a curious sadness working through the tenderness. She cupped Elowen's chin. "Don't tell me you plan to leave tonight."

"It is indeed a quest to find Hugh. Who better suited than the Three?" Elowen found that while she meant to sound sarcastic, there was more genuine truth to her words than she'd anticipated. Perhaps it was a result of the courage she'd accumulated tonight, first at the bar, and now with Vandra's kiss. She believed herself. And she believed *in* herself. More than she had in years. "I must go tell Clare at once."

"Hold on a moment." Vandra wrapped her hand around Elowen's arm. She knew that Elowen would feel every bit of her worry, and through her insistent grip, she seemed to welcome that understanding. "How can I be sure you are safe?"

Elowen sensed the danger of this moment. Not in the literal sense—she still felt quite safe—but the danger of what it would mean to accept this concern. To let Vandra worry would be to let her have a piece of Elowen's heart. Elowen could never give over all of herself, but maybe she could give a little. Maybe there was a way to let Vandra in without getting hurt.

"You're right," she said, wrapping her arms around Vandra's waist. "If only I had a private guard to watch out for me before I go. One of Thessia's best."

Vandra glowed with pleasure. "That settles it." She headed for the chair beside the bed, where she began unlacing her boots. "I will rest here, watching you."

"Perfect," Elowen said, meaning it. "I will go let Clare know I am joining the quest. And then I will return to my chambers and sleep comfortably, knowing I am protected."

Elowen had no idea what awaited her tomorrow, but for one night, she had everything she needed.

18

Clare

We, the remaining three of the Four, accept your quest," Clare announced. "We will ride out from Queendom and rescue Sir Hugh for our queen and for Mythria."

He wondered if there was some manner of officially signing up for royal quests. Galwell had always handled the logistics. Was there some registry or something? Otherwise, how would the queen know who she had dispatched on what quests and ensure their progress? *Not important*, he reminded himself.

He settled for lowering himself to one knee.

He felt awkward. Never more like an impostor. He muscled past it, welcoming the feeling's familiarity—if he did not know how to play noble hero, he'd learned in long nights on dungeon floors how to deal with discomfort. Someone, he reminded himself, had to hold them together.

He did not share how much the very fact of a *them* surprised him. Reuniting the group after the women's departures from this very room yesterday had felt like grasswalker wrangling—unwise, unless one wanted to get one's head chomped off.

Instead, Elowen had appeared in his quarters late last night, stating she had changed her mind and would join the quest. Predictably, she offered no explanation for her new resolution. He was reminded of when she'd complained for weeks about quest food-stuffs, only to announce she'd come to consider the flatbreads they rationed one of her favorite foods. Clare, of course, had not questioned her.

He had, however, noticed the happy flush painting her cheeks. He wondered who'd done the painting.

For her part, Beatrice had not even looked at him once today. He understood her disdain. He'd awoken the old Clare yesterday—rude, forward, uncompromising. The rogue, not the hero. He'd promised himself and promised her he would embody nobility and gallantry, and instead he confronted her in her washroom.

If he were a worthy man, perhaps he would not have abandoned her after the funeral. Perhaps he could have handled the revelation with grace, even care. Even love.

Perhaps they never would have hurt each other the way they did.

He could not know. He just knew he meant every word when he promised her this quest was their only hope of healing.

The queen gazed upon them with recovered composure. "Queendom thanks our noble heroes for their valiant efforts," she stated. "Rise."

Noble heroes? Valiant? Isn't she laying it on a little thick? Clare could not help wondering. People only called him *valiant* when they were joking.

Nevertheless, he rose to the queen's command.

The moment he did, Thessia dropped her regal demeanor, her shoulders slumping in relief. "Oh! The three of you! Working together! I've had no rest, not one wink, for days. Last night, just with the possibility of the greatest heroes in Mythria venturing to save Hugh, I was finally able to get some sleep. I know you three will bring him home." Thessia laughed, pacing in front of her throne.

Clare could not help smiling. He recognized her response. He knew how real, soul-salving relief could hit one with giddy delight. He'd skipped home when Farmount's wisest animal healer had informed him Wiglaf's cloud-cough was curable.

"We're going to get some grand songs out of the quest, I know it." In her enthusiasm, the queen was now digressing. "'Four Face the Darkness' is quite familiar now. Don't get me wrong, I love Sir Noah Noble's songwriting. I just worry he's rather a one-ode wonder, you know? Well, then," Thessia went on eagerly, "what is your strategy? Your magnificent plan?"

No one spoke.

Several moments passed until Clare realized the question was for him. Which was unfortunate, for his mind was entirely empty, clear like the cloudless Mythrian summer.

His companions rounded on him. Elowen did not conceal her impatience. Beatrice offered him nothing except her smirk. "Go on," she urged. "You *are* our leader, Sir Grandhart."

He felt Thessia's eyes dart expectantly among them. "If I may," the queen finally prompted with impressive delicacy. "I'm no hero, but perhaps you would wish to speak with the last man to see Hugh—his Man of Honor for our wedding."

Clare pulled his gaze from Beatrice, desperately wrestling away the memory of how she'd looked last night, naked and dripping wet. It was one of the hardest fights he'd ever faced.

Perhaps Thessia should lead the quest, with how poorly he was doing. Yes, he was certain there was a quest registry somewhere, and his name would get a demerit mark or something. Perhaps a skull or a picture of gryphon droppings.

"Yes. Yes," he concurred hastily. "Is he here? Witnesses shall serve as our first recourse."

"Why, yes," the queen said. Clare ignored the gentle edge in her voice. She gestured to a guard, who left the room. When she returned to her throne, she regarded the group. "You must be eager to get underway," she went on. "How fun it will be to go on a quest together again! Tell me you're not thrilled. *I'm* thrilled, and my fiancé is literally missing. He's going to be so delighted when you three rescue him."

Clare coughed. He did not want to speak dishonestly to his queen.

Beatrice took a deep breath.

"Oh, if only you had my heart magic," Elowen spoke up, experiencing none of their compunctious discretion. "Pure eager joy fills the room."

"Yes. Quite," Beatrice said, not to be outdone in dry disdain.

The queen narrowed her eyes. However, she did not have the chance to interrogate them further, for her guard reentered the hall. The brown-eyed man he escorted looked nervous—until his gaze fell on the heroes. His expression changed to one of starstruck wonder.

Finally, Clare felt on firm footing. He could do this part—winning over fans. Grinning like they were old friends, he clapped their witness on the shoulder. "Good sir," he said warmly. "What is your name?"

"Arthur. Great Ghosts," the man replied. "You're really Clare Grandhart. You're even more handsome than the portraits depict."

Clare could practically *hear* Beatrice rolling her eyes. He grinned gracefully, used to unprompted compliments. "You flatter me, Arthur." He went on. "I understand you're a good pal of our man Hugh, and you were with him the night he was kidnapped. What can you recall of the eve in question?"

The mention of his friend sobered Arthur. He stood straighter, his expression solemn. "I remember . . . men joining our party. It was the night of Hugh's bachelor party," he clarified. "We were . . . fairly deep in our cups by then, though."

Fighting flagging hope, Clare looked Arthur right in the eye. "Is there nothing you can remember?" he pressed. "A description? How many there were?"

Arthur hesitated. "We were playing Drinking Swords," he confessed. "Sir Hugh is . . . very good at Drinking Swords."

Clare winced, understanding the import of the revelation. The game involved participants walking the length of the courtyard or room with shots of liquor perched on their weapons' flat edges, compelling opponents to drink whatever they could keep up without spilling. It was favored among university students for the enjoyably high-stakes opportunity to get very drunk, very fast.

He was racking his mind for new approaches when he heard Beatrice sigh. She strode past him, speaking with sharp haste. "Arthur, you know who I am, right?"

"Of course," the man replied rapturously. Clare would've reacted the same way, he knew. Her assertiveness was, quite sincerely, his favorite of her many marvelous qualities. His resentment of her decisions would never let him forget how his heart would pick up, his entire life sharpening, when he got to watch her this way.

Over the course of long nights on their decade-old quest, she'd shared her past with him. He knew what her upbringing had made her, even if she didn't—strong. When the Four had faced challenges, she was often the first to propose they fight, doing what was difficult or daunting. She would volunteer. She was relentless. She was deeply selfless.

It scared him sometimes. It never failed to fill him with wonder. Part of him desperately wished to tell her what a hero he saw in her.

It was why, when he'd realized she'd seen herself as nothing more than a sacrifice, disposable, something irreparable had snapped in him. It enraged him—it was like sacrilege, he felt, how she had disregarded her incandescent life.

The memory of their last kiss seared into him. How she'd squabbled with him in the cave where they'd camped. How she'd pulled his lips to hers. It wasn't hungry need or hasty fear. It was perfectly her—decisive. Determined.

She'd left him with the most hope he'd ever felt in his life. Until the coming days. The funeral. The revelation of what she'd intended. Even if he could forgive her, deeper within himself, he knew he could not cope with the fear. He didn't know how he could gaze into her gorgeous eyes without remembering how close his heart had come to collapsing.

He'd done wrong, he knew he had. He just couldn't imagine doing otherwise.

When she smiled, welcoming Arthur's reception, he found himself irrationally jealous. He hadn't seen her smile *once* in the past days in his company.

"Arthur, may I use my magic to view the night through your eyes?" she asked gently.

Inspiration lit Arthur's face. "Yes! Of course! Anything for Hugh."

Thessia smiled softly at his words. Her fiancé was a well-loved man.

Which only heightened Clare's nervousness. One way or another, they had to find Hugh. He watched anxiously while Beatrice grasped Arthur's hands. Invoking her magic, she closed her eyes, and Clare found himself utterly fixated on the notch between her collarbones, moving steadily as her breathing deepened.

No, he chastened himself. What had they reminded each other? This quest was *not about them*.

Emerging from her magic, she straightened, newly urgent. She spoke to Elowen. "Come here," she said. "Watch this."

Clare was prepared to mediate, expecting Elowen's resistance to physically touching Beatrice. Yet whatever had colored Elowen's cheeks evidently persisted into leaving her mood downright pleasant (by Elowen standards). Without protest, she crossed the room and clasped the other woman's hand. They closed their eyes and entered the magic.

"Well?" Beatrice inquired when moments had passed and they opened their eyes. "Did you notice what I did?"

Elowen straightened her sleeves, stepping back from Beatrice. When she nodded, she was the very image of grave contemplation. "Yes. The men who took Hugh are same men who attacked us in Keralia."

Clare realized what the revelation meant. "We have a lead!" he exclaimed.

Elowen frowned, and Clare could tell it was not mere Eloweniness darkening her mood. He realized the connection to the attack in Keralia did not strike her with the fortune of coincidence. "Yes?" he prompted her warily.

Elowen sighed in reluctance. "Vandra was able to ascertain the men who attacked us were members of the Fraternal Order."

Vandra—the reference caught Clare's interest instantly. In order to have shared her findings after following their attackers, Vandra must've spoken with Elowen *recently*. Last night was the only night Clare was not with Elowen. Which meant . . . Vandra was the reason for Elowen's ebullient mood!

The next moment, he realized he was the only one grinning.

Oh—right, he realized, his excitement dying. It was not regular kidnappers who took Hugh. It was the Fraternal Order.

The queen had gone deathly pale. Not even the ghost of her

good cheer lingered. "No," she uttered. "No. Not *them*." Clare recognized the anguish of fear stretching her delicate features rigid. He knew what she was remembering—*who* she was remembering. "Not Hugh. Please no."

The rest of the group unfortunately shared her dismay. "This is no meager rescue quest," Beatrice said.

"No," Elowen added gravely. "If the Order has Hugh, it is for a plot."

He could not find fault with his companions' conclusion. Attacking them first, and now abducting the future king from the heart of Queendom itself? Not the acts of resentful Fraternal Order members wreaking restless vengeance. Whatever the Order was up to, it was real. It was purposeful.

Which meant it was very, very dangerous.

"Todrick van Thorn is dead," Thessia protested, her voice wavering. "There is nothing more they can do."

"Desperate men do not think that way," Elowen replied quietly.

"If . . . I don't . . ." Beatrice was retreating, her ferocity vanquished. "We can't face them again."

Watching his once-dearest friends wrestle with their fears, Clare was gripped by a force he'd never felt. Part panic, part passion, part fury. He was not fully in control of himself when he strode into their midst.

"No, don't you understand? It *must* be us," he insisted. "Each of us needs to face the Order." He stared right into Beatrice's eyes, reminding her of their conversation. "For peace." He looked next to Elowen. "For revenge." He rounded, facing the queen. "For Galwell and for Hugh."

He swept his eyes over his companions, a hush following his gaze.

"We faced the greatest danger the Order ever posed," he reminded them, his voice low with power. "And we destroyed it. We can pick off their splintered remains. We are three of the Four," he finished, "and in provoking our vengeance, the Order has sealed its doom."

He practically *felt* the reverence descending over the room. Everyone looked—inspired.

He'd done it. *He'd* given the speech!

For once, Clare felt he had honored Galwell's legacy. He'd finally, if only for a moment, lived up to the greatness Galwell, for whatever reason, had seen in him. *He* could lead them. He could help his friends.

He could even, perhaps, find the hero he sought in himself.

Despite not wanting to get his hopes up, he started imagining everything the coming days could hold. They could fight fierce raiders or grotesque monsters—song-worthy stuff. Perhaps, he contemplated, he would even face someone in single combat. In the days of Mythria's founding, heroes often settled whole battles in one-on-one duels, the height of epic challenge.

Elowen spoke up. While her wry delivery offered little in the way of enthusiasm, Clare knew her well enough to hear the new vigor in her voice. "I . . . may know someone who could lead us to the Order," she announced. "Someone who recently followed and spied on them. We'll need to add a fourth to our quest."

The number rang out a little painfully. Nevertheless, Elowen continued, dauntless.

"Vandra," she said.

19

Elowen

Hope colored the mourning Queendom.

Hundreds of Mythrian citizens had gathered to see their heroes reunited. On the castle's main balcony, Vandra and Thessia stepped into the shadows while Elowen, Clare, and Beatrice remained in view of the reverent audience. It should have been awkward, or agonizing. Somehow, it was peaceful. When Clare reached for Elowen's hand, Elowen accepted. So did Beatrice on the other side. The three raised their clasped fists to the sky as the crowd below them bowed.

This gathering was once planned as a celebration of what they had accomplished ten years ago, defeating the darkness and ushering Mythria into a new era of prosperity. This was the anniversary of Galwell's death. Of Mythria's renewal. It was meant to be the biggest Festival of the Four yet.

And now, amid flags and festival floats done up in their honor, it was the start of an entirely new quest. Elowen could not focus for long on the emotions of the crowd because her own feelings were so potent. Beneath her sadness, and her uncertainty, she felt something very surprising.

She was proud.

Elowen did not want the responsibility bestowed upon her. Yet, thanks to her heart healer—as well as the night she'd shared with Vandra watching over her—somewhere deep down, Elowen finally recognized she *needed* it. There had been an ellipsis at the end of their last quest, and for ten long years, Elowen had lived inside it, forever waiting for what would come next.

Next was now, finding Hugh. There was a symmetry to it that satisfied Elowen. No matter what happened, she would not be solely defined by having saved the realm ten years ago. Perhaps she'd be defined by failing to rescue Hugh, or by being eaten alive by stingbugs. There were infinite possibilities ahead.

Which was why, when they reached the first overnighter of their new quest, the distinct anti-glamour of camping did not put Elowen in poor spirits. Quite the opposite. The inky sky was lit by a full Mythrian moon, casting a serene glow. The grass that grew where they intended to set up their tents for the night had a pleasant roughness to it. Exfoliating, almost. Elowen saw all of it as an opportunity. Years alone in the trees had trained her for this. She could put to use her hard-earned patience and her ability to make the most out of very little.

Importantly, though, she was *not* alone anymore. That in and of itself was a large source of excitement. Elowen had gotten Vandra to join their rescue team. They were officially on the same side, and if all went well, everyone in Mythria—but especially Vandra's parents—would know Vandra as the source of good she'd always been.

"Do you have a preference for where you'd like our tent to go?" Elowen asked Vandra. She believed herself to sound *very* casual. In reality, she vibrated with anticipation. She'd been tired the night before, worked up by all that had unfolded. Now she had the time and energy she needed to pay full attention to Vandra, and she was consumed with wondering if, when, and how they would come together again.

Vandra scanned their surroundings. When she'd agreed to join the quest, she'd retrieved her beloved black horse, Killer, who now stood a few paces away, grazing. They'd picked a heavily wooded area for obvious reasons. Lots of trees meant ample cover. It did not leave them exposed to the elements, or worse, an attack. "Somewhere private," she said, and Elowen's heart raced faster.

What else would they need privacy for?

Beatrice trudged past them with her hands in the air, attempting to conjurate something. "The spell service here is terrible," she announced despairingly.

Elowen knew how to get good spell service in wooded areas. It was perhaps her greatest area of expertise. She followed Beatrice to offer assistance, but three steps into the endeavor, she decided that was the behavior of friends, and Beatrice was not her friend in this. They just shared a common interest, and that interest happened to be saving the realm. Evidently, someone had to do it, and very few people had the expertise they did. Their personal politics did not need to interfere anymore. If anything, Elowen being generous would strain them further. It would be misinterpreted somehow.

Turning back to Vandra, Elowen reworked her question. "Should we find an adequately secluded spot?"

Clare interrupted, tapping Elowen on the shoulder. "I've forgotten my nighttime facial oils," he whispered.

"Have you?" Elowen asked, confused.

Vandra let out a *tsk*ing sound. "I told everyone to double-check their satchels before we left."

"It's a very small jar," Clare protested. He turned to Elowen again, imploring her with his gaze.

"I can only sense emotions, not read minds," she reminded him.

Sighing, he moved closer, tilting his chin up to catch the glow of the violet night. "On my forehead," he said, directing Elowen's attention. "There are fine lines that require treatment. Perhaps you have something comparable I could use?"

Elowen had rejected the opportunity to help Beatrice. Clare did not afford her the same choice. Placing a hand on his shoulder, she felt his genuine despair. "I don't use any special facial oils. I wear heavy cloaks so the sun cannot infect me with joy."

Clare turned to go, his head hanging low.

"You've aged well," Elowen called out after him. He would never appeal to her specifically, but she understood him to be a handsome man in the same way she understood when a garment was of good quality.

Her words placated him more than she expected. He whipped back around, beaming with delight. It was entirely possible Elowen had never given him a real compliment before. She thought of the younger Clare and how fearful he used to be of his own softness. Now he showed it with sometimes reckless abandon, and Elowen's heart ached for the younger man he'd once been, and how much it would have meant to him to receive a compliment from a younger Elowen.

Ghosts. Elowen had really opened herself up more than ever before. If she wasn't careful, she was likely to weep over something like the cleansing of rain or the unassuming innocence of flowers.

Instead of asking Vandra a third question, Elowen took Vandra's hand, pulling them into the comforting depths of the forest.

"Won't you be sleeping nearby?" Clare shouted after them.

"Perhaps raising your voice isn't the best strategy at the moment," Beatrice reminded him, still aggravated from her search for spell service. "And neither is splitting up from us," she said, more to Vandra than Elowen.

"We're not splitting up," Elowen responded, looking somewhere near Beatrice's general direction. Very businesslike. A consummate professional.

"We won't be very far," Vandra assured them. "If someone attacks, I will be there to rescue you within moments."

"Oh, we don't . . . I can protect . . ." Clare shook off his warring thoughts. "Thank you," he said.

"Vandra and I just need some space to ourselves for the night," Elowen explained, realizing after the fact that they'd already resolved it and she didn't need to provide more context.

Clare gave a look of impressed understanding. "Go on, then," he said with a grin. "We don't want to keep you from your fun."

Thessia had provided them with magicked tents that required little work to assemble. The two women found a sufficiently private location at the base of an imposing crestoak, and they opened the small contraption that held their dwelling. From it sprang out a charmed little room, quite literally. The walls had been magicked so they could not be burnt by flame, and the floor had a very thin layer of cushion. Though it was modest, and far from what would be considered comfortable, it still provided more than one expected from a night of camping.

Vandra climbed inside the tent and lay on her belly. "Certainly pays to have a mission funded by the queen. Could you have imagined such extravagance ten years ago?"

Elowen slid in after her, sealing the tent's door closed behind them. "I recall more than one night using twigs as a pillow."

Vandra's eyes twinkled. "Ah, yes. So many twigs. So little time."

There was no doubt anymore that they both had the same thing on their minds.

Now they had not just the protection of a sufficient sleeping place, but the permission to be together without hiding. There was nothing stolen between them anymore, except for the words Elowen wanted to say. They'd been robbed from her, plundered by her own uncertainty.

"Who'd have ever imagined we'd be on the same side," she said. It was as good a place to start as any.

Vandra brushed a curl off Elowen's cheek, closing what little space existed between them. "You know my loyalties on that job were only to the money I was supposed to get, and I didn't even receive it. I felt no passion for Bart's hope to become Mythria's hero instead of Galwell. I'd have joined you on the last quest. All you had to do was ask."

Elowen's face flushed. She fumbled for purchase, stunned by the admission. As far as she understood, it had been set in stone. It never once occurred to Elowen that Vandra's position last time was just that—a job. One that could have changed.

Back then, she'd understood Vandra to be dangerous and deadly. Someone who worked for whoever paid the highest price. Now she knew it was so much deeper than that. She also knew what it was like to have someone else decide who you were without your input. She regretted how long she'd spent doing that to Vandra.

"I'm sorry I never did," she told her.

"Worry not," Vandra said. "We can't change the past. And I'm sure it wouldn't have worked anyway. I'd have taken all of Grand-hart's sponsorships. All the songs about the Four would have been written of the Five, changing every rhyme scheme. The public would adore me too much. It would have been exhausting."

Elowen smiled. "I'm glad you've joined us now," she said, nudging in closer. "We have fun together."

There was that word again. *Fun.* The same one Lettice had used when she asked Elowen to go to the Needle. It's what Clare had said as they'd walked away. Elowen used it now as a test, hoping Vandra would enlighten her on the meaning.

In some ways, Vandra did. She kissed Elowen lightly, letting her lips linger after she finished. "We do."

Elowen's mind raced. If all she had to do was ask, she needed to know the right question. "Would you . . ." she started. She had to get this right. She couldn't destroy what they'd started. It was too important to her. She needed to find a way to do this without hurting Vandra. "Would you want to be my questmate . . ."

"Darling," Vandra interrupted. "I already told you I am."

"With benefits?" Elowen blurted right after.

"Oh." Vandra's eyebrows raised. She cocked her head to the side, lost in thought. That dreadful place. Elowen still had a hand on Vandra, and she felt Vandra's apprehension, but she knew not what caused it.

"It's okay if you don't," Elowen rushed out, terrified she'd ruined this by being too forward. "I realized that I should ask, though, since you made a rather compelling point about what I *didn't* ask last time."

Vandra rubbed her face. "I did do that, yes."

Elowen scooted away and sat up, her back pressed against the fabric wall of the tent. "If you'd prefer we didn't have more fun together, I understand. We're not who we used to be."

"I'd love to continue having fun with you," Vandra said. "If that's what you want."

"It is," Elowen eagerly confirmed. "Very much so."

"Then we are questmates with benefits," Vandra said. Or asked. Elowen wasn't sure.

To clear up the confusion, she lay down beside Vandra. "Yes," she said with great emphasis, running a hand along Vandra's back.

Vandra curled into her then, rolling to the side so that she could nuzzle her rear into Elowen's front.

"After all, you've just gone through a breakup."

"Oh. Yes," Vandra said, stiffening for a moment. "My breakup. That's right."

If Elowen didn't know better, she'd think they were cuddling. But questmates with benefits didn't *cuddle*. Surely this was just foreplay.

"Let us not think of the past. It's better to make the most of the time we have." Vandra pulled Elowen's arm around her like a blanket. "Who knows what tomorrow will bring."

Elowen shuddered. The last quest had brought such loss. She could never withstand another tragedy of that magnitude. As she pressed her nose into Vandra's hair, she fought the urge to tap into Vandra's emotions. To feel her then would be to know too much. And questmates with benefits didn't ruin the moment with their worries.

So Elowen held Vandra. In a casual way. Certainly not an intimate embrace alone in the wilderness, using each other's bodies as pillows, not just for comfort, but for safety.

Mercifully, the embrace did eventually turn lustful. Vandra rolled over. Elowen pressed her mouth atop Vandra's with what she hoped felt like casual desire. Like their nights together ten years ago, when they spoke with their bodies instead of their words, distracting themselves from the constant anxiety of their daily tasks by finding solace in each other at night.

"What are your limits?" Vandra asked between kisses. "I will only do what you are comfortable with."

Limits? Elowen wondered dimly. She flushed, embarrassed by the depth of her own desire. Her wants were untamed. "I have none," she answered. "Do you?"

"None," Vandra responded.

With that, Vandra's hands came up under Elowen's blouse until she reached Elowen's breasts. Elowen could not help but gasp, feeling the depth of Vandra's tenderness again. It stole her breath. It felt so wonderful to be touched that she pulled Vandra closer, her hands attempting to find Vandra's chest in return. Vandra, with her expert reflexes, put a stop to it, pinning Elowen's hands in capture.

"Be patient," Vandra said. "Let me work."

It had been ten years since Elowen had been intimate not just with Vandra, but anyone. Ten very long years closing her eyes and imagining a moment such as this. Elowen wanted to give as much as she received, and that made her rush, trying to match Vandra's every action with an equal and appropriate response. She sighed, fighting the urge to resist.

"You are so lovely," Vandra cooed as she pulled down the fabric of Elowen's blouse to expose Elowen's breasts in full. They spilled out over Elowen's bodice. "Fucking breathtaking," she said, her fingers pinching and squeezing all the right spots.

"I want you so much," Elowen gasped out, unable to contain herself. How could she possibly receive pleasure before giving it, especially when she had direct access to knowing how deeply Vandra wanted her? "I'm desperate to touch you back."

"Darling," Vandra said, removing Elowen's bodice, then coaxing Elowen's top over her head.

All that remained were Elowen's bottoms. And her shoes.

Ghosts. She still had on her shoes.

"Have you considered that your want is a turn-on for me?" Vandra continued. "That making you wait riles me up? Every second you can't touch me is another second I grow wetter, watching you squirm, knowing how badly you desire me."

Elowen had not in fact considered it, and the new knowledge

sparked low in her belly. She was slippery now, more than ready to receive the attention Vandra was so eager to give.

"Will you be a good girl and let me work?" Vandra teased, coming up to Elowen's mouth to steal one more kiss there. It was sweet, lingering, playful. So very Vandra.

"I will," Elowen promised.

Vandra tore her way down Elowen's body, removing Elowen's shoes and leggings until Elowen lay completely bare. Elowen did not feel nervous or exposed. She knew she couldn't be. Not when she experienced how complete Vandra's lust was. It protected her as much as it freed her. There was no holding back. She felt deeply desired, and so full of lust that it dizzied her.

"Delicious," Vandra said, admiring Elowen as if she were art.

She moved her mouth down until she landed on the exact spot where Elowen wanted her the most. Vandra's tongue pressed into the wetness, coaxing moans out of Elowen with every teasing circle. Elowen wished she could last longer, if only to draw out Vandra's own pleasure, but her willpower was not strong enough. She cried out, gasping as her orgasm rolled through her in waves.

As soon as the calm descended upon her, Elowen's focus sharpened. It was time for what she really wanted most—the privilege of making the careful Vandra Ravenfall lose control.

They swapped places in the tent, with Vandra on the bottom, Elowen sitting on her hips. Though Vandra submitted, she never looked away from Elowen, staring deeply into her eyes as Elowen made slow work of undressing her.

When Elowen's curls fell into her face, blocking her view, Vandra reached up, tucking them behind her ear. "There you are," she said, running her thumb along Elowen's chin.

Vandra's clothing may as well have been poured onto her, molded to her shape with an exactness only the most skilled hand magicians possessed. Elowen relished in removing it article by article, using her hands and even her teeth to pull the fabric away, each piece bringing her closer to the glorious umber of Vandra's bare skin.

When she had Vandra fully exposed, her desire to pleasure her was still present, but a surprising tenderness overtook her, too. Elowen did not want to be playful. She wanted to be careful. This was delicate.

She laid herself atop Vandra, bare skin to bare skin. Though Vandra did not possess Elowen's magic, Elowen still wanted to send back all the warm affection she'd received. She wanted to protect Vandra, too. Their heartbeats thrummed against one another.

"You're so soft," she whispered, letting her hand wander down as her mouth pressed onto Vandra's, stealing gentle kisses. "You feel wonderful."

She did. Touching Vandra, pleasuring her, was indeed a wonder akin to the great natural majesties of Mythria. Elowen made slow work of it. She pressed her nose onto Vandra's so that every sharp breath and shaky whimper would blow against her own skin.

Elowen had hours of this in her. She would never tire.

It was only when Vandra grew truly desperate, bucking into Elowen's hand, that she dared to increase her tempo. When Vandra finally fell apart, Elowen joined her, for the friction she'd created between them, lined up exactly right, had been enough to get her there.

Or maybe it was just Vandra. She was more than enough.

In fact, to Elowen, she was everything.

20

Beatrice

"A re you *sure* we can't stop at Harpy & Hind first?" Beatrice asked.

Heroically fighting a headache, she slumped over her horse, whose jostling gait was not helping. She did not feel like the conquering valiant the realm needed. She felt hungover. Which was frustrating, as, surprisingly, she wasn't.

Instead, four hours of sleep in the forest had left her feeling much the same way. While their enchanted tents were preferable to slumbering on the ground, sleeping in the woods—in the cold, with the murmur of wildlife surrounding her, on the slim bedroll provided—was sleeping in the woods.

Years of the finest feather mattresses farthings could purchase had left her unaccustomed to camping. When the minstrels wrote the songs of their new "reunion quest" the way Thessia wanted, she very much hoped they would leave this unflattering detail out. *Grandhart the Gallant, Elowen the Epic, and Backache Beatrice* was not how she wished the verses to remember her.

"You do realize we're in the middle of nowhere," Elowen replied uncharitably. The other woman looked irritatingly composed despite them having risen with the first pinking hues of dawn only to follow Vandra for hours into the forest.

Where Elowen's ire often left her with a complicated cocktail of guilty understanding and impatient combativeness, exhaustion now left Beatrice with only the stiff drink of the latter.

"No, actually, I have no idea where we are, and I doubt you do, either," she snapped. "Never mind it. If a few hours' detour gets me a honey-foam milkbrew, I promise I will be better prepared to rescue Hugh. He does not deserve a heroine running on four hours of sleep. What if they cut off his finger while I'm caught in a yawn?"

Elowen preened. Her scarlet locks practically shimmered in the sunlight pervading the forest cover. "I got four hours of sleep," she replied loftily, "and I feel wonderful."

From up ahead, Vandra laughed with satisfaction. "Yes, well, Beatrice did not have multiple orgasms last night," she reminded Elowen.

Clare grunted. With the grim fulfillment of a consolation prize, Beatrice noted he looked worse for the wear like her, hunched on his horse. The eldest of the group and used to comfort himself, he was, she concluded, likewise ill-equipped for the aches of questing.

Of course, *he'd* rallied the group into this ridiculous quest, not her. She hoped he was very much enjoying what he'd wrought.

"Okay, was that really necessary?" he ground out, his weary voice like gravel. *Not sexy gravel*, she counseled herself. Just ordinary gravel. "Sincerest congratulations on your mutual pleasure last night, truly. But . . ." He stalled, summoning the right words from his exhausted vocabulary. "Don't rub it in."

"I'm afraid that's rather exactly what we did, darling," Vandra cooed.

Elowen swallowed her smile.

Clare's demeanor only darkened. He looked—jealous, she found when she unfortunately met his eye. Very unfortunately.

Each severed the glance they shared in mutual annoyance. How, she found herself wondering, did his eyes still look like pure crystals, even when the rest of him looked like the rough rock surrounding them?

In meager mercy, Vandra slowed her mount. She leapt from the horse, still laughing to herself.

"The bad news," she went on, "is I'm afraid we are nowhere near a Harpy & Hind, nor are we near anything at all. When villains select a location for their evil lair, they tend to prefer seclusion."

"Don't act like villains don't love foamy milkbrews as much as the rest of us," Beatrice muttered in her discontent.

"You just know the Fraternal Order has pumpkin-gingerroot cream on tap in every one of their lairs," Elowen joined in.

Beatrice snorted with laughter. Elowen did the same—until each woman remembered herself. Embarrassed, they darted their gazes elsewhere.

Beatrice's heart pounded. Did they just *joke* together? It felt painfully like childhood, when they would poke fun at the often exceedingly literal Galwell. When they were friends, close to sisters.

When they loved each other.

"The *good* news is," Vandra continued, enthusiasm audible even in her hushed voice under the forest canopy, "we have reached our destination!"

She swept her arms aside—gesturing, the group saw, in the direction of the mountainous ravine where the mouth of a dark cave opened.

Vandra's pride in her presentation went undiminished when no one reacted with cheers, relief, displays of undaunted vigor or other common quest-like reactions. Indeed, Clare frowned.

"Wait, we're . . . here?" he mustered, like comprehension itself was an unwelcome labor in the morning light. "Already? I expected our journey would get more . . . I don't know, epic," he groused, dismounting from his horse with wincing movements. Elowen and Beatrice followed suit. "We weren't even beset by monsters. Or betrayed! What material will there be for the songs?"

Vandra shrugged. "I followed the Fraternal Order after they attacked in Keralia. The first night, I overheard them discussing their plans while they camped. Mentioning a chair lashed down with ropes. Pretty customary hostage stuff," she clarified, perhaps without need. "They said they were headed for crystal caves in the east. Of the three crystalline formations in the realm, there's only one cave complex large enough for occupancy of over three people, the one east of Mount Mythria. I feel certain they have Hugh here," she concluded.

"Easy in and easy out," Elowen replied. Something prickled in her voice, something Beatrice could recognize but could not read, like the writings of Old Mythria one could find on walls in old villages like Elgin. "The faster we find Hugh, the faster we can go home," Elowen went on. "Perhaps we'll reunite for another quest in ten years, but I shall savor the time apart."

The mere mention of the prospect made Beatrice frown involuntarily, reminding her of the pain in her joints and the hammering in her head. "A quest at thirty is unpleasant enough," she declared. "I shan't do forty."

"You *have* aged poorly," Elowen retorted, and there it was—the point of the prickle. It was obvious she was making up for their moment of mirth with redoubled viciousness. Yet, Beatrice found she did not care, for Elowen's overcompensation only reminded her of the short lapse in their enmity. Of how, for just one moment, Elowen forgot her hatred and laughed with Beatrice.

"Yes, well, I'm certain ten more years of isolation will only improve your sociability," Beatrice replied, unable to muster the other woman's disdain. The memory of their companionship lingered with her like a favorite song stuck in her head.

"Ladies!" Clare sighed, rubbing his forehead. "Stop with the squabbling, my Ghosts above. We're about to save a man's life. The fiancé of our dear queen! We'll be heroes! Again!"

"Actually"—Beatrice nodded with her chin—"looks like Vandra will be the hero this time."

Everyone followed her gesture. Yes, down the ravine, the erstwhile assassin was proceeding on her own, undoubtedly fed up with her questmates.

"Well, shit," Clare murmured. Not even four hours of orgasm-free sleep could vanquish the quiet delight with which Beatrice watched the long-legged man jog in pursuit of Vandra. "I shall lead us!" he called out in reminder.

She shot Elowen a wry glance—which she was startled to find returned. Indeed, she could swear Elowen almost smiled. No grudge withstood the appeal of mocking Clare Grandhart's vanity.

They chased his long stride. "I should lead," Elowen challenged. "I deserve vengeance for my brother."

"Personally, I feel I should lead," Beatrice ventured. "Because . . . well, because why not? I would do an excellent job."

They entered the mouth of the cave, which was only a small rocky space with a narrow tunnel leading down into unseen depths. Clare sped down the terrain, and the women followed, sending stones flying under their feet.

"Perhaps Harpy & Hind could sponsor your leadership," Elowen returned. "'The Great Mythrian Milkbrew Quest, brought to you by—'"

She was cut off by a very vexed-looking Vandra, blocking their path. "Literally, *how* did you ever foil me? You three are helpless," she said, sounding exhausted. "Please be dears and shut up as we *sneak* into the bad-guy lair."

Clare, Elowen, and Beatrice muttered chastened apologies.

Silently, they continued down the tunnel. Where it flattened out, the ceiling was low, causing the group to crouch and crawl toward an opening. When finally there was space to stand, Beatrice found Clare's hand offering to help her up. She prepared a rejection, but the words died on her lips, for the chamber they found themselves in was the most stunning place she had ever seen.

Crystals covered the enormous cavern. Everywhere they glittered, amethyst, aquamarine, pure glass like diamond. They captured the light entering down the tunnel from the cave entrance, illuminating everything. Stalactites, jaggedly geometric, descended like gleaming fingers from the ceiling, which was covered in sharp, perfect gemstones.

They reminded her of Clare's eyes.

Gawking, she was hardly conscious of putting her hand in Clare's to rise. The room—did caves have rooms? Chambers? Hollows? She did not know—was massive, with winding ridges of rock proceeding down into the depth of the cave, where Vandra waited.

"Quick question," Beatrice whispered. "Where *are* the bad guys?"

"We must proceed deeper," Vandra replied.

"I'm not certain that's a good idea," Clare huffed.

Elowen rounded on him. "Galwell wouldn't lose his nerve."

"I'm not *scared*," he replied hotly.

"I still say we get brews in us first, honestly," Beatrice interjected. "The caves could go on for miles. I require energy."

Elowen ignored her. "If you're not frightened, what is it?" she demanded of Clare.

He rubbed his hand, either remembering Beatrice's touch or the sharp rocks they climbed over. "Galwell would have posted one of us outside to ensure no one cuts off our exit," he explained. "I forgot."

"If you could just *shut up*, we could do the raid my way," Vandra said, frustration returned, stronger than before. "Stealthily. I'm quite good at doing these kinds of things on my own, if you haven't heard."

"Yes, but four draws more attention than one," Beatrice pointed out. "You're not on your own right now. You're part of a crew."

While she intended the point practically, she noticed the revelation's effect on Vandra, who looked stunned, perhaps even moved.

"I'll go guard the cave entrance," Elowen grumbled. "It was always my job anyway."

While Galwell always left Elowen on guard duty—protective of his sister—Elowen's mood indicated she wished she could do more. Beatrice found herself pulled to protest for Elowen, then remembered the gesture would probably not endear her to Elowen.

She did not, unfortunately, get the chance. None of them did.

Like magic, seemingly summoned by Clare's warning, men emerged on the outer rim of the cave, their silhouettes sharp in the sunlight. The four heroes were closed in.

On instinct, they gathered, back-to-back, defending each other from exposure. Beatrice found herself facing where the cave continued deeper into the rock.

No one moved, however. The Order members confining them did not press in.

The reason came in the echo of footsteps from within the cavern. *No.* Her eyes were deceiving her. The man who approached was a ghost walking forth from her nightmares, a wraith wrought of her worst memories. While her hopes for the quest were not high, she could hardly contend with the new depth of their peril.

From the darkness stepped Myke Lycroft.

His emergence made horrible sense. He'd gone into hiding after the Order was defeated and his best friend and leader Todrick was slain, remaining unseen despite the queen's efforts to visit justice on him for the forging of the Sword of Souls and his role in the Order's dark ploy. His reappearance now was . . . well, *worrying* was one understatement Beatrice would not permit herself. The possible coming of the end of the realm as they knew it was closer to the truth.

He was older, like all of them. Hiding had hardened him. He no longer looked like the young man in his friend's shadow. He looked like he'd spent the past decade planning . . . this.

Nevertheless, what had unnerved Beatrice on their earlier encounters unnerved her now. His predecessor Todrick van Thorn had *looked* villainous, with his rapier smile, his inky swoop of hair.

Myke Lycroft—he looked like a hero.

His golden hair was silky straight, even, dared she say, fluffy. His grin was winning, even welcoming. He looked like he would help you mend your fence or join your horseball squad if you were short one player. Like he would win your confidences or cheer you when you were upset.

In most men, she would have found his charm inoffensive. In one whose heart she knew held such wickedness, it horrified her.

"Finally!" he chided them. "What a reunion!"

He strode into the cavern, clearly enjoying each step.

"I was going to let you get farther into the caves, you know," he informed the unfortunate heroes. "But the four of you are more incompetent than I expected. I mean, my word! I've waited here for days! Do you know how miserable it is with nothing to do except play Ogre's Chess with your henchmen for *days*? I was starting to worry you wouldn't find the witness I left you." He fixed impish eyes on them. "The one I knew *you* would use your magic on."

He spoke to her. *To Beatrice.* Dread hit her like stone.

It was a trap.

With presence of mind she could concede was impressive, Clare called out, "Let Hugh go!"

Myke laughed darkly. "Grandhart, stop pretending you're a hero," he sneered, with whip-crack disdain cutting his charm in half. "It's fucking embarrassing. I can't take you seriously."

He swept his eyes over Elowen and Vandra like he was noticing them for the first time.

"Indeed," he went on, instructing Clare casually, "why don't you grab Miss Elowen and the Deathrose Guild assassin and save yourselves." He waved his hand. "I won't need the rest of you. I'll have my men escort you out."

Miss Elowen and the Deathrose Guild assassin. The rest of you.

His eyes landed on Beatrice, and ice froze in her veins.

"Welcome to your capture, Beatrice *de Noughton*," Lycroft said.

21

Elowen

Beneath the fear, of which there was plenty, Elowen sensed embarrassment.

They had strolled—no, *argued*—their way into this setup, and worse, they hadn't made a single plan. This was exactly why Elowen had spent the last ten years in the trees. Up there, no one was ever at risk of being kidnapped by a vengeful twit who looked like his favorite activity was spitting on his own shoes so that they better reflected his cloying smile.

Clare moved to protect Beatrice, pulling a sword from his scabbard and leaping in front of her. "You'll never take her," he said menacingly. "I won't let you."

Myke put a hand over his heart. "That's sweet." He turned to one of his henchmen and whispered, "He's a poor excuse for a hero, but I do love when romantics make their grand gestures. Chokes me up a little, I can't lie." He wiped a real tear from his eye.

"I'm not . . . This isn't romantic," Clare said, sharpening his scowl. "Not a single one of us will let you take Beatrice."

Elowen and Vandra exchanged a glance. They were outnumbered and surrounded on all sides. Elowen figured the best thing they could do was stall until someone came up with an idea. She forced herself to speak in the hopes of buying some time.

"What exactly do you want with Beatrice anyway?" she asked Myke.

Beatrice, still behind Clare, peered over his shoulder to examine Elowen. Elowen gave her a glare that said *What?* then went back to scowling at Myke, who seemed to appreciate a chance to lay out his plan.

Myke took out a small, spiraling dagger and pointed it at Beatrice. "She will use her magic on Hugh to get into his memories," he said, using his strange little weapon as an accessory to his storytelling, swooping it around to emphasize his points. He was so broad with his use of it that some henchmen had to duck out of the way as he gestured. "Turns out, he was one of the young foot soldiers who helped hide the Sword of Souls ten years ago. And since we knew he wouldn't use his big-boy words to tell us where it's at, we decided to take matters into our own hands."

As far as everyone knew, the Sword of Souls had been vanquished, though it dawned on Elowen how naive she'd been to believe that. Of course it wasn't the kind of weapon that could be destroyed—it was powered by the pain of hundreds of trapped souls, after all—but she'd been so wrapped up in her own grief that she'd accepted that narrative without further examination. Elowen should've known better than anyone that adventures didn't have neat endings. There was no real resolution. Much like the Fraternal Order, the sword was never actually gone, just out of sight.

"Once we know where it is, we will use it to bring back Todrick." Myke paused to smile, relishing in the horror settling across the room, a choking vine weaving through everyone's understanding of the situation, squeezing tighter with every passing second. "Yes. You heard me right. Todrick van Thorn will rise again, and he and I will use our combined powers to rewrite this realm into the place we'd always envisioned together."

Myke spoke like this would be a good thing. In his mind, it was. He had warmed since mentioning Todrick. It was the same way

Clare got when he brought up Galwell, a fondness and respect coating every word—though Clare looked up to Galwell, and Myke saw himself as Todrick's equal. He genuinely believed reuniting with his best friend and using their magic to take over the realm was an ideal scenario. They could finally be the worst versions of themselves, and not a single other person would be strong enough to stop them. Their dream for the realm was a nightmare to everyone else—a place where their men ruled with infinite power and little compassion, forcing Mythrians to comply at all costs.

"Don't look so surprised," Myke chided. "Did you all really think I would spend the rest of my life as a failure? That I would hide away in my grief, never to be seen again? No, my foes, after years of listless despair, I began planning. Without Todrick, I am half as happy, half as interesting, and half as powerful. Why would I ever want to live this way forever?"

Elowen schooled her face to remain calm. She'd done exactly what Myke had not. She'd hidden. And now the worst person on this side of the Ghost's Gate was showing her how wrong she'd been to go on like that for as long as she had. Ten whole years she'd spent adrift, the same as Myke Lycroft. But she had never started plotting a way to return to her glory. If anything, she'd been shrinking herself smaller and smaller, desperate to be seen as nothing at all.

Myke pressed a hand to his heart. "Now that I finally know how to bring Todrick back, nothing will stop me from doing just that."

Sword extended forward, Clare dashed toward Myke to engage in combat.

The henchmen reacted not by capturing Clare, or even Beatrice, but by grabbing Elowen of all people. What did she have to do with this? Even Myke had said she was expendable! One of the men wrapped his gloved hands around her arms while another pressed a cold sword to her throat.

"Make one more move and I'll have them slash her throat," Myke warned.

Clare stilled, torn. Vandra's keen eyes darted back and forth, searching for a solution. Beatrice's face, which had been rather stoic, fixed itself into something that looked almost like remorse.

Myke clearly believed that the remaining three of the Four still had loyalty to each other. He didn't understand how fractured they'd become. This was a mess in all ways it could be, and now Elowen had somehow gotten herself tangled up in the heart of the battle when all she'd meant to do was kill time until a viable plan emerged. If she ever got freed, the first thing she was going to do was lay into Lettice for ever letting her believe she was capable of going on another quest.

"Take me, then," Beatrice said, offering her wrists for tying. "If you leave Elowen alone, I will go without resistance."

It was Elowen's turn to give Beatrice a look of shock, and Beatrice took the opportunity to return the same *What?* expression and continue on with her business. After a nod of approval from Myke, the two henchmen released their hold on Elowen to saunter toward Beatrice instead. They could have committed a little longer to being interested in Elowen, but this wasn't the moment for her pride to interfere.

"No!" Clare shouted. His features darkened as his desperation morphed into anger, surely remembering how Beatrice had tried to sacrifice herself in the last quest. It struck Elowen how cruel their shared history was, destined to repeat itself over and over.

Within that same history, Elowen saw a solution.

Impulsively, Elowen dashed over to Myke and shoved him

toward Beatrice. Beatrice grabbed him by the hair in an instant, thrusting herself and Myke into one of his memories. It was so fluid it looked planned, another echo of their past. The henchmen paused, confused, as Myke thrashed about, his dagger swinging in every direction until finally, he surrendered.

Clare and Vandra capitalized on the lull by charging toward a massive column of shimmering amethyst. It would be large enough to create a barrier between the henchmen and the others, and it also seemed to hold the entire cave together. Elowen joined them, knowing that they needed as much force as possible to dislodge it. They were making decisions together using only instinct. And it was *working*.

The load-bearing column cracked. Elowen shoved again, channeling every bit of her pain and fury into the action. The Fraternal Order would never have this. They wouldn't win.

After another satisfying crack, the column began to sway, preparing to tip over.

Vandra turned to Elowen and smiled. "Good job, darling."

One of the henchmen, taking advantage of Vandra's distraction, grabbed her, right before the column crashed to the ground. Vandra and the two henchmen got stuck on one side of it, with Clare and Elowen on the other. Shimmering crystal surfaces began to tremble without the support of the smashed amethyst.

"You need to run!" Vandra yelled. "The walls are about to fall down!"

"I can't just leave you!" Elowen shouted back. Crystals started pouring down, first in drizzles, then in sheets, like a dazzling prismatic rain.

The henchmen shook dislodged dirt off their clothing with grins on their faces. Elowen could sense their growing excitement.

They took great pleasure not just in the unfolding chaos, but the promise of killing the one and only Vandra Ravenfall, even if it meant they'd die doing it.

"I will be fine!" Vandra said. She kneed one of the henchmen in the groin while elbowing the other. "Get out of here immediately!"

It was Clare who stopped Elowen's hesitation. "She has survived this long without you. Trust that she can survive this, too. We must go."

Startled, Elowen broke from Clare's grasp to grab Beatrice by the shoulder, yanking her off Myke to guide them toward the tunnel. She wasn't *saving* Beatrice, per se. She was just doing the logical thing.

The shower of crystal destruction followed them as the three retraced their steps, exiting the way they'd entered. Beatrice was slower than usual, and Elowen almost chastised her for it, until she looked back to see Beatrice grabbing her side. Myke had no doubt nicked her with his dagger, and in true Beatrice form, she'd said nothing of it.

"Let me," Elowen whispered, careful not to let Clare overhear. He was busy leading the charge, shoving fallen crystals out of the way to clear their path to freedom. Elowen almost said *Let me help*, but that's not what this was. If Beatrice was hurt, she was going to be insufferably silent about it, and it would slow everything down.

"Fine," Beatrice hissed. The pain must have been immense, or she'd never have agreed so quickly. She held out her hand for Elowen to grab.

When Elowen latched on, she closed her eyes, taking the opportunity to use the full extent of her powers. If she focused, she had the ability to completely absorb other people's emotions. She could pull out the feelings and take them on as her own, then dissolve them into nothingness inside her.

She did not want to take on all of Beatrice's pain. That would have been exhausting—and yes, painful—but it also would have taken too much time. She took off a bit, softening the edges, and even that much made her break out into a sweat. Beatrice really was carrying a lot.

Beatrice seemed to almost say thank you, but must have thought better of it, and they charged forth.

When they emerged from the cave, the fresh air tasted bitter on Elowen's tongue. She gulped it down, heaving, all of the adrenaline hitting her after the fact. She shook as violently as the crystal caves did, while the sounds of shattering walls still rang through the hollow hill.

Elowen had let Vandra die in there. And worse, Elowen knew she could not send herself back into the trees to get over it. It hadn't even worked the first time. She was not over a single thing that had happened to her ten years ago, from Galwell's death to her stolen moments with Vandra. She'd already held too tightly to all of that, and now she'd made it worse. She'd asked Vandra to come. She'd let Vandra protect her. And she'd done nothing in return but put Vandra in danger.

She has survived this long without you, Clare had said as the walls were coming down.

And she didn't survive knowing me again, Elowen thought. The first seed of devastation began blooming in her chest, pressing against her lungs, threatening her ability to breathe.

"Are you all just going to stand there gawking, or should we get on with our quest?"

Elowen whipped around, finding Vandra feeding Killer some straw she'd plucked from the ground outside the cave. The fallen amethysts had scattered through her dark, flowing locks like some of the fashionable hair jewels that were popular many years back, and the fractured crystals clung to her cloak in constellatory patterns. She was radiant in all ways she could be, from her clothing to her smile to her mood.

"How did you—" Elowen asked, faltering. The sight of Vandra stole all of her breath.

Vandra petted her horse's mane. She wore no distress in her emotions, or even the slightest hint of worry. "There was a faster exit on the other side. Without you three around to distract me, I found it quite easily."

If Vandra wasn't upset, why was Elowen? And why did it bother her so much that Vandra was fine? It was exactly what she wanted, and yet, Elowen found herself sulking as she walked over to the horses, confused by her own pain. Perhaps it was the implication that Vandra had an easier time without Elowen. Even though Elowen herself had just thought it, she didn't appreciate Vandra confirming the assumption.

"It isn't all good news, though," Vandra continued. "Myke is still alive. I could not reach him in time. He went out a different way than all of us. We need to be on our way at once."

Climbing atop his steed, Clare mumbled, "This was all for nothing."

Elowen had been too distracted by her own feelings to first notice how angry Clare was. It was much like the caves—a shimmering fury on the verge of collapse. For the first time, Elowen felt like she was seeing a reflection of herself in him. This was what it was like to be around someone who did not shield their hurts. Where others may have been put off by this, Elowen found herself charmed.

Good for Clare. The realm needed more curmudgeons.

"It wasn't actually," Beatrice said. She hoisted herself onto her horse with a grin that only faltered when her injured side had to bear some of her mounting. There was no time to manage her pain further or bandage the wound. She would have to endure.

"How so?" he snapped back.

"I went into Myke's memories and found out where Hugh is," she said with no shortage of satisfaction. "He's near the Straits of Baldon."

When she'd thrust Myke toward Beatrice, she'd hoped Beatrice would comb his memories for Hugh's location. And she had. They'd executed a wordless plan to perfection. Elowen might have been excited, if she wasn't so confused.

So much for conjurating Lettice to yell at her. Elowen might need to conjurate her for the very reason most people used heart healers—to talk about her romantic feelings.

22

Clare

They rode for an hour deeper into the woods, following no path except Vandra. Rocks and caves marked the way descending into the forested darkness, the cover of the dense foliage choking out the light.

The decline followed the group's spirits. Though they'd escaped their enemies, Clare felt no rush of victory. He found himself in his head, replaying the past hours. The return of Myke Lycroft did not upset him the most. Not the reemergence of probably the vilest man in the realm, intent on recovering the Sword of Souls. Not even the inevitable peril of Mythria, and so on and so forth.

No, what upset him was Beatrice. *Beatrice*, who'd done exactly what he wished he could not have predicted.

He welcomed the release from his rumination when Vandra slowed her horse, her eyes scouting the forest in evaluation, searching sharply for hidden risks. Evidently deciding they were far enough from the possibility of the Order's pursuit, she stopped the questing party.

"I'll water the horses," she declared, dismounting Killer in front of the mouth of the dark cave where she'd paused them.

"I'll help," Beatrice volunteered with unusual haste.

Vandra shot her a look. "Don't be ridiculous," she said. "You're injured."

Clare's head whipped to Beatrice. Fear clenched suffocating claws into his chest. *Injured?* Wasn't what she'd pulled in the cavern overwhelming enough? Would the Ghosts never give him peace?

"What? When?" he demanded. He could not, he found, pin down which question he needed spoken first. They rushed out of him in clumsy chaos. "How—why—why didn't you say anything?"

"It's nothing. I'm fine," she replied. He recognized the shortness of someone wishing to forestall a conversation.

Yet when she leaned to dismount her horse, she stopped short, wincing. He saw her knuckles whiten on the reins.

He was off his horse instantly, rushing over the rocks, reaching her the fastest he possibly could. While fear's clutches hadn't released him, what joined them was even more powerful. *Anger*, lancing into his soul, hissing into him like fresh-forged steel. *She's injured. They hurt her.* His vision red, he scoured her for signs of harm.

He could find nothing before Beatrice waved him away, irritated.

"Get off your horse," he ordered, knowing she would only continue obstructing him.

She held her chin high.

"I'm fine here," she informed him. "I'll sleep on the horse. It'll be more comfortable than the bedroll."

He was livid.

Fear did not merely grasp him now. Like the darkest magics, it possessed him. "You need tending," he ground out.

She held his gaze, furious, until finally his suggestion prevailed. She started to dismount—then promptly winced, wobbled, and looked woozy and weak from the exertion. She lost her balance, sliding from the horse right into Clare's arms. He wrapped his grip under her legs with gentle desperation, holding her aloft.

"*Ghosts, I'm fine,*" she insisted, yet her voice held no confidence.

He ignored her, not wanting to risk depositing her on her feet only for her knees to give out under her. He glanced to Vandra instead. "Healing supplies?" he demanded. The rest of his vocabulary was gone.

Vandra wordlessly tossed a small pouch from her belt, which landed in Beatrice's lap. Vandra's efficiency left him grateful—in one who'd quite recently made her money killing people, her instinct for compassion startled him.

The projectile's presence only sharpened Beatrice's glare.

"I'll just help Vandra with the horses, then," Elowen interjected. The women skittered off, obviously wishing distance from the sparring soon to occur.

Clare could not fault them. If *Elowen*, whose dourness was incomparable, feared the oncoming clash of Clare's anger and his patient's stubbornness, the fighting was certain to prove fearsome.

Which it would. Good Ghosts, Clare was going to nurse her so furiously. He was going to unleash the full strength of his fury on helping ease her pain. In the healing caress of his experienced fingers, she would know his wrath. Yes, he was going to nurse the living shit out of her.

"How dare you—" she seethed.

He marched into the cave, carrying her as one would a mellifluously yowling lyricat left out in the rain.

The cave welcomed them ominously. No crystals grew here. The obsidian walls consumed light, leaving only the shimmering indication of the moisture dripping down the dank walls. It was no place for escapades or escapes, no place for heroism. It was the manner of underworld fit for fugitives, for last resorts and lost hope. The sort of place where wounded creatures would go for quiet to—

No. He would venture into despair no further.

He lowered Beatrice. Gently, he set her down on the rough ground.

"Don't. Move," he uttered. "Except to put pressure on your wound."

She eyed him, glaring. He met her gaze unafraid. Or, unafraid *of her.* Indeed, her resistant resentfulness was nothing next to the cavalcade of horrors conquering his heart. *Injured. Injured. Injured.* What the fuck did *injured* mean? He was riven in half, needing to know and horrified of what he might find. What if he exposed her wound only to find her vitally punctured, impossibly pale? What if minutes or moments from now her gorgeous eyes went unfocused, her precious chin drooping to her chest?

What would happen to him?

He was grimly pleased when she leaned back on the wall in silent, bitter surrender.

In the dark, he could not properly minister to her wound, and if she'd lost blood, cold would only draw her strength. While he did not wish to wait long, he needed firewood.

He ventured from the cave, returning in haste once he'd collected handfuls of dry wood from the woodland ground. As he stacked kindling on the edge of the cave and sparked the flame, feeding it wood until it raged strong, he fought to do the opposite in himself. He controlled his heart rate and his breathing despite the roar within him.

She's injured. Lycroft struck her.

It was not the whole of his ire.

She was willing to sacrifice herself again.

Remembering how she offered herself to the Order in the crystal caves, he violently snapped a piece of wood for the fire. He could not handle the idea of her acting this way again. Discarding her life for others, offering herself up whenever the mouth of danger opened.

He was still fuming when the fire rose high into the cave's darkness. "Let me see it," he said upon returning to Beatrice.

"I'll do it myself," she replied, but her hand remained on her side, like she did not know where to start. She *was* maintaining pressure on the wound, he was gravely relieved to note. For once, she was doing what he'd asked.

He knelt in front of her. Fear had ceded to fury while he lit the fire. Now they resumed their clash on the field of his heart. Hands wavering, he pulled her cloak aside, fumbling over the heavy fabric of her bodice.

"Gentlemen are supposed to ask permission before they do *that*," she remarked wryly, until she gasped with pain on the final word when his hands found the damp tear in the garment.

In her.

"We've firmly established I'm no gentleman, Beatrice. Not with you," Clare retorted. Gone was every pretense, every self-presentation, every grasping reach for idealized heroism. Only one wish consumed him—her, safe.

The gash, his fingers' gentle inquiry found, stretched long. Until he could examine her skin, he could not know the wound's depth. He reached for the front of her bodice, where buttons and stays held the covering in place. His frantic fingers hesitated on instinct.

Beatrice had the gall to roll her eyes.

"If I told you to stop," she challenged him, "would you?"

His mouth flattened. Now was *not* the moment for jabs concerning his honor or lasciviousness. "*Are* you telling me to stop?" he shot back.

She was silent. When she shook her head, it was the permission he needed to start viciously unbuttoning. The work was intricate and slow, but he did not want to destroy the garment. No concern for immodesty nor fashion restrained him—the clothing was the closest she had to armor. "You've obviously had practice undressing women," she commented once he'd undone the first fasteners easily.

Unceasing in his work, he glanced up at her. "Don't pretend to be surprised," he growled, "and don't try to distract me from my anger." *You'd have it easier convincing Vestryian nobles to cease espionage of each other*, he wanted to say. *Nothing could ever distract me in defense of you.*

He did not need to. The wry fire in her eyes faded. She understood. In the wake of their conversation in Queendom, of course she did.

Watch the worst moment of my life.

Undoing the final buttons, he tugged the bodice off—careful not to rip the piece—exposing her chemise and leggings underneath. Dark red bloomed across the white linen at her side. While the fabric, mercifully, was not too dense with crimson, he nevertheless wondered how long she'd intended to ride with the wound open.

"It's—" Beatrice ventured.

"Not a word."

Silenced, she permitted his ministrations.

He grasped the hem of her chemise. The moment he feared.

When he would wake up from the nightmare, or step further into one. Incongruously, Galwell's were the words he heard in his head. *Legends never wait.*

He exposed the wound.

It wasn't deep. Thank Ghosts, the gash wasn't deep.

He exhaled, wondering whether she heard the shudder of relief. The boning of her bodice had caught much of the blade's clean slice. He saw no deep penetration—nowhere the knife could have punctured her insides or her crucial veins. If he could mend her, preventing inflammation, Beatrice would live.

If.

Despite relief's rush, the knot in his chest hardly loosened. Not hesitating, he reached into Vandra's pouch, finding bandages and tinctures taken from hand magicians with gifts for healing. Methodically, calling on skills he'd not used in years from his bounty-hunting days, he commenced work cleaning and applying spelled salve to the gash. He welcomed every wince, every undulation of Beatrice's skin, for they meant she drew breath.

When he finished, only bandaging the wound remained. Beatrice raised her arms, fighting pain's grimace.

"Take my chemise off, please," she ordered him.

He hesitated. On her warm side, his hand lingered. On her skin. Cream pale, with familiar freckles like gems in white gold.

The whole while he tended to her, he wasn't thinking of her in a way to elicit desire. Her body was only the precious vessel of her life, something to be protected and healed. But her words distracted him powerfully. They reminded him of what else her body could do.

Noting his response, she smirked. Even in pain, her expression lit the cave like fire never could. "Don't pretend to be modest now," she mocked, reveling in repeating his sentiments back to him.

He scowled. Indignation flared hot in him—he would not stand for teasing, not after what she'd done.

Swiftly, like he was pulling out an arrow, he lifted her chemise over her head.

Despite her exposed chest, his eyes didn't dip. He kept them on hers. In firelight, they shone, brown, luminous, brown like—brown gemstones. Did brown gemstones exist? If they did, he could not remember the name of them.

He felt ridiculous, distracting himself, playing poet in an effortful diversion from the naked skin in front of him. He was no poet. Not even when her eyes made him rhapsodize like one.

He needed her dressing done, her wound managed, her chemise returned—her perfect chest no longer inviting his kisses. *Ghosts, no—*

"Thank you," she said casually. "It'll be easier to bandage now."

He ground the words out. "Much easier, yes."

Only if he commenced could he complete the miserable work. He grabbed the bandage and started wrapping her rib cage, covering the wound—which was, wonderfully conveniently, right beneath her bare breasts. She was the one whose open wound stung with spelled healing salve, whose gash his every constriction compressed. Yet why did he feel *he* was the one getting tortured?

Every wrap of the bandages brushed his knuckles under her curves—heaving, he counseled himself harshly, only with every pained inhalation. He was so close to her he could feel her breathing on his neck. She lit his body with fire. With desire. With rage. He did not know where one gave way to the other.

He grew hard in his leggings, infuriating himself further. One shouldn't yearn with insatiable sexual hunger for one's nursing patients. *Certainly* not for one's former lover who shook one's very soul with incurable habits of venturing into danger.

Finally finished, he tied the bandage off on her uninjured side. When he yanked the knot sharply, she sucked in a surprised breath. His tending complete, she pulled her chemise back over her head with effort.

It was not the end of his work here.

"Don't ever," he ordered her, "do that again."

She hesitated. When she replied, he found the confrontation in her voice unconvincing. "I can't promise I'll never get injured," she informed him. "Neither can you."

He shook his head with quiet vehemence.

"Not that," he said. He would indulge no coyness. Indeed, Clare Grandhart had never felt more serious in his whole life. "You endangered yourself. You gave yourself up. You were going to go with the Order."

When he met her gaze, he was surprised to notice her flinch.

"You were going to sacrifice yourself. Again," he went on. "I—I can't . . . You—" The comedown of realizing her wound did not endanger her life, combined with the unrelenting fearsomeness of what she'd done, caught him up short. He composed himself, continuing. "You're not a sacrifice. You're a *person*. Your life is no less precious than those of queens or knights or nobles. You can't throw it away."

His elegance was gone, but he kept going. He had to.

"I didn't say it to you when we first faced the Order, and Ghosts know I've lain awake more nights than I care to count thinking about what would have happened if Galwell hadn't found you out. If you had—succeeded because I never told you . . ." he said. He felt he was carving each word in rock. Headstone or victory monument, he could only hope he knew. "I guess I'm . . . saying it now.

I don't know how to live in a world without you in it, so fucking stay in it. Please."

Embarrassed, he swiftly made to stand. He did not know how desperation reconciled with rough charm. How it fit in a rogue, or a leader. Or a hero.

He stopped when he felt her hand on his arm.

"I didn't know," she said softly.

"Now you do," he replied. His voice remained furious, guarded, covering the fear, the hurt underneath.

She took in his declaration, her eyes turning sad.

"We're heroes, Clare. Or, we're supposed to be," she said. "If it comes down to one of us or Mythria, we have to be ready to make the choice. If it comes down to one of us or the other . . ." Somberness descended over her. "When we defeated van Thorn, we knew any one of us might not come home. My life isn't worth *more* than Galwell's."

He hated the impossibilities she was stating like fact. He rose to his feet. "I can't tell you what to do," he replied, grasping onto the rare certainty he could find in heroism's foreboding fog. "If I could, you never would've married *him*. You would've—"

He halted himself. Desire, he was realizing, waged its own war on his wiser judgment. It unexpectedly had much in common with fear, he found. It pushed him, warped him, possessed him, challenging the edifice of the character he imagined for himself. Fear and desire both were no heroes.

They were rogues. Like him.

"Never mind that," he corrected himself. "What I mean to say is, if it makes a difference to you to know you matter to me . . . well, now you know. You matter to me."

He could hear Vandra and Elowen approaching, voices loud and cheerful. The contrast with the hush in the cave could not have rung out sharper. The long look Beatrice gave him was inscrutable, or perhaps he was just hopeless at reading her.

"It makes a difference," she said. Her voice was so quiet, so vulnerable, it sounded fragile.

Clare nodded, finally feeling the fires of his anger die down. He did not come on this quest to have this conversation, but he felt grateful for the opportunity nonetheless. Incredibly grateful. *Ironically* grateful—for he felt a piece of him that had been wounded for ten years was finally, finally healed.

Interrupting his realization, Vandra sauntered into the cave, holding wine bottles.

"Do you all fancy getting completely drunk?" she asked.

When his eyes met Beatrice's, he knew instantly she shared his reaction. Wine in the midst of questing and confessionals?

For once, an uncomplicated question.

"Absolutely," they replied in unison.

23

Beatrice

I t may not have been pretty!" Vandra proclaimed. "We may not have Sir Hugh. But no one has died, and we know where to journey next."

Over the campfire, she thrust a wine bottle forth in grandiose exhibition.

"Which calls for celebration!" she cried.

Everyone cheered. They sat around the fire, knees hunched to chests on old logs Clare had hauled inside. The gentle flames warmed them, uniting the questing crew in hard-won comfort.

Questing crew? she wondered wanderingly. The phrase was profoundly ugly. *Questing group?* No, worse. *Questing party?*

She drank deeply from the bottle in her hand. The wine was hers, procured from Thessia's royal stores upon her very reasonable explanation of how heroes simply could not quest without wine. Thessia had winked and loaded her horse up on the way out of Queendom.

Vandra had discovered the stash of three wine bottles while watering the horses. Beatrice had not intended to share, but Vandra was right. For perhaps the first evening of the journey since she'd left her lonely hometown, Beatrice felt hopeful.

No, not just hopeful—*grateful*. Vandra, Elowen, and, yes, even Clare had saved her today. Sharing her quest wine was only fair.

Clare gulped his down enthusiastically. With firelight flickering on his features, he looked the way she felt. His eyes shone with renegade light, one part exhaustion, one part happiness. "For three washed-up heroes and one reformed villain with messier histories than the Winter War," he contended while Vandra returned to her seat, "I would say survival itself is victory!"

"Huzzah!" Beatrice found herself cheering with Vandra.

"Huzzah!" Clare echoed.

"Elowen, say *huzzah*," Vandra urged, passing her bottle to Elowen.

Elowen sipped, her cheeks reddening like they always had when she and Beatrice stole drinks from Elowen's parents in their youth. She had commenced the night surly, either due to the events in the crystal caves or ordinary Elowen-iness, until, with the wine, she'd loosened up. "I do not need to say *huzzah* to participate in the sentiment," she said primly.

"Yes you do," Clare replied with the same seriousness. "Come on now."

Passing his bottle to Vandra, he stood, swaying slightly. The wind coming into the cave ruffled his hair. His shirt was unbuttoned. He looked the way he did on the cover of *Mythria Magazine* when he was named Sexiest Man Alive for the third time. Beatrice remembered the year well. The week magazines hit the scribestands, she'd "forgotten" items on errands in the village every day in order to eye the cover without purchasing one for herself.

"*Huzzah!*" he roared into the night.

Everyone clapped. Beatrice was tipsy enough to laugh. Ghosts, it was wonderful. Beatrice was no stranger to feeling drunk, but she'd forgotten how it felt to *laugh*.

"Go on then, Elowen," Clare prompted. "One good huzzah!"

"No," she replied. "The moment has passed."

"It certainly has not!" Beatrice interjected. On every other night she would have worried Elowen would hear judgment or painful pressure in her refutation. On other nights, she might have meant them. Inebriation and hope erased the second-guessing from her mind.

Vandra leaned back on her elbows. Her eyes lingered on Elowen in adoring amusement. When Elowen's gaze caught hers, Elowen's cheeks went their familiar shade of Vandra-induced pink.

It was enough. Elowen relented, standing with wine in hand. She drank deeply. She wiped her mouth. Then for no reason whatsoever, her demeanor shifted entirely, dramatic grandeur consuming her. She looked—she looked rather like Domynia on *Desires of the Night*, full of commanding inspiration.

"*Huzzah!*" she announced into the echoing cavern.

Everyone applauded. Elowen sat, looking uncharacteristically pleased with herself.

Beatrice felt loose, even happy, and not only from the wine. Clare's confession had been . . . nice. Earlier, in the crystal caves, she and Elowen had worked together. She knew they would never be what they once were to each other, but perhaps one day, they could be something. She could settle for *something*.

Sharing laughter with them now was—improbably—lovely. It was funny, how the darkest of seclusions could change into the warmest of refuges with the presence of the right people.

She passed her wine to Clare. Feeling free, she dipped her foot into the slipstream of memory. Where often its currents felt cold and unforgiving, she now found them welcoming. "Remember," she posed, "the night Clare got kidnapped?"

Clare humphed. "*Kidnapped* is a strong word. I prefer to consider it unplanned, involuntary espionage in the Order's carriage."

Elowen—Elowen!—hiccupped a giggle.

Vandra, however, laughed loudly. "You were kidnapped," she confirmed. "I would know." The other women's eyes rounded innocently.

Clare's narrowed. "*Why* would you know?"

Vandra grinned. "I may have tipped them off," she confided with remorseless glee, "and I may have spooked your horse so he ran off and you were right where they needed you to be."

Clare put down his drink. "No." He sounded legitimately scandalized, which was hilarious. "You didn't."

"I'm sorry, Grandhart. Add it to my tab of villainy," Vandra replied.

Shaking his head, Clare gestured in Beatrice's direction. "Prove it," he challenged Vandra. "Let Beatrice take me into your memory of the day."

While Beatrice often resented others invoking her magic without her permission, she found the present proposal wonderful. Clare getting kidnapped? His horse on the run? Vandra snickering out of sight? Everyone in Queendom would want a head-magical glimpse of such a sight. She could probably charge for admission!

It was, however, Vandra who faltered. Her eyes shot to— Elowen. "There are parts of the day I wish to remain . . . private," she explained.

Elowen's cheeks went even pinker, indignation rose-hued with drink's sweet disposition. "Don't say you *seduced* me to distract from Clare's—" She reconsidered midsentence. "Oh, wait, that's exactly what you did."

"A very fun day's work," Vandra conceded.

Elowen softened. "You're forgiven. I remember the afternoon in question." She smiled, her gaze clinging to Vandra. "It was worth it."

"Hey!" Clare protested.

Inspired—okay, disappointed Clare would not insist on replaying proof of his "unplanned, involuntary espionage"—Beatrice reached for Vandra's wine and held it high. "I propose a game!" she cried. Her mind fought the wine to chase the idea sparked by Clare's challenge. "Truth," she said dramatically, "or Dare."

Clare groaned. "We're not children."

"You whine like one," Elowen muttered.

Beatrice refused to listen to the interruptions. Oh, she was loving her devious diversion now. "Truths," she explained excitedly, "will be confirmed with Elowen's magic. She'll feel it if you're defensive. Dares . . ." She paused for emphasis, pleased to find her compatriots—*questriots*? Ugh, no—watched her now with curiosity. "Dares will consist of the revelation of embarrassing or interesting memories using mine."

Clare frowned skeptically. "I'm not sure that's more fun than something like Strip Carousel."

"While I commonly endorse games involving removal of clothing," Vandra replied, "no one has playing cards. Go on," she prompted Beatrice, who was preparing to redouble her case when Elowen spoke up.

"I find it sounds greatly amusing," Elowen declared unhesitatingly.

Beatrice faltered. She'd expected Elowen's resistance on, more or less, principle. The other woman's instant support stopped her silent.

"Why don't you go first, Beatrice?" Elowen went on. "Truth? Or dare?"

Beatrice feared neither, in honesty. What were embarrassing memories or embarrassing revelations to her? How much more embarrassed of herself could she possibly feel?

"Truth," she said, knowing the choice would involve the use

of Elowen's magic, not hers. It was her quiet *thank you* of sorts for Elowen's support. In the crystal caves earlier, and now, in Elowen's unprompted cheering of the Truth or Dare idea itself. It would bring them together, just slightly.

Firelight flickered in the look Elowen gave her former friend. "Who called for divorce? You or Robert de Noughton?"

"I was wrong," Clare commented, leaning in. "This game is indeed delightful."

The question, combined with the quantity of wine she'd consumed, set Beatrice's stomach churning. Supportive or not, Elowen was, as it happened, skillful in the manner of embarrassing Beatrice. She'd forgotten quite *how* skillful. Nevertheless, she counseled herself, *she'd* wanted to play this game. She couldn't be a coward now.

Very well, then.

"Robert," she replied. One word would do, wouldn't it? The game was Truth, not Truth and Feeble Explanation. She drank from her bottle, knowing the only way out was deeper in.

"Oh, Beatrice," Vandra said heavily, not helping matters. "You let yourself be dumped by that bore?"

"It's not like I was in love with him," Beatrice protested. "I was just fine . . . existing," she found herself elaborating. The words managed to make perfect sense and none.

Clare's voice, quiet in the dark, grated next to her.

"Robert de Noughton is the greatest fool in Mythria," he said. "He didn't deserve you."

Not even perfectly sober could Beatrice have responded comprehensibly to the compliment. Unspoken gratitude would need to suffice for the way his words eased the confession's embarrassment from her. She glanced in his direction, finding his faraway gaze on the fire.

The moment passing, she held her wine back to Vandra. "Your choice?"

"Dare, baby," Vandra replied, predictably.

"Very well." Drink did not dull or muddle her magic. Instead, she'd found rather the opposite. The looseness of inebriation made the folds of memory easier to slip into. "Show us," she proposed, "your most humiliating defeat in combat."

Vandra laughed. "I have no humiliating defeats," she replied.

"I sense embarrassment," Elowen sing-songed.

Everyone saw Vandra stiffen. "You've been away from people too long, love," Vandra shot back hastily. "You're getting mixed up."

Beatrice grinned. The poised Vandra, flustered like a child caught shattering their mother's vase during playtime.

"Why don't we let the magic determine the truth?" Beatrice replied sweetly. "Or would you prefer to welcome defeat right now?"

Vandra's hesitation stretched until finally she drank, grimacing with the swallow of wine. "*Fine*," she said. "Let's get this over with."

In delighted victory, Beatrice took her outstretched palm. The four of them joined hands, permitting Beatrice to draw the group into her magic. When the veils of the past unraveled, they were in the mud. Stables were nearby. The focus of the memory, however, was the hulking hroxen in front of them, lumbering on six legs, growling in promise of the destruction it intended to wreak in every direction.

Including Vandra's, where she stood, sword in hand—wearing only her underclothes.

Her fighting stance did not intimidate the enormous hroxen. With one roaring swipe, the beast knocked Vandra flat in the mud. When she hauled herself to her feet, wiping filth from her eyes, the creature was gone, charging off unhindered. Past-Vandra looked dismayed, her underclothes filthy.

The vision ended sharply when Vandra yanked her hand from Beatrice's. "That's certainly enough," she commented.

"You're evading." Elowen narrowed her eyes.

"Why were you half naked?" Clare had the unclouded intuition to ask.

Now Vandra looked down. "The creature surprised me when I was . . . attending to someone. In the stables. Obviously the moment was completely ruined. She did not even leave her address."

Clare laughed, one loud guffaw. "Embarrassing on several fronts, then."

His chiding earned Vandra launching a bottle his way, relying on his instincts to catch the wine without spilling, which he did. He grinned in welcome of the challenge to come.

"You must know I won't go easy on you, Grandhart," Vandra warned.

"Ooh, perhaps we'll finally figure out the *truth* of his magical gift," Elowen speculated.

Clare lifted his chin. "Do your worst," he replied. "Dare."

"Worst performance in the bedroom."

The very idea cooled Beatrice with displeasure. Yet, she consoled herself, the dare was not the most terrible Vandra could have demanded. Indeed, the present premise was probably the one occasion on which Beatrice would not despise the idea of Clare's intimacy with other women.

"Personally, I don't wish to see that," Elowen interjected.

Clare, however, looked unperturbed. He leaned back, visibly cocky. "None exists," he informed them. "I'm always spectacular. Honestly." He held out his palm for Beatrice. "Go look. You'll find nothing."

She hesitated. She did not really want to clasp his hand.

Vandra watched them, her eyes darting from one to the other. She looked unnervingly like she'd managed to win a game with no winners.

"Very well," Vandra said with a much darker sparkle entering her eye. "What about something else?"

In the uneasy quiet, Clare waited, refusing to concede.

"*Best* night of your life," Vandra proposed.

Beatrice caught the way Clare went quiet. His reaction, she found, consumed her. The whole realm vanished right down to the way he—

"Once again," Elowen chimed in, halfway drunk, "I must insist we leave as soon as Clare's butt makes an appearance."

In the next instant—yes, relief flickered with the firelight on his features. He was glad he could grasp onto Elowen's humorous jab instead of—of—what? "How are you certain my butt is involved?" he protested in playful indignation.

Elowen's glance was withering. "Of *course* it's involved."

Clare snorted.

Then his gaze went to Beatrice. The vulnerability in his crystal eyes held everything.

She wondered whether she'd cheated disaster or lost something precious when he rounded to face Vandra. "Let's return to the first one," he requested hastily. "Worst performance."

Vandra slowly shook her head. Oh, the perils of having friends who were wicked.

Beatrice watched Clare, clinging on to his every movement, his every shift, the merest inflection fleeting over his features. She was, she found, at once terrified and desperate to know what night Clare held fondest in memory. With the way his eyes held hers, pleading preemptive mercy, she knew *she* was part of the night in question.

What was it Galwell had said in the scene she replayed in Keralia?
Legends never wait.

She outstretched her hand.

Clare placed his palm in hers. Whatever drink did for the fluidity of her magic, Clare Grandhart's touch did tenfold. The past unwrapped with an ease she'd never felt, like the memory *wanted* her to return there.

Where the conjuration found them was not unlike where the four of them sat. Rough stone walls. The quiet of night. The cave of Clare's memory was hushed except for the soft sounds of sleep.

Except past-Clare wasn't sleeping.

Beatrice's breathing hitched. She knew what night he'd conjured. She'd never revisited the memory herself, yet she required no magic to remember every detail. For Clare's dearest night, she realized in heart-racked wonderment, was one of her own.

Earlier, the Four had escaped cursed fog in the forest they were navigating. The fog embraced them without warning, enshrouding Clare first. Only Galwell's grip had wrenched him free. If the fog had consumed him, he would have died. While Beatrice could only watch in helpless horror, he very nearly did.

When nightfall ushered them into the cave, Beatrice had let down her walls. Her persistent resistance of him, her everything. She positioned her sleeping roll near his, needing to be close to him. To remind herself he wasn't gone.

With Elowen and Galwell and her pride in the cave with them, she couldn't speak, couldn't say what she was feeling. *I was scared today. Don't leave me.*

Instead, she faced him in the darkness and took his hand in hers. While his eyes widened in silent surprise, she held on tight. With the comfort of his closeness, she could permit herself something like slumber.

Her own memory ended there.

Clare's, she found, did not.

While the Beatrice of the past slept, her grip relenting on their entwined fingers, he watched her. He looked . . . The only word she could find to describe his expression was enraptured. While she dreamed, he'd let down his own guard. His cocksure carelessness, his rugged ribaldry.

His eyes wide open, gazing upon her sleeping face, he looked like he was seeing the stars for the first time.

The memory ended there. The four of them emerged from Beatrice's magic, their rowdiness subdued. Not surprisingly, no one quite knew what to say.

She looked to Clare instinctually, and found him watching her. The sparkle of his eyes was not like the memory. Not hostility, either, nor embarrassment. In one of her youth's only years of consistent schooling, she remembered learning how the immeasurable pressure underneath mountains could change metallic ore into glittering gemicyte stones. What improbable gems had the past decade pulverized Clare's regret, his resentment—his passion—into?

He severed their gaze suddenly. Into the stilted silence, it was he who managed to dispel everyone's discomfort. *Clare Grandhart, king of jokers.*

"I think we can agree that was *much* worse than my naked butt," he commented.

The wink he shot Beatrice let her know he was only jesting. It left her impossibly grateful. No matter the rigor of exposing his deepest feelings, he wanted her to know he held their happiest moments dear.

She was touched. "Well," she replied, her heart light, "your naked butt *is* fairly spectacular."

"*Sliiiiiiime*," Elowen said.

Clare tossed his head back and laughed. The others joined in. Magic Beatrice never, ever expected started to work, for she found herself disregarding her effort to find the right name for her group. Questing crew, questriots—it didn't matter.

They were her *friends*.

The game drew on for hours into the night. Everyone unveiled his or her share of revelations. Elowen's first kiss—the daughter of their village's finest weaponeer, when they were fourteen. Vandra's first paid mark—the Duke of West Waverly, who tortured his peasants when they could not pay his tithes.

Drunkenness inspired them. With minutes passing, they found themselves growing less guarded. It was harmless, except when it wasn't. Beatrice noticed it in Elowen first. The hunger pervading the other woman's eyes was one she would never permit in daylight.

It worried Beatrice. It blazed in her so brightly Beatrice knew someone was sure to be hurt.

Like dark magic, upon her noticing, Elowen passed the wine right to Vandra. "Truth for you," she said.

Vandra frowned. "That's not how this works."

Waving her hand, Elowen dismissed the objection. "Have you," she pressed, "ever been in love?"

It was the rare demand to elicit no reaction from the rest of the group. No scandalized cheering. No laughter. Only quiet. When Vandra's eyes tightened, Beatrice suspected she was less drunk than she'd let on.

"Yes," Vandra said.

Elowen looked like she expected the revelation—or perhaps like she knew how she would feel no matter what Vandra said. "With who?"

Vandra's pause opened chasm-like, promising to swallow the four of them. Finally, she set the wine down, the glass clinking disharmoniously on the rocky ground. "I think maybe I'm done playing for the night," she declared. "This game grows dull."

Elowen pouted. "You're no fun," she slurred.

Grimacing, Vandra rose to her feet. "I rather remember being *only* fun," she said bitterly.

Beatrice could hear the double-edged sword of the remark. While she did not know its hidden meaning, Elowen undoubtedly did—she frowned into the fire, saying nothing, letting her paramour leave without following her.

It saddened Beatrice. Elowen was eternally closed off, portcullises down, drawbridges up in her fortress of sorrow. Beatrice wished she could encourage Elowen to simply follow Vandra. To speak to her. To show her feelings. But Elowen's heart magic only went one way, and Elowen had no interest in extending herself the other.

Gazing emptily forward, Elowen finished the wine Vandra had set down. Knowing what doldrums waited in the depths of drink, Beatrice caught the deepening change in Elowen's eyes instantly. She looked—defeated. The dull edge of despondence.

"I have a dare for either of you," she intoned. "Favorite memory of Galwell."

Of course the night would end here, Beatrice thought. Especially now, with Vandra gone, the empty hole in their group opened large.

With her own senses dulled, however, she did not feel the stab of panic the mention of Galwell ordinarily induced in her. Instead, what descended over her like cursed fog was only wistful sadness.

Then Clare held out his hand. "I have one," he said softly.

Beatrice interlaced her fingers with his. He did the same with Elowen. Beatrice's magic coursed into them, the cavern vanishing.

The tavern in which they found themselves was worse for the wear. No fault of the establishment's, Beatrice remembered. Crimes of intimidation had been growing more common. In the vision, the tavern owner was boarding up the windows for security.

Fear was sweeping the land with the widening of the Order's hold—the way they emboldened their followers to strike at everyone who looked different from them, who spoke different, who felt different. The realm was witnessing how easily rich men who loved themselves could change into cheerful cultists who hated everyone else.

In the pub, the Four were getting drunk. Beatrice could not remember what they were celebrating or commiserating—the night was gone from her own memory. She felt inexpressibly grateful drink had not wiped it from Clare's.

Even Galwell, who rarely drank, held a goblet of mead in his hands. Ever perceptive, ever sympathetic, he noticed the mood in the room. While the rest of them imbibed, he hefted himself on weary legs from his seat.

He crossed the tavern, where one of the musicians on his off hour sat with his lute. When the musician nodded in unspoken permission, Galwell carefully lifted the polished instrument. He played familiar chords. Then, in the midst of everyone, he sang.

"*My home is Mythria,*" he started slowly. "*My love is here.*"

Heads rose from goblets. Conversations died in solemnity. Only Galwell's resonant voice filled the room, singing the first lines of the realm's famous reverent hymn.

Until one more voice joined him.

The tavern owner, pausing in his work, hammer in hand, voice wavering.

"My home is Mythria. I hold her dear."

With the first chorus, everyone joined them. Not one person *didn't* know "My Home Is Mythria." Poor singers and melodious, young and old, drunk and keen-eyed—everyone was singing. Everyone was united.

Including them, even Elowen. Beatrice, watching herself, heard Clare next to her—the true Clare, not the memory—join the chorus. Elowen did the same. Finally, her eyes wet, Beatrice sang, harmonizing with the voice of her past self.

They remained in the vision until the song was over. When Clare removed his hand gently from Beatrice's, the magic ended.

Except it didn't, not exactly. She found herself wrestling with shadows, struggling with the strange sensation that the vision they'd just left was what was real, while the cave in which she found herself was the conjuration. The nightmare, haunted by the echo of the voice they would only ever hear in memory.

"It should've been me," Beatrice heard herself say.

No one spoke until Clare, paused in the effort of reemerging from her magic, looked to her. "What?"

She knew what the wistful sadness was now. It was clarity. The cold zeal of the conviction she hid even from herself. She spoke it plainly now.

"I should have died instead of him," she said. "He was . . . the hero. The inspiration. The everything. I'm just . . . me. But the truth is, I'm glad to be alive, and I hate myself fiercely for it."

Clare watched her, his expression like stone.

It was Elowen, however, who spoke. "Don't," she said.

Her voice was firm. Beatrice was not certain she'd heard right until Elowen went on, removing her doubts.

"I'm glad you're alive," she said. "Even though I'll miss my brother every second for the rest of my life, I wouldn't ever wish you to trade places."

Elowen rose. Their game was over.

Touched beyond words, Beatrice sat in front of the warmth of the fire long into the night.

24

Clare

When he was younger, Clare Grandhart invented Hang-over Corn-Toast. Never did his recipe find widespread endorsement—not unless one counted various well-fed groups of wayward men in the eastern reaches of the Vast Plains where he grew up. Indeed, never was he credited for the culinary master-work.

Yet invent them he had.

One started with ordinary corncakes, obviously. However, he would then fry them together with runny dawnjay egg yolks, where they would combine in the pan with the porous cornbread into his fluffy yet filling delicacy.

Stumbling back to the cave from where he'd relieved himself in the morning light, he remembered Hangover Corn-Toast fondly. In his youth, Clare could have drunk twice what he did last night, fortified himself with one plateful of his marvelous food, and considered himself ready to stake out competing mercenaries on the Vast Plains' hottest reaches for hours without retching once.

Everything felt possible back then, drink-related or otherwise. He could fall in love so easily. He could get his heart ground underfoot, then move on to the next lover the next fortnight, hav-ing washed his sorrows into drunken oblivion.

Now, however—

Ugh.

Clare Grandhart was feeling too old for lots of things lately. Loving—not just romantically—was harder when you knew its painful costs. Fame and fortune were starting to feel like place-holders instead of prizes. Heroism was proving fucking impossible. Drinking?

Well, it made heroism look easy.

Clare had woken fortunately without vomiting, but with the powerful need to urinate. Sunlight pervaded the foliage cover, leaving his head splitting. He was certain no quantity of Hangover Corn-Toast could save him from how he felt now.

His only consolation was knowing he was not unique in his discomfort—he'd heard several instances of Elowen retching during the night. Of course *Beatrice* held her wine comfortably and slept in peace.

Outside the cave, Clare found Vandra the only one up, packing her tent onto her horse. She looked sullen, her eyes dark-ringed, not glancing his way when she passed him.

While he had no capacity to offer comfort in his present state, it dispirited him. Discouraging Vandra was not easy—whatever was going on with her and Elowen had evidently wounded her deeply—and Clare sympathized.

He sometimes privately felt he understood Vandra in ways the others did not. No one was *always* cheerful. High spirits could mask low moods. He knew sadness was hard, of course. He just knew happiness was sometimes harder, for no one expected you ever to hurt.

He sat outside the cave entrance near his horse, wincing in the freckled sun, with absolutely every muscle in him focused on holding himself upright.

Food. He grasped desperately onto the notion. If he could not have his Hangover Corn-Toast, perhaps protein from their conservative rations would help. Stomach rolling, he reached into his horse's pack for his ration of jerky.

Right when he was lifting the jerky to his lips—

He was attacked, a horrible screeching sound splitting the sky and his skull. He cried out loud, enveloped in a clash of claws and a flurry of feathers. "Please," he heard Elowen call miserably from the cave, "if you're being murdered, Clare, kindly scream more quietly."

"It's not me," he managed to reply, wrestling with the furious wings. "It's—"

He constrained his attacker into compliance.

"Wiglaf!" he exclaimed.

For on his forearm, jealously eyeing the jerky—and looking invigorated from his attack—sat Clare's pet eagle.

Delight filled Clare. No headache, even the considerable one he had now, could overcome the joy of Wiglaf's surprise visit. He respected his eagle's independence and knew of Wiglaf's preference for occupying himself with winged pursuits from week to week. Nonetheless, while Clare did *not* feel homesick for his Farmount terrace's comforts, he had missed his feathered friend.

"Hi, buddy," he enthused. "How you doing? Oh, look how long your talons have gotten!"

He often felt the eagle could understand him perfectly, every word. Reinforcing his conviction, Wiglaf chirped in what was obviously gratitude.

"No, no, no," Clare replied gently. "You've got to file those down before you perch on Dad. I'm sorry." He lowered Wiglaf, who reluctantly hopped onto the rocky ground. "You're very handsome, though," Clare went on. "Who is the prettiest eagle there ever was?"

Wiglaf lifted his beak, his invitation for "chin rubbies."

Of course, Clare obliged.

Wiglaf produced the soft cooing in the back of his throat that Clare knew were groans of ecstasy. They were Clare's very favorite sound.

"Yes, that's the spot, hmm?" He scratched vigorously, feeling the contours of Wiglaf's perfect fluffy chin.

They were engaged in the same when Elowen and Beatrice emerged from the cave, blinking in confusion. While Elowen looked unenthusiastic to meet the morning, Beatrice's expression transformed. She burst out laughing, her smile catching the bright sunlight.

"Well, this is adorable," she commented. "May I meet him?"

"Of course," he greeted her. "He loves new friends."

His headache disappeared. He suddenly felt twenty years old. Invincible, joyful, hopeful. Falling in love was easy, and Clare Grandhart felt strong enough to challenge an entire mercenary camp single-handed.

*　*　*

They rode for the Straits of Baldon under the unrelenting sun.

The landscape changed. The forest ceded to the dusty stone of the east. Eventually, they found one of Mythria's endless everypurpose roads, wide enough for lanes of wagons carrying commerce or families or entertainers or whatnot. In recent days, Clare speculated, they would've run hectic with Festival of the Four-goers. Now, though, word that Queendom was in mourning must have spread fast. The road was deserted.

The ground flattened, the rocks disappearing onto open flatlands. On they journeyed, waiting for the first glimpse of the watery straits past coastal cliffs.

Wiglaf's presence improved everyone's spirits, even Vandra's. The eagle flew with them half the day, then grew bored, setting off on his own feathery quest—though not before Beatrice had surrendered half of her jerky over to his eager beak.

Watching her stroke his head, Clare found himself imagining the future overmuch.

He could not help himself. Was he fundamentally hopeful in nature? He feared he was. Yet when he watched Beatrice, effortlessly caring for the little creature who shared his home, it was like . . . It was silly, he chastened himself.

It didn't work. Watching her, it was like he could hear strains of romantic songs playing over his own personal conjuration of imagined memories.

It would never come to pass, he reminded himself. Not long from now, he would part from Beatrice and Elowen once more. Nevertheless, he clung on to the possibility that their relationships perhaps did not need to remain . . . like they were. Perhaps he could invite them to his home for—dinner parties, or concerts, or whatever they preferred. Or he could plead with Thessia to send them on more quests! He'd quest wherever she wanted if he could do it with his friends.

He just knew he was not ready to say goodbye to them yet.

Every mile their horses walked carried them closer to where Hugh was held hostage—to the inevitable end of their journey. Whether they ended the quest as heroes or failures, they would need to return home.

"Hold," Vandra uttered.

The word pulled Clare out of his wandering malaise. He followed her gaze out to where—a lone man was walking down the road in their direction.

His clothing was ragged. His head was hung low in exhaustion.

His gait was weary, until he looked up. When he saw their questing party, he started running right for them.

"Ambush?" Vandra queried, reaching for her weapons.

Clare raised his hand. "No—" He peered forward, scrutinizing the running man.

It was impossible. Or, no, merely very unlikely. Yet with every step closer the stranger made, Clare's certainty grew.

He hopped off his horse.

"Hugh!"

The man who reached them with huffing paces was, indeed, the future king of Mythria. The object of their quest. Clare's friend, furthermore. Clare studied him, looking for—magical interference? He didn't know. Sir Hugh Mavaris looked exactly, wonderfully *right*. Bronze skin and thick black swooping hair. Crooked nose, straight mouth. World-ready roughness encasing the gem of kinghood.

While he was filthy and his normally perfectly trimmed beard had grown out, he looked, incredibly, uninjured. Clare welcomed him, and they clasped forearms.

"You're alive," Clare marveled. "You're—you're rather okay, it appears."

Hugh ignored him in desperation. "What's the date? Have I missed my wedding?" he asked with urgent horror.

Clare laughed, pleased to deliver happy news. "It's in three days. Fear not, my good man."

It left Hugh literally weeping with relief. His friend really was exhausted, Clare noted. They would need to help him rest on the return to Queendom.

The return to Queendom. Clare's mind shifted to what the fortunate happenstance meant. They'd . . . finished their quest. Were they heroes?

Or were they just . . . done?

While he was very happy Sir Hugh was safe, Clare decided he could not ignore the disappointment he felt. The quest hadn't offered him the chance to prove to himself he could live up to Galwell's legacy. To prove he was, when needed, the hero he pretended.

What was he left with instead? Cheap victory and the road home. He would return to Farmount and his daily existential shadows.

"How did you escape?" Vandra asked Hugh.

Clare felt instantly embarrassed. The question was imperative. Was Hugh pursued? Was the Order near? *He* should've covered the important details. Galwell would've. Instead, he'd lost himself fretting over how unfortunate his comfortable, famous life was.

"I didn't," Hugh replied. "They let me go."

The hollowness in his voice was haunting. It left everyone concerned.

"Why?" Beatrice pressed. "You didn't give up the location of the sword, did you?"

Hugh's face fell.

"I didn't need to." He spoke with grave hesitation. "Myke Lycroft, he . . . he had this dagger. Coated in dried blood. While he held the weapon, he explained, he himself could use the magical gift of whoever's blood was on its blade. Holding the dagger, he . . . went into my memories. He saw the sword's final location for himself."

Horror descended over them. *He went into my memories*, Hugh said.

In Clare's hurtling thoughts, the past days rewrote themselves. They did not *escape* the Order in the crystal caves. The Order got everything they needed. Myke Lycroft did not need Beatrice. He just needed Beatrice's *magic*.

Myke, forger of the Sword of Souls, was a magical weaponeer whose hand magic could create weapons with enchanted properties.

He'd had one on him yesterday. One he slashed Beatrice with, allowing him to use her magic.

They'd journeyed out to where Hugh was held, imagining they had the Order on their heels. Instead, the whole while, Lycroft had exactly what he wanted. They'd played into his hands perfectly.

They'd failed.

Except we didn't, did we? Clare remembered. Their quest was the retrieval of the queen's fiancé, who was with them now, protected, entirely safe. They may have failed in the quest they should be on, but they'd succeeded in the quest they'd set out on. They could go home.

Which they would, he knew in his stomach with queasy dread. It was hard enough getting the four of them to venture out to rescue Hugh. When it came to defending the whole realm? He would need to content himself with—with victory, he supposed.

He heard himself speak up. "We have Sir Hugh," he said. His voice was low, bent under the weight of Mythria. "We could take him home to Thessia. It's what each of you signed on for. I know I cannot expect more—"

Elowen ignored him.

"Where is the sword, Hugh?" she demanded.

"Can we retrieve it before the Order?" Vandra joined in.

Clare felt a lump grow in his throat, deeply moved. It was, he promised himself, the last time he would ever underestimate the nobility of Elowen True or Vandra Ravenfall.

Hugh shook his head. "They've already obtained the sword. Worse, they . . ."

He gazed out over the desert landscape. When he continued,

the calm in his voice sounded practiced from his soldiering youth, learned on fields of carnage.

"They massacred the closest village. The Sword of Souls was dead. It needed sacrifices," he intoned. "Now, it's powerful once more."

The stomach-churning horror of the Order's work was nearly incomprehensible. Sacrifices? The entire village? "It's done, then? They've raised Todrick?" Clare asked shakily, forcing the words.

"No . . . not yet. Soon." Hugh hesitated like he could read danger in their eyes. "I know where they plan to bring Todrick van Thorn back to life."

The group's gazes went to . . . Beatrice, the only member of their party who hadn't spoken up. Who was injured, Clare reminded himself. No matter his gratitude for Elowen's and Vandra's vengeful zeal, he would not begrudge her the right to end her own quest here.

In the moment she stepped forward, Clare knew her decision instantly. She'd never looked hotter, he found. Like their fucking conquering general, commanding the field.

"Tell us where," she said. "We will stop them."

25

Elowen

"Bit of a bummer, isn't it? The bad guys tossing me off the moment they figured out how to get their realm-changing weapon. Makes a man question his own worth," Hugh said.

Elowen didn't want to laugh. But Hugh's fullhearted grin—and the bravery of asking such a question while the five of them were quite literally trudging through sinking sand—worked in his favor.

"I'll say," Elowen responded.

If Hugh had been smiling widely before, his whole face broke open then, bright as the moon at its fullest. Elowen had expected him to be dull—or worse, egotistical—but she found he was neither. He had a humbleness about him that surprised her. More than once he'd had to ask for help getting out of the sinksand, and he always said a gracious thank-you when Clare, or Vandra, or even Elowen, came to wiggle his leg so that he could pick up his foot and step forward.

It pleased her very little to admit that she liked Hugh. The joke he'd made at his own expense had lightened the tense mood. Realizing its effectiveness, he kept up the bit as they trekked toward the place where he swore the Order was headed.

"Death by sinksand would be a most embarrassing way for me to go," he said. "Especially since I'm the one who said we should travel this way. I see now why the Wagons-For-You drivers never use this route, though it's technically faster."

"When are *you* ever using Wagons-For-You?" Beatrice asked him, not hiding her shock.

"You'd be surprised," he said. "Whenever Thessia and I desire a quiet night out, Wagons-For-You drivers have been far more discreet than our royal ones."

Quite frankly, Hugh was their missing puzzle piece. In a literal sense, of course, but also, on an emotional level, the group needed his presence. Without him, the sinksand of their own relationship drama threatened to pull them under. Having an outsider around allowed all of them to focus on him instead of each other. Hugh didn't complain, not even when the sand opened into a vast expanse of punishing dunes, dry heat blazing down on them. He withstood everyone's questions with impressive ease, keeping the conversation light by always finding ways to make himself the butt of the joke.

Thanks to Hugh, the journey flew by so quickly that Elowen did not notice the shift in landscape until they'd arrived.

Vermillion Vale glimmered in the near distance, a glitzy, sparkling stretch of attractions and accommodations. Whether it was a skyscraping obelisk meant to evoke the Pillars of Askavere, or a shimmering fountain as large as the Waterfalls of Crestrose, Mythria's most impressive history had been replicated to stunning effect in Vermillion Vale, each building crafted with one goal in mind—entertainment. Mythrians came to this city to see the realm's past in the most carefree light, so far removed from the original context that it was easy to keep the drinks flowing and the fun never-ending.

Fun. There was that complicated word again, burdening Elowen anew. It was fitting to be in the realm's premiere fun location with her fun questmates. But what did fun have to do with the bleak task at hand?

"This is where the Order plans to resurrect Todrick," Hugh explained. "They want to gamble in the city's largest inn first."

"Of course they do," Elowen sneered.

She peered down at her clothes. Her cloak was covered in dirt and sand, and her hands had a thin layer of grime on them. She looked as she felt, worn down. When she glanced over at her four travelmates, they seemed the same. They'd all been through it.

"We do not give off the appearance of people who are ready for a raucous day of gambling ourselves," Elowen noted. When no one responded, she couldn't help but remind them of the obvious. "Plus, while we are all recognizable, Hugh is the most famous person in Mythria right now."

At the use of his name, Hugh put a firm hand on her shoulder. "Fear not," he said. "We are far from the weariest-looking bunch to stumble down the pathways of the Vale. But you make a good point about my fame. Luckily, I've learned things from my time with the queen. There are many ways to hide in plain sight."

"'Tis true," Clare confirmed.

Elowen could not tell if Clare was jealous of Hugh or admired him. Clare tended to be the most famous person in any room, what with his decade-long commitment to upholding his public image. But Hugh's fame was *royal*. When he started dating Thessia, the gossip pamphlets became obsessed with dissecting every morsel of knowledge they had on him. And they really were morsels. Hugh was a bit of an enigma to the public, which only heightened the intrigue. They knew he'd grown up in Paramar Bay, and as a young boy he'd survived a usually fatal sledgeling bite while playing hide-and-seek with his brothers. But no one in his family was willing to talk to the scribes and provide any more information on his personal life or how it was that he'd ended up a Mythrian foot soldier in the first place.

Clare procured a horseball cap from his bag, then tugged it over Hugh's dark mop of hair. "There," he said. "He is disguised."

Elowen arched an eyebrow. Hugh looked exactly the same, only now he had a ridiculous ballcap on his head.

"Thank you, my friend. I am," Hugh assured them. As he scanned the group, Elowen sensed a melancholy feeling from him. It reminded her of a child longing for their parent. Or perhaps when someone realized they'd eaten the last bite of a meal before mentally preparing to be done with it.

"What is it?" she asked.

Hugh cocked his head in confusion.

"Forgive me if this is untoward. I just sense some sadness from you," Elowen explained.

Hugh brightened at this notice. "My own bachelor party was unfortunately cut short by my kidnapping. We were supposed to celebrate here in the Vale." He scanned the group again. "Would you all mind if I thought of this as my bachelor party?"

Elowen stifled another laugh. Hugh's bachelor party was composed of a grumpy recluse, her dangerously charming former assassin questmate with benefits, her struggling divorcée ex–best friend, and Clare Grandhart.

Seeing the humor for himself, Hugh smiled again. "It's a bit untraditional, but since you all traveled far and wide to save me, I'd be honored to have you among my party."

"Of course," Clare replied with his signature enthusiasm.

"Delightful," said Vandra. "I'm in."

"Sure," confirmed Beatrice.

Elowen was the last to respond. "We'd love to," she told Hugh.

He threw his arms around his nearest questmates, which happened to be Elowen and Clare. "Incredible! Let us indulge in some well-intentioned debauchery before I commit to a wonderful life with my true love." He dropped his voice to a whisper, though no one besides Elowen and Clare was close enough to hear it. "Also known as finding out exactly where the Fraternal Order plans to resurrect their evil leader."

He gained the laugh he hoped for. He'd certainly earned it.

Hugh led them to Vermillion Vale's most expansive inn. It was built out of a white quartz that made the building shine brightly under the sunlight, though inside, there were no windows at all. Day was indistinguishable from night, which seemed to be the point, for it was not long past noon, and every gambling table was occupied, with patrons nursing bottomless drinks. There were people dressed in bright colors, people dressed in very little, and even people dressed up as famous people. Anything was possible in Vermillion Vale. The hustle and bustle was so overwhelming that Elowen almost missed it at first because of all the feelings she accounted for with her heart magic. It was only when Beatrice gasped that she noticed.

There were Clares.

Everywhere.

Someone was dressed as Clare on the very day that Todrick was slain. Another was Clare from any of his six Sexiest Man Alive cover shoots. There was Clare's ridiculous shadow play cameo character, when Clare must have believed that a goatee suited him.

Every time Elowen blinked, three more people dressed as Clare would spawn. Two of them—Spark's Sport Potions Clare, and a Clare that had somehow merged with his eagle, Wiglaf—were sparring with foam swords, yelling "Good form, sir!" at each other over and over.

Among the sea of Clare impostors, the real one's face paled. If it was possible, he did not look himself, despite a hundred different echoes of his existence filling every corner of the inn. "It appears as though we've stumbled upon the annual Clare Convention," he said, self-consciously wiping sand off his tunic.

"Annual Clare Convention?" Elowen repeated, hoping that saying it again would somehow make the situation less absurd.

"It's usually later in the year. With the ten-year-anniversary of the Four and all, it seems the Clares moved it up," Clare said sheepishly.

"That makes sense," Hugh told him.

Wiglaf Clare paused his jesting to examine the real Clare. Elowen's stomach dropped, thinking them exposed. The longer Wiglaf Clare looked, the clearer it became that he did not comprehend what he was seeing.

"He's trying to figure out which Clare you are," Elowen muttered in amazement.

"How about the real one," Beatrice deadpanned.

"This is good," Vandra said. "They will assume all of you are impersonating the Four to pay homage to Grandhart. And that I'm doing a jaw-dropping impression of the cunning new woman from the latest quest."

It was true. By being themselves, they were somehow not themselves at all. And Hugh was in a ballcap, so apparently they were all effectively disguised.

"The downside is, it will be difficult to distinguish Order members from Clares," Beatrice noted.

"No Grandhart worth his salt would ever join the Fraternal Order," Clare protested.

"If there are duds among the apparent diamonds, we have to spread out to find them," Elowen said, sensing an opportunity to handle some of her personal matters while also attending to the realm-saving ones. "Why don't Vandra and I search the card tables and see if we can scrounge up any information? Then someone else can roam the pools, and others the tavern?"

Elowen did not wait for a response. It wasn't often that she found herself giving orders in the first place, and she correctly assumed the event was exceptional enough that everyone would comply without protest.

Elowen walked ahead of Vandra, combing through Clares for the seediest-looking men she could find, figuring they were the most likely to be Order members. It wasn't a perfect plan, but it seemed the most logical way to find evil among Grandharts.

Plus, Elowen wanted Vandra to see her as a woman who took initiative without hesitation. A competent person who didn't fear every miserable, daunting unknown ahead.

She stopped near a stackjack table where four of the most composed men she had ever seen had gathered to play. All of them had blond hair and aventurine-colored eyes, and they wore matching sandy tunics. If they were not Order members, they had surely started a cult of some kind. They'd have made decent Clares, actually, if they weren't so committed to the ominous poise they'd cultivated.

"Let's listen to them," Elowen said, lingering nearby. "They look the part."

"Why not join them?" Vandra asked in return. "We can get better intel that way."

Elowen flushed. "I don't know how to play stackjack."

"No one knows how to play stackjack." Vandra headed for the table, forcing Elowen to follow. "Care if I jump in?" she asked the men.

They startled at her presence. She had all of the command Elowen lacked, and the fearlessness, too.

"We've got room for two more," the stackjack dealer confirmed, pushing stacks of colored chips toward Elowen and Vandra.

"All you have to do is stack," Vandra told her.

"And jack, I presume?" Elowen bit back, already tortured. She hated this confusing game and the way that she could never seem to make herself enough. No matter how she tried to change, her emotions always pulled her back down. She didn't know how to play, but she knew she'd lost before she'd even begun.

"What brings you all to town?" Vandra asked cheerfully, ignoring Elowen. The four men stared, no one answering. Vandra stared back, smiling at each of them while making such meaningful eye contact that one by one, the men looked down, intimidated. It was skillful, the way she asserted dominance without uttering another word.

"We are constituents of the Collective of the Resurrected Ghosts," one finally muttered.

Ah. They had not found Order members at all. They'd somehow stumbled upon monks. *Gambling* monks.

Elowen, like most Mythrians, saw the Ghosts as what they were, dead heroes from their past, forever honored for how they'd brought Mythria to life. These men saw them as something much grander. They really believed the Ghosts walked again, reborn to save Mythria once more. Where the Ghosts were, none of them could say . . .

Sighing, Elowen got up to leave, but Vandra tugged her back to the table. "You wanted to ask me something, didn't you?"

Elowen fumbled for words.

"That's why you broke us off, yes?" Vandra continued,

whispering into Elowen's ear, "These men are too focused on Ghostliness to care about our personal drama, and I'd like to play a round of stackjack. We can sit here and freely discuss whatever is on your mind."

Vandra had figured out Elowen's entire game plan. It was utterly stressful, being seen. Worse, because Elowen had no money, Vandra had to pay for both of them to play. Vandra put forward a handsome amount of farthings, and Elowen gulped, knowing already that she'd drain every last bit of it.

"You know what they say, you have to bet big to win big," Vandra told the monks, winking.

And so they began their game of stackjack, which did indeed involve stacking, yet was also somehow about counting? Elowen could not bring herself to understand. "I thought you didn't like to play games," she dared to say, balancing a red chip atop two blue ones.

"Fourteen," the stackjack dealer announced. Whatever that meant.

"I never said anything of the sort," Vandra rebutted. She put four yellow chips beside Elowen's red. "Truth or Dare got boring, so I stopped participating. This one has clear stakes, which I enjoy."

"Seven," said the dealer.

The monks strategized their turns as Elowen glared at Vandra. "You avoided answering my question, then," Elowen said. "That wasn't you being bored. That was you being evasive."

"And what did I have to gain by being honest?" Vandra asked.

One of the monks put down a single blue chip.

"Twelve and three," the dealer called out.

"You know exactly what there is to gain," Elowen said, the heat in her cheeks spreading to her neck. She needed to say more, but she couldn't bring herself to offer it up.

Frankly, she was terrified. She was also difficult. And she had yet to make the right move at the right time. She'd crossed the line when playing Truth or Dare, overwhelmed by the depth of her own feelings, especially because Vandra always moved through the realm with such ease. Nothing ever seemed to overwhelm her. An entire cave had collapsed with her trapped inside it and she'd somehow gotten out unscathed. During the game, Elowen had hoped to find Vandra's weak spot. Love, it seemed, was everyone's weak spot. And that was the wrong instinct for Elowen to have. Why did she want to make things harder? A woman like Vandra would only ever be dragged down by loving Elowen.

In the time it took for Vandra to craft her response, the three other monks played their hands. Vandra was so unflappable. It unnerved Elowen to no end, which then bothered Elowen that she could not remain cool in response. Feeling Vandra's emotions would never be enough. She wanted to crawl inside her brain and understand how Vandra always kept her composure.

"I like games where I understand the outcomes," Vandra said. "With stackjack, we can either win or we can lose. There are no other choices. There is no consolation prize or secondary loss. Whatever you put in is what you give up. Nothing more, nothing less."

At that moment, Elowen shoved forward all the red chips she had, placing them on the single blue chip the monk had put down earlier.

"Two," the dealer said, perplexingly.

"When we played Truth or Dare, it seemed to be a chance for all of us to laugh together, which I welcomed after the hell we'd been through," Vandra continued. "Everything had become so dreadfully serious. But *you* changed the rules. You made it about something personal. I didn't know what you wanted from that moment, because you were the one who told me that we were questmates with benefits. What you were asking me went far beyond something as casual as two people who romp together for *fun*, so I decided not to play anymore, because I no longer knew exactly what I was risking." She paused, leaning closer. "So tell me, Elowen, what am I risking?"

"I don't know," Elowen fumbled out defensively, hating herself even more. She should have stayed quiet, giving herself a moment to think. But she turned feral when she was scared. She lashed out. And truly, if Elowen could not even do something as simple as admit the depth of her feelings, how could she ever do something as complex as love Vandra in the way she deserved?

Vandra sighed, then waved her hand at the dealer. "All aboard," she said.

The four monks, plus the dealer, held their breath. Elowen sensed great anticipation.

Vandra gathered up all her chips, then stacked them one by one atop Elowen's last play. With every new chip added to the pile, the suspense grew. Whatever Vandra was doing, it was gutsy.

Before she placed the last chip, she looked at Elowen. "Bet big to win big," she said. She put the red chip atop the tower, and the whole thing fell, eliciting a loud gasp from the table.

"Thirty," the dealer declared.

Elowen assumed Vandra had somehow become victorious. But the dealer pushed the coins toward Elowen instead.

Vandra stood up. "Congratulations," she whispered. "You've won again."

At that, Vandra walked away, leaving Elowen and her mountain of coins at the stackjack table with four disgruntled monks and a thousand words left unsaid.

26

Beatrice

There were simply . . . too many Clares.

Indeed, *one* Clare was very nearly too many, in Beatrice's consideration. Yet she now found herself overwhelmed by Clares of every manner in every corner of Vermillion Vale. Of *course* his legend earned him his own convention.

The real Clare was, of course, delighted. Once the surprise of the development wore off, he settled into pointing out every version of himself like they were visiting the exotic creatures of the Beastuarium.

"Oh, there's me from the masquerade we had to go to!" he cheered. "How clever. Ghosts, next to him is my deluxe-edition Hero Card outfit. Not the ordinary portrait for common collectors. The deluxe," he explained.

She'd had enough.

Beatrice halted them in the center of the casino floor, rounding on the infuriatingly real Clare. "You do realize we're here looking for Order members," she snapped. "Not . . . Clares."

He was unmoved.

"I'm capable of both, thank you very much," he informed her.

She was formulating some jab on the theme of him overestimating his capabilities—it was going to be quite savage, in fact—when the future king interjected enthusiastically. "Oh, you must note this one," Sir Hugh commented, pointing. "It's you when you escaped the Grimauld Mines."

"Where?" Clare whirled.

Beatrice frowned, robbing the boys of their fun. "You're a bad influence on him," she informed Hugh.

Hugh hung his head in good-natured contrition. "Very sorry, Lady Beatrice," he replied.

She did not correct him on the *lady* part, wishing not to remind everyone once more of her divorce.

Indeed, she could not withstand more reminders herself. She knew she was being short with her companions because Vermillion Vale left her ill-tempered. The reason was not simply the countless walking imitations of her vain ex.

No, it was because she had honeymooned here with Robert de Noughton.

The casino floor itself—where opulence became oppressive, where every surface shined with gold inlaid in obsidian like some monument or mausoleum—reminded her of the cowed, wounded woman who went wherever Robert wanted because she was too full of self-loathing to imagine living the life *she* wanted. Guilt for surviving Galwell, guilt for being *happy* she survived him, had made her feel like she deserved punishment.

So she'd punished herself. She'd indulged in deprivation. Life with Robert, starting here, was the perfect prison.

Not this time, she told herself. Her life wasn't the same anymore.

She noticed Clare spontaneously join a group posing for a portrait conjurist, grinning like one of the many impersonators and not the real hero himself.

She could not help smiling. His joy was contagious.

Watching him, she could not deny how on this quest, she'd

started to . . . want things again. Quietly, she knew she could not return to the life she was only pretending to live.

He caught her eyes on him. *Oh, of course he did, damn him.* Was his magical gift knowing whenever he charmed someone? It would suit.

Refusing to let her gaze skitter, she held his. She was not rewarded when cocky smugness settled over his features. With the conjurist's image finished, he strode over to her.

"Hello," he said.

She was indeed starting to *want* things once more. With his half-grin luminescing like the enchanted candles flanking the entrance, she felt pulled to him.

No—she *always* felt pulled to him. Now it was more. Now it was dangerous inevitability. The knowledge of what would happen *when* his inimitable Clare-ness pulled her in. She found her body turning toward him, reminding them both where they once fit together.

"Hi," she replied.

Deftly he pulled a drink from the tray of a drinkmaid passing them. He handed the goblet, effervescing with lavender foam, to Beatrice.

"Are you a time-walker?" he said with his customary combination of joking and not. "Because I see you in my future."

She laughed, remembering the very first words Clare Grandhart ever said to her. The laughter brought unexpected nostalgia. No-longer-Lady Beatrice had more experience dragon-jousting than with feeling nostalgia. Yet Clare's jesting invocation of their first night reminded her of how the fabric of her past was not sewn entirely in sadness. Heroism and sacrifice were not the start and end of their story. There was *humor*. There was lust. There was joy.

Perhaps, she considered, such reminders were why she found herself remembering how to want. Perhaps he was helping her remember *what* to want.

Nevertheless, she refused to reveal her fondness for his reprise. "It really is a terrible line," she chided him.

He raised an eyebrow. "I remember it working out pretty well for me once."

"Only *pretty* well?" she returned.

Was she flirting with him? She was. His eyes widened in delighted surprise. He leaned even closer, close enough to whisper in her ear.

"Beyond my wildest dreams," he murmured.

She shivered, not needing her magic to remember the night he described. The feeling of his mouth on hers, his fingers pressing her over the edge . . .

"Friends! Dear friends, look!"

It was Hugh. He pointed, directing their reluctant gazes to one Clare impersonator dressed in floral-patterned pantaloons.

"It is Clare when the Castle Corpus raid called for him to pretend to be one of the Lord's Jesters!" Hugh described with enthusiasm.

Clare closed his eyes, the reminder of his pantaloons at this particular instant paining him.

With the moment interrupted, Beatrice remembered herself. How could she imagine herself pulled to him? How could she credit Sir Clare Grandhart with perilous inevitability? He was no witch of Megophar, capable of warping the heart with honeyed potions. While her past with him did hold lust and joy, she needed only remind herself they were not the greater parts.

She *needed* to remind herself. If she didn't . . . well, she knew exactly where things would lead.

She stepped back, frustrated. "We should split up," she declared. "Cover more ground in our search."

"Or . . . we could ditch Hugh?" Clare proposed, pretending inspiration had struck him. "Perhaps the Order would take him back."

In no mood—or, desperate to be no longer in the mood—Beatrice frowned. "We hated each other only days ago," she pointed out.

The remark did not have the desired effect. Clare shrugged, his grin insouciant. "Did we?"

His impossible rejoinder silenced her. *Did* they? She was furious with Clare even now, and she knew he was upset with her. Over the past couple of days, he'd eviscerated any doubts on the matter. Yet . . . those feelings somehow loomed scarily small now. Figurines casting long shadows in the wrong light.

She did not enjoy it. She'd given up so much, lost so much. She did not know if she could stand giving up her resentment of Clare Grandhart.

"You search the shops with Hugh," she said decisively. "I'll go to the pools."

His face hardened at her rejection.

"Very well," he replied.

Turning, he headed where she'd directed, grabbing Hugh on the way. The inn's luxury shops waiting to vend everything from Vestryian masks to scarves of the softest magic-woven fabric to cheap sunshifting spectacles shaped like preening soliswans. While Clare's departure was what she intended, she could not help feeling hurt.

She set down her drink, the foam collapsing into lavender nothing. Walking out to the pools, she wondered if they had been doomed from the start. Perhaps she and Clare were destined always to hurt each other, over and over.

Inevitability.

Just not the sort she wanted.

Stepping out into the sweltering heat, she ducked past a shirtless impersonator emulating Clare's muscliest magazine cover. Could she not have one moment without Clares of any kind?

She pressed on, feeling like she had felt on her honeymoon—surprised how one could find oneself miserable in paradise. For the Vermillion Vale pleasure pools *were* paradisiacal. In their uncommon shapes, enchantment kept the water ever perfectly warm. Shimmering magical waterfalls in pink and crystal-blue hues poured into their depths from conjurated rocks.

Beatrice was commencing her reconnaissance when she halted—utterly unprepared for the man whose eyes she caught near the closest pool.

It was not Clare. It was not one of Clare's many, many fans. No, it was the only person she wanted to see less than her ex.

Her *other* ex.

Impossibly, *Robert de Noughton* was poolside in the Vermillion Vale heat. He stood facing Beatrice while a woman rubbed tanning potion on his shoulders. He and Beatrice paused, each obviously as shocked as the other. The other woman went motionless, watching Beatrice, who received the impression of forest prey who wished to remain undetected.

Beatrice understood quickly what was going on here. He'd returned to their honeymoon destination with . . . Beatrice's replacement.

Robert eyed her with embarrassment, perhaps even concern for hurting her feelings. Which was eminently reasonable—yet Beatrice did not feel the hurt she expected. She found her pride unwounded.

"Robert," she said without spite. "I would say I'm surprised to find you here. Except, well. You know."

"Erm," said Robert.

She intended the remark in jest. Robert rather looked like she'd hauled him in front of the Inquisitorial Guild. She softened her voice. "Would you like to introduce me to your . . . ?"

She did not know what word to fill in for the newcomer.

"Betrothed," Robert provided, wincing. "Sorry."

Beatrice shrugged, carelessness coming easily. It was marvelous, she found. "We're past apologies, I'd say," she remarked. "You should live your life. No mourning period needed."

Robert smiled gratefully. She did not resent his happiness, nor did she wish him ill. She had known evil men. While Robert de Noughton was not a great man, he was not an evil man, either. With patience and the wisdom of his mistakes, he might make a decent one.

And her?

She'd never loved Robert. She couldn't have. She needed to heal in order to let anyone into her heart.

She did not know if she had yet. Healing, she understood now, was its own quest, over uncharted ground, with demons of the heart menacing her intrepid steps. She could not know what her destination would resemble or what perils she would encounter on her way.

She knew she had started, however. Which was magical in itself.

No longer would she let the ruination of her marriage with Robert plague her path. If she'd learned anything from the costs of saving the realm, it was how short—how devastatingly fragile—life was. Devoting years to regret and mourning would get you nowhere.

Robert composed himself. With nervousness's retreat, he looked happier. "I wish to introduce you to my betrothed," he said. "The future Lady Marion de Noughton."

The other woman clasped Beatrice's outstretched hand, blushing. "I am *such* a fan," she enthused. "I hope this isn't awkward to say, but you're my hero. I was in university when you saved Mythria, and hearing tales of your bravery inspired me to take on leadership roles of my own in school."

Genuinely touched, Beatrice could not help smiling. "That's very kind. No awkwardness at all," she reassured Marion. "I wish you every happiness."

"Thank you, Lady Beatrice," Marion said.

"It's just Beatrice now," Beatrice replied with instinct she found growing more instant. For the first time, though, it did not feel like an evasion or a rejection or a contradiction. It felt like . . . her. She was Beatrice.

It was enough. At last, it was enough.

What irony, she found herself noting. In the city where she first got used to the name Lady Beatrice de Noughton, she now let its legacy go. What happened in Vermillion Vale, stayed in Vermillion Vale, in the end. New to noblewomanhood, she'd wandered through this same inn, perhaps even the same enchanted pool deck. It was funny how retreading old roads could lead to new destinations.

"What are you doing here in the Vale?" Robert inquired.

"Oh, you know, saving the realm," she replied honestly.

Whether welcoming her candor or presuming she was joking, Robert laughed. He laughed! Not nastily, either! Beatrice commended herself on the healing this no doubt represented. She could laugh with her ex-husband.

"It suits you," he said warmly. "You look well. Like yourself."

Beatrice's smile softened.

"I know," she said.

She started to go. Never one for the cues of concluded conversations, Robert went on cheerfully. "Well, I hope you'll save the realm before tomorrow night. There's this splendid banquet being thrown. Every nobleman in Mythria was invited. It's why we've come."

She stilled. *Every nobleman in Mythria.* "Where?"

Robert puffed up, which she did not mind. If pride induced loquacity, she welcomed his self-congratulation.

"The Night Dragon," he informed her.

Unlike Vermillion Vale's older establishments, the Night Dragon, she'd heard from Elgin's younger residents, was the shiny new gem of the Vale. *Fake* gem, some would say, purchasing renown with gaudy luxury and constant revels.

If one were interested in promoting one's renewed Order—or in having the realm's most powerful people in one room for easy magical mind manipulation—and if one were the vexatious Myke Lycroft, the Night Dragon would lend the perfect flash to one's fete.

"Thank you, Robert," she said. "Thank you *very* much."

She hurried from the conversation, knowing she'd uncovered where the resurrection of Todrick van Thorn would be held.

She'd done it.

Now she just needed to find her friends. Clare, she discovered promptly, made the task very easy. There he was, on the rock waterfall directly in front of her, courting guests. It was very Clare. His idea of espionage was finding the nearest crowd to impress.

Impress them he did, in fine form, orating with one hand on his belt. He'd undone the top ties of the white tunic he rode in wearing. Flush with the thrill of her discovery—not to mention the exhilarating confidence of finally knowing *herself*—she rushed up to him.

His back was to her. When she pulled on his bicep, he turned, smiling in surprised delight.

The sight, Clare with the turquoise of the waterfall surrounding him, was enchanting. His smile made his familiar features wonderfully boyish, his blue eyes brightening in the light.

Certainty of every sort raged in Beatrice.

"I know we said we should split up, but I've changed my mind," she declared.

Then, feeling daring—no, feeling fucking *heroic*—she kissed him.

He paused, stunned. When he kissed her back, it was fiercely. His embrace swept her to his chest. His lips were hungry, passionate, consuming with the fervency of longing. For one perfect moment, it was everything.

Until she noticed Clare . . . did not smell like Clare.

She should have found herself wrapped in the morning mist of the Galibrand Straits, ocean water scented with sunlight.

She wasn't. Instead, the kiss smelled like perfume oils. Pinroses overhung with sweat. Which meant . . .

Oh, Ghosts no.

She withdrew in horror. The Clare impersonator she'd just smooched smiled, oblivious to the misunderstanding. Not only did he share Clare's height and dress, she noticed now the strange immateriality of his features. He possessed, she realized, some manner of hand magic allowing him to manipulate his face to resemble the real Clare's.

She needed to get free from the crowd of people who'd just cheered their kiss. She started to bow, pretending she was just performing, here for the Clare Convention. It was working, guests clapping while she retreated hastily, when—

Her eyes locked with Clare's.

The *real* Clare.

He'd just entered the pool grounds with Hugh. From the confusion warping his features, he'd definitely just watched her kiss someone else—someone she thought was him.

Beatrice wished the hroxen from Vandra's memories could swallow her whole.

Alas, with no hroxen in sight, she settled for running away. She fled through the pool deck, embarrassment overwhelming her. It was ridiculous! Knowing Clare was following her, wanting to make fun, or gloat, or whatever *Clare* reaction he would have, she continued like the Deathrose Guild itself was pursuing her.

Her mind racing like her steps, she knew her only chance was to venture from the path. Except . . . what surrounded the path were luxurious pools.

Very well, then.

Refusing to lose her nerve, she ducked directly into the nearest waterfall she saw. The water was indeed magically warmed. How lovely. Within seconds, she was utterly drenched.

Nevertheless, the measure worked. Past the curtain of water, she watched. No Clare emerged. Finally, feeling unwelcomely like she was undertaking the Castle Corpus raid herself, she concluded she was safe to venture out.

Despite her clothes dripping, she held her head high as she reentered the casino. She needed refuge, some manner of—

Elowen.

No complicated history could vanquish her relief when she noticed the other woman sitting at one of the nearest gaming tables.

Upon glimpsing Beatrice's sopping state, Elowen startled. "Beatrice! Were you attacked?"

"Much worse, I'm afraid," Beatrice replied, sitting heavily on the open seat. She ignored the dealer's look of disapproval. "I have been humiliated."

Elowen evaluated her—no doubt preparing some means to jeer or further rub Beatrice's face in her shame.

Instead, Elowen burst out laughing.

Beatrice glowered. "It is *not* funny."

"It very much is," Elowen confirmed. "What did you do? Oh, don't tell me it has to do with the Clares running around everywhere."

Deception, Beatrice knew, would get her nowhere with Elowen. She settled for sitting silently. Yet even quiet was confession, she realized from the change in Elowen's scrutiny. She'd handed over emotions of dread or regret to Elowen's heart magic, she guessed.

"Oh, Beatrice. What did you *do*?" Elowen repeated.

"*I kissed one!*" Beatrice exclaimed.

Elowen's eyes went uncommonly round. "Did you know—?"

"Of course I didn't," Beatrice replied miserably. "Worse, Clare saw. Our Clare," she clarified. Oddly, sharing her misfortune was easing the jumble in her head somewhat. She faced Elowen, ready for her reaction.

Elowen had ceased laughing. Real sympathy entered her expression. It was like seeing a sunrise, Beatrice found. Not pleasurable, exactly. Yet lovely in its rarity, its profundity, nonetheless.

Elowen stood. "Come," she said. "I can't help with the humiliation, but I can help you to our rooms so you can change out of your very wet clothing."

Without hesitation, she rounded on her heel, leading the way.

Beatrice followed her best friend.

"I'm—I'm sorry," she said. Yes, chasing impulses had gotten her into this disaster. Perhaps, however, it could make something of the catastrophe.

Reaching the lifts where powerful enchantments ferried guests from floor to floor, Elowen glanced over her shoulder. "For what?"

Oh, what a question. Beatrice was sorry for so many things, she did not know where to start. How could she apologize for the death of a brother? She couldn't. She hoped Elowen understood the unspoken sorrows filling the futile silence. "For pulling you from your cards," she managed.

In the long gaze Elowen gave her, Beatrice knew she heard everything unsaid.

Elowen looked up finally, into the lighted shaft where the lifts rose high above them. "I was losing anyway," Elowen informed her. She paused. "It's . . . okay."

Beatrice nearly wept. For everything was *not* okay, she knew. She did not deserve Elowen's forgiveness. The words were false mercy, the uncommonest of graces from Elowen. Yet selfishly, she was happy to pretend for just a while.

The lift lowered to their feet. Beatrice stepped on, standing where she never expected she would again—at Elowen's side.

27

Clare

Without hesitating, Clare punched himself in the face.

He'd stormed up to the impersonator, enraged, not stopping to consider the crowd watching him or the possible consequences of punching someone in the midst of Vermillion Vale's finest luxury inn. Public considerations had never stopped him from punching other men in the past. Why start now?

The impersonator reeled, perhaps expecting stage-fighting instead of the devastating slug to the jaw he received. Clare—the real Clare—found the punch did not ease the pain in his chest. Neither did the distraction of the shock to his knuckles, nor the instant red mark forming on the other man's cheek, unsettling the enchanted symmetry of the impersonator's face.

The other man shook off the shot, stunned, until his eyes fell on Clare himself. Delight sprang onto the impersonator's features. The opportunity to fight in front of the growing crowd, it seemed, was worth the wound.

Perhaps this was what Clare impersonators often did in front of audiences. Clare wouldn't know. With hurt vibrating in his heart, the entire Clare Convention, which until the very past moments had delighted him, felt impossibly misguided.

Who would ever want to be him?

He was consumed. The man in front of him had just kissed Beatrice. Pure rage powered him. Clare crouched into his customary fighting stance, the one depicted in his non-deluxe Hero Card and with which he'd fended off Leonor the Overlord, former horseball guarder and the Order's onetime main enforcer.

The other man did the same.

Clare lashed out, jabbing with his left fist, his preferred opener.

The other man did the same.

Both punches connected. Clare found himself to be the one reeling now. If punching himself in the face offered him no joy, he enjoyed this even less.

He reached instinctually for his usual countermove, using his foot to sweep out the opponent's legs. When the impersonator matched his move exactly, the clash resulted in their feet connecting, sending *both* men crashing to the ground. The crowd cheered with laughter, of course.

"You're very good," the impersonator commented. "You've studied Clare's moves."

"Didn't need to study them," Clare replied.

Past the fog of rage, the complication of the duel was emerging. In every formidable fight, the idiosyncrasies of Clare's enemy shaped his strategy—regional customs, psychological maladies, personality streaks. You could read much about an opponent's life in their fighting style, he'd learned. Where one grew up, whether one wrestled with older siblings or cowered from parents or fought for money or survival or sport. It was poetic, Clare found in his contemplative modes.

In this moment, he found it irritating.

Squaring off with someone impersonating his own moves, he was effectively playing Ogre's Chess against himself. Recognizing what the fight required, Clare was forced to reevaluate. He would have to do everything *opposite* his own instincts, doing what he ordinarily never would.

He would have to go rogue.

The predicament's one gift was his innate knowledge of the not-Clare's next move. He ducked the blow he knew was coming, then struck forth himself, fast and sloppy—the desperate move of inexperienced fighters, impulsivity he grew out of early in his hardscrabble youth. It worked, sort of. He connected with the impersonator's cheek, nearly breaking his own thumb because his fist was not closed properly.

The sting did not stop him. What *did* stop him was the not-Clare's boot bludgeoning into his gut. The blow knocked the wind out of him, sending him crashing to his hands and knees in the puddles on the waterfall's rock.

Grudgingly, he recognized the kick for what he probably would have done in the face of his own flailing previous punch. Ghosts, the guy was good. The crowd roared. "Clare versus Clare!" the impersonator crowed, exciting them further. "Who will prevail? The ultimate showdown!"

The showiness discouraged Clare. His opponent would not want to be outdone, which would make the fight harder.

Yet he did not have what the real Clare did. *Fury*, fresh-wounded.

The real Clare's fists, like the Sword of Souls itself, were weapons forged in pain, for he had just watched *someone else* kiss Beatrice. The other man could not possibly feel the wrath Clare did, for he was only putting on a spectacle. No one could know the envious rage he felt.

Okay, that's not entirely true, he corrected himself. He was quite certain plenty of people in Mythria considered themselves to be in love with Beatrice of the Four.

None of them knew the depth of Clare's devotion, however. He recalled the way Beatrice had looked in this man's arms. She had wanted to kiss *him*, he knew. He couldn't make out what she'd said, but when she'd comprehended she had kissed an impersonator and saw the real him watching, she'd fled, realizing her mistake. Which meant the odds of her wanting to kiss the real him now were . . . low.

This man had stolen the one fucking kiss he might have gotten from Beatrice.

He'd spent ten years dreaming of her lips. Ten years of trying to forget every memory of Beatrice and yet waking up with her face first in his mind. Ten years of—he could now concede—slime-ish longing.

All for the one chance he might have had with her to be stolen by a two-bit performer in a costume. The man needed to pay. Clare hauled himself to his feet.

"*You owe me a kiss,*" Clare ground out.

"I— What?" the impersonator replied, startled.

The remark had made more sense in Clare's head. Never mind it. He weaponized the man's distraction, surging forth, tackling the impersonator to the ground. They rolled on the wet flagstones of the pool grounds, wrestling for the upper hand. The display looked *very* dignified, Clare felt certain. Very heroic. When the man headlocked him, hard, Clare escaped only by bending his opponent's fingers close to breaking.

He fought free, panting, his tunic soaked, hair mussed. On the ground, his own likeness struggled to recover. "She didn't want to kiss you, you fool!" Clare roared down.

Only hearing the furious emphasis of his words did he understand how much he meant them. How the sight of this man dressed like *himself*, reckless and wretched on the ground, summoned them. *Of course she regretted the kiss.* He was not the man she deserved or could ever want. Not the hero anyone could ever want. He felt stripped raw.

"You don't deserve her," he spat, lower.

The impersonator's eyes narrowed. He hauled himself up warily, understanding this was *so* not about him anymore.

Which it was not. Clare, who had wrestled with fear and with desire, faced now the newest of his heart's rogues—rage. Visiting his despair on one who simply *looked* like him was meaningless, but he did not care. It did not register in his fury-racked head, which saw only the perfect opportunity for reifying self-loathing into pounding fists.

He did not know how he would ever cease. He would pulp his opponent to weeping pieces in the name of punishing himself. Ghosts, the hatred was filling him up. The unfathomable, indefatigable knowledge *he'd* fucked up the past decade, which he could have spent repairing his relationship with the woman who held his heart. Of course she'd fled—he hadn't done anything to make her *want* to kiss him. To stay.

Like he wasn't now.

He faltered, shame consuming him. *What was he doing?* If Beatrice beheld him now, lashing out meaninglessly in misery, would she find him the man she desired? Or would disdain drive her even further from him?

Unfortunately, his opponent seized the moment. He launched forward, knocking Clare to the ground. "Only one of us will win the beautiful Beatrice's heart!" he challenged with dramatic flair.

It was, put mildly, rather the wrong thing to say.

"Don't even speak her name," Clare warned.

"How can I not? She is my—our—true love!" the not-Clare protested.

Clare fought his way free. He rolled away and stood, panting from exertion. "She's *my* true love," he growled.

Hearing the edge in his voice, the crowd hushed.

Then recognition dawned. The whispers started. Spectators were realizing his "performance" was uncommonly convincing, his "costume" and "likeness" uncommonly perfect.

"It's the real Clare Grandhart."

"It's really him."

"Clare Grandhart has declared his love!"

"Oh. My. *Ghosts*. Claretrice is happening!"

Dread unfolded in him like dragon wings. Oh, the scribesheets would love this. The Vermillion Vale incident would probably pay their editors' salaries for the entire year.

The impersonator, realizing, fell to his knees. "Forgive me!" the man implored.

Feeling the crowd's fascination, Clare reverted to his other improvisational skills—newer, yet oftener used. Affecting an appreciative bow, like the fight was all performance, he flashed the crowd a grin.

Inside, he felt ragged. A decade of aspiring to be a better man *abandoned* when he beheld Beatrice kissing another. His resolve was worth nothing. His promises to himself were worth nothing. His honor was worth nothing. It was not the poor impersonator's fault—Clare acted out on his own.

In embarrassed haste, he helped the man to his feet. "Your form was excellent," he praised the impersonator honestly.

The man's eyes widened. He received Clare's words with reverence. "You mean it? I studied all the stories, all the accounts of your fights, all the conjurated reenactments, hoping to learn your style."

"You mastered it," Clare assured him. "I felt I was fighting a younger version of myself."

The impersonator nearly wept with joy. Clare was glad—encouraging his very recent opponent eased the guilt of visiting his own inner turmoil on the poor performer. He gestured for the audience to applaud the impersonator, who welcomed the reception, calling out to the guests, "I'm performing with my fellow Clares tomorrow eve! The Night Dragon Inn!" Then, in genuine gratitude, he waved at Clare himself. "I could never have been here without my personal hero. Clare Grandhart, you honor me!"

The guests clapped louder, unsurprisingly exhilarated. Clare knew he should . . . make a speech, or something.

His eyes straying to where Beatrice had fled from him, he found he could not. He didn't feel like Mythria's hero. He was just the old Clare. The rogue, the bandit, the mercenary. The man Beatrice could never love.

"The honor is mine," he mumbled.

In the echo of the crowd's cheering, he stumbled from the pool grounds back inside the inn. He knew where he was going, more or less. Clare did not need to fight. He certainly did not need to face Beatrice, whose discomfort he could imagine perfectly well.

What he needed was a drink.

Fortunately, he found himself in the finest place in Mythria for one. Like every Vermillion Vale inn, this one was outfitted with more taverns than one could count. Clare wandered to the nearest casino-side counter, where old horseball matches were conjured in poor quality over the cheap bar. He ordered himself a stiff mead.

He'd not drunk his first swill when—wonderful. Someone walked up to him. "Nice show out there, Grandhart," the speaker greeted him.

"Thanks," Clare replied, distantly wondering if he recognized the gravelly voice. Fans he'd encountered previously would sometimes get offended if he did not remember them. Whatever. "I'm not signing autographs right now."

If the fan did know him, his refusal might offer cause for genuine concern. Clare Grandhart not signing autographs was like how one knew a flying stallion was gravely ill if the creature would not open its wings.

Indeed, the reality was not far off. His chances with Beatrice, he knew dully, were likely ruined for good. For once in his life, Clare Grandhart wished only for solitude.

"Oh, we don't want an autograph from a loser like you," Gravel Voice replied.

Now Clare looked up.

He clocked instantly the *we* in the intruder's rude reply. Grinning like wolverlings emerging from the forested dark, four men in very expensive garb surrounded him, cracking their knuckles. In the center of them—

Leonor the Overlord loomed.

Clare sighed and set his drink down. No wonder he'd recognized the voice.

He found his misfortune nearly comical. In the Four's final fight with the Order, Clare's heroic duty was marshaling the frightened remnants of the queen's forces against the Order's army.

It had put him in confrontation with Leonor, the former professional horseballman whose combination of muscle, strategy, and noble lineage had elevated him to leading the Order's forces. The manner of man who would have cheated to win horseball matches, yet never needed to. Clare knew only a hero with his own fighting finesse could conquer the Overlord. He'd incapacitated Leonor, but not without the hardest fight of his life.

Could his past stop catching up with him? Please? he implored the Ghosts silently. First his oldest and worst self leaping out of him—now his old worst enemy? Could his past please just give it a rest?

"Let me guess," he grumbled. "I've finally found the Order."

Leonor the Overlord grinned.

"Wrong again, Grandhart," he said slowly. "We have found *you*."

28

Elowen

Fate of the realm hanging in the balance or not, Elowen needed to watch *Desires of the Night*.

It had been on a short hiatus since the big Domynia reveal, and this was the triumphant return. Stealing away into the gaudy chambers Hugh had rented for their fake bachelor party, Elowen left Beatrice and made herself a fort in her bedchamber. Hugh himself had gotten very drunk and passed out in the living quarters, which made it quite easy to keep track of the soon-to-be royal. Perhaps that was fitting for a bachelor party.

Elowen had spent so many years watching *Desires* from her cozy, cramped treehouse that she couldn't bear the thought of viewing the shadow play in such an opulent space. She tied the bedsheets onto the golden pillars that framed the room's heart-shaped bed, and she built a small hideaway within the larger room. It wasn't perfect, but it shielded her in the way she needed, granting her some semblance of seclusion.

With a snap of her fingers, she brought the shadow play to life, scaling the conjuration so that it aligned with her wall of bedsheets. When *Desires* was on, Elowen did not have to be Elowen, which was a great relief after the exchange with Vandra at the stackjack table. It was utterly exhausting to be herself. She became instead an unseen member of the family at the heart of the play instead, allowed to laugh, smile, and fight alongside them in whatever way she pleased.

The sight of the living Domynia brought tears to Elowen's eyes. What a joy to be back in this made-up realm full of wish fulfillment. No one could ever understand how full Elowen felt there, immersed in a story that wasn't her own. Elowen had made such a mess of her actual reality. She'd been difficult, and emotional, and she'd caused harm to a woman she cared about deeply. None of that mattered to the characters on *Desires*. Elowen could offer them her whole heart and never once hurt them because of it.

The play picked up at the embrace between Domynia and her lover Alcharis. It was bliss. A perfect reunion made sweeter by the evident love between the two. Just what Elowen needed.

Suddenly, Domynia's lover pulled back, their energy shifting. They had questions. How was it that she was alive? How were they supposed to deal with that? And why had she behaved so poorly before her untimely death?

Elowen gnawed at her lip, concerned. "I'm not sure I like where this is going," she said.

She used to speak aloud to herself all the time. At the moment, she found herself to be a rather inadequate companion for the conversation she wished to have. She needed someone else to bounce ideas off of, someone who could challenge her thoughts or provide clarity.

As the play progressed, Beatrice's prediction in the wagon started coming true—Alcharis grew more and more upset, struggling with how to forgive Domynia for the past. Domynia could not come up with adequate responses, only furthering the rift.

"Is this written for me?" Elowen asked. More like accused. It felt a bit *too* personal.

When Domynia stormed off, unable to continue her painful

conversation, the walls of Elowen's fort—once cozy—became suffocating. Her comfort play no longer provided her comfort. It reminded her instead of all the problems she was avoiding.

Elowen used to find avoidance a comfort in and of itself. Staying out of things relieved her of the responsibility of resolving conflicts. Now it hurt worse to be silent. She could *feel* how she was letting Vandra down, and every moment she waited to fix it was another moment wasted.

Elowen stopped the conjuration and threw back the bedsheet. She could not stay here, attempting to live as she used to live. Why had she convinced herself she wanted to? This way of existing no longer suited her.

She had to find Vandra.

As if called into place by Elowen's thought, there Vandra stood, already in the chambers. She had a real gift for doing that.

"Oh," Elowen said, surprised and a little embarrassed. She'd hoped for time to come up with an official plan. She figured she'd do that while roaming the inn looking for Vandra. "How long have you been here?"

"Long enough to catch you talking to yourself," Vandra responded.

"I didn't even hear you come in."

"Perhaps someone's told you once or twice that I'm quite good at being stealthy. It's sort of my whole deal."

"That's right," Elowen said, faking a dawning realization. "I do think that's been shared before. I must have had you mixed up in my mind with the woman who wants to tame all the wild brushwalkers."

"Funny you should mention it, that's *also* me," Vandra responded. Her arms, once crossed, unfolded.

"Really? I don't suppose you're also the woman who puts spicy dollpeppers on her sugared hotcakes?"

"The very same."

Elowen bit back a smile. They'd never done this before, been playful together. Elowen didn't know she was capable of it. But if she'd learned anything since coming down from the trees, it was that she was capable of just about everything she once thought she could no longer do, and that emboldened her to keep pushing.

"I don't suppose you're the woman with the most generous spirit I've ever known, are you?" she asked. "If you are, you might be just the woman I was hoping to see."

Vandra tapped her finger on her mouth. "Hmm. I have been told on a few occasions that while I have no patience for those who cause true harm, I can be a bit too forgiving of those I hold close to me, but I've worked on that in heart healing. I'm not sure if that makes me the woman you seek. That woman sounds like a push-over."

"Far from it," Elowen responded. "Her generosity is her greatest attribute, because she understands that joy is the first thing that other people will try to take from you, and she rarely lets them steal it. Unfortunately, I believe I am someone who has succeeded in taking it away."

Vandra plopped down on the tufted chaise beside the heart-shaped bed. "This poor woman you speak of. I do suspect she may be very wounded indeed. What did you hope to say to her? Perhaps I can pass along the message. If I have the time. I'm very busy, what with saving the realm and all." She looked at her charmed nails, examining the pink shade.

"It's rather personal," Elowen told her. "Not something I'd go sharing with just anyone."

"I wonder if that's part of the problem?" Vandra responded, still assuming the role of a third party to this conversation, and still looking at her nails. "That you won't share things? With anyone? Ever? At any time?"

Elowen deserved this. She did. She'd tried to build walls around herself, and she'd succeeded. What she hadn't accounted for was the fact that she'd also put in some windows along the way, so she could admire everything on the other side. That's where Vandra lived, in view but out of reach. Elowen needed to own up to that, or she'd remain alone in a trap of her own design, losing the only woman she'd ever wanted to let inside.

"Vandra," she said, dissolving the game they'd started. She had to be herself in this moment. Own it fully. "You're right. About all of it. I've been so afraid to get hurt that I've ended up hurting other people in the process. Namely you. I have hurt you by withholding my own truths before knowing yours. It's what I'm used to, figuring out how someone else feels first so that I never have to say what is in my own heart. You're the only person who has ever really confused me. No matter what emotion you're feeling, I can never figure out what it means, and that terrifies me, because it makes me afraid that I'm wrong for what *I* feel."

The corners of Vandra's mouth pulled down into a frown. It was a simple kind of sadness, laid bare. Elowen felt it as candidly as Vandra displayed it. The only way to get through the agony of it was to keep going.

"I've been back in the realm for only a little while, but I can now see how little I've survived off of for the last decade," Elowen continued. "I've held myself back from so much, terrified to let other people in, because I know what it is to lose someone important. It's only recently occurred to me that if I'm never honest with you, I've already lost you anyway. And I cannot for the life of me understand why I would accept an existence without you when having you around is an option that's available to me. What a fool I am, letting you walk away without saying what my heart has sung since the very moment you entered my life."

"And what is that?" Vandra asked, her frown fighting to withstand the tears that welled up in her warm brown eyes.

"That I love you," Elowen said.

She had never told anyone she loved them before, and it stumbled out with such finality, such certainty, that Elowen couldn't help but smile. Ghosts. She *loved* Vandra. Love! This was why the poets spent ages trying to put this feeling into words, for this feeling had a hundred other feelings tucked inside it, like a flower that bloomed within itself, new layers beneath every petal.

"I love you," she repeated, adoring the way it flowed from her lips. "I love the way you wake up, and for only a few moments, you're not the Vandra everyone else knows. You're still tired, and you're a little suspicious of everything. Then the light gets into your soul, and I watch the brightness wash away your doubts. I love that you have so much knowledge of Mythria, and you're never afraid to share it, even when it challenges what someone else says. I love how you know firsthand that this realm has some really bad people in it, but you still choose to greet each day with kindness. And it *is* a choice. You're not kind because you don't know better, you're kind because in spite of the bad people, there is still so much good here, and you're committed to experiencing it."

Elowen ran out of breath. Vandra's mouth had fallen open, and she moved to say something in return. Elowen held a finger up as she took a deep inhale. She wasn't done yet.

"You are a very intentional person, which I also love about you," she continued, still a bit breathless. This whole love thing was exhilarating. "There is no place you go or job you take that happens on accident. Except, perhaps, for me. I think I am the biggest accident that's ever happened in your entire life. When you and I first started meeting up, you had no idea I could ever be someone capable of loving you. That wasn't the point for either of us. Truthfully, I didn't know that about myself either. But now it seems comical that I've gone this long pretending like it might not be possible. Because the love I have for you is constant. It existed long before I noticed it, and I understand now that everything else I feel happens in relation to it. I also understand that you don't have to feel the same way back. The point in telling you this is not to convince you to feel it in return. It's to show you that I no longer plan to live my life the way I once did. I plan to be honest with myself and with others, even when it might bring me pain. I plan to let this love keep me brave until the Ghosts take me home."

Elowen could have kept going, but she chose to stop there, finding it to be as good an ending as any other. She'd said what she felt, and the hard part now was letting Vandra process it in her own time.

In all the years Elowen had known her, she'd never seen Vandra stunned. When she attempted to get a sense of Vandra's emotions, she found something like a buzzing in place of the feelings—a shuddery, tingly unfamiliarity that mimicked a bug flying too close to your ear. It was, she realized, her own heart getting in the way.

"Vandra?" Elowen finally said, unable to withstand the charged silence any longer. "Would you like me to leave?"

At that Vandra tumbled into her arms, as if she'd been charmed into stillness and the spell had been lifted. Vandra kissed Elowen's neck, her cheeks, her mouth. The tears that had welled in her eyes were spilling onto Elowen's skin.

"Does this mean you accept?" Elowen asked.

Vandra paused. "You silly, silly woman," she said, smiling through her tears and hitting Elowen playfully on the shoulder.

Bewildered, Elowen pulled back. "What?"

"You haven't asked me anything!" Vandra told her.

The buzzing cleared, and Elowen could finally think. She'd said so much. More than she'd ever said to anyone ever, and still she'd failed to include the most important part of all. "You're right," she said. "See? You're very good at pointing out what people have missed."

"Enough!" Vandra interrupted. "Ask me!"

Elowen wrapped her arms around Vandra's waist. "Vandra Ravenfall, would you like to be my girlfriend?"

"Yes!" Vandra responded, kissing Elowen on the mouth. "I would!"

Elowen showered Vandra in kisses in response. Love was complicated, Elowen knew, but in that moment, there was an exquisite simplicity to it. She moved to lay Vandra onto the bed, but Vandra stopped her.

"What is it?" Elowen asked, concerned.

"I cannot bed you until we've finished the newest *Desires*," Vandra told her. "I need to know what everyone is going to do about Domynia's return."

Elowen laughed then, holding Vandra to her chest as she did so. "Of all the things I expected you to say to me right now . . ."

"I told you before that I was a real fan," Vandra protested. She readjusted the blanket fort and climbed inside it. "It's not my fault you didn't believe me!"

Elowen climbed in behind her. "I'm sorry for all the times I ever doubted you." She kissed Vandra's forehead. "Truly."

"Is this a good time to tell you I did not recently go through a breakup?" Vandra said.

Elowen scoffed. "You *did* lie!"

Vandra rolled her eyes. "Oh, please. It was a harmless one, and

I am owning up to it now, aren't I? Everything else has been completely true. I said it because I hoped to make you jealous. You were being so difficult to me, even more than I anticipated, and I needed a way to get through to you. For what it's worth, it worked. You did engage me more when I said it."

"I'm glad no one has broken your heart recently," Elowen responded, kissing Vandra's nose.

"Only you, my darling," Vandra said playfully. "We spent ten years apart, and I knew I could live without you, but when I saw you again, I realized I didn't want to anymore. I'm glad you've finally realized the same thing."

Elowen laughed. "I'm afraid I realized it about the same time you did. It just took me far too long to do the right thing about it."

Elowen snapped her fingers twice to return the conjuration to view. The two women cuddled into each other as they started the latest shadow play from the beginning again. Elowen found herself much more capable of tolerating the contentious reception to Domynia's return. She understood now that painful emotions often needed to be felt in completion to be released. When they weren't, they tended to clog up one's heart, making them bitter. Domynia's lover had to get it all out. Every last bit. It was the only way to heal.

Elowen shot upright so fast she ripped the bedsheet ceiling from the post, covering herself with it in the process. "Ghosts!" she said, scrambling to break free.

"What is it?" Vandra asked. She stood up to lift the bedsheet off Elowen's head.

"The Sword of Souls is made up of countless trapped souls," Elowen said.

"Right," Vandra confirmed.

"And those trapped souls are in pain," she continued.

"Of course."

"And pain is an emotion."

Vandra caressed her cheek. "My love, where is this going?"

Stunned by the use of *love*, Elowen fumbled to continue her thought.

"Oh! I'm sorry," Vandra said. "Now is not the time for me to say I love you in return, is it? Forget I mentioned it! You were on such a roll!"

Elowen kissed Vandra for strength. "That's fantastic news, thank you. I love you, too, as you know. But back to my point. I've figured out how we can stop Myke from using the pain of the souls inside the sword. If I can get my hands on it before he uses it, I can absorb all the pain inside it, rendering the weapon unusable."

Vandra's eyes sparkled. "My love, that's brilliant! How did you think of it?"

"Watching *Desires*," Elowen said, delighted.

"Only you could accomplish such a feat," Vandra told her sincerely.

Elowen grinned. As she evolved, Elowen's shadow plays did not always comfort her, but they did continue to provide her with *exactly* what she needed.

29

Clare

Clare Grandhart was getting his ass kicked.

In fairness, the fight was ten against one. Furthermore, his hand was already bruised from his duel with the intrepid impersonator.

Not that he was making excuses.

He had been thrown out of the tavern, which, like most in Vermillion Vale, unfortunately opened onto the indoor gambling hall, not the outside road. Instead of landing on soft terrain, Clare wound up crashing onto one of the nearby gaming tables with a thud. Chips went flying. Cards were flung from gamblers' grasps. With startled cries, panicked guests fled. Clare hoped none of their hands had been good. He'd known the pain himself of a wayward fight interrupting a winning streak.

Other pains found him now. His whole upper half hurt, courtesy of the Order's flurry of fists. He winced and hauled himself up. When one of his assailants lunged, he managed to redirect the man's momentum, ramming his head into the gaming table.

The victory was short-lived. Three more Order men descended on him, kicking him in the ribs.

Clare wondered how much worse one day in Vermillion Vale could possibly get.

"Where's all that heroism I keep hearing about?" Leonor the Overlord mocked, striding up while his companions continued their handiwork. *Is it handiwork if they use their feet?* It mattered not. "Ten fucking long years of Clare Grandhart being declared Mythria's finest," Leonor went on. "Look at you now."

Replying was difficult under Clare's circumstances. Instead, he fought to stand from all fours.

He did not get far. Leonor kicked him hard, right in the gut. The man was muscle personified, which, Clare knew, drove his resentment for Clare uniquely. One of Mythria's most popular horseball players until his personal politics leaned into overthrowing the queen, Leonor was exactly the sort who had once imagined Spark's Sport Potions sponsorships for himself. Nothing warped men like perceived entitlement deferred.

With the kick, Clare fell onto his side, wheezing. The casino floor where his foes were surrounding him—the well-lit gaming tables now empty, the guests having fled—was unyielding, the slick stone offering him no purchase. He was faring poorly, if he was honest with himself. He used to know how to take a beating, how to block out the pain and will himself to keep moving.

He'd gone too long without real fighting, however. In the comfort of luxurious Farmount, his days full of indulgence, he'd lost his grasp on the man who had once earned his fame and fortune.

He was not living up to the heroism he chased, which he'd proven perfectly well outside. What's more, while heroes did find themselves in predicaments like his present, he could not picture Galwell on the ground, gasping, clumsy, outnumbered.

Yet he was not Clare Grandhart, either. Not the *old* Clare, the outlaw who could withstand punches without flinching.

Which left—who? If he could not fight, and he could not lead, and he was not worthy of the woman he loved, he was . . . no different from the performer he'd wrestled outside.

He was just one more Clare impersonator in an endless crowd of them.

"When the Order is restored to its rightful place," Leonor continued, evidently enjoying the fine practice of villain speeches overmuch, "when Todrick rises and rules the realm the way it should be ruled, people like you will be relegated to where you belong." He stepped over Clare. "Beneath . . . my . . . boot," he said slowly, savoring the words, while his heavy heel pressed Clare's face into the polished stone floor.

Out of Clare's existential embarrassment, panic surged forth. He tried to buck, wrestling to escape, but hands held him down everywhere. Tears sprang into his eyes while the pressure mounted on his jaw.

Until the very moment he knew he could withstand no more.

Then, release. Leonor's boot lifted. "Let's head out, boys," the Overlord directed his men. "I reckon we'll not even need to tie him up. Grandhart is more pathetic than I thought."

The Order men removed their hands. Clare half-wished they would resume punching him. Shame inflicted deeper wounds now. He seethed on the ground. When he struggled to right himself under the casino's unflinching lights, his punished muscles would not cooperate.

Leonor laughed. "Told you." He knelt down in front of Clare, looking him in the eye. "You should have joined the Order when you had the chance. But I suppose you'll help us in the end. You're to be our gift to Todrick," he explained. Somber reverence grasped the man's voice. "One final soul for the Sword of Souls, taken from one of the Four responsible for his death."

Clare's vision blurred. He fought to hold on to consciousness. His opponent's words didn't help. *One final soul.* It was perfect, really. He had to commend the Order for their flair for poetry.

Behind Leonor, the doors of a lift opened. People inside gasped when they saw Clare, and then the doors closed on their frightened faces.

No one was coming for Clare Grandhart.

Yet he would not give up. He thought of Galwell, who never ran out of strength. While the hands of the Order's men hauled him up, his mind strayed to more of his heroes. To Elowen, who had faced so many fears in so few days. To Vandra, who was fighting for a better life despite her past. To Beatrice. Who despite every hurt they'd inflicted on each other had wanted to kiss him today.

He did not know whether he could ever be worthy of his fame. He just knew he needed to be worthy of his friends.

With every bit of vigor he could muster, he rose up. Head-butting backward, he connected with the nose of the man holding his arm. It worked marvelously. The man cried out in pain, releasing Clare. Freed, Clare limped toward the lifts.

He focused on the lift doors. The magic lanterns' light illuminated the gold frame. The effect was ethereal. Salvation itself.

Right as he reached his destination, someone grabbed him and shoved him up against the closed doors, ready to smash his face in. "It's over," the Order man growled. "You're done."

Clare grinned. Surprise stopped his assailant's fist. "You've forgotten one thing," Clare said, feeling like Galwell about to storm the Order's stronghold. "I'm Clare fucking Grandhart."

His catchphrase didn't need eloquence. Not when it had heart.

As the words left his mouth, he went limp. The lift doors opened, and he fell inside, exactly like he planned. His maneuver unsteadied the man enough for Clare to kick him off, sending him stumbling.

It left Clare sprawled on his back on the lift floor—which was when he realized the lift was not empty.

Over him stood Beatrice.

Understandably, she looked shocked. She'd changed her clothes, he noticed. Would she have caught his eye were she clad entirely in rough-spun cloth? Yes. Was the white blouse she wore belted into her leggings desperately distracting?

Definitely.

Their gazes met, both of them stunned silent for a heartbeat. The last time they'd locked eyes, she'd run from him, from the kiss she wished he had not witnessed. Perhaps, he intuited, enclosing herself in a small lift with him was not the refuge she'd intended.

However, he did not have the chance to wonder if she would leave him again. In the next instant, she was pulling her arm back to land a solid punch on Leonor, who was trying to climb into the lift.

The hammering strike pulverized the Overlord's nose. He withdrew clumsily, crying out while blood poured down his face. While Beatrice urgently pressed the spelled runes on the wall, prompting the doors to slide shut, they could hear Leonor howl.

"Fall back!" he commanded his men in wretched frustration. "It's only a matter of time!" he yelled at the closing doors, to them. "Tomorrow there'll be no hiding from the Order!"

Beatrice tensed, her fighting stance ready, her eyes flashing. She was poetry in combat, Clare found himself observing. His favorite sorts of poetry were lyrics of hard-fought victories—and, in recent years, love songs. Watching her, he could not decide which one rang louder in his pounding head.

Her gaze rounded on him. No poetry echoed in *her* ears, he noted. Sharp evaluation swept over him.

"You're hurt," she commented.

"The Order is here," he explained. "They jumped me." He was grateful for the safety of the lift.

She knelt, wiping blood from his lip gently as she examined his face for injury. "I figured," she murmured.

Beneath them, the lift rose. Carrying them up, into the sky. It filled Clare with an odd euphoria. "You kissed me," he stated.

Her finger paused. Her eyes narrowed.

"Is now really the time?" she asked.

Yet hidden within her irritation, he heard—*yes*. She wanted to know how he felt on the subject. "We could find ourselves in this lift with Todrick himself and I would still consider the matter of you kissing me to be the most pressing issue on my mind," he said.

She laughed a little at that. How he loved her laugh. It was like the glimpse one could catch of the crescent moon in daylight on summer evenings when the sun had not entirely set.

"You're concussed," she said, covering for how he'd charmed her.

When she reached up to turn his head to the side, continuing her examination, he grabbed her hand.

"I'm thinking more clearly than I have in ten years," he replied.

If she wished to reject him now, she could. He would not, however, have her mistaking his devotion for a medical malady.

That silenced her. Swiftly, she stood, ending her inspection of him—rather prematurely, he felt. He knew no healer or heart magician who could relieve pain the way the charge in her eyes erased every hurt from his pummeled body. He felt new. He felt fucking *fantastic*.

Rising to his feet, he followed the wondrous feeling. He stepped toward her, pressing her against the railing in front of the transparent spelled wall of the lift. Past them, Vermillion Vale lay spread out under the sky. The lift ascended slowly, showing off the Vale's panorama. The road of glittering inns and taverns lit up with iridescent colors in the setting daylight.

"The doors . . . are going to open." She exhaled.

"I don't care," he said.

"Someone could come in."

"I don't care."

She was intoxicatingly close. He could smell her, the scent he would never forget. Something sweetened with secrecy, flowers opening in moonlight. He could not help his hands finding her waist. She didn't shy away or withdraw. Instead, she . . . wavered. Like she was warring with herself.

"You're bleeding," she remarked, valiant in her fight.

"*I*," he repeated. "*Don't. Care.*"

He ran his nose along the curve of her neck. Under him, he felt her shiver. And—

The lift doors opened. The knife of disappointment cut into Clare, deeply enough he nearly gasped. Instead, the sound came out half frustration, half something else. No part of the utterance, however, seemed to reach the reason for their interruption. Outside the lift stood a pair of gentlemen in elaborate formalwear, the sort under which even Clare's handsome earnings would strain.

One held in his hand purple liquor. The other nodded his head exuberantly to music only he could hear. They were, Clare intuited, on their way to the inn's rooftop revelry club.

Not on this lift, they weren't.

"It's occupied," he shot over his shoulder, still hunched over Beatrice.

Their dauntless interlopers—damn them—weren't deterred. In the corner of his vision, he even noticed one of them roll his eyes. The prospect of a canoodling couple didn't bother them, Clare guessed, when such dalliances were common in the Vale.

Nevertheless—did the name of Sir Grandhart command no respect? And just how often would Vermillion Vale's cast of unpredictables prevent him from kissing Beatrice?

He was preparing to round on the young nobles, ready to let them know exactly what he thought of their cravats, when Beatrice reached past him. With one purposeful finger, she stabbed the spelled rune to close the doors.

"Sorry, boys," she said, her voice diamond hard. "You heard him."

The lift doors closed on the gentlemen's indignant frowns.

Clare's heart raced. Hearing her like this, feeling her this way . . . He wondered if it was possible for these sensations to incinerate everything in him, leaving a creature of pure desire. Her eyes found his. The lift restarted its gradual climb higher. He leaned closer . . .

Yet no matter how fierce his need, no matter how many punches the Order's men struck, one question clung in his head. No longer could he leave it unspoken. It had the power, he understood, to define his life.

"Why did you try to kiss me?" he asked.

In response or on instinct, she opened her legs, just enough for him to press his between hers, bringing their bodies close. He knew he was hard. Embarrassingly hard, under other circumstances.

Now? He didn't care.

"I—I guess I wanted to. I . . . always want to," she ventured.

He'd heard of the rush dragon riders felt racing for the sky. He suspected he knew the feeling. Combined with the closeness of her, it produced a humming growl in the back of his throat.

"Then why did you run?" he pressed.

His hand rose up her front, finding her breast. When he felt her fingers rise to his chest, he very nearly lost consciousness. If he *was* concussed, she was not helping. If he wasn't—well, it did not matter. He felt like he was. Dizzy, uncomprehending, wrecked.

"When—" she started, then swallowed. "When I kissed . . . him, there was a moment where I wondered if you—he—you would laugh. Or worse, gallantly and gently reject me like the gentleman you've started pretending you are. When he kissed me back, I was . . . *relieved*."

He had gone still, listening closely. Only the fragility of her voice now was capable of distracting him from her warm figure under his hands. He'd rarely ever heard her sound vulnerable in this way.

"I felt like I'd saved the realm or survived some impossible odds," she went on. "But when I saw *you*, I realized I'd won nothing. Everything I feared could still happen. It was . . . too much to face."

In his embrace, she seemed to shrink. It was quietly devastating, watching the strongest-hearted woman he knew collapsing under the weight of the shadows stalking her soul. He needed to help her—not out of heroism or chivalry or obligation. No, he *needed* to. Desperation consumed him whole.

"Perhaps I'm a coward," she confessed. "I probably am. When it comes to you, I've been the greatest coward for ten years."

With her final words, his path illuminated. Hearing in them the naked purity of honesty, he knew he did not need to encourage her, or inspire her, or flatter her.

He need speak only the truth.

"Then kiss me," he implored her, "and see what I do. See where this will lead."

Her eyes rose. How he loved what he found in them. *Yes. Loved.* Defiant pride lit her perfect features, moonlight meeting firelight now. Her response was exactly what he'd hoped, and counted on. For while she could chasten herself like no one else in Mythria could, he knew she was *no* coward.

Slowly, she slid her hands *down* his chest. To his belt.

No coward indeed.

He pressed into her, meeting her vigor, feeding her fire. In kind, she leaned forward, her lips inches from his. The precarious proximity was enrapturing, nearly hallucinatory. He felt himself on the edge not only of consciousness now. He was on the very edge of sanity.

When she kissed him, he lost himself entirely.

With how hard he pressed her into the wall, he would fear hurting her—except she was strong, he knew. She was his warrior, his champion. His general, his crown, his realm.

Desire drove her forth. She pushed back, warring with him, each of them fighting the other for the lead in the kiss. Feeling her insistence, he opened his mouth to hers. Yet wanting to win something for himself, he grasped under her, hiking her onto the railing inside the lift so her legs could wrap around him.

Higher and higher they rose, the view outside ever more magnificent. The entirety of Vermillion Vale playing host to their passion.

He placed his hands on either side of her, pinning her possessively. She kissed him hard until he wrenched himself from her, needing to speak. "I think it's pretty obvious," he murmured, "I'm not fucking laughing. Or rejecting you. I'll say yes to . . . whatever you want."

She raised an eyebrow, evidently intrigued by the suggestion.

Then the lift doors slid open once more.

He groaned, pretending his heart was not hammering. How in the realm could this keep happening at the worst possible times? What would he do if *poor lift logistics* pulled her from him? How would he survive? "Ignore it," he implored. "Ghosts above, Beatrice, ignore it."

In reply, she—*no*. She *smirked*. He'd shown weakness. He'd demanded mercy from his fellow fighter, his kissing duelist, his devoted opponent.

She pushed him away, walking past him. In defeat, he gripped the railing, his knuckles white.

"Our room is this way."

He looked up, finding her where she'd spoken. In the hallway, watching him. Expectant. *Waiting* for him. Her smirk was more smile now, less sly.

"Aren't you coming?" she asked.

Her meaning was unambiguous.

Clare was not ashamed to stumble out of the lift after her.

30

Beatrice

Beatrice's heart pounded. Her head felt full of lightwings, glimmering radiant on summer nights, their colors iridescent. Her every step lifted with eagerness.

Clare followed her.

When she entered the group's suite, she found Vandra and Elowen's door shut. Hugh slept soundly on the couch. In the inn's luxury, Beatrice noted how unlike questing her present circumstances felt. The finery of their lodgings was the farthest imaginable contrast from the caves where they'd camped, the isolated intimacy nothing like the constant closeness of one's companions.

It wasn't just the rooms that differed, either. *She* was unfamiliar to herself. Her nervous joy held the intensity of walking into combat, yet the exact opposite emotion. Her only fear was how excited she felt.

Of course, she was aware of what remained ahead of them. They still needed to plan their strategy for stopping the Order now that Beatrice knew where and when their enemies would hold the resurrection. They would need to weigh approaches, consider risks, evaluate options . . . But those things could wait, her heart decided for her. When one had saved the realm once, one did not necessarily expect to survive a second time.

Right now was for living.

She continued to the bedroom the footman had delivered her

baggage to when they checked in. The enchanted fire rose to life on her entry. This was, however, Vermillion Vale, so the fire was spelled to stay romantically low, smoldering in promise of occupants' eyes doing the same. The bed was ridiculous, velvet and heart-shaped.

It did not matter.

When Clare entered after her, he closed the door. He passed his hand over the rune magicked to prevent sound from emanating out of the room.

Delicious anticipation clenched in Beatrice. Clare's breathing was heavy. His eyes were dark in the firelight.

She found herself shaking. She'd not removed one item of clothing, yet the hushed room made her feel incredibly exposed. Nervousness and anticipation danced in her, setting every fiber of her soul to singing.

She'd promised herself for so long she could never forgive Clare Grandhart. Taking this step with him—it would mean more than forgiveness. It would mean giving herself to him once more, knowing where desire would likely lead.

Twice now, they'd let the walls down between them on the eve of peril, thinking they wouldn't survive. Would tonight be just one more passionate prelude to danger and sacrifice? Or would it be the beginning of something new? Which thought frightened her more?

She fought her misgivings. Her reeducation in wanting consumed her. Oh, how she *wanted*.

Right now was for living.

Clare showed no such fraught nerves. "Where?" he demanded, his voice rough. "The bed?" When she hesitated, he strode forth. "Don't say you've changed your mind already. I knew we should've never left the lift."

She managed to shake her head. "I've been trying to change my mind for ten years. It hasn't worked yet," she replied. "It's not going to happen now."

"Are you saying you've lusted after me all these years?" he asked.

She rolled her eyes, charmed as she always was by him. "If we do this," she replied, ignoring his question, "be warned. Your room is across the hall, so while you could sneak out in the morning, you wouldn't get very far."

She wondered whether he heard the strain under the joke. How the remark hid real fear. Not of him fleeing in the morning, obviously. Of—losing him, in one way or another. Of passion and joy crumbling once more into resentment and pain.

His expression said he did. He responded not with nonchalance, not even humor. Instead, sincerity etched over his features— his ruggedly gorgeous features, she could freely admit now. He stepped one step closer, right up to her.

"I'll be by your side as long as you'll have me. I know your magic lets you relive the past . . ." he started to say, then looked down.

In his silence, she glimpsed what she nearly never could in Clare—the weight of years. Of carrying himself without help. She'd learned pieces of his life when they first grew closer. She knew he did not have parents he could speak of. She knew his first venture into the Grimauld Mines ended in the slaughter of his companions. She knew he'd lost his best friend when Elowen lost her brother. He lost the rest of them when Galwell's funeral splintered the Four.

She'd learned more in recent days. How he'd never expected to return from his second journey into Grimauld. She'd come to understand how much rested on the formidable shoulders of the man in front of her. How much loneliness. How much loss. Like the rest of them, he'd carried the feelings for years. Unlike the rest of them, he'd somehow done so smiling.

"We *all* relive what's happened to us. Over and over," he whispered. "No amount of revisiting our memories will change the past. We can't return there, not really. All we have is right now."

He gazed up, right into her eyes.

"*That's* what we can change," he concluded. The vengeance of hope in his voice—it was more perfectly Clare Grandhart than any jest or gloating remark. He outstretched his hand. "What do you say, B?"

Her hesitation was gone.

She lifted her chin, lining her lips up with his. Yet instead of kissing him— "I have one condition," she said.

His lips quirked in a grin. "Of fucking course you do."

"I know you're pushing yourself to live up to Galwell's legacy," she went on. "Pretending to be the noble hero Mythria needs. But"—she pinned his flickering eyes—"I don't need that. I don't . . . want a gentleman."

His eyebrows rose.

"I want Clare Grandhart," she said. "The man I met in a seedy shithole tavern, who smelled like sweat and had a foul mouth and didn't hold any of himself back just because it would be more genteel if he did."

For once, Clare said nothing. She did not receive the cockiness, the self-congratulation, or the vindicated wink she expected. No, he looked—stunned. Like, she realized, while he fought and doubted himself in vain efforts to make himself *better*, he never imagined someone could want him for who he already was.

Then, of course, came the cockiness.

"Given this *enlightenment*," he drawled, smirking, setting sweetness clenching in her once more, "I feel compelled to share I punched the impersonator who kissed you. Turns out I'm not much of a gentleman, even when I try."

She laughed—feeling somewhat like they were still on that lift, except it had no ending, carrying them ever higher into the wondrous night.

"Well then," she replied. "Don't hold back, Grandhart."

He was on her instantly.

The force of his passion overwhelmed her, dizzying pleasure rendering her weak. His hands, feeling her breasts. His mouth hot on hers, devouring. His massive frame dashing her into the ecstasy of lovely surrender. Suddenly he was ripping her clothes, the seams splitting under his experienced grip as the garments fell to the floor.

He paused only to growl in her ear, "How am I doing?"

She knew what she needed to say.

"Passably," she replied.

"*Hmmm*," he grumbled. "*Passably* won't do." He hoisted her up, throwing her over his shoulder while she shrieked. "I have to say," he went on with glib casualness, "I'm surprised. I know you had a schoolgirl crush on old Galwell. He *never* would've behaved this way in the bedroom."

Groping for something like the upper hand while her front half hung down his back, she settled for slapping his ass. "Why do you even remember that?"

He stopped short, like something in her words had jammed in his clockwork. The next moment, he was depositing her down, onto her feet in front of him, to her great dismay. "You're joking, right?" he asked when he could look her in the eye. "When the girl you can't stop thinking about mentions having a crush on the other man you're currently questing with, the detail tends to stick with you."

She found her expression softening. "It shouldn't," she informed him. "Like you said. Schoolgirl crush. When I grew up, I realized what I really wanted. Ghosts help me, but it's you, Clare." Drawn to him, she lifted her chin. "Not you pretending to be someone else," she said. "You, as you are."

Finding him speechless, she spared him having to reply and pulled him into a deep kiss. He kissed her in return, with more than hunger—she felt the song his lips played of longing, of gratitude, of weary wonderment. Of deep, real joy.

While he kissed her, he reached behind her, where he opened the bathing room doors.

She withdrew, questioning. She'd not even noticed where he set her on her feet, figuring the hallway in front of the bathing room was only one inadvertent waypoint on their journey into the bedroom.

Clare looked to have other plans. He murmured his explanation into her neck. "It drove me *wild* watching you take that bath in Queendom. Now I'm going to do everything I've been imagining doing to you since."

Heat rippled through her. In the past nights, she'd done some reimagining of the encounter herself. She guessed their wildest dreams were going to converge.

In reply, she strode into the bathing chamber, inviting him to follow her. The bath—closer to a small pool, sunken into the stone floor—was full. Upon their entry, the pink waterfall cascading from the ceiling had commenced pouring hot water into the pool. Crystal-blue steam rose from the shimmering surface.

Clare stripped down to nothing in front of her.

Ghosts, she'd forgotten how large he was. Her mouth went dry.

Ignoring whatever indulgent desire she knew her face held, he strode into the water, then turned, waiting for her.

He did not need to wait long. She walked steadily and with purpose right into his arms.

On his skin she found remnants of the fight downstairs. Cuts, scrapes, new wounds joining old scars. Her own recent injury stung in the hot water, reminding her of its half-healed state whenever she moved her side.

She welcomed the pain, for the pain made the experience more real. She was not walking in some fantasy, unmoored from herself. Nor was Clare. They were *them*. They could find this pleasure even in hardship. They had not fallen into each other's embrace—they had fought their way there.

She felt Clare's hands cascading over her naked curves while the hot water unwound her muscles. Every fear, every worry, every resentment disappeared, desire softening her shape into one of pure hungry hope.

Clare filled her need. He was, indeed, no gentleman. His fingers found her under the water, demanding her pleasure. With urging strokes he coaxed her heart ever faster.

She wrapped her legs around his waist, feeling the length of him. The contact sent his head rocking back, his eyes closing. That wouldn't do. Beatrice gripped the back of his neck. "Afraid to watch, Sir Grandhart?" she asked, knowing what wicked fire she was playing with.

Clare's eyes flew open, the crystal blue she'd spent years dreaming of fixed on her once more. "So this is how you're going to be." His voice made everything in her clench.

"How?" she repeated breathlessly, his thumb pressing in a place that made her grateful the water was holding her up.

He brought his lips to her throat. "Difficult," he rasped.

Beatrice gripped his hair firmly enough to pull his head back. "I'm with Mythria's Sexiest Man Alive. I want to see his eyes."

Sinking a finger into her, Clare did as he was told. He didn't close his eyes. Didn't blink. When finally they could withstand the deprivation no longer, Clare slid into her, each of them gasping in the warm water, and still he watched.

It was not enough for Clare Grandhart, the rogue. He moaned into her shoulder, pressing his lips, his tongue, his teeth into her skin. He touched every part of her and told her where to touch him in return, his requests urgent and raw.

She gripped him under the water, raked nails down his chest, clung to his broad frame. Every stroke pushed them farther, and closer.

She'd only ever known Clare Grandhart on quests. Sharing a journey in the intrepid hope of reaching the end of the road. Now was no different. It was like they were racing in unison for the greatest destination either of them had ever known.

As he got closer to the edge, she expected Clare to grow more frantic, harder, faster. Instead, his movements seemed more intentional. He pushed her to the bath's wall, pressing them tighter together, like he needed to touch as much of her at once as he could. "I'm watching you, Beatrice. You're fucking spectacular," he ground out, his fingers interlacing with hers.

His words were her undoing. While he held her, they found their release together. Fears vanished, years collapsed. Everything erased in one shattering culmination of light.

What surfaced then was—contentment. For the first time in so many years, Beatrice wanted to be nowhere but the present.

But the future loomed.

In the unguarded lull, life found her. She spoke freely, spontaneously, like she was on the verge of giggling. "The resurrection is happening tomorrow night," she said, a little breathless. "The Order is throwing a revel at the Night Dragon Inn."

Unsurprisingly, Clare looked startled. "Beatrice, love," he replied delicately. "Is this some manner of polite way for you to kick me out of your bath? Because if—I wasn't good, then I'm brave enough to hear it."

She splashed him. *Wasn't good?* she wanted to say. *Every love song written in your honor has not done you justice.* She knew such comments would only enlarge his self-satisfaction, however. "Quite the contrary. I'm telling you because we have some time," she settled for saying. "All night, in fact."

Clare grinned. His widest, most wonderful grin.

"Now what, exactly, could we do with so much time?" he inquired.

She withdrew from him, sliding in invitation under the waterfall. "We have a lot of years to make up for, Grandhart," she said.

Clare stalked closer in the water.

"Best start right now," he replied.

31

Elowen

Over breakfast, Elowen wore a huge smile on her face, and frankly, she expected some fanfare because of it. When was the last time any of them woke up to the sight of her *beaming*? But Clare seemed determined to outdo her in terms of cheer. He was unusually chipper, even for him.

For one, he could not stop humming one of the songs that had been written about him, a love ballad called "The Grandest Heart" that spoke of his yearning to give his heart to someone as grand as him. That would not have been odd alone. Clare always appreciated the art made about him in a very genuine way.

The odd thing was he would not—no, could not—stop patting people on the back. When Elowen salted her plate of dawnjay eggs? A pat on the back. Vandra bent over to relace her boots? A hearty pat on the back, and a "Those are great boots" from him.

All Beatrice did was walk into the room, and Clare not only patted Hugh on the back for it, he whistled, as if the very sight of her was worth celebrating. Elowen had assumed the perfume of love she'd picked up on that morning was her own. Love could tunnel your vision in such ways, she'd learned. Make you ignorant to your own surroundings. Which may have been why no one else noticed her cheer. They were in their own respective tunnels.

"Good morn, my beautiful questmates. I bring you fantastic

news," Clare announced once Beatrice had completed their assembly around the breakfast table. "Thanks to Beatrice's incredible, magnificent, *ingenious* detective work, we know the resurrection will be held at a revel the Order is throwing at the Night Dragon tonight."

"And I have figured out how to disable the weapon," Elowen said, interrupting. Stealing Clare Grandhart's thunder was not easy to execute, and it amused her to be the one capable of doing it. She appreciated that while the moment took him by surprise, she sensed no bitterness or resentment on him.

"How?" he asked, his curiosity overriding the initial shock.

As she explained her idea to absorb the pain inside the Sword of Souls, Clare and Beatrice grew so stunned, they stopped eating. Vandra did, too, but only to give Elowen her full attention and support. The only oblivious party was Hugh, who did not quite grasp how notable it was that Elowen was not only commanding the breakfast chatter, she was offering solutions. He savored his meal, even letting out small sighs of delight as Elowen spoke.

"That's marvelous," Clare said when Elowen finished. "I can't believe none of us thought of this earlier. How did it occur to you?"

Elowen's cheeks warmed. "It came to me when my girlfriend and I were watching the latest episode of *Desires of the Night*."

It was Vandra's turn to beam. She tucked her chin into her shoulder and gave a coy little wink like *Who, me?*

Hugh, once again just a bit tapped out of the whole situation, swallowed his last bite of stoneflour loaf and said, "Forgive me for not knowing this, but who is your girlfriend?"

The table laughed again, though not with the same verve, for Hugh did not deserve to be anyone's target. The question itself was just too innocently amusing.

"Vandra," Elowen told him. "As of last night."

"Congratulations." It was Beatrice who offered this. Elowen gave her a small nod in return. "And not to dampen the mood, but last night, Clare was jumped by the Order."

"That does dampen the mood," Vandra confirmed.

Beatrice gave her a wry glance before continuing. "They want to kill one of the Four with the sword as their final sacrifice before reviving Todrick. It will be a very dangerous affair to be caught at that banquet."

"I know," Elowen said. "Especially since I'm thinking that Vandra can pretend to turn me over to the Order so that I can get close enough to the sword to drain it."

Vandra clapped her hands. "I am so good at pretending to be the bad guy. Many have told me my work is convincingly excellent every time I have done it. Just ask the queen herself!"

"That's how I met Vandra," Hugh offered. "She was pretending to threaten me. Turns out it was a test of my honor from Thessia. After everything she has been through, she can never be too careful." He laughed it off. "Lucky for me, I passed."

"You were great," Vandra said. "Even when I started plucking your eyebrows." She leaned in closer to him. "They've grown in quite nicely since."

"Thank you," he said.

Beatrice was frowning, Elowen noticed. Elowen had been so distracted by displaying her own competence that she nearly missed the fact that Beatrice was worried about her.

"We can pull it off," Elowen said. The we she used was intentional. Uniting. They were on the same side for this. "Together."

"How?" Beatrice asked, her concern growing. "We can't exactly follow you into a Fraternal Order revel without being instantly recognized."

"Worry not!" Clare said. He picked up a large satchel he'd tucked beneath his feet, and he stepped away from the table to open it. "Today is a very special day, for today is the day you tap into the Grandhart within."

He reached into the satchel and pulled out what appeared to be a costume, tossing it into Beatrice's lap.

"You and I will join the army of Clares invited to entertain at the revel. They don't yet know they've been hired to work for the Fraternal Order. We can safely infiltrate the event, and no one will be any the wiser," Clare said.

"What about me?" Hugh asked. He made no effort to mask his devastation at the exclusion.

"Hugh, my good sir," Clare said softly. "You are about to be the king. We cannot risk your safety in such a way."

Hugh straightened up. "I insist you do." He looked around the table, making pleading eye contact with each person. "You are the greatest heroes Mythria has ever known, and I have no bigger dream than to assist you in this quest."

"Ghosts, he's good," Vandra said quietly.

Grinning, Clare tossed Hugh a costume. It was very easy to charm Clare Grandhart into agreeing. Hugh ended up with a crumpled Clare outfit that Elowen recognized instantly from Clare's guest spot on *As the Realm Spins*, a different shadow play that she sometimes watched. The ensemble came complete with a small patch of blond ready to be affixed to Hugh's chin, and a rather floofy yellow wig to cover his dark curls.

For one stunning moment, there was complete silence. And then in a collective, loud and sudden as a flock of birds fleeing a tree, the group laughed. No, they *roared*. Tears spilled from Elowen's eyes, she laughed so hard. Vandra had to grab her stomach, for she'd developed a stitch. Beatrice started clapping in delight. Even Hugh could not contain himself.

Clare, for his part, remained good-natured as ever. "Whatever do you find so amusing? Is it not a thrill to step into the expertly waxed boots of our realm's most renowned mouthpaste sponsor? Have you never wondered what the tunic of a man who has modeled scandalous undergarments made of faux-grawk skin feels like?"

His comments were kindling to the fire, reigniting the laughter when it threatened to die out. Every single person at the table was united in their amusement. Somewhere beyond the joy Elowen felt, she ached with longing, like she was so fond of this moment she already missed it somehow, even though she was living it. It reminded her of all the past joys she'd had to hoard like precious rations, keeping her amused up in the trees when nothing else did. She let out a deep breath, her laughter renewing. She wanted to savor this unity as long as possible without letting her mind wander to what it would be like to lose it.

"Thank you, Clare. I look forward to seeing Hugh help save the realm in a goatee and neck scarf," Elowen offered.

Everyone's laughter died, spotlighting the kindness of Elowen's words, trying to find the catch within them.

"I'm serious," she said. Beneath the table, Vandra squeezed her thigh, boosting Elowen's courage. "This is a wonderful idea, and I am very glad you've thought of it."

In the same way he'd reacted when Elowen told him he'd aged well, Clare clasped his hand to his heart. "That means so much," he said.

The table quieted again, considering the plan in full. It was highly dangerous. Yet so was everything else they'd ever done.

There were surely reasons it shouldn't happen, but saying them aloud seemed redundant. Everyone knew it was the best shot they had at defeating the Order for good.

Elowen would become the full hero this time, just like her brother had before her. But she wouldn't let anyone misrepresent her as they often did with Galwell. She would write this story on her own terms, and she would live to tell the tale herself.

32

Clare

Clare had nearly wept when he saw a Harpy & Hind in the dining plaza of their inn.

It was ordinary, with no unusual features or reflections of the grandeur of Vermillion Vale. Clean counters of maple-colored wood, stained with rings where patrons had placed drinks. The same pleasant lute music from a youthful conjurated musician in one corner. One of countless H & H shops one could find everywhere in the Vale.

Yet for Clare, it could have been the Ghost's Gate itself.

He had hardly slept, understandably. Bedding Beatrice—figuratively speaking, for in fact they'd wound up doing the deed nearly everywhere *else* in the suite—surpassed even the greatest dreams sleep could offer.

Nonetheless, flush with fulfilled passion, he'd met the morning with zeal. He'd even gotten in some exercises in the suite's living room with the conjurated exercise coach he paid for on subscription.

Only in the lift down, facing the new day, did weariness hit him, weariness he knew only one restorative could conquer. He'd procured what he needed now. Steaming cup in hand, painted with Harpy & Hind's ubiquitous insignia, he sat with the impersonator he'd punched yesterday.

Yesterday. Even the very concept felt enshrined in a golden glow. The greatest day of his life, he reckoned.

Yet it was no longer yesterday. It was today. Today demanded nut-milk caramel foam brew and a consultation.

The impersonator was named Cris, he'd learned. *Clare and Cris*. Their names even sounded similar. It was not the only connection—when he was not using his hand magic to resemble Clare, Cris honestly *still* looked like Clare, although his eyes were brown, not blue, and his nose was much straighter.

Cris held his own large nut-milk caramel foam brew. When they'd ordered, he'd confessed to having first tried the confectionary concoction knowing the drink was Clare's signature brew, only to have genuinely loved it.

No surprise, Clare withheld from saying. *Nut-milk caramel foam brew is the finest brew ever envisaged.*

Clare sipped deeply. Cris sipped even more deeply.

Clare had explained they would face the Fraternal Order. Yes, the same evil men who had menaced Mythria in the Four's first quest, possessed of the same powerful magic. "You can count on the Clares, Sir Clare," the impersonator promised while they enjoyed their caramel foam.

Clare did not remark on the surrealism of the statement. Instead, the other man's conviction made his stomach start to hurt, which admittedly was not difficult given what he was consuming. They had spent the morning strategizing and discussing what lay ahead.

"And remember," Clare cautioned, "it's going to get dangerous. When we're in and the fighting starts, have your men *get out of there*."

His new companion frowned.

Clare prepared himself for the worst. Since first approaching his erstwhile fist-fighting opponent with this perilous proposition, he'd been waiting for the moment the impersonator would get cold feet and withdraw from the venture.

"And leave you and Beatrice and Elowen? My lord, we would never," Cris replied firmly.

Clare felt himself exhale with guilty relief. He knew he ought not cheer this man's entry into danger. Yet, still, they were going to need all the backup they could get.

"We do not just dress up like you to stand for conjurers or sign autographs. We live in your example," Cris went on proudly. "We'll fight at your side."

The stomachache returned. Perhaps he ought to have ordered plain cold water, just this once.

If Todrick rose to power, he reminded himself, it would not only be Cris and the Clares who would find themselves in grave danger. Oppression and cruelty would claim countless lives and ruin countless more. Without submitting Cris into peril now, worse consequences would be visited on the entire realm.

Would the notion have comforted Galwell? Perhaps.

It did not comfort him. All he could do was smile weakly at Cris, hoping his impersonator did not die tonight.

"You are a real hero," Clare said in honesty. "Thank you."

He rose from his seat, unable to withstand more of his new friend's good cheer—just another reminder of the joy swords could strike down in combat.

He strode for the door, where Vandra waited, her expression questioning.

"They'll get us in," Clare confirmed. "They'll fight, too."

His recruiting counterpart studied him, her eyes sharp despite not partaking in Harpy & Hind. She was, he'd learned, one of those who *loved* to preach of how much finer she found brews produced by independent brewers. *Very well*, he'd replied, *when the*

Hind designs commemorative drinks for our next victorious quest, you may request they exclude you. Vandra had humphed.

"This doesn't please you," she noted, reading his face.

They continued down the inn's lane of vendors. Vandra carried the leather bag storing the weapons she'd sourced for them, the clang of metal inaudible in the din of music and guests.

"No, it's good," Clare replied. He could hear how he was convincing himself. "We need all the help we can get. The queen's army would never reach us in time."

Vandra nodded patiently.

In her silence, he recognized encouragement to continue. "It's just . . ." he ventured. "I don't like the thought of these men getting hurt just because they're following my example. Who am I to lead people?"

Her laughter was not the reaction he expected. Okay, he knew he was no Galwell. Yet he did not imagine the idea of his leadership was downright humorous.

Or, not until now, he didn't.

When Vandra went on, her voice uncommonly gentle, he realized he'd misunderstood her. "You followed Galwell into danger," she pointed out. "Perhaps it was harder for him to lead you than you thought. He did sacrifice himself to save Beatrice."

Clare fell silent for a moment. Vandra was right. Clare had been so focused on the ways he'd fallen short of Galwell that he hadn't considered what parts of heroism Galwell himself might have struggled with. Perhaps, he realized, worrying he would not measure up to Galwell had carried him ironically closer to his glorious friend.

"Can I confess something to you?" he asked, emboldened.

"I'm no monk, Grandhart," Vandra replied.

He paused. "Does that mean . . . no?"

"Oh no, please tell me," she said eagerly. "I love secrets. I was just saying you don't need to ask permission. Your life isn't a burden to me." She punched him on the shoulder, hard enough other men would have yelped. Clare recognized genuine love in the gesture. "We're friends, aren't we?"

He smiled. "I'd say we are."

While the corridor wound past vendors of shining masks, he found his words. Clare was no poet, scribe, or orator, no heart healer or philosopher. He'd had very little practice in confessing how he felt.

"I don't know how Galwell did . . . any of it," he started. "I woke up with Beatrice in my arms this morning, and I don't want to go into battle with her. I want to take her and Elowen and you far from danger. I want to let someone else fight Myke."

The words would not come easily now. Clare forced them, finding inspiration in the struggle. If he did not know how to speak, he *did* know how to fight.

"I'm not a hero." He hung his head. "Those men costumed as me are closer to the real thing."

Only several steps forward did he realize Vandra no longer walked with him. He stopped. Turning, he found her waiting—insisting they would go no farther until he heard what she had to say.

"Clare, heroes are great and all," she said firmly. "But there are other things a person can be. Other destinies. Other legacies. Look at me, for instance." She smiled, without wry charm or subtle sarcasm. "I'm not one for glory or nobility. I don't always do good. But I try. I follow my own code. I'm no hero—I'm something I'd rather be instead. *Myself.*"

Meeting her gaze, he really listened. Vandra Ravenfall was, incredibly, *not* jesting. Not coy, not ironic, not making gentle fun of him. She was utterly serious.

It meant the realm to him.

Myself. He remembered what Beatrice had told him last night. How she wanted him, only him. One of his very favorite moments of the entire eve—which was saying something.

Of course, if Vandra wasn't going to joke, he would have to. "I hate to break it to you," he informed her, "but you're absolutely a hero."

Vandra shook her head, looking not displeased. "Take it back."

He grinned. "It's the truth. You don't have to be here, but you are."

The humor faded from Vandra's expression. Her eyes locked on his, sword-sharp with intensity.

"And so are you, Clare," she said. "What if you let that be enough for once?"

33

Beatrice

eatrice. Come out already."

She knew she needed to heed Elowen's demand. It was not unreasonable. Her friends could not defeat the Order if she did not get over herself—or, namely, the ridiculous garments she found herself wearing.

She would have chosen a knight's heavy steel encasements instead of her present fashion. Thigh-high boots that took forever to lace up. Lightweight leggings. A flowing chemise in emerald green with billowing sleeves. Her hair under a short golden-colored wig, which had cured her of any desire to spell her hair blond.

She was "Horseball Clare."

He'd volunteered to play in a charitable tournament Thessia had organized for Mythria's renowned celebrities to flaunt their skill on the field. Beatrice had hated how, when she saw the news in scribesheets, she immediately knew how much the opportunity would have meant to him, having wished when he was younger to play professionally.

Staring at herself in the mirror over the fireplace in her room, Beatrice now found herself wishing he'd never had the chance to ride in Thessia's tournament.

Clare himself had chosen her costume. Why he'd chosen this one, she had no inkling. However, she suspected it was the leggings.

"We're going to be late," Clare added.

"You can't be late to a party," she called out in weak protest.

"Fair point, but you *can* be late to the resurrection of dark evil," Vandra replied.

Beatrice frowned at herself. Vandra had her there.

"The carriage is here," Clare exhorted her, restraining his eagerness poorly. "It's time we depart."

She groaned.

"Fine," she submitted. Standing in front of her door, she prepared herself. This was undoubtedly worse than walking into combat. "No one can laugh," she warned.

Forcing aside reluctance, she emerged into the suite.

She found her crew seated in the spacious sitting room. Everyone—well, everyone stared. Vandra and Elowen were not in costume, needing none for their part in the plan. Clare was dressed in his non-deluxe Hero Card costume, having wished for flashier garb but grudgingly conceding the common costume would disguise him best, and Hugh was happily decked out in the rustic stylings of the character Clare played on *As the Realm Spins*.

"Oh, Beatrice," Elowen said. "The wig . . ."

"*I know*," Beatrice replied peevishly. "The rest of you better not let me die looking like this."

"It's not so bad," Vandra consoled her, grimacing.

Clare rose from his seat.

Ignoring them, he strode up to her. The man certainly could stride. With one gentle, rough finger, he lifted her chin. "You . . . look . . . magnificent," he said.

She forgot herself entirely. Her costume. Even, if she was honest, her fear of what the night held. She went utterly weak.

"Is it weird I'm incredibly turned on right now?" Clare went on. Only the deep kiss he swept her into rescued the moment from ruination. The crew responded in customary form. Vandra wolverling-whistled. "Okay, can we finally stop pretending we didn't know you were together now?" Elowen remarked. Self-conscious, Beatrice pushed Clare off her gently. "I mean, heart magic here," Elowen continued. "I knew all along, but still."

Hugh sniffled.

Everyone found the future king crying. No one knew what to say. "Hugh, we'll get through this," Vandra ventured. "You have a wedding to make. Fear not."

Hugh shook his head. "No," he clarified. "I don't fear for us. I've just rooted for Claretrice for . . . so many years." He wiped his cheeks, overwhelmed with joy.

Beatrice rolled her eyes, yet found she could not muster her ordinary disdain for the nickname.

Clare, of course, grinned in delight. When she caught sight of his expression, she could not help smiling in return.

For the past decade she'd struggled with what she had lost when the Four had won against the Order. She'd spent the past days wondering what she might win or lose if they vanquished their foes once more.

Perhaps, she considered now, the very presence of the people in this room meant something else entirely—victory against the phantoms of the past, no matter the outcome of the impending fight. Happiness. Friendship. Even love, perhaps. The spoils of the war won in her heart.

It gave her courage. If she could face the darkness within, she could face the darkness ahead.

"Well, shall we save the realm?" she invited them. "Again?"

* * *

The carriage was long, sleek, and luxurious. Lacquered paint the color of night reflected the shining magical lights of Vermillion Vale.

Beatrice had only ever ridden in one like it once, when Robert had booked one to carry them home from a feast where he'd wished to impress the inviting lord in the neighboring village. He'd nodded off in his cushioned seat, and she had stared out the window in grateful silence.

Now the group piled in, everyone jostling with nervousness. The spacious interior fit them and their weapons roomily—and, they found, compartments in the doors held sparkling wine and chocolate-covered nightberries. Enchanted lighting illuminated the space in changing displays of pink and purple.

It was, she would say, not quite the war chariot she'd expected.

Clare, evidently feeling similarly, looked to Hugh. He held up a wine bottle in unspoken inquiry.

"It was part of the carriage rental package here," Hugh explained sheepishly. "And . . . well, I wanted one. This is my bachelor bash, after a fashion."

"Personally, I could use a drink," Elowen volunteered.

"Me too," Beatrice chimed in.

Clare shrugged, clearly finding no fault with the premise of pre-combat libations. He poured the bubbling drink into the provided glasses.

While he passed them out, the carriage started down Vermillion Vale's wide main road. Outside their windows, sparkling color shows and spelled tavern signs lit up the night. The clamor of crowds joined with the echo of music in one exhilarating chorus.

Beatrice found herself strangely moved. Vermillion Vale was

nowhere poets wrote of, yet . . . she found so much beauty in the night surrounding her. The Vale overflowed with expression, with hope and struggle. With people. With life.

"To heroes." Hugh raised his glass.

Clare nodded. He hoisted his drink. "To us."

"To Galwell," Vandra offered solemnly.

Beatrice looked to Elowen. "To friendship."

Elowen smiled. She raised her glass in everyone's waiting silence.

"To tomorrow," she said.

They downed their drinks. *To tomorrow.* Yes, they would fight *for* tomorrow like they would drink *to* tomorrow.

The Night Dragon was not far, the luxury inns of the Vale closely located for easy passage of guests from one to others. With the carriage drawing them closer to their fate, everyone fell silent.

If they failed, it would fall to other heroes to defend Mythria, if other heroes even remained. If they failed, the people Beatrice cared for most in the realm would be gone. The inspiration she'd just felt changed into desperation. It was easier, in a way, living in Robert's manor, never having anything it would hurt to lose. Just days ago, a silly robe was the most important thing to her.

Now . . .

She met Clare's eyes. While he likewise looked lost in dark contemplation, he managed a wink.

It comforted her. If Clare Grandhart could still wink, everything was not lost.

She reached for one of the chocolate-covered nightberries. She loved nightberries. Enjoying the pop of sour sugar in her mouth, she faced the group.

"So what does everyone want to do tomorrow?" she asked cheerfully.

Elowen laughed. Clare did the same. "I was envisioning massages and manicures," he joined in with eagerness. "Spa day. I haven't gone this long without a visit to my favorite manimagician in years."

Vandra grinned. "I was hoping to catch a concert," she shared, reaching for the nightberries. "I hear the Brethren are playing."

"I would be interested in that," Elowen said meaningfully.

"It's a date," Vandra replied.

"Well, *I* would like to go shopping," Beatrice declared. "I've recently lost all my possessions in a divorce."

"How dreadful," Elowen commiserated.

Hugh watched them, openmouthed.

"Is this . . . what it's always like?" he asked.

Beatrice offered him one of the nightberries. "What what's like?"

"I've never saved the realm before," he explained. "I guess I didn't picture it like this."

The other four exchanged amused glances. In some respects, their current situation didn't resemble their first venture in saving the realm. Instead of dark clouds over castles, they rode through the glittering lights of entertainment. Instead of road provisions, they enjoyed luxurious delicacies. Otherwise—in the important ways—

"Yeah. This is pretty much what it's like," Clare said.

Hugh remained skeptical. "If I didn't know you'd done it once before, I'd be a tad worried," he confessed.

His concern charmed Beatrice. Hugh was good-spirited, even jovial—yet she knew Thessia would not love him were he not cautious and gently inquisitive when needed. In his position, she would likely feel the same.

She clapped a hand on his shoulder.

"Hugh, we're the experts on the subject," she promised him. "Our professional advice? Have as much fun as you can."

On cue, the carriage slowed. They had reached the Night Dragon.

In the ironic echo of Beatrice's words, the group's companionable cheer faded into somberness. "Well, this is where we depart," Vandra noted. "We'll see you inside."

Beatrice fought to hide the way her stomach sank to the carriage floor. Vandra opened the door, revealing the Night Dragon's unceremonious rear entrance, then proceeded nimbly out. Elowen followed. As she was halfway out, however, Beatrice grabbed Elowen's hand.

Elowen halted. Her eyes gleaming like the lights of the Vale, she found Beatrice's gaze.

Beatrice did not know quite what she wanted to say. She only felt the wretched reprise of their first quest, remembering when last they'd parted from each other for battle. She'd pushed Elowen away, forcing them to fight, in order to conceal her deception from Elowen's heart magic. She'd hurt her friend.

"You know, these past days," she said, knowing she needed to hurry, "it's been . . . an honor to be your friend again. I—"

Elowen squeezed her hand.

"I know," she said. "I feel the same."

Beatrice was certain she did. "Be safe out there," she implored Elowen.

The other woman's lips quirked. "I will, as long as you don't do anything foolish like—I don't know, try to sacrifice yourself?"

Grateful, Beatrice returned her friend's smile. Elowen released her hand and leapt down into the luminous night.

When the carriage started once more to move, carrying them to the main entrance, Beatrice sat back in her seat, allowing herself the comfort of leaning into Clare. He wrapped an arm around her, his scent enveloping her—journeys and magic and home in one.

It did not last long enough.

The carriage drew them around to the front entrance. The inn's liveried footman opened the door gracefully. Outside, the Night Dragon waited.

What she could not offer the place in commendation of its design, she could in the properness of its name. The luxury inn looked like none she'd ever seen. Where others sought to invite with glittering gold or promise peace with lush waterfalls, the Night Dragon was sculpted of swooping, stabbing contours of ebony rock. The place *wanted* to intimidate, hoping the provocative intimation of danger would entice guests looking to revel on the edge.

Very subtle, she wished to say to the Fraternal Order.

From the look of the gathered crowd, the ploy was working. The inn was flush with guests, young revelers wearing every manner of expensive or flamboyant clothing. Nighttime spectacles hid eyes unfocused with drunkenness or edged with magic indulgence. Drum-heavy music pounded from within.

Waiting off to the side, the flank of costumed Clares stood. The real Clare, who'd coordinated with Cris earlier, had shared this was where the impersonator troupe had planned to meet up for their Night Dragon event. More Clares were walking up, joining their compatriots in the growing crowd. It was the logical location for Beatrice, Hugh, and Clare to rendezvous with the Clares, they'd decided.

With Hugh, she followed Clare over, joining the impersonators. To the cadre's credit, they looked ready, jaws set, eyes clear with vigor.

They would need it, she knew.

Near the front of the group, Beatrice spotted the man she kissed yesterday, standing proud with his compatriots, hand on his sword. Their conversation died when the three drew nearer.

Clare Grandhart, the one and only, stepped forth, squaring his shoulders. While she loved the rogue most, Beatrice found she didn't dislike the commanding posture he struck.

"Fellow Clares!" he called out. The conquering knight. The captain in charge of himselves. "Let's get this revel started!"

34

Elowen

The revel room packed in more bodies than Elowen had ever seen inside a single place. Clares had been hired to pass out drinks and work the bar in character. She couldn't make out Beatrice, Hugh, or the real Clare among them. Live musicians used a magical amplifier that made their tunes so loud Elowen's body actually shook with every note. It smelled like body odor and perfume oils had gotten into a war that neither side could ever win. And the entire room was green from the crystal lights that shot out like swords, slicing through the tightly packed crowd.

On a raised platform, Myke Lycroft made sure he was visible to everyone in the entire space. He held the Sword of Souls, delighting in not just the physical weight of it, but the heavy emotions inside. It disgusted Elowen to sense the joy he felt. He lifted the sword up to the crystallized lights, downright aroused by its power, then tilted his head down to chat with someone below him.

Elowen nearly fainted when she realized who was on the other side of the conversation. Todrick.

The *corpse* of Todrick.

His body had been charmed to hide signs of decay, but even that could not erase the uncanny stillness of him. The strange sheen of his cheeks. The brittle dullness of his lifeless hair. He had been rendered to smile, frozen in a state of horrific bliss.

Elowen and Vandra had only a moment to compose themselves

before their uncostumed presence would become notable. Elowen could not afford to panic. Instead she grabbed Vandra's hand, squeezing her fingers quickly beneath her cloak.

"May the Ghosts keep us safe," she whispered.

"We don't need the Ghosts. I will keep you safe," Vandra replied. And then she cleared her throat and burst forth, dragging Elowen by the wrist. "*Myyyyke*," she sing-songed, raising her voice to be heard over the chaotic music. "I come to you bearing gifts!"

Elowen did not have to pretend to resist. She channeled her every anxiety and fear into this moment, and her body reacted as it normally would, by pulling back, desperate to recede into the shadows.

"Vandra Ravenfall," Myke said back. "To what do we owe this misfortune?" He gestured down to Todrick as if Todrick was an active participant in the conversation.

"It's only misfortune when I'm not on your side," Vandra cooed once they reached the ground, where dead Todrick sat with his hollow half-smile, staring at them with empty eyes. "Lucky for you, I've seen the error of my ways, and I've come to pledge my devotion to the Fraternal Order. To prove I'm honest with my word, I've brought you something valuable."

Vandra's voice was sinister in its sweetness, but Elowen knew the heart of the woman behind the deception. She didn't need to feel Vandra's emotions anymore to know that the love between them was strong enough to withstand whatever lengths they had to go to for access to the Sword of Souls.

Elowen—fearing her comfort with the situation showed on her face—started tugging once more against the grip that Vandra kept on her wrist.

"I heard you wanted one of the Four to be the last soul killed

with your sword before you resurrect Todrick," Vandra continued, lassoing Elowen closer. "What better member than Galwell's
little sister? She's so surly, isn't she? Perfect for the job."

"Let me go," Elowen hissed.

"Never," Vandra replied.

Myke clapped in delight. "Fantastic!" he cheered. "No, *poetic*.
She's just the person indeed. It would be like murdering Galwell
all over again. They even have the same hair. But I know someone
who would delight in killing her even more than I would, which is
saying a lot."

"Is that so?" Vandra asked carefully. Elowen sensed her confusion. She also shared it. *Someone wanted to kill her even more than
Myke Lycroft?*

Myke leapt off the platform in rather impressive fashion, sail-
ing to the ground and landing in a fighter stance. Then he dusted
off his tunic and turned to Todrick. "My brother from another
mother," he said, kissing Todrick on the forehead. "Welcome to
your party."

Myke plunged the Sword of Souls into Todrick's torso.

In the blink of an eye, souls began coursing through Todrick,
reanimating his lifeless frame. His ghastly skin regained color,
starting at his ankles, visible in the gap between his shoes and his
too-short pants. There was also a dark glow around him.

This was what happened when life was born from pain.

For a startling moment, everyone froze, transfixed by the ominous glow. It was oddly fascinating, how unnatural it was. When
realization dawned that Todrick returning to this realm meant
only terrible things, chaos soon followed.

The army of Clares surged forth, brawling with members of the
Fraternal Order. A captor wrenched Elowen away from Vandra.

Everything happened within seconds, devastating their entire plan in the blink of an eye.

As the captor drew Elowen further from the crowd, surely escorting her to some locked chamber until Todrick was rested enough to end her life, Elowen still radiated calmness. She'd spent years anticipating something as awful as this. Somehow, living it did not scare her. She knew the depths of her own fears with breathtaking intimacy. She could catalog them by their scent, their taste, their color. They were hers to hold forevermore. They would never be removed. Not entirely. But she'd worked so hard to push past them and *live*. She would not let the Fraternal Order send her back to the depths of despair with one swift capture. Not easily, at least.

Not without a fight.

"Hello," she said to the burly man who held her by the arms. "Wow. You're so handsome. Can I ask you a question?" She played docile, appearing friendly. Charmed, even. A move straight from Vandra's playbook. If she never got to see Vandra again, Elowen would always find ways to keep her close.

The man leaned in so he could hear Elowen better over the roar of the crowd. "What's that?" he asked. "You're much better-looking in person, you know."

As soon as he got near enough, Elowen took her chance. She cranked her neck back and headbutted the *shit* out of the man. Her vision doubled. It was a small price to pay for what her work did to her captor. He lumbered back like a felled tree, rendered unconscious from the force of Elowen's blow.

Head spinning, Elowen ran toward Todrick.

"No, my love!" Vandra called out, wrestling two Order members nearby. "It's too dangerous!"

"Everything's dangerous!" Elowen yelled back. "I can't live in fear anymore!"

With one roundhouse kick, Vandra knocked over the Order members she'd been wrestling. For a moment, Elowen thought Vandra planned to stop her.

But, no. Vandra would never.

She started clearing Elowen's path instead, mowing over Order members who might interfere.

Elowen followed the path of fallen bodies until she reached Todrick, who looked to be about half alive. His legs and arms were flush with color, but his chest and head were still bluish and cold. Elowen didn't have much time.

She just hoped she had enough.

Elowen scanned the crowd, making sure there were no other imminent threats to her safety. She found no danger. She did, however, find Beatrice.

The terror in Beatrice's expression was clear. Elowen required no heart magic to decipher it. It did not concern or upset her. Instead, it was a comfort, like a blanket that wrapped around her. No matter what had happened between them, they loved each other. They were family, and they always would be.

I'm sorry, Elowen mouthed.

I'm sorry, too, Beatrice mouthed back.

With that, Elowen put her hands around the Sword of Souls.

35

Beatrice

In one horrible flash of light, Elowen and the sword went flying in opposite directions.

Beatrice watched her friend hit the ground hard. Elowen did not move.

Instinct like none Beatrice had ever felt ignited in her. She wanted to run to Elowen—but an Order member grabbed her, his expensive cologne reeking. He ripped her wig off.

"It's Beatrice of the Four!" he called out, attracting more attention.

Suddenly, Order men descended on her from every side, like carcass hawks wheeling over their next meal.

Beatrice fought, ducking under blows, slashing forward with the quarter sword she'd hidden in her riding boots. In the fray, the braid she'd concealed under her wig came loose, whipping behind her with every movement. Improbably, the pounding of the revel room's music helped her, providing the rhythm for her dance of destruction.

Emerging from the melee, Beatrice saw with enormous relief that Elowen was conscious, if barely. She was crawling with feeble, hungry strength toward the Sword of Souls, which glimmered weakly. Its power was diminished, but not yet gone.

Elowen was close. *So very close.* In seconds, she would have her hands on the weapon. She would be able to finish what she'd started, vanquishing the sword's magic. She would complete their quest.

Only—into her path stepped Todrick van Thorn. *Fully revived.*

She'd forgotten how formidable van Thorn was. He effervesced with evil. The revel room's cutting lights shone off his dark hair. The vigor of viciousness sparkled coldly in his eyes, like he considered nothing around him to be real, only a game.

Dressed in funereal shades of night, he surveyed the chaos into which he'd been resurrected. He grinned.

Nearby, Beatrice noticed, Vandra was climbing onto the stage where the musicians played. She lined up her shot from the elevation, loosing an arrow directly at Todrick.

It glanced off his heart, ricocheting with the smallest shimmer of dark magic, leaving him unharmed. He was . . . *No.* The sword had not only reanimated him, Beatrice realized, heart plunging in horror. The foulest man in the history of the realm did not merely live. He was immortal, the sword's magic coursing through him in protective power.

"I've missed this," he declared.

The first words from Todrick's mouth quieted the fighting nearest him. He held men's gazes—they were not used to hearing the undead speak. With magic or without, however, his presence was commanding.

"I've missed the fear," he went on. "The pain."

He shrugged grandly.

"Why pretend? In the moment of my death, what infuriated me were the hours, the days I'd spent ingratiating myself to others. Pretending I wanted only what was *right for Mythria*. The way the realm should be ruled." He shook his head. "Pretenses of philosophy. Of noblesse."

He reached for the sword of the man nearest him.

When the fighter handed the weapon over, Todrick promptly ran him through with it.

"I'm done pretending," he stated. With every word, Beatrice watched how he captivated even while he unnerved. The worst part was she understood how it worked on them, the Order's men. The resentful, the dissatisfied, the self-righteous, the proud. She felt how he drew them in, a blackhearted beacon. "I want this *for me*," he drawled. "The domination. The oppression. It's fun. I like it."

He dropped the sword. With the clang of cold steel, Beatrice felt herself flinch.

"I'm going to enjoy ruling you," Todrick told the room. He laughed in delight. Tossing Clares and Order members alike out of his way, he strode forward with unnatural power.

When his eyes fell on the sword, however, he frowned. Elowen may have been too late to stop his resurrection, but she'd weakened his weapon. The sword no longer held the power he needed to rewrite reality for all of Mythria.

If his glee was unnerving, the darkness of his disappointment was downright frightening. He rounded on Elowen with disgust. "You stupid girl," he hissed. His voice held no velvet, only venom. "You'll pay for that."

When he started for Elowen, valiant Clares rushed him. Van Thorn waved his hand once. His pursuers stopped. Their postures suddenly relaxed.

Beatrice had fought Todrick before. She knew what was happening. Using his head magic, he'd rewritten the reality surrounding him. Anyone close to him no longer believed him to be their enemy.

Beatrice locked eyes with Clare, who was fending off Order men across the room. Both of them were too far away to get to Todrick.

Myke reached him instead.

In the midst of the fray, Myke pulled the wickedest man in Mythria into a hug.

Beatrice felt her eyebrows rise. She expected Todrick to push Myke off, intent on resuming his vengeance. Van Thorn did not. Rather, he clasped Myke close, returning the embrace warmly.

"Thank you, my friend," she could hear Todrick say.

"I missed you, brother," Myke replied, full of feeling. He wiped a tear from his eye. "You bring out the worst in me. I have so much I wish to tell you."

"I wish to hear everything. Soon," Todrick promised.

Watching, Beatrice found the moment oddly . . . moving. Yes, they were evil and needed to be stopped. But they were best friends, too. Myke had spent years planning this reunion. He was not merely restoring his partner in villainy—he was reviving his dearest friend.

Beatrice could not help looking to Elowen, who was fighting to stand. Watching the villains embrace, unlikely inspiration found her. She should never have abandoned Elowen for ten years while grief devoured her. She should have been like Myke and fought to bring her best friend back to the world.

If she survived this, she would do better.

When the men parted, Myke put a dagger in Todrick's hand, the silver glinting. The weapon enchanted to steal powers, Beatrice intuited.

Visceral fear gripped Beatrice. She pushed forward, jabbing elbows into faces, carving her path with swings of her sword. On the other end of the room, Clare was doing the same. There was no lyricism in his combat now, only frenzied ferocity. He couldn't get free, and she couldn't move fast enough—she would not reach Elowen in time.

The next instant, she saw she would not need to. Vandra leapt down from the stage, crouching when she hit the black marble floor. She ripped a shield out of someone's hands and slid the sharp metal across the floor with enough force to knock both Myke and Todrick off their feet.

It gave Elowen the chance to stagger toward the sword.

The sword.

The powerful weapon held their only hope of defeating the invulnerable Todrick. Except it wasn't powerful anymore, not after Elowen had depleted its magic. It would need sacrifices. *Souls.*

The realization hit Beatrice with horrible clarity. *Their* souls could be enough to power the sword—hers, Elowen's, Clare's—ensuring it held enough magic for Vandra and Hugh to slay Todrick.

It was the choice Galwell had made. How could you let someone die when you could be the one to save them?

Everything in the room seemed to slow. The rhythm of the music disappeared under her heartbeat. The darkness of the Night Dragon closed in on her, narrowing on the consuming enormity of her choice.

But . . . it was one Beatrice wouldn't make. Maybe Galwell was simply better than her. She was not willing to sacrifice her friends *or* herself. Not anymore. She needed what she'd found these past days on the road with her companions, mending her shattered pieces. Not a last stand, a doomed repetition. *A path forward.*

She thought of Elowen's forgiveness of her, of how she'd forgiven Clare. Forgiveness, she realized, was the first step of something none of them had done for the past ten years—focusing on a better future instead of living mired in the past.

We all *relive what's happened to us. Over and over.* Clare's words returned to her. *No amount of revisiting our memories will change the past. We can't return there, not really.*

Beatrice could, though. She did every night.

The clash had changed the room from revel into battleground, Clares fighting Order men in one ceaseless clamor. Clare continued valiantly forth, but his pace dragged while he wrestled more opponents than even he could handle. Vandra struggled to wrench her bow free from men who'd seized the weapon's shining frame.

While Beatrice watched her friends fight off foes, get back up after being knocked down, continue to fight without giving up, she stood still.

She closed her eyes, everything around her fading as she sank into her powers. The veil of the past rose, gossamer curtains greeting her. For ten years she'd endlessly relived what had happened on one devastating day, over and over. On this quest, she'd learned the virtue of making new choices, of fighting her expectations, of forcing herself to forgive and grow and change and understand instead of repeating old mistakes.

How could you change the future?

By doing what you couldn't in the past.

In her magic, she returned to just minutes ago. She rewatched in her own eyes as Vandra dragged Elowen toward Myke. Distantly, she felt blows bruising her, blades cutting her. She resisted the pull of the present, fighting to remain in her magic.

Vandra was speaking to Myke. In seconds, Beatrice knew Myke would plunge the sword into Todrick. But right before their plan could collapse, Beatrice did what she had never once imagined possible.

She stepped out into the past.

The shimmering curtain of magic resisted her movement. Head

pounding—muscles fighting reality itself—she pushed, straining her power. *I can do this*, she counseled herself.

She ran. When Myke leapt from the dais to where he would stab Todrick's corpse, Beatrice was there, waiting, right where he landed. Using his surprise, she wrenched the Sword of Souls from his hands.

Under the crystalline lights, she looked to Elowen. Elowen looked to her.

In their locked gazes, perfect clarity passed. They needed no practice making wordless plans. They'd done it since they were children.

Beatrice threw the sword right to her, changing the future.

36

Clare

Clare stood among the Clares, blending into the crowd in their inconspicuous guise of revel room servers, waiting for their moment. He caught Cris's eye. His impersonator nodded with confidence Clare wished he shared.

He remembered raids with his old bandit crew under the cover of the Vast Plains nights. He remembered executing Galwell's plans fearlessly, fighting like five men in deadly strongholds. The legend Clare Grandhart inspired men across the realm. He could inspire himself, too. When Elowen grasped the Sword of Souls to depower the weapon, he would lead their charge.

But instead, Myke jumped from the dais—like he intended to resurrect Todrick now.

Clare's heart clenched in his chest. This would ruin everything. If Myke drove the enchanted sword into Todrick before Elowen could get her hands on the weapon, Mythria was more or less doomed.

Yet—

Beatrice was there, somehow. Clare's mind struggled to comprehend what he was seeing. It was not what they'd predicted, not what they'd planned. With fast force, Beatrice wrested the sword from Myke's hands and threw it perfectly to Elowen.

The Fraternal Order reacted immediately. With weapons drawn, unsheathed in one collective shriek of steel, they moved to shield Myke and the disgusting corpse of Todrick, whose gaunt, lifeless smile never changed.

Clare knew what the moment demanded. Fuck the plan. He preferred improvising anyway.

"Clares!" he called. "Now!" He pulled a sword from under his cloak and raised it high into the air, signaling the performers to retrieve their own very non-prop weapons that Vandra had sourced for them.

They rushed in to defend Elowen, who gripped the sword, magic swirling around her hands and surging up her arms. Green incandescence emanated from her, overpowering even the revel room's dazzling swaths of light.

It's working, Clare realized. They were going to defeat the Order. Todrick wouldn't come back.

Euphoria rushed into him. No revel could ever compare to the sheer rush of victory. While the fray unfolded, metal clashing on metal in the darkness, the clang of swords joining with the heavy power of the music, Clare felt unstoppable.

Until he glimpsed Beatrice.

She was stumbling away from the fray. Her knees gave out beneath her, and she crashed to the floor. Something was very wrong. He didn't know what had happened, but she must have used her magic somehow to anticipate Myke's movements. She was drained now. Vulnerable.

Fear ripped through Clare, sharper than a blade. When he started for her, though, Order men blocked his way. He shoved forward desperately. In the distance, Leonor loomed, heading right for the weakened Beatrice, who was only barely managing to fend off an attacker. He needed to get to her.

He couldn't. While perhaps he could have fought free of one of the Order men holding him, he could not fend off both.

The man on his left crumpled without warning. Clare glanced up, finding none other than Cris standing over the man. Seizing the moment, Clare pushed off his other opponent.

The relief on his face was the only expression of gratitude he could muster for Cris, who needed nothing more. "Go to her, man. We've got this," he said.

And indeed they did. Clare needed spare them only half a glance to see them handily dispatching more attackers. In fact, around him, the Order was falling to the Clares. They were *winning*.

Clare ran for Beatrice, leaping over a chandelier crashing to the floor in the mayhem. The ebony stone cracked under the wrought-iron limbs while illuminated gems flew everywhere. Clare hit the ground crouched with the sharp stones crunching underfoot.

When he straightened, he found himself cut off by none other than a furious Myke Lycroft.

The battle raged around them. Myke's cheek had been slashed, blood cascading down half his face. In his eyes was righteous fury. The Order was failing, and he knew it. Todrick was dead for good.

Myke would take whatever vengeance he had left.

He licked the blood from his lips, his hand finding his sword.

"I challenge Clare Grandhart to a duel to the death!" he called, his voice riven with desperation. "Man to man—how matters *should* be settled."

Skirmishes subsided. Eyes fixed on them. Myke's challenge held import, harkening to the days when heroes would duel in their legends. It was funny, Clare could recognize. In a way it was the ultimate recognition of what he'd been seeking for a decade—the chance to prove he was the hero everyone needed him to be. It was the sort of moment songs could be written of. The sort of moment to make Galwell proud.

But Galwell was dead. Who fucking cared if he was proud or not? Clare's life was not determined by what strangers or the dead wanted of him. It was determined by *him*. By the people he loved.

Clare made to pass Myke, no longer interested in legacy.

Myke watched him, confusion warping the villain's frantic features. "Is this what Mythria's great hero has become?" he spat. "Fight me or reveal yourself to be a coward."

Clare kept walking, his sword lowered in concession. "Call me a coward if you wish," he replied. "I don't care what anyone, especially lowlifes like you, think of me." Striding past Myke, he let his shoulder knock into the other man's roughly.

He was not Galwell the Great. He was Clare Grandhart.

"You all saw it!" Lycroft screamed out. "Grandhart is no hero! He won't meet me in battle!"

Clare let him shout. His only care was Beatrice.

Finally, he reached her. His victory. His everything. The end of his quest. For Clare, the center of Mythria lay weakened on the floor in front of him. While his reputation crumbled, he knelt at her side.

"Hey, love," he whispered, his voice rough. "You ready to go home?"

Beatrice nodded. While she looked dazed, she seemed uninjured. "I think . . . you're the best Clare here, Clare." She giggled, intoxicated by the overuse of her magic.

Clare smiled, his heart full. "That's good enough for me."

He hoisted her up into his arms. Rising to his feet, with Beatrice's head resting softly against his chest, he glimpsed Elowen on the dais. She raised the Sword of Souls aloft, the weapon gleaming with dangerous light. In one massive release of magic, the souls exploded out of her like daylight shattering the darkness.

While Vandra crouched defensively, the blast knocked Order men off their feet.

Elowen dropped the sword, looking stunned. Not just stunned—*victorious*.

Clare used the distraction to head for the service door, while Vandra straightened. In the chaos-consumed room, Vandra picked up the Sword of Souls. She strode up to the dais—up to Todrick—raising the unenchanted blade.

Where she lopped the dead leader's head clean off.

Reaching the service door, Clare's final glimpse of the revel room was van Thorn's ossified ebony hair thumping unceremoniously onto the floor.

Night greeted him outside. The cool was wondrous in contrast to the heated furor inside the Night Dragon. High into the sky rose the lights of Vermillion Vale, with no inkling of the destruction beneath them. As Clare set Beatrice down, Order men fled out the doors, evading capture, knowing dishonor's stain would mark them forever. It served them right. He expected Myke Lycroft was among them, returning to his existence in exile—the only life he deserved.

The revel was over. Vandra emerged, stumbling out with her arm around Elowen. In Vandra's free hand, the Sword of Souls remained, safely out of the Order's clutches. The women's faces exuberant, they shared a victorious kiss. Clare could not help returning the wolverling-whistle Vandra had given them in their suite.

It made him easy for Elowen and Vandra to find when they parted. They walked over. "Is she all right?" Elowen asked, eyeing Beatrice.

"She's magic drunk," Clare replied fondly. "She'll be fine."

"What *happened*?" Vandra voiced the question Clare suspected was on everyone's minds.

From the ground, Beatrice spoke up. "I stepped out inside my memories. Changed the . . . future."

The group's eyes widened. "Is this the intoxication, or are you serious?" Elowen asked gravely.

Beatrice pouted. "You know I'm an honest drunk, El," she reminded her friend indignantly. With visible effort, she dragged her gaze to Clare. "Guess I really am a time-walker." She smiled sweetly up at him.

It undid him entirely.

He could not wait to kiss her. Or just to hold her close, knowing she was safe. Or to jest with her, saying, *Lo, remember when we saved the realm? Twice?* He did not know where he would start.

He did not know how he would ever end.

Since they'd set out on their quest, he'd wrestled with the rogues within him. Fear, fury, desire. Yet he knew now the greatest of them was love. For nothing quelled heroism like knowing there was something grander still in this realm for him—something no duel, no victory, no quest could match. He did not need to be great. He needed only to be good enough for the people he held dear.

They'd triumphed, but more importantly, they had found their way back to each other. He and Beatrice, Elowen and Vandra. They would write their legend in days of friendship, nights of love, lives of loyalty.

What could be more heroic than that?

Elowen knelt, pulling Beatrice into an embrace. Clare and Vandra exchanged knowing looks.

"Where's Hugh?" Beatrice asked abruptly. "We still have to get him home in time for the wedding."

Clare faltered. Where *was* Hugh? Everyone looked around, searching the crowd still streaming out of the revel room. Clare's gaze found Order men, Clares in every manner of costume, some people limping while others ran, even someone who suspiciously resembled Beatrice's ex-husband . . . But there was no sign of Hugh.

Until he appeared. His shirt was bloodied, his hair perfectly tousled, his biceps rippling in his torn tunic.

He looked fucking heroic.

"Gang! Guess what?" he called out. "I've slain Myke! He challenged me to a duel, and he was very unskillful!"

The four of them stared in surprise. Finally, Clare huffed a laugh.

"Get in here, Sir Hugh." Clare waved the future king over warmly, drawing him into their group hug. "I think," Clare informed him, "you're officially the new hero of Mythria."

37

Beatrice

N othing compared to the dessert table.

Beatrice stood with Elowen, gazing over the vast spread of sugary confections produced for Thessia's wedding. The friends were dressed in glittering gowns—Elowen's forest green, the same dress Beatrice remembered from the weddings they'd attended before their first quest, and her own shimmering pale pink. Queendom's castle matched them for finery, from the flowers decorating every corner and entrance to the fine silk garlands draped in every corridor.

Beatrice examined the sumptuous sweets with indecision. When you were the queen, she guessed, your nuptials would compel every dessert you could imagine, and some you couldn't. Thessia's royal event planners had held competitions for the finest culinary hand magicians in the realm to dazzle them with delicious inventions. Everyone in Mythria had watched the conjurations.

The results waited in front of them. Elaborate, high-reaching sculptures of Mythria's castles constructed entirely of sweetened cream enchanted in unmelting soft ice. Sugar flattened into parchment-thin sheets folded into flowers and other sculptures. Pearlescent jelly globes with colored sweet liqueurs swirling within. There were even imitation wedding rings with gems of candy.

Elowen scooped some iced cream—strawberry, its pink sheen suggested—right out of the wall of the nearest sculpted castle. "I think," she commented, slipping the spoon past her lips, "I made a mistake living in the trees for ten years."

When Beatrice bit into the round pastry she'd chosen, caramel liqueur flowed from the fluffy center. *How in Mythria did they get the liqueur inside without moistening the cake?* She would need to watch the competition conjurations when she returned to her room.

"I'm leaving Elgin and moving to wherever has a bakery that sells *these*," she declared.

Elowen giggled. It made Beatrice smile like no wondrous confection ever could. Her friend had laughed more freely in the days since they'd defeated the Fraternal Order in Vermillion Vale and returned victorious to Queendom.

She laughed with Vandra, she laughed with Clare—she'd even laughed with Beatrice on their sleeping rolls from the quest, laid out on the floor in Beatrice's room in the castle, where Beatrice had invited her in imitation of the "sleep outside" parties they would have when they were children. They'd stayed up until sunrise watching their favorite *Desires of the Night* episodes and catching each other up on their lives.

They piled their plates high with cakes, creams, and citruses and brought them back to their table, where Vandra was seated, drinking wine.

Vandra, who took formalwear very seriously, had had a magenta one-piece suit custom-made for her. Queendom's finest fashionist had cut every line perfectly, leaving Vandra looking like she was dressed in blushing daggers.

She pulled Elowen into her lap, making Elowen giggle once more.

"You just missed the royal scribe," Vandra informed her. "He wants to make some sort of dramatic reenactment conjuration of our heroics."

Beatrice snorted. "Ghosts aid him," she commented, hand hovering with indecision over her plate. Chocolate-covered plum with silver-painted shell, or dragon sculpted out of folded sheet sugar? "I certainly don't need to relive any of it!"

"Let him interview Hugh," Elowen suggested. "He's the real star."

Vandra reached up, gently brushing Elowen's hair behind her ear. While Elowen had politely yet firmly resisted the queen's maids' efforts to decorate her face with rouges and gem dust, she'd consented to just a little magical enhancement of her hair. It shone like winter sunsets.

"I don't know," Vandra replied gently. "While Hugh has the glory of defeating Myke, no reenactment would be complete without a certain heart magician releasing all the souls trapped in the Sword of Souls."

Elowen didn't shy away or cower from the attention. She preened. "I was quite magnificent," she conceded. "Elowen the Excellent, perhaps."

Vandra gazed into Elowen's eyes. "Elowen my everything," she offered softly.

Beatrice smiled. Wanting to give the women their moment, she excused herself on the premise of wanting more chocolate plums, which was not entirely fabricated.

Like Sir Hugh's victorious duel, stories of Elowen's feat of magical power had grown in recent days to the stuff of legend. Beatrice could not put into words the pride she felt watching her once-fearful friend contend gracefully with fame and fans.

No one, however, had spoken of Beatrice's time-walking.

She'd requested her friends conceal her newfound power. As far as Mythria knew, the plan all along was for Beatrice to race toward Myke and rip the sword from him.

In honesty, she knew the renown—not to mention the new requests she'd receive—were not the deepest reason she wanted secrecy. She did not know how she felt about her new magic herself. How did one rewrite every memory of one's life, knowing in each of them, part of oneself remained hidden within?

One day, she would know.

Just not yet.

She wandered through the courtyard-turned-flower-festooned-revel while the musicians struck up one of the newer songs captivating Mythria. "King of Heroes" was written in honor of Hugh himself. When the singer picked up the first verse, she nodded along to the pleasant melody.

A hand found her waist.

"May I have this dance?"

Clare Grandhart's voice was sugarless, yet the sweetest sound she had ever heard. She turned, finding him waiting behind her, his formal tunic glittering with black crystals in the moonlight. He'd let his hair grow out on their quest. It was now long enough to fall *very* rakishly across his forehead.

Hardship had filled the past years. With Clare in front of her, she reveled in the joy of something wonderfully easy. She smiled, placing her hand in his.

"You know the steps to this one?" she asked playfully when he led her onto the dancing parquet.

The courtyard was full, unsurprisingly. The wedding was *the* event of Mythrian society. Noblewomen Beatrice recognized from Robert's banquets chatted over sparkling wine. Sir Noah Noble danced with his date. Nearby, none other than Cris demonstrated impressive dancing, dressed in his Clare regalia. Like many Clare impersonators, he formalized weddings in Vermillion Vale. He'd utterly charmed Hugh, who had excitedly suggested to the receptive Thessia the impersonator formalizing their ceremony. He now wore ring candies on each hand.

Clare smirked. "For a period, I was the most popular bachelor in Mythria," he reminded her. "Unable to sit a single dance out at any social occasion."

His phrasing distracted her from the enticing proposition of mocking his vanity. "For a period, but no longer?" she inquired.

Clare swept her into the dance, of which he did, indeed, know every step. The parquet was open to the night sky, the stars sparkling in the darkness like the gems he wore.

"Hugh has held the honor since we defeated the Order," he explained. "However, I suppose since he was very recently married off, his reign is now over."

"He cuts quite the hero," Beatrice mused. Her eyes found Clare's. "It doesn't bother you?"

Under her scrutiny, Clare's smile softened. "It was a relief, honestly." His eyes drifted to the center of the courtyard, where Thessia and Hugh swayed, lost in each other, both dressed in stunning gold and white. "Free of the expectations, I've started to remember who I am," he said.

Beatrice said nothing. The notion filled her with indescribable joy. She'd known the Clare who preceded his legend, who considered himself no hero. He was the greatest, loveliest man she'd ever met.

"But . . ." he went on hesitantly. Clare danced backward from Beatrice.

With the dance's next step, he strode back up to her. Gazing sideways, his stare never left her.

In his pause, she heard—embarrassment? Shyness, certainly. On Clare Grandhart, wings or horns would've surprised her less.

"What is it?" she asked.

"Well, I'm . . ." he started. "I'm honestly not sure I am a bachelor anymore," he went on.

Her eyebrows rose. Her heart picked up its pace. Yes, hope was dangerous. She was Beatrice of the Four, however. She could face danger.

"Are you asking me a question, Grandhart?" she prompted him.

He was, or wanted to. He opened his mouth, squaring his shoulders. He looked just on the verge of working up the courage—

When rain fell from the night sky.

The droplets started small, strengthening quickly. In minutes, the rainstorm was dousing guests fleeing from the floor. Everyone ran for cover—except Thessia and Hugh, who danced in the downpour like nothing could dampen their joy.

"Oh, come now," Beatrice remarked. "Can this couple not catch one break?"

The moment the words left her lips, the rain stopped.

Or—not *stopped*. The raindrops changed into pink and white rose petals, drifting gently down onto the wedding. Cries of relief and awe went up around them.

In the stunning enchantment, the floral rain decorating the night in descending petals, Beatrice felt moved. Magic need not hurt or reveal or even save the realm. Magic could be happiness. Magic could be lovely.

When she faced Clare, her heart full, she found his eyes on the sky. Feeling something flutter over her fingers held in his, she lifted their joined hands.

In the faint luminescence of Clare's palm, *rose petals swirled*.

She gasped.

"You're a hand magician!" she cried.

Clare pulled sparkling eyes to hers. He looked strangely regal, white petals coming to rest on his shoulders like cream medallions. "An embarrassing gift for an extremely dashing scoundrel," he replied.

Beatrice laughed. She pulled him closer, spinning with the music while every step kicked up flurries of petals under their feet.

"I wouldn't say it's embarrassing," she said. "Changing threats into flowers could be quite useful."

"That *would* be indeed," Clare returned. "Imagine I magicked the Sword of Souls into rose petals. But no, my gift is all but useless. I can *only* change water into rose petals." He shook his head. "It's a parlor trick, if anything," he admitted. "Only good for perfume or scented baths."

Beatrice threw her head back and laughed. With the dance's next step, she pressed herself close to Clare, who watched her reaction in confusion.

"I *love* scented baths," she reminded him. "Didn't you know?"

He blinked. Delight lit up his eyes like every star in the rose-filled night. He held her tight, embracing her with every spinning step, continuing the dance like he would never let her go.

When the song changed, however, he slowed them reluctantly. Her reply, she noted, had given him his passionate, careful courage. "Beatrice, what I was saying before . . . I would like to talk to you about our—I mean, my hopes for our future," he explained. "Perhaps tonight, in private. Would you . . . come back to my room with me?"

She kissed him deeply. Under his scents she loved—of dance sweat, of clear mornings—she noted the softest hint of roses. Her outlaw king of flowers.

"I cannot tonight," she informed him. "There is something I

must do. But I was thinking I would move in with you. You like Farmount, yes?"

His brow furrowed. Not with displeasure, only surprise. "What?"

"Oh, apologies," Beatrice went on. "May I move in with you? Or you can move in with me in my cottage—I care not. I just want to be with you—"

He crushed his lips to hers, rogue and reverent. In the kiss, she could feel him smiling.

"Yes. Yes, Ghosts, yes," he rushed to say. "Come to Farmount. I . . . picked my flat, my neighborhood, with you in mind. You'll love it. It's wonderfully lively. You'll never be bored, and I . . ." He faltered, only momentarily, summoning the same courage. "I will try to make you happy."

It really was easy with him. Knowing what to say, how she felt.

"You already do," she promised.

Clare Grandhart grinned, wide and free.

"Wait," he said after a moment. "What is it you must do this night?"

She squeezed his hand, where roses danced still.

"I cannot say just yet," she confessed. "Do you trust me?"

Clare looked like he found the same ease in replying. "With my life."

She leaned in to press a gentle kiss to his cheek. "Please let Elowen and Vandra know I had to go," she said.

When Clare nodded, she released his hand. She walked from the parquet, past the desserts, out of the courtyard.

With her she carried only the song playing when she left, one commemorating their first quest and Galwell's devotion to Mythria. She hummed the musicians' refrain even as she continued into the castle and the sounds of the wedding faded. All the way up to her chambers, she carried the sweetly somber melody with her.

In her room, she did not light the torches.

Instead, she sank onto her bed. Like she'd done on hundreds of other nights in the past decade, she lay still.

The shimmering sheet of the past descended over her. Ramparts replaced comforting castle walls. In place of rose-petal rain, dark lightning convulsed with evil magic.

Focusing on the day the Four first defeated the Order, she entered the memory one last time.

Where she'd just danced in her lover's embrace, a bloody battle raged. She returned to her past self, standing above on the ramparts. Turning, she knew what would happen next.

Todrick van Thorn emerged from the castle, zealous in the darkness. He held the Sword of Souls, the enchanted weapon shining with pain. He planned to use it to extend his magic over the queen's army surrounding the palace, the first step in his grand design.

Beatrice was ready to die on the sword's point to stop him.

He paused when he noticed her. Humor's ghost entered his pretty, horrible features. "You," Todrick said.

She opened her arms wide.

"One more soul," she promised him. "If you can claim it."

His eyes sparked like the lightning.

When she'd first lived this day, she did not know Galwell had climbed the ramparts behind her. She knew now. Todrick would swing the Sword, and Galwell would charge in front of the blow, which would crash deep into him, ripping muscle, shattering bone. He would die, slowly. Painfully.

Living her memories, she felt the same devastating inevitability. The pull of the past was strong.

Yet she knew now—she was stronger.

She stepped *into* the unfolding chaos. Evading the swing of the sword she'd meant to kill her, she feinted to the side, into—the solid form of the oncoming Galwell, pushing him out of the way.

"Galwell, *now!*" she cried.

The effort of screaming words she'd never said nearly made her black out. Every second of change wore on her. She felt her pulse weaken, her vision cloud.

No. She fought to hold on. Just a little longer.

In her warping sight, she watched Galwell, the effortlessly expert swordsman, stab his own sword cleanly into the surprised Todrick. The strike was fatal.

She knew what would come next. Myke Lycroft would come up the stairs. He would find his slain friend. He would weep on the Sword of Souls, vanquishing its power. A magical explosion would decimate the ramparts. While they and Lycroft would escape with their lives, Todrick's corpse and the sword would fall down the cliffs outside Queendom.

Then . . .

Then, she didn't know.

For Galwell the Great *lived*. He rushed to her side, leaving his sword sticking out of his fallen foe. His eyes scoured her for injuries he would not find, for her weakness was owed to no slash or strike. Her magic fought the past, destroying her with the effort.

Sparing Galwell's life and giving him the years he never had would require much of herself. *Too* much. If she continued here, it would kill her.

It was a price she would have paid, once.

With the companionship of friends she considered family and the greatest, loveliest man she'd ever known, she had come to understand Galwell's life was not worth more than hers. She would not embrace defeats she felt she deserved. Nevermore would she sacrifice herself into the darkness. She would fight for the light.

She couldn't change the last ten years without draining herself. So—

When Galwell knelt next to her, she grabbed his hand.

And with the last flash of magic in her, she pulled him out of the past.

38

Elowen

Elowen found herself at the Needle once again, sitting in her usual spot near the back and nursing a sprymint fizzy.

This time, however, she was not alone. Far from it. It was so late it had become early again, and most of the wedding guests had tagged along with Elowen, Vandra, and Clare for some after-hours fun. There were at least twenty people too many inside the pub, all dressed in wedding finery, but it wasn't the kind of over-crowding that bothered Elowen. Or maybe she was just too happy to care about the fact that she didn't like to be around this many people at once. She'd have to discuss it with Lettice during their next appointment. For the moment, she appreciated that she didn't fully understand herself, and she likely never would.

Vandra filled the seat beside Elowen, their ankles intertwined as they both took in the scene. Wedding guests were dancing and singing, led by none other than Clare Grandhart, who'd made it his personal mission to fill the pub with good cheer.

"You were right," Vandra said. "This is the best place to people-watch."

Elowen leaned into her. "Of course I was right," she confirmed. "When have I ever been wrong?"

"*Never*," Vandra answered playfully.

"Correct. Which means I am also right about where we should reside," Elowen said, placing a hand atop Vandra's. "There is plenty of room for you up in the trees with me. Morritt the brush-walker would love to have you. Your enthusiasm for creatures of his kind would be a refreshing change of pace for all involved."

Vandra let out her throatiest laugh, relishing in the attention it drew to their private conversation. "Darling, is this your way of asking me to move in with you?"

"Only if you say yes," Elowen said. "Otherwise I'd prefer we forget this ever happened."

Vandra clinked her glass to Elowen's. "Consider it scrubbed from my memory!"

Elowen flushed. Had she really misjudged the intensity of their relationship? Though it was relatively new in some respects, it was also over ten years old in others. And Vandra was the only person in the realm that Elowen wanted to see as much as possible. If they didn't live together, Elowen feared she would possibly never get enough of Vandra.

"My love," Vandra said, catching the concern in Elowen's eyes. "I jest! I want nothing more than to live with you."

Elowen let out a sigh of relief.

"Just not in the forest," she added, kissing Elowen's forehead.

"Perhaps you've forgotten, but I do not have any money," Elowen said. "That is the only home I have, and the only one I can afford."

"I'm quite confident Thessia is more indebted to us than ever," Vandra replied. "And I have been residing in palace quarters for free this last year, saving up as much as possible in the process. We are well equipped to find a home that is not yours or mine, but ours."

"*Ours*," Elowen echoed, smiling. "I like the sound of that." She leaned in closer, letting her breath tickle Vandra's ear. "Are you sure you don't find the unique charms of the cursed forest appeal-ing?"

"About as appealing as you'd find living in a crystalline skyscraper in the heart of Vermillion Vale," Vandra whispered back. "When it comes to us, there will always need to be some compromise. We can find something that appeals to us both."

Elowen pressed her forehead to Vandra's. "You're right. We can."

"Besides, I want to take you to meet my parents in Devostos. You can join us for our monthly dinners. I'm overdue for one, what with saving the realm and all."

"They may not know what you do, but surely they know who I am," Elowen said. "And I'm so dreadfully bad at lying, as you know. How will I explain how we met?"

"I plan to tell them the truth," Vandra replied. "About all of it. I have been searching for a life that would make them proud, and I've realized I already have it. They may not understand everything I've ever done, but that doesn't mean I have to hide it anymore. I am happy with who I am, and more than that, I am ecstatic about who I love. I am ready for them to know me. *All* of me."

They went silent, closing their eyes and letting their breathing sync. It would never stop amazing Elowen how she could feel like this around Vandra—cared for, safe, and *loved*. At the end of the day, it was all she really needed. The rest would fall into place.

Someone tapped her on the shoulder with a strange amount of insistence. "I'm sorry to interrupt. I just have something very important to share."

It was Beatrice. She looked windswept and disheveled in a way that confused Elowen. It almost seemed as though Beatrice had been on another quest. Not many would be able to recognize the way that looked on another person, but Elowen found herself to be uniquely qualified, and therefore accepted the impression that Beatrice did in fact appear recently quest-ridden.

At once, Beatrice hugged her. It was a fierce hug, tight and all-consuming. Elowen stood up from her seat to squeeze back as hard as she could. This was a hug of bonds that could be fractured but never broken. It was a hug of love that went beyond friendship and into the territory of family. Thanks to both heroics and childhood history, they were forever linked together, and the years they went without acknowledging their lifelong connection also lived inside this hold.

Elowen began to cry for the time they'd lost, and all the time they'd soon spend making up for it.

"All my childhood, you gave me a home, resources, even a family," Beatrice started, still holding Elowen. "I used to feel indebted to you in a way I didn't know how to contend with. But now I understand when you love someone, giving to them is a gift for yourself as much as it is for the other person. I have never owed you anything, and I know that now. But I want to give you a gift all the same."

The crowd began to quiet. The energy in the pub shifted. Elowen sensed shock and . . . was it reverence? People began backing up, creating a pathway that led straight to where Elowen and Beatrice stood. Elowen watched this unfold with great curiosity, wondering what could possibly inspire the level of awe that had overtaken the entire room. She examined the expressions of the wedding guests, searching their faces for clues. Some of them even began bowing, deepening her confusion.

"*Elowen.*"

Her heart felt him before her eyes saw him, for his voice flooded the gaping hole that had lived in her chest for ten long years. Elowen stumbled back. Her hands roamed for the seat she'd just vacated, needing something far sturdier than her own wobbling legs to hold her up. The seat did not find her. Galwell did.

Galwell.

Her mind repeated his name, hoping it would help her make sense of his presence. Her brother stood before her, the very same as he'd looked when she'd last laid eyes on him, down to the carmine cloak atop his shoulders and the dirt smeared across his tunic. His strong arms caught her before she recognized she'd been falling. He held her to his chest, and she crumpled, racked with sobs that came from a place beyond all emotions she'd previously known, so primal she could not label it.

As ten years' worth of grief worked its way to the surface, her brother ran his hand atop her hair in soothing strokes, just as he used to when she was a young child attempting to climb trees and stride through lakes the same way he did, not yet old enough to understand his athleticism was a part of his hand magic. When she'd fall from a tree, or get caught in the current of the water, he always circled back to help, holding Elowen tight as he assured her she'd one day match his strength. She believed then she'd never be as strong as him. It was impossible.

She knew now, with his steadfast arms around her, that her strength had always matched his. She'd had the strength to withstand his loss and continue on with her life. And now, upon his return, she had the strength to accept it. She did not need to ask how this was possible. She'd been raised on shadow plays after all, where no one important stayed dead forever. And in the magical realm of Mythria, with friends as powerful as hers, the same proved to be true.

"You," she said, turning to look at Beatrice, Galwell still holding her.

"Me," Beatrice confirmed, weeping.

Beatrice had figured out a way to bring him back through her time-walking magic. Galwell the Great lived again. She had pulled him from the past somehow, lifting him out of his last living moment and bringing him to their present.

Now that she'd made some sense of it, Elowen was able to breathe again. She pulled her head from Galwell's chest and looked up into her brother's eyes. "If you've come to us from ten years in the past, I am thirty years of age, and you are twenty-seven. Which makes me older than you now," she said teasingly.

The entire crowd laughed, Elowen's joking truth loosening the knots of uncertainty in the room.

Galwell only smiled, pressing a hand to Elowen's cheek. "And yet, it was only yesterday for me that you were my little sister. I see now in your face how much has changed."

Elowen scoffed. "Ghosts, Galwell. Are you saying I look old? Now I know how Clare feels when he worries over his wrinkles, even though they suit him just fine."

"Clare Grandhart has wrinkles?" Galwell asked.

"I do." Clare emerged from the crowd, tears streaming down his face. He pulled Galwell into a hug that was so fierce, it almost knocked the wind out of Elowen, who was experiencing every last bit of Galwell's breathless confusion colliding with his deep appreciation for this reception. "You remain as sturdy as ever," Clare noted, squeezing Galwell's bicep. "Ten long years I've spent trying to replicate this, thinking on many occasions that I've come close. What a fool I am."

"Have you forgotten my strength is magicked?" Galwell asked in earnest.

"My brother," Clare said, his eyes welling anew. "I've forgotten nothing about you."

The sincerity of Clare's words reignited Elowen's weeping, too. Poor, sweet Galwell could not decide who needed more tending.

"I only meant that you are now wiser than I will ever be, and

I can see that in your eyes," he said to Elowen, returning to the original point as only he could. "You have lived through great sadness." He peered closer. "Am I the source of it?"

It was another impossible question. Galwell held the most prominent role not just in Elowen's sadness, but the sadness of Mythria itself. And now he walked the roads of Queendom once again, where statues had been built to grieve the loss of him. How could anyone ever begin to explain that?

"You're back now," Elowen said instead, her tears flowing without pause. "There is so much I need to tell you. It's been ten whole years since last we spoke."

"You should start with the wedding," Vandra interjected, pressing a hand on Elowen's shoulder. She stuck out a hand for Galwell to shake. "Galwell True, it's unbelievable to see you again. I'm not sure if you remember me. I'm—"

"Vandra!" Galwell said, wrapping her up in a hug. "How could I ever forget such a lovely thorn in my side?"

"That's right," Vandra said, her smile brightening from the recognition. "In your mind, you only saw me yesterday. I'm happy to report I'm no longer your adversary. Sorry about all of that. It wasn't personal. I hope I look even better than you remember."

"You look exceptionally well, yes," Galwell confirmed. "Are you the one who has just been wed?"

For as much as she'd tried to hold on to every little detail she could, it had been ages since Elowen thought about the way Galwell asked such straightforward questions, no pretense or motive behind them, only honest curiosity.

"Perhaps someday soon," Vandra responded, stealing a glance at Elowen. "But no, I am not the bride of the hour."

"It's Thessia," Elowen said quickly.

Galwell pressed a hand to his heart, and the crowd of onlookers—

lacking the knowledge that Galwell had never really loved his once bride-to-be—gasped.

"She's wed another?" he asked.

Yes, it would certainly take some practice to adjust to his line of questions. "A royal foot soldier turned knight named Hugh," Elowen continued. "He is a great man." With this, she gave Galwell a keen look, and Ghosts, it was surreal. Her older brother, who was now her younger brother, understood her. He understood that no one else in the room knew about his lack of romantic feelings for Thessia. He understood that this wedding was a good union and a cause for much celebration.

"That's wonderful, then," he said. Though he looked at Elowen as he spoke, the comment was more for the rest of the pub, who'd spent ten years grieving Queen Thessia's lost love alongside her. "My sincerest congratulations to our princess."

"Queen," Elowen corrected.

Galwell bowed, even though Thessia was not at the Needle to receive the gesture. "Our queen, yes. Forgive me. There is much I must relearn."

Elowen grinned at her brother. Her living, breathing brother. When would the shock wear off? Likely never.

"Worry not," she said to him. "I will help you adjust to this beautiful new realm, for it is a beautiful new realm for me, too." With that, Elowen flagged down the pubtender. "I think it's high time we get Galwell a drink," she said.

The crowd cheered.

Elowen wrapped an arm around her brother. She had her girlfriend on the other side, and her best friend just behind them. Who knew what would come next? Certainly not Elowen.

She only knew that no matter what, she was strong enough, brave enough, and loved enough to face it.

39

Clare

The carriage rolled to a stop. Clare felt himself torn in half. He didn't want this adventure to be over.

Elowen and Vandra, nodding off after their late night at a roadside tavern, were across from him. While Clare would have expected himself to feel likewise weary, for they'd all gone out last night, no exhaustion weighed on him. Not when the green Mythrian road passing them reminded him constantly of what waited ahead.

Next to him—Galwell.

With clear eyes, the once-lost hero watched the countryside, his auburn hair lifting in the wind passing through the open windows. Clare had just gotten him back. It was going to be hard to say goodbye so soon. While Clare had not known Galwell long in life, great friends did not need long to leave profound impressions on grand hearts.

But on his other side was the reason Clare looked forward to the journey's end. Beatrice. Their life together.

Galwell looked up, pulled from whatever contemplation held him. "Let us help with your luggage," he half-offered, half-commanded.

"We don't have much," Clare said.

"We'll help anyway," Galwell replied readily.

It was strange how *not* strange it was to be with Galwell again.

Never mind how he was now younger than the rest of them—having been taken from his present into ten years into his future—he still had that same commanding presence. He still felt like a figure Clare would look up to, even if now Clare perhaps had less need to.

They climbed out of the carriage, the road crunching underfoot. The day was dazzling, the landscape glorious. Galwell and Vandra unloaded the two small bags Beatrice and Clare had accrued on their voyage and stowed them on the horses they would ride west to Farmount.

The road crossing where their paths diverged was unremarkable except in the way everywhere in Mythria was remarkable. The dappled hills shone emerald in the sun. The cloudless sky reached out endlessly like hope itself.

When the packing was done, the group stood in a circle, looking at one another, knowing goodbyes were coming.

Elowen and Vandra were accompanying Galwell back to the siblings' home village so Galwell could see his parents. It was too intimate a moment for Clare and Beatrice to intrude on. Galwell deserved privacy as he adjusted to a changed Mythria. He, like all of them over the past ten years, would need to decide who he was when the battles were over.

Besides, Clare was eager to show Beatrice their home.

"It is strange." Galwell spoke first, for some things never changed. "I feel like we are concluding the quest to save Thessia. But for you, this is the conclusion of an entirely different quest. I don't know how one says farewell after sharing what we've shared." His gaze found each of them. "You do, though."

Beatrice smiled sadly. "Not really," she confessed. "After you . . . died . . . we didn't exactly say goodbye."

Galwell blinked. "Then how did you part? I know you grieved, but surely you had each other."

"What Beatrice is politely trying to tell you," Elowen said, "is that we acted terribly. We all quarreled and—"

Vandra cut her off. "Beatrice and Elowen had a shouting match at your funeral, and Clare went off and slept with someone. Do I have it right?"

Clare winced, chagrined. "That's about it." He did not want to meet his noble friend's eyes. While he'd rued the way the Four's friendships had ended, at the time he'd found himself almost grateful Galwell couldn't see them then. *What would he say?* Clare had not ever expected he would confront the answer.

So when Galwell only laughed, Clare's gaze shot up in surprise. Galwell shook his head lightly.

Clare went on, uncertain. "While I aspire to comedy most of the time, that particular moment was not my most humorous."

"No, of course not," Galwell said, sobering. "It's just a little funny how much of a mess you all made mere moments after I was . . . buried? I assume you buried me. Should I visit my own grave?" he asked. "Would it still be there?"

"Galwell, I literally discovered I could time-walk days ago," Beatrice reminded him. "I don't have any answers for you."

Galwell nodded, accepting this for the moment.

"We needed you, Galwell," Elowen said more softly. "Without you, we were lost."

Galwell straightened, a shimmer of that heroic spark entering his eyes once more. "No, you did not need me," he replied, warmth under the firmness of his voice. "You saved Mythria without me. You saved *each other* without me. You suffered unfathomable loss. You dealt with unimaginable peril. Despite it all, you returned to each other." He put his hands on Beatrice's and Elowen's shoulders. "I could not be more proud. The next time I die, I will do so knowing you will be okay."

In the moment's hush, each of them was moved. Everyone's eyes welled with tears.

"Well," Clare said, "as the eldest now of the Four—sorry, the Five"—he nodded to Vandra—"I hope I die first."

Beatrice rounded on him. "Oh, so because you're the oldest, you now have special privileges?"

"When it comes to our demise, yes."

Vandra stepped forward. "We'd best wrap this up before we spend the day debating who gets to go in what order."

Galwell grinned. "It's marvelous. You all grew up."

Clare knew it was silly, their childish bickering inspiring this observation. Yet he knew Galwell was right. In the light of the peaceful day, they stood, no longer lost, lonely, furious, wayward souls. They were strong enough to venture into their fears. They were strong enough to forgive their failings. They were strong enough to love themselves.

"So," Clare spoke up cheerfully, "next time we all get together, what should we do?"

"I'm happy with whatever, as long as it doesn't involve saving the realm," Elowen remarked.

"Or camping," Beatrice added.

"Oh, camping wasn't that bad." Vandra smirked, her eyes on Elowen.

"A dinner party, perhaps," Beatrice proposed. "At our home in Farmount. As soon as you can come."

Elowen nodded. Galwell, however, looked over with curiosity. "Beatrice, did your cooking improve while I was dead?" he inquired sincerely.

Beatrice frowned, and Clare guffawed.

"How about," Clare offered, "whatever it is, we just do something fun."

"I can agree to that," Beatrice said, her voice softening.

With teary hugs and claps on the back, Beatrice and Clare climbed onto their horses. Clare found himself wondering what the poets would write of days like this one, with no villains to defeat or battles to fight—only the Five, forever one. He worked to remember every detail, knowing no song would memorialize them for him. *The day drawing long over the plains . . . The wind whispering in the grass . . .*

Above them, Clare heard the familiar cry of Wiglaf circling. With his friends behind him, his bird in the sky, his girl at his side, he rode toward the setting sun, his heart light.

It wasn't farewell. There would be more of life's journeys ahead. Ordinary, but no less epic. They would face them as they had faced everything.

Together.

Acknowledgments

If you, dear reader, have reached these acknowledgments and are only now discovering the personage named E. B. Asher is, in honesty, three people—surprise! We will henceforth be using the pronoun "we" to refer to the authors.

Thank you to the Electric Eighteens of Los Angeles, our debut group, for bringing us together when our very first novels were published in 2018. Without group events and ARCs to exchange, we would never have met, the foundation of our friendship would never have been laid, and this book would never have been written. The Ghosts smiled down upon us when they brought us together.

To our agents, Taylor Haggerty and Katie Shea Boutillier, thank you for rolling with the wild idea we pitched to you, despite our having no previous experience in this genre. Your faith and enthusiasm—and invention of the term "rom-quest"—gave us the chance to invite readers into our beloved Mythria. You two are shadow play stars in our hearts.

We're ever grateful to our editor Sylvan Creekmore for welcoming this story into the Avon family and for not shying away from working with three authors at once. Editing this book with you was a complete delight. Your keen insight into the story—understanding it sometimes better than we did—and appreciation of all of the Clares was invigorating and incredibly meaningful. We feel very fortunate for this book to have passed into the wonderful new hands of Priyanka Krishnan. Thank you for adopting these characters, and us, and treating us like we were your own. We would choose you both to captain our horseball team any day.

Kate Forrester and Ploy Siripant, thank you for a cover that could only have been crafted by the finest hand magic. You exceeded our literal fantasies. The Sword of Souls has never looked more stylish.

It's been a dream to work with the team at Avon. In marketing and publicity, thank you so much to DJ DeSmyter, Kalie Barnes-Young, and Samantha Larrabee for getting this book into readers' hands. Thank you to our production editor Jeanie Lee, assistant editor Madelyn Blaney, copyeditor Linda Sawicki, and proofreader Sophia Lee. If it were real, we would buy each of you a cup of Harpy & Hind brew.

We owe our sincerest gratitude to the many kind authors who gave us support, enthusiasm, and early praise for this book. Emma Alban, Megan Bannen, Ted Elliot, India Holton, Suzanne Park, Jodi Picoult, and Adrienne Young—we would sing songs of your many glories in Mythrian revels.

As always, we're very indebted to our friends and family. You inspire us daily. Thank you for listening to our ideas about Mythria at every stage. May your baths be full of Vesper oils and your plates piled high with the sweetest corncakes.

Finally, to all the readers, booksellers, and librarians who've picked up this book and helped spread the word, we remain forever grateful. You are the real heroes of Mythria.

About the Authors

E. B. Asher is the pen name for authors Bridget Morrissey, Emily Wibberley, and Austin Siegemund-Broka. Bridget Morrissey is the author of the romance novels *That Summer Feeling*, *A Thousand Miles*, and *Love Scenes*, as well as two novels for teens. She lives in Los Angeles, where she coaches gymnastics. Emily Wibberley and Austin Siegemund-Broka are the authors of the romance novels *The Roughest Draft*, *Do I Know You?*, and *The Breakup Tour*, as well as several novels for teens. Married, Emily and Austin live in Los Angeles, where they continue to take daily inspiration from their own love story.